DOWN CAME DEATH

CHAPTER 1

Six weeks into the job at Summit Mountain, June 10th started out like any other day. The resort had officially been open to members for two weeks, and slowly, the customer count visiting the coffee shop to get their morning cup of Joe had been increasing daily. A typical morning shift started at 6:00 a.m. for a 6:30 opening, unless Larissa had closed the night before. If that was the case, then the majority of closing items would also need to be completed before opening. This included taking out the trash, and sweeping the floors.

This particular day was forecasted to be a cold one, with highs in Bozeman only reaching the low forties for the day. On average, the city was 4,820 feet above sea level. By the time you finished your climb into the mountains south of the city, you were around 7,850 feet. You could always count on it to be ten to fifteen degrees colder than the town below. Even in June, temperatures in the high country could plummet from one day to the next. An early summer snowfall was always a possibility.

Even though the resort was located at the base of a large mountain, there was still significant elevation to climb once you turned off the main highway from Bozeman to reach its entrance. After clearing the guarded front gates, you briefly traveled a tree-lined road until it opened up to the main parking lot. Compared to a typical grocery store parking, it was about half the size but large enough to accommodate about fifty vehicles. The coffee shop was on the other side, to the left of the resort's main entrance. It was a standalone building with a brick front and a double glass door entrance. Once entering, you immediately saw the large chalk-written menu along the back wall, with the cash registers and ordering stand underneath. Normally, you never noticed the centerpiece of the shop until you turned to leave. A large stone fireplace, boxed in by two couches and a love seat, provided the majority of the seating. With so many nice areas to sit and view the mountain around the resort, most customers grabbed their order and left. The couches were normally occupied by older couples who owned a condo at the resort.

Opening with Emma today, was Sammy, who had recently arrived from California to work for the summer. When working the opening shift, Emma would always arrive first. All her life, her father would stress if you aren't five minutes early, you're not on time! Punctuality in the household was of utmost importance. Sammy, who didn't have the discipline displayed by Emma, was more of a free spirit and would shortly follow.

Even though they had known each other for less than six weeks, they really hit it off the first day they were paired together. In their mid-twenties, both shared a love for random tattoos and body piercings. Of the two, Sammy was outgoing, boastful, and loud. You never had to guess what she was thinking, often telling you before you realized what was happening. Emma was the quiet one, normally calm and very reserved, almost sheepish.

The majority of the shop's employees worked four days a week. A typical schedule would involve three twelve-hour shifts, plus a half-day, which started at 11:30 a.m. until 5:00 p.m. On this day, both ladies were working the 6:30 a.m. to 6:30 p.m. shift, with a third showing up to help with the lunch crowd. This particular morning, a line was already forming outside the door around 6:20.

"Looks like it's going to be a busy one, Emma," Sammy exclaimed. As she headed to unlock the front door, she could see four or five people standing outside, shivering. Three she recognized as fellow resort employees whom she had met at the restaurant across the parking lot. As she reached to unlock the door, she felt the wind coming through the cracks. Opening the door, she gasped as the frigid temperature from the wind hit her face and body, quickly passing through the short-sleeved t-shirt she was wearing. "Jesus Christ, that's cold," she blurted out to the frozen customers anxious to escape into the building. "No shit, Sherlock," one of the customers replied, pushing his way into the building.

"Terry, you're such an ass," Sammy quipped back.

Emma, wearing a long-sleeved sweater, stood behind the counter, a good thirty feet from the front door. "What are you complaining about? It's not that cold," she jokingly greeted the first customers.

The ladies quickly got into a rhythm, churning through coffee with an occasional order of hot chocolate. Whenever a customer opened the door, Sammy was reminded that her chosen wardrobe did not match the weather. Dressed in a tight, light blue short-sleeved shirt with matching blue yoga pants, each breeze passing through the door hit her like a freight train, sending a shiver through her body.

Sammy reached out, to touch Emma's shoulder, turning her slightly. "Emma, look how hard my nipples are!"

Emma, looking slightly annoyed, turned back towards the customer at the counter. His cheeks were bright red. Emma wasn't sure if he was blushing at Sammy's comment or if this was from the wind.

"Emma, I'm not kidding, they're so hard it's starting to hurt," Sammy continued, "My whole body is aching, and I can't warm up."

Emma was feeling the opposite. Her combination of a sweater and skinny jeans was a little too warm while working around the heat of the coffee and espresso machines. She welcomed the little bit of coolness delivered from the air rushing in and colliding with the sweat on her neck. However, she was starting to feel her sinuses act up, getting a slight headache. Emma told Sammy she was going to the back, to take her sinus medicine. Knowing help would arrive around lunchtime, she hoped it would numb the slight pain before it turned into a throbbing headache.

"Look what I found!" Emma proudly stated, holding up a red jacket on her return to the counter area.

"You're the best," Sammy answered while snatching the jacket out of Emma's hand.

As the morning edged towards the lunch hour, the sky had darkened, and the wind intensified. As the constant flow of customers continued through the doors, the sound of the wind whistling and howling was audible to all. "Hopefully, Larissa will show up on time so we can take our lunch break." Emma thought to herself.

"This jacket isn't working, I'm still cold," Sammy uttered.

"I'm sorry, what?" a slightly distracted Emma responded.

"I'm still cold!" she repeated.

Emma didn't know what to say, but her mouth, of its own free will, uttered, "Sorry." This was somewhat of a common recurrence with Emma, a bad habit she was trying hard to break. It often triggered an anxiety attack. "Why am I apologizing? She was cold; I found her a jacket. Tough luck if it's not good enough," raced through her mind. As her anxiety started to build, she quickly tried to remember the exercises her therapist had taught her about a year ago. Eventually, she was able to calm herself down by slowing her breathing.

"Earth to Emma, hello, Emma, do you read us?" Sammy called over to her co-worker, who appeared to be in a trance.

Emma turned towards Sammy, who pointed to the customer standing in front of Emma. "Yes, Sir, may I take your order?" she finally replied.

The clock showed 12:05 with no sign of Larissa. The line of customers now stretched from the counter to the front door. As Emma surveyed the people in front of her, none looked cheerful. All looked cold and hungry. A sinking feeling overtook Emma as she started to realize Larissa wasn't going to show. She could feel her dull headache start the beginning stages of becoming a very bad sinus headache.

"I'm going to wring her neck when she shows up. Does Miss Brazil think the rules don't apply to her?" shouted an angry Sammy.

"It's very frustrating when you're running a business with a skeleton crew, one of which is a prima donna," Emma thought to herself.

As 1:00 p.m. inched closer to becoming a reality, still no Larissa, but the customers were definitely real and appeared to be never-ending. "I'm going to pass out if I'm not able to take a break soon, this is ridiculous!" Sammy turned and shouted to an invisible employee somewhere in the back of the storage room.

Over the next hour with no Larissa sightings, Sammy's anger was quickly reaching the boiling point. Any filters she had been using to mask her agitation around the customers had disappeared within the last hour.

Emma's head felt like it was about to explode, but knowing that no matter how much they complained, it wouldn't change or improve the situation, she was trying her best to stay positive. However, each time Sammy flew off the handle, a vice grip clamped down on Emma's shoulder blades and neck, intensifying the pain in her head.

Finally, around 3:00 p.m., Emma received a call from Larissa. "Hey guys, sorry to do this to you, but I just woke up and don't feel that great. Probably not going to make it in today."

"Is that the little bitch?" shouted Sammy for all to hear.

"Yep, and guess what? She doesn't feel well enough to work today," Emma said sarcastically back.

Sammy angrily, grabbed the phone. "Sorry, but we have customers to serve, so go fuck yourself," and slammed down the phone. As Sammy turned around to face the front of the store, she felt every eye focused on her. Suddenly, she felt a strong wave of nausea building. "Emma, I gotta go right now, I'm about to throw up." Sammy politely moved Emma out of the way and made a dash to the back door. As soon as she flung open the door, she was immediately hit by a 40-degree temperature drop from inside, taking her breath away. Instead of vomiting, now she was attempting to regain her breath. The thirty-degree air was not what her system was expecting or wanting. After what felt like ten minutes (but was actually less than a minute), she stepped back inside.

"Sammy, are you okay?" asked a concerned Emma. "You ran out like a bat out of hell!"

"Yeah, I'll be alright. I'm just so frustrated with this job and terrible co-workers. Present company not included. Sometimes I just want to get up and get the hell out of here."

"I know, you would think Larissa would be considerate of other," Emma started before being interrupted by her highly agitated coworker.

"Let me stop you right there, Emma," Sammy said while holding up a finger of disapproval. "You need to realize the majority of people aren't like you! They don't give a flip about anyone but themselves. It's the 'Me! Me! Me!' and screw you mentality that everyone has that drives me crazy. Suckers like you and me who actually give a rat's ass are an easy mark to be taken advantage of, and I'm so sick of it."

Emma could see Sammy starting to get ramped up again. "Sammy, time-out, it's not worth it! Chill! It's slowed down a lot from earlier. Go take your break and calm down; I'll hold the fort down until you get back."

"Are you sure? I don't want to take advantage of the situation."

"Sammy, in your current state, do you really want to work or take a break?" Emma sarcastically replied back. Receiving no answer, Emma added, "Yep, that's what I thought."

"You're the best," Sammy said, while giving Emma a big hug. "I'm going to have a cigarette and go over to the cafeteria to get a bite to eat. I'll be back in 45 minutes tops!"

"Take your time, I'm not sure if you have been paying attention, but the snow's really been coming down over the last couple of hours. I don't think many more people are getting out in this mess." Emma turned to walk back to the counter but quickly paused, turning around to tell Sammy, "Hey, will you take some of the trash over to the dumpster while you're out?"

"Sure thing," Sammy said, grabbing a bag as she walked out the back door.

Emma made her way back to the front of the store where she saw Charles. Charles had been a regular since Emma first started, usually appearing a couple of times a day. Charles, or Charley as he preferred to be called, was retired, in his early seventies, single, and could spend hours talking about basically nothing, at least that's what twenty-something Emma thought.

"Good afternoon, Emma! Where's your partner in crime?"

"She just went on break. What can I get you, Charley?"

"Hot cocoa, please. It's freezing outside! You know, I've had a place here for the last ten years; we always get a little bit of snowfall in June, but not like today. I bet we've already had about three inches of accumulation, and the forecast calls for twelve before it stops sometime overnight. I had planned to drive down to Yellowstone this morning; glad I didn't go, might not have made it back. Emma, have you been to Yellowstone yet? It's beautiful this time of year, but you gotta watch out for the bears! They're just now getting over the hangover from their winter hibernation and will eat anything they can catch. Did I ever tell you about the time I was chased by a momma bear? I was mountain biking around Spanish Peaks, came around a corner, and there were two cubs in the trail. As I slowed to process what was happening, I briefly caught a brown flash out of the corner of my eye, and then Bam! I felt my body momentarily leave the ground before crashing back to the ground. I felt like I had tumbled halfway down the mountain before I came to a stop at the base of a tree. However, once I was able to regain my senses and get back to my feet, Momma bear was only about fifteen yards from me."

This was probably the third time Emma had heard the story, and she quickly tuned Charley out. Her throbbing sinus headache had gathered momentum. If she only had the chance to crawl back into bed, she could ride it out. As

Charley continued to speak, his voice was like a hammer pounding into her head. She once again tried the relaxation exercises she was taught, focusing her thoughts on the plans she and her friends had made for the upcoming weekend. Finally, the sound of her name brought her back to the present.

"Emma, are you listening to me," Charley asked.

This finally pushed Emma over the edge, and she snapped at the old man, "God damn it, Charley, you repeat this story every time you come in here! Yeah, I'm listening, you ran past the couple yelling 'bear'." she responded.

"Emma, I haven't gotten to that part; you're not listening," a dejected Charley responded.

"Charley, it's been one hell of a morning; I'm just struggling to keep it together until the end of the day. Please take your order and just leave," she replied.

Emma wasn't the only one struggling with her emotions. Sammy had been fighting to hold back the tears as she exited the back door; this was not what she had signed up to do all summer. Maybe, she thought, a nice warm meal would calm down the nerves and take away the anxiety that had built up over the course of the morning.

As she walked into the resort's restaurant, she heard a familiar voice. "Hey, Sammy, late lunch today," Terry shouted from the kitchen area.

"Yeah, late lunch. We're down an employee, just Emma and me working the line today."

"I'm assuming you know who is missing," Terry chuckled.

"You mean the name that shan't be mentioned," Sammy shouted back with her best attempt at a British accent.

"What shall I get you?" Terry asked before offering, "The New England clam chowder would be great on a day like this!"

"Sounds pretty good, I need something to warm my innards!" She replied. Sammy filled up a cup from the soda fountain and went to find a table in the back of the restaurant. Within minutes, Terry appeared with her bowl of chowder. "Terry, I'm sorry I called you an ass this morning." Sammy offered.

"No problem, I've been called worse. I'll leave you to enjoy the chowder," Terry responded as he walked away.

Sammy sat quietly for a moment, still feeling dazed from the hectic pace of the morning. She stared straight ahead, looking across the many empty tables scattered across the dining floor. Only a few were occupied by fellow resort employees. Outside, she could see what was once scattered snow flurries turning into consistent heavy snowfall. The twenty or so vehicles in the half-full parking lot, all had a four-inch covering of snow on the roof, hood, and trunk.

The sudden noise of a metal pan clanging against the floor moved Sammy's stare to her right, where she could see Terry standing with two other employees. Terry had a very aggravated look on his face, and she could tell by his body language he wasn't happy with either of his companions. Sammy couldn't hear what was being said and quickly lost interest, turning her attention back to the food. Staring into the clam chowder, she thought. "Why is my life such a never-ending series of disappointments?"

Sammy grew up in Northern California, about forty-five minutes north of San Francisco, in the town of Gallinas. It was an unincorporated town located along the route of the Northwestern Pacific Railroad. Growing up without a father, she and her mother often struggled. Her mother held two jobs just to cover the rent and buy food. In school, she never really felt passionate about anything and always tended to hang towards the back of the class. During high school years, she didn't participate in any clubs or groups, preferring to finish her classes, head home, plop down on the couch, and turn on the TV.

While watching TV, she would fantasize about traveling to far locations, living a nomadic lifestyle, and never staying in one place long enough to get bored. Like most students entering senior year of high school, she started to think a little more seriously about her future. One thing she did know; she would not be remaining in Gallinas. After high school, she decided to move to Portland, Oregon, for a year, which quickly turned into three. After which she moved to Seattle, but quickly found out it was too expensive to live on a restaurant worker's salary. On to Yakima, then Spokane, down to Twin Falls, Idaho, and before she knew it, she was sitting on break eating clam chowder, and it had been ten years since she had graduated.

As she finished her chowder, she could see the snowfall was intensifying. "Hopefully, this will slow down the traffic into the coffee shop," she thought. She quickly paid for her meal and headed back across the parking lot to where Emma was holding down the fort.

Walking toward the back entrance of the coffee shop, she saw the trash bag she had left by the door, suddenly remembering her promise to take out the trash. The wind was picking up again, making Sammy's red shoulder-length hair dance around her round face. Walking the fifty or so yards to the dumpster wasn't what she really wanted to do, but a promise is a promise. She also decided to quickly grab another bag from inside before starting her journey.

Emma thought she heard the back door open, but the line of customers prevented her from leaving the cash register area to check. Looking out the front window, she could see several inches of snow covering the vehicles in the lot. Hopefully, the resort members would start to stay in their rooms until the storm passed, allowing her to seek relief from her pounding head.

Unfortunately, this never materialized. Even though the heavy snow continued, over the next hour, Emma was slammed with customers. "Where's Sammy!" she angrily shouted under her breath when she thought no one was looking.

Finally, a lull in customers gave Emma the opportunity to take something for her head. She walked to the back room, popped a couple of pills, and turned off the lights before sitting down on a chair to relax. She focused on her breathing exercises, attempting to slow down her elevated heart rate. Anxiety attacks had become commonplace for her over the last couple of years, leaving her a shell of the person she used to be.

Perhaps thirty minutes or more had passed since Emma disappeared into the back room to deal with her head. The front door had been silent, with only the sound of the wind occasionally making an entrance. Finally, she was starting to feel somewhat normal again. That's when the reality of her one and only friend at the resort abandoning her kicked in. How could Sammy do this to her? They were a team! Anger started to build inside Emma. She was tired of being the one everyone else took for granted. Momentarily, she thought about grabbing her things and leaving, but reality was she needed a paycheck. Angrily, she picked up the phone and called over to the restaurant.

"Thank you for calling Summit Mountain Bistro, this is Terry, how may I help you?"

"Terry, this is Emma over at the coffee shop, is Sammy still there?"

"She stopped by about two hours ago, said you guys had been swamped all morning."

"I'm running on fumes, will you tell her to please head back," Emma pleaded.

"Would love to," Terry said. "However, she left here well over an hour and a half ago."

"What the fuck!" Emma slammed the phone down, "Sammy, if you're napping in the back, I'm going to kill you!" Emma shouted towards the back of the shop. No response. Will this nightmare never end, she thought to herself. Unfortunately, before she could think about her next move, she felt the wind rush in as another customer finally came through the door.

As the clock struck 6:30 p.m., Emma finally was able to exhale. "What a day—a no-show and a mental meltdown." Even though Emma was still upset with Sammy, at least the pain in her head had subsided. Locking the front door, she scanned every visible inch of the shop. Something told her

Sammy was in the building. A couple of weeks earlier, Sammy had pretended to leave, but in fact had hidden in the storeroom. On that night, as Emma took the trash to the back door, Sammy popped out, scaring Emma senseless.

"Well," Emma said to no one, "looks like I'm closing solo tonight." Emma went to the back, to grab a broom to sweep up the front. "Sammy, if you jump out from behind one of these shelves, I'm going to kill you!" Nothing! "Okay, something is not right," Emma told herself. Looking around the storeroom, she wondered, "Did she come back after the break? I thought I remembered hearing the door open. I definitely didn't hear her say she was back." Looking at the bags of trash next to the back door, something looked different; "Maybe fewer trash bags," Emma wondered. Did she grab a couple of bags when she left, or did she come back and grab two? Maybe she just set them outside the back door. Emma slowly opened the back door, fully expecting Sammy to shout, "Gotcha!" Not a sound.

As Emma surveyed the surroundings behind the shop, all she saw was a blanket of snow. "Wow, it snowed a ton today," she thought. There were no visible footprints, no tire tracks, just a pristine, untouched covering of snow. Emma went back inside, now realizing there was no Sammy, and the store had to be cleaned before she left for the night. After another thirty minutes of sweeping and cleaning, the store was ready for the morning crew. All that was left was to take the trash to the dumpster.

The trash container was about fifty yards behind the coffee shop. Because of the never-ending threat of bears in the neighborhood, company policy after closing time was two people take out the trash at all times. "Well," Emma thought. "Tonight we have three employees taking out the trash—me, myself, and I!" She grabbed two bags and headed towards the dumpster, quickly realizing getting there wasn't going to be easy.

The June snowstorm had dumped about fifteen inches of snow on the ground since her arrival that morning. Every step was a struggle, sinking deeper and deeper into the snow, as she went. Wearing only black sneakers with ankle-height socks, the snow felt like ice as it touched her uncovered skin. "Goodness! This is a pain." she muttered, now dragging the bags of trash across the top of the snow. After ten minutes of slipping and sliding, with her sneakers wet and cold from the snow, she arrived at the dumpsters.

Directly in front of her sat two bags of trash buried halfway in the snow. "Okay, Sammy wouldn't have brought two bags over and not thrown them in the dumpster. Last night, did Larissa drop the trash here? Well, regardless of who, I can't leave it here." Emma reached up to push in the lever allowing her to drop the trash down the chute; it didn't move. She tried again, still no movement. Emma vaguely remembered from her training something about what to do when the mechanism to the trash drop was frozen. Working only during the summer, she hadn't paid much attention to rules regarding freezing temperatures, but knew a hammer was always a good tool to have when things were stuck.

Over the next thirty minutes, she made three trips back and forth between the store, and dumpster, retrieving the remaining six bags of trash. On her last trip, she also brought a hammer. As she slowly dragged the last two bags, her gloveless hands were really starting to ache, replacing the pain in her feet which went numb about fifteen minutes ago.

She took a firm grasp of the hammer before raising it above her head. Already, her body was starting to tense up, knowing the pain she was about to endure once the hammer struck the cold metal, transferring the energy back through her frozen hand and arm. Before another thought could cross her mind, she swung the hammer down solidly, striking the latch before dropping her tool and screaming out in pain. It took her a few moments before the pain started to pass. She reached to check the latch, "What the fuck?," she screamed out when the door didn't open. She could feel her eyes watering up but wasn't sure if it was from the cold or her emotions. She just wanted to go home and put an end to this nightmare of a day.

She looked down at the snow, her eyes focused on the hole created when she dropped the hammer. Tears ran down her cheeks a few inches before freezing to her skin. Realizing the longer she waited the colder she would become, she reached for the hammer, picking it up and swinging like a woman possessed, striking the latch at least three times before she dropped to her knees exhausted. She sat motionless in the snow. The wind, which was at her back, picked up again, blowing her shoulder-length brown hair into her face. Finally regaining the energy to stand, she could see a piece of the latch had broken off. Emma, for the first time all day, had a big smile on her face as she easily pushed open the broken door.

The smile quickly faded from Emma's face; she was really starting to feel the cold. Her shoes, socks, and jeans were soaked from the snow. Her hands and feet were both numb and felt like they had been pricked by a thousand needles. Her arms and shoulders were exhausted from dragging the bags, but somehow she was able to summon up a last bit of energy to throw them in the dumpster. Soon she was down to the two bags which greeted her when she first arrived at the dumpster.

As she bent over to grab the bag, she saw a slight reddish discoloration in the snow under where a bag had laid. "What had leaked from the trash," she wondered. She took her hand and brushed away a little more snow, and the spot was bigger and redder. "Oh, this is blood!" Emma shouted as she fell back on her rump. A combination of exhaustion and a day full of negativity put her imagination in overdrive. "Oh my god, there's a dismembered body in this bag." She quickly started going through the pockets on her coat, frantically searching for her phone. Finally, she realized it was on the counter in the shop. Jumping to her feet, she made a mad dash back to the coffee shop, making it halfway before her legs gave out, and she face-planted in the snow.

With the adrenaline in her body starting to kick in, she was quickly back on her feet. Once back at the shop, she could feel the burning in her lungs from the cold air. "Okay, Emma," she told herself, "hold it together, you're overreacting, don't make a big deal out of this yet, we need to know the facts." "What facts? I'm not a detective. To heck with overreacting, I'm calling the Sheriff." Emma took a couple of deep breaths, picked up the phone, and dialed 911. After a ring or two, the line picked up, "Gallatin County 911, what is your emergency?"

CHAPTER 2

After hanging up with the operator, Emma went over to the Bistro to grab a bite to eat and wait on the authorities. As she sat at a table in the back of the restaurant, she wondered how this awful day could get any worse. She then began to feel guilty about complaining, with her one and only friend potentially dismembered and stuffed into a trash bag.

Looking down at the table, she could finally see how red her hands were from the cold. As they slowly started to warm, they began to shake. She wondered if it was her nerves or just the effect of the cold.

"This will help you out," a voice suddenly interrupted Emma's thoughts, before placing a bowl of chili in front of her.

"Thanks," she responded before looking up.

"I'm Terry, I run the restaurant. You called earlier, didn't you?"

Emma didn't personally know Terry but had been warned by Sammy to stay clear of him. According to Sammy, you could be laughing and joking with him one minute and the next he would just be mean. Not physically, but his words would cut like a knife. She had diagnosed him as bipolar.

"I'm Emma," she finally responded.

"When did Sammy show back up?" he asked.

Emma sat quietly for a moment, wondering how much info she should share. If she was overreacting, she would be ridiculed by everyone at the resort. The police should be arriving soon, so that much she had to share.

"She didn't," Emma shared.

"What! That's crazy," Terry blurted out.

Emma just shrugged her shoulders before eventually telling him she actually called the sheriff's office and they should be arriving in a little while.

"Wow. That's crazy," Terry repeated before walking off.

"Yep, Emma, you said too much; should have kept that to yourself," she thought, looking over the almost-empty parking lot. Well, anyways, might as well relax. If the Sheriff was coming from Bozeman, it would be at least another hour before he would arrive.

The trip into the mountains from Bozeman normally took about an hour. However, this evening, the wipers on the Sheriff's vehicle had been in constant motion the entire duration of the trip, removing the sheet of snow, which quickly reappeared after each cycle of the wipers. Finally, the snow eased up about the time they turned off the main highway.

Nightfall was setting in, and the temperature was really starting to fall when the Sheriff, followed by one of his deputies, navigated their four-wheel-drive Chevy Tahoes through the guard station, down the tree-lined road, and into the parking lot.

The info the dispatcher had provided was vague: a female caller reported a coworker went on break but never returned. Normally, a call like this would be a low priority, but it had been a slow day at the sheriff's office, and with the bad weather moving in, Mikeal decided to at least check things out. When the Sheriff arrived, a good two hours had passed since Emma made her 911 call. The two Tahoes came to a stop side by side in front of the coffee shop. The sheriff's deputy was the first to exit his vehicle, followed by Mikeal Lancaster, Sheriff of Gallatin County.

Deputy Devin Bordeaux had been with the sheriff's office a little over eight years. Clean-shaven, with a full head of blonde hair, his 6' 2" frame made him slightly taller than the Sheriff. Originally from Louisiana, he had been an avid outdoorsman. After working four years with the East Baton Rouge Parish Sheriff's office, he accepted an offer with Gallatin County and made the move north. As it approached 10:00 p.m., darkness was starting to settle in at the resort. "Sheriff, I'll take a look around back," he said before setting off with his flashlight leading the way.

The final instructions Mikeal had received from dispatch were to meet the caller in the restaurant at the resort. With his flashlight out he briefly inspected the right side of the coffee shop before turning his attention to the restaurant. "I'm looking for the lady that made the 911 call," the Sheriff asked the first person he saw after entering the restaurant.

Before she could answer; Terry walked out of the kitchen. "Sheriff, you're looking for Emma. Follow me, I'll take you to her."

"That won't be necessary," Emma said, suddenly appearing at the front of the restaurant. "I saw the Sheriff walk in the front door. I'm Emma, pleasure to meet you," the young lady said, extending her arm to shake the Sheriff's hand.

Mikeal quickly assessed the young lady standing in front of him. Slim build, approximately 5' 7", green eyes, and long brown hair pulled back in a ponytail. "Pleasure's all mine, Emma, but please call me Mikeal. Is there someplace quiet we can go; I'd like to take down your statement."

"By the way, Sheriff," Terry interjected, "I'm probably the last person that saw Sammy; I'm guessing you want my statement too?"

"Great, but let me focus on her statement, and I'll follow up with you when I'm finished." Mikeal's eyes scanned the room as he followed Emma back to her table and a half-eaten bowl of chili. "Crazy weather, even for Montana standards, isn't it," Mikeal opened with.

"Yeah," Emma responded. "Looks like I'll be spending the night here. My Honda Civic was perfect for the flat, non-snowy Florida roads, but not so much in Montana."

"You're from Florida?" asked Mikeal. "I visited Panama City once."

"A little north of where I grew up in Tampa," Emma answered.

"So, what brought you out to Montana, lot different here than in Florida."

"Yeah, I guess I was just looking for a change, been a little difficult on me since graduating high school."

"Difficult, in what way?" he asked.

"I don't know, just trying to figure out what I'm going to do with the rest of my life."

"Well, you're still young; you have plenty of time to figure it out. I was almost thirty before starting a career in law enforcement. It wasn't even on my radar, then I kind of fell into it. So you never know, maybe one day you'll just stumble into something like I did."

"Maybe," Emma responded. "Only time will tell."

"So, Emma, walk me through today, even the boring parts. You never know, sometimes what you may think is a minor detail could be important."

"OK, I got to work around six this morning."

"Were you the first one in, or were others already here?" Mikeal asked.

"Coffee shop is always the first thing to open in the morning, and I'm usually the first to arrive," Emma responded. "Sammy arrived about ten minutes after I did."

"Just to confirm," Mikeal asked, "She's the potential missing person?"

"Correct, Sammy Hudson, or I guess officially Samantha Hudson," Emma stated.

Mikeal pulled out a little notebook, writing Samantha Hudson across the top followed by AKA Sammy. Emma's eyes followed every stroke of his pen as it went up and down, not realizing as she became more engaged in the interview, her body language had changed. Feeling proud of remaining calm as she answered the Sheriff's questions, she was now leaning in towards Mikeal ready to provide more information.

"How would you describe her physical traits?" Mikeal asked.

As Emma spoke, Mikeal wrote the following on his notepad: approximately 5' 6" (Emma actually only implied she was slightly shorter), brown eyes, shoulder-length reddish hair, round face, and average weight.

Without looking up from his paper, Mikeal continued the questioning, "What was she wearing?"

"She had a matching dark blue t-shirt and yoga pants," Emma replied.

"The yoga pants were blue as well?" Mikeal confirmed.

"Correct."

"What type of mood was she in when she arrived, happy, sad, tired, agitated?" Mikeal continued.

Emma pondered on this for a moment. The start of the workday she's normally on autopilot and rarely takes notice of those around her. "I guess she was OK, wouldn't call it happy getting up so early, but she wasn't sad or irritated, at least she wasn't when she first arrived."

"What do you mean, when she first arrived? Did her mood change once she started working?" the Sheriff asked.

"Well, we both became a little irritated when we arrived and noticed the night shift didn't complete all of the closing routine."

"What exactly does that mean," Mikeal responded.

All these rapid-fire questions were starting to unnerve Emma. The calmness she had experienced only minutes ago was starting to fade. Under her sweater, she could feel sweat building up on her arms and on her back.

She pulled back from the table, crossing her arms and resuming her normal slouched position. Finally, she responded to Mikeal's question, "The big thing was floors needed to be swept and trash taken out. It sounds petty, describing it back to you, Sheriff, but this wasn't the first time they left things for the morning crew! After a while, it starts to be a pain."

Emma's voice started to rise, and Mikeal could sense she was starting to become agitated with the questioning. "Look, it's getting late, and I know you've had a long day. We can pick this back up in the morning," Mikeal offered.

Emma sat quietly for a moment. Her next shift didn't start until 11:30 a.m., and she would really like to sleep until at least 10:00 in the morning. Finally after an awkward silence of a few minutes, she agreed to continue the interview.

"OK, so you both were bothered by the closing crew; anything else happened this morning out of the ordinary?" Mikeal resumed.

"Yes, Larissa, who was part of the closing crew the night before, was supposed to come in at 11:00 A.M. to help out with the lunch crowd, but guess what, she didn't show up. This was when Sammy really started to flip out. Even with the snow coming down, we were really busy this morning, almost non-stop. We didn't take breaks; it was a grind. Once the crowd slacked off, I told Sammy to go take a break and get something to eat. That was the last I saw of her. I got busy listening to a customer's bear story, and the next thing I know, customers were stacking up again, with Sammy nowhere in sight. I called over to the restaurant, but they said she had already left."

"What time did you call?" Emma thought for a moment before trying to backtrack in time, "Let's see, Larissa called around 3:00, so it would have been after that before Sammy left. I'm not sure, definitely after 5:00, but maybe as late as 5:30."

As she spoke, Mikeal was busy jotting this timeline down. "Who did you speak with at the restaurant?" the Sheriff asked.

"The guy you met earlier, Terry."

"What exactly did he say to you?"

"Basically, she had been there but left about fifteen minutes before I called."

"Interesting," Mikeal said aloud. "That's the coffee shop on the other side of the parking lot, correct?" Emma nodded in affirmation. "What is that, about a minute walk, maybe with two to three inches of snow, a couple of minutes?"

"I guess, never timed it," replied Emma.

"What I'm getting at, Emma, is if she left fifteen minutes before you called, she would have easily been back at work, maybe she wasn't going back to work," the Sheriff thought to himself. "Is Sammy's car still in the parking lot?"

"I don't know," Emma responded. "I didn't think to take a look."

"Do you know what type of car she drives?"

"It's a white four-door Nissan, I believe."

"Do you know the model?"

"Not really, Sheriff," Emma responded. Internally, Emma was starting to feel another anxiety attack coming on. "I can't believe I didn't check to see if her car was gone! I'm such an idiot," she thought to herself.

"Emma, you okay?" the Sheriff asked.

Emma was really starting to feel unwell. The sweat previously restricted to her arms and back was starting to flow down her neck, and she could feel the pace of her heart accelerating as her problems with anxiety started to kick in.

"Oh, I'm sorry, Sheriff, I was mentally trying to picture Sammy's car, dammit," she thought to herself, "there I go saying sorry about everything."

"Don't worry about it," Mikeal tried to calmly reassure her. "Your description is plenty to go on."

"What about the blood?" Emma blurted out.

"Where did you find blood?" replied Mikeal.

"If Sammy got in her car and left, where the hell did the blood come from by the trash cans!" Emma said almost shouting. Without realizing it, Emma had stood up from the table and slammed her hands down on the table.

"I understand how upsetting this must be for you, but I'm just trying to develop a clear picture of what happened. I'm not saying she left in her car, just listing it as a possibility; in due time, we'll figure it all out. But since you brought it up, tell me about finding the blood," Mikeal calmly asked.

Emma sat back down at the table, tears starting to appear at the corners of her green eyes. Mikeal offered her the napkin laying on the table, which she refused, choosing instead to dry her eyes with the sleeves of her sweater. She took a couple of deep breaths before continuing, "After I served the last customer and locked the front door, I went to the back, fully expecting Sammy to jump out from behind a shelf and make me wet my pants. After looking around the back, I realized I was still alone. So I started to complete the closing routine by myself. After sweeping the floors and washing the dishes, the only thing left was to take out the trash. Normally, we're not allowed to take the trash out by ourselves because of the bear threat, but the trash had piled up from the night before, so I didn't think I had any other option. It took me several trips to drag all the bags through the snow to the trash. Oh, yeah, I almost forgot, when I took the first two bags, there were already two bags sitting beside the dumpster."

"Is that normal in bear country to leave bags sitting in the open?" the Sheriff said, already knowing the answer.

"No," Emma responded. "But when I tried to open the latch to put the trash in, it was frozen shut. I figured maybe Sammy started to take out the trash but couldn't open the latch, so she left it. I went back to the shop, picked up a hammer, and was able to pound on it till it opened. After throwing in the bags I dragged to the dumpster, I reached for the original two bags; moving the first is when I saw what looked like blood in the snow. That's when I ran to the phone and called 911."

"Do you want me to take you to the dumpster so you can see the blood?" Emma asked.

"No, it's too dark now. I'm afraid we would possibly trample over some potential evidence," Mikeal stated.

"But what about putting up lights and calling in the forensic team?" dejectedly, she asked.

"I think you've watched too many NCIS episodes, Emma. We're a small county Sheriff's department; we don't have all the equipment. I've got my deputy blocking off the area; it'll be fine until morning. Plus, that will give you a chance to go home and get some rest."

"Sheriff, I'll be sleeping in the back of the coffee shop tonight, I'm not sure how much sleep I'll get."

"Nonsense," Mikeal replied, "I'll have my deputy drive you home and bring you back in the morning. Grab your coat, and let's walk outside and see if Sammy's car is still here."

"My shift starts at eleven tomorrow; please don't pick me up too early," Emma responded as they both got up and headed to the door.

"Sheriff! Sheriff! What about my statement?" Terry yelled as he ran out of the kitchen.

"Hold your horses, in due time. I'm going to be here for a while."

"No offense Sheriff, but my shift is over and I'd like to get home," Terry responded.

"Fair enough, give me ten to fifteen minutes to look outside, and I'll be back to take your statement, and you can be on your way."

"Okay," a dejected Terry said before returning back into the kitchen area.

Stepping outside was still a shock to the senses, even for the Sheriff who by now had called Montana home for a little over a decade. "Jesus, the wind goes right through you," Mikeal exclaimed. "Emma, you sure you're not a mental case, leaving Florida for this!"

The Sheriff didn't know it at the time, but his statement really hit home for Emma. Not quite two years before, fed up and confused on her direction in life, Emma attempted suicide. In her off-campus apartment back in Florida, feeling all alone, she took a half bottle of pills and attempted to slash her wrist. Fortunately for her, the only sharp blade she had was from her razor. Half asleep from the severe cold and allergy medicine that she had ingested, she struggled to break the blade free from the plastic razor handle. Finally, after about fifteen minutes, she was able to free the small blade. She had googled the correct way to slash one's wrist, not sideways as shown in the movies. She made the first cut and was surprised to see it wasn't that deep. So she made a second cut, then a third and a fourth. "This isn't working out," she thought to herself. "Only a little blood, but man this hurts like hell."

"Emma. Emma!" the Sheriff finally yelled. "Are you spacing out on me again?"

"I'm sorry Sheriff," Emma quickly thought up an excuse. "Stepping out into this chill reminded me of growing up in Michigan."

"I thought you were from Florida?" Mikeal asked.

"Sheriff, is anybody really from Florida? Everyone's a transplant from the north or Cuba," she responded.

"Where do you normally park?" the Sheriff asked.

"We park towards the back of the lot; that's my Honda Civic over there." Emma pointed towards the back of the parking lot where there were only two other vehicles remaining, neither of which was a Nissan.

"Alright, no Nissan here, and that's a truck. You sure she didn't also drive a truck?" asked Mikeal.

"I don't know, I've only seen her in that car."

"Alright, well, I know the guy back in the restaurant wants to get home, so let's call it a night. We can pick back up where we left off tomorrow morning. Let me find someone to take you home." "Devin!" the Sheriff yelled across the parking lot. "I need you to give this young lady a ride home."

Emma watched as the younger deputy walked over to Mikeal. Out of hearing range, they briefly chatted before he turned back towards his vehicle, pointing Emma towards the passenger door.

As Emma climbed into the deputy's Tahoe, the Sheriff walked over to her side of the vehicle. He paused for a second, looking down at his phone before telling Emma, "I'm pretty sure your friend's alright; we'll get this all figured out tomorrow."

As the taillights of the Tahoe faded out of sight, the Sheriff returned to the restaurant. Terry was the only one left in the restaurant, occupying one of the first tables behind the reception stand. As Mikeal walked towards the table, he physically sized up Terry. Remembering his first encounter shortly after arriving, Mikeal mentally noted that Terry was a couple of inches shorter than the sheriff, who was an even six feet. Terry had tight, curly brown hair, which almost covered the bottom of his earlobes. Mikeal wasn't 100% certain, but he believed this to be a perm. Brown eyes and a mustache rounded out his description.

"I'm sorry to have kept you waiting, Terry, isn't it."

Still slightly miffed from his first interaction with the sheriff, Terry didn't offer to stand and greet him, remaining slouched in his chair before replying sarcastically, "Yes Sheriff, I'm the head Chef at the Bistro."

Mikeal sat down at the table, across from Terry. First, unzipping his green down sleeveless jacket, followed by repeating the process with his matching fleece outer jacket. Finally, reaching inside the jacket, he retrieved his notepad. All of it completed before saying another word to Terry. "Okay, so Terry, what time did Sammy come in here today?"

"I think it was around three, but I'm not exactly sure. Normally, we're slammed around lunchtime, but with all this snow, there really wasn't anyone here."

Mikeal could tell the excitement Terry had when he first arrived had disappeared. The sheriff had dealt with these types many times before. If you make them the center of attention, they'll talk for days, but focus first on someone else and it's game over. They'll deliberately make a conversation painful.

Mikeal wrote down approximately 3:00 P.M., before moving on to his next question, "Once she arrived, what did she do?"

"Yeah, she had soup."

Okay, not really what Mikeal was asking, but he smiled back at Terry before clarifying, "When she came in, did she talk or sit with anyone?"

"I don't recall, but there weren't many people eating around then, so probably not."

"When you spoke with her, did she seem to be acting normal or rational?"

"Well Sheriff, I don't really know her. We've spoken maybe a couple of times, but she did seem to be worked up about a co-worker not showing up."

"Oh yeah, what did she say?" Mikeal asked.

"Evidently, the trash wasn't taken out last night, and they were swamped this morning, and Larissa didn't show up," Terry answered as though it was taking his last remaining energy to get through the interview.

"Emma also mentioned Larissa; what can you tell me about her?" asked the Sheriff.

This question seemed to breathe new life into Terry, bringing him out of his slouched position and raising the energy in his voice, "She's a really pretty co-worker, and, you know, the other girls are jealous of her. She can come off a little lazy at times, but I think that's just her culture; she's Brazilian. I hear the other girls in the coffee shop complaining about her all the time, but she seems fine to me."

"About what time did Sammy leave the restaurant?"

Unfortunately, Terry didn't find the next question as interesting, returning to his slouched position, "Sheriff, I'm not sure. I had gone back into the kitchen. I guess she was here for about thirty minutes."

Mikeal quickly jotted down 3:30 P.M. in his notepad. "Emma said she called over here looking for Sammy. Did you talk with her?"

"Yes, I did," Terry answered.

"What did you tell her?"

"She wanted to know if Sammy was still here, and I told her she left fifteen or twenty minutes ago."

Mikeal returned to his notebook, scribbling down the approximate time Emma called.

"Terry, you mentioned a few minutes ago you didn't see her leave? So how do you know she had been gone fifteen to twenty minutes?" Mikeal asked.

"It was just a guess, Sheriff, but they only get an hour for lunch. I think Emma called around four, assuming thirty minutes to eat, it seemed about right."

Mikeal looked at the notes on his pad from his interview with Emma. The times didn't add up with Terry's version of the timeline.

"Emma indicated she spoke with you sometime between 5:00 and 5:30, that's at least an hour later than what you're telling me," Mikeal confronted Terry.

"Sheriff, I told you it was only a guess," Terry calmly replied.

"Would you agree then, if it was closer to 5:00 when Emma called, based on your recollection, Sammy had left fifteen or twenty minutes earlier, the actual time she left would have been between 4:30 and 4:45?"

"I would agree," Terry answered before replying, "Are we done here?"

"Alright, well I'm not going to keep you any longer, thanks for your help."

Terry stood up without responding, grabbing his jacket from the back of his chair before walking in the direction of the front door. Mikeal finished jotting down a few more notes before standing and moving in the same direction as Terry.

Terry motioned for the sheriff to leave the building, before keying in the alarm code and also exiting the building. "Do you need a ride home in this weather?" the Sheriff asked Terry.

"No, I'm good, Sheriff," pointing to the jacked-up four-wheel-drive pickup truck parked next to Emma's completely snowed-in Honda Civic.

CHAPTER 3

Sheriff Mikeal Lancaster looked like a mountain man, but he wasn't from these mountains. He was an East Coast transplant who moved west to Montana over a decade ago. Standing a little over six feet tall and weighing around two hundred pounds, he was no longer the fit and lean individual he had maintained throughout his thirties. Well into his forties, his curly blond hair was cut close to his head and was beginning to be overtaken by patches of grey. Unfortunately, this grey had overtaken his beard, making him look ten years older than his actual age. He grew up in the Snowbird Community outside of Robbinsville, North Carolina, on the outskirts of the Smoky Mountains.

Western North Carolina and Eastern Tennessee were the only areas in the United States, where Native Americans and European immigrants governed side by side. When the government was seizing land from the Cherokee Indians in the early 1800s, they would round them up, promise them a better life out west, and then march them thousands of miles to Indian Territory, which is now modern-day Oklahoma. As we all know from the limited teaching we are provided on Native American History, this was known as "The Trail of Tears." When it came to removing the Cherokees from Western North Carolina and Eastern Tennessee, they ran into a problem. The area now referred to as the Great Smoky Mountains contains the highest elevations and some of the most remote areas east of the Mississippi River. This provided the Cherokee an advantage over the U.S Cavalry. The Cherokee had lived in this region for many generations and knew the area inside and out. Due to the rugged terrain, just pure numbers of soldiers were not as effective as in the Mississippi Territory (which included what we now know as the states of Georgia, Alabama, and Mississippi). After more than a decade of trying to remove them, they reached a compromise, creating a reservation in what is now known as Cherokee, NC.

In addition to setting aside land for a reservation, they also created smaller "Communities" in the region for the Indians to remain and govern. Snowbird was one of those communities.

Growing up, Mikeal was considered lazy by most adults, never had an interest in formal education, dropping out of school when he was sixteen. However, this couldn't have been farther from the truth. His interest and focus were in nature, specifically hunting, trapping, foraging for wild mushrooms, and basically learning to live off of what the land can provide. It was often said he was a man born one hundred and fifty years too late.

His friends and cousins knew a different side to Mikeal than most others. As a young man, he wore his hair long, was very quick-witted, and eager to spin a tall tale with the best of them.

Ultimately, his lack of education started to catch up with him. He had lived in a single-wide trailer on land owned by distant relatives, where he was able to grow a decent selection of vegetables during the summer months. His skill as a hunter provided him with meat year-round, and for at least a couple of years, he was able to barter with others for repairs and other items requiring cash money.

A chance run-in with someone he knew from elementary school gave him an opportunity to make a little cash. This friend was a Bounty Hunter, who specialized in rounding up Mountain Folk, who, with a little cash in their pocket, would head to the big cities of Asheville or Knoxville. Usually, it was young men in their early twenties, only partially civilized and definitely not versed in what goes on outside the rural community of Snowbird, who would get in trouble with the law. Further, they didn't take the time to learn how the bail system worked. Often, after being released, they fled back to the mountains, swearing they'll never return to the city. Unfortunately, the laws required them to eventually appear in court.

This created a very profitable business for Mikeal's friend, who was looking to expand his business empire. At first, Mikeal only served as physical backup, earning twenty dollars a day. Most days he never left the car, watching his friend apprehend the subject with little resistance. After a couple of weeks, his role evolved to reconnaissance, where he would silently move through the woods, locating a remote cabin or homestead. Armed with only a phone, binoculars, and a photo, he would often spend days in the woods waiting on the bail jumper to show his face.

Eventually, Mikeal would have the same responsibilities as his friend who ran the business. Over the course of several years, Mikeal developed a reputation as the best tracker of man or animal in this region of Western North Carolina. One of those who was starting to take notice was John Wolf, Chief of the Snowbird Community Police Force. John and Mikeal had been friends for a number of years. The Chief, in his mid-forties, was about twenty years older than Mikeal, but they both shared a love of the outdoors and hunting. The Chief, however, had never been a fan of Mikeal's sense of humor.

The Payne brothers, Billy and Tommy, had a long list of illegal accomplishments, mostly related to their family's moonshining business. Like Mikeal, they were very familiar with the area, and just as the Cherokee eluded the Calvary over two hundred years ago, they disappeared into the mountains, and the authorities could not find them.

Chief John Wolf and his officers had been searching for the Payne Brothers for the last two weeks with no luck. Mikeal, sensing a potential large payday, also had been tracking the brothers. It was actually one of John's officers who suggested they work together with Mikeal.

It wasn't normal procedure to work this closely with a Bounty Hunter, but the Chief figured after two weeks of turning up nothing on the Payne brothers, where was the risk? He had also known him long enough not to be put off by his sense of humor.

The drive out to Mikeal's place was one turn after another as the road hugged the spine of the Appalachian Mountains. Eventually, John made it to the dirt road turn-off which led to Mikeal's trailer. After leaving the paved highway, the dirt road quickly dropped in elevation to the highway, bottoming out at a creek. It was lined by straight tall pine trees which were covered in kudzu, blocking out a considerable amount of daylight. Crossing over the creek, which only held a stream about three inches deep, the road began to rise again before making a sharp turn to the right. The road flattened out for about fifty yards before the Chief knew to turn left into Mikeal's driveway.

The trailer sat back from the road a good distance, surrounded by more pine trees. It wasn't flat, but a sloped lot. The front of the trailer was supported by three levels of cinderblock, compared to a single level holding up the back. John parked his cruiser and walked towards the front steps. He could see Mikeal sitting on the front porch, which was only wide enough to fit a single chair.

"Mikeal, I have a proposition for you," Chief John exclaimed as he walked up to the front porch steps.

"Prostitution? Isn't that illegal, Chief?" He replied back.

"You heard what I said. Are you interested in hearing it, or am I just wasting my time?"

Getting up out of his chair, Mikeal said, "Chief, you know I don't hear well out of my left eye!"

"Left eye my ass," John said as he threw out his arms to give Mikeal a big bear hug.

"How have you been doing, Chief? Only a couple more months to hunting season. You been doing any scouting?"

"Nah, haven't had any time lately. I'm out all day and then spend a couple of hours at night completing paperwork. What time I have left, I try to spend with Meg and the girls."

"That's one of the benefits I have with my current situation," Mikeal chuckled. "No wife or kids, but I have all the time in the world, just how I like it."

"Sounds great," the Chief said, "but don't forget about this luxurious single-wide with cardboard windows and no electricity you live in. It's amazing you can maintain this level of living with hardly any money coming in."

"Well yes, you do make a good point," Mikeal sheepishly grinned, "Cash flow from my investments is sometimes an issue."

"Getting back to my proposal, are you interested in making at least five hundred dollars a week?"

"You have my attention," Mikeal answered back.

"You know the Payne Family, particularly the boys, Billy and Tommy?"

"Oh, I see, that's what this is all about." Mikeal responded. "Well Sheriff, you shouldn't worry about those brothers. I'll have them rounded up in a couple more weeks. Besides, the reward of five grand is a little better than your offer of 500 a week."

"Mikeal, if we work together, we will have them before the week is out. I'll also guarantee you if we catch them, with your help, you'll get your five grand," the Chief added.

"Chief, your word has always been true. If you agree to share intel with me, we have a deal," Mikeal replied, extending his hand to shake on the deal.

"Done!" The Chief commanded.

The Chief then proceeded to bring Mikeal up to speed on the facts. They were being transferred from one county jail to another when the transport van got a flat tire. While the deputy was out changing the tire, they were able to kick open the door and scurry down the embankment and out of sight.

"We figured they would come back this way, but after two weeks, we haven't made any progress locating them. I'm starting to think they didn't come back to this area," the Chief finished.

"Chief, these mountains are home to those two boys. Of course, they came back; where else would they go? They're not exactly city slickers," Mikeal replied.

"Oh, I forgot to ask earlier, do I get paid regardless if we capture them dead or alive?" Mikeal asked.

"Well, preferably alive. Those old boys may be as crooked as a stick, but I'm not aware they ever hurt anyone. If we don't catch them, I'll still pay you five hundred a week for up to two weeks. Either way, you'll return to your luxury estate with money in pocket."

The Chief ended the conversation by telling Mikeal, "It's too late to get started now; I'll pick you up at daylight. We'll pay a visit to Ma and Pa Payne."

The next morning, true to his word, the Chief was back in Mikeal's driveway at dawn. "Are you ready to earn your money?" the chief asked Mikeal as he opened the car door.

"Locked and loaded and ready to go," he replied.

"Whoa, we need to back up a minute here! I never said anything about you being armed."

"What the hell!" A pissed-off look overtook Mikeal's face. "You expect me to help you without any personal protection? I thought you knew me better than that."

"Relax," the Chief said, "I'm only messing with you."

"You piece of shit Redskin," a less than amused Mikeal shouted back!

"Hold on a minute," the Chief said in a serious tone. "We can joke, but I better never hear you use those words directed at me or my people again! You piece of shit white brisket-eating, trailer park piece of trash!" A slight mischievous smile came across the Chief's face.

"Alright, you're right, I should've never gone there, you tree-hugging son of a bitch!" Mikeal deadpanned back.

"Are you ready to visit the Payne family, Mikeal?"

"Yep, let's see what these white sons of bitches say about their two pieces of shit sons."

After driving about thirty minutes, the Chief turned off the pavement, heading down a washed-out gravel road wide enough for one vehicle to pass. After passing a few houses, the road became even smaller, with tall hedges on both sides and signs posted saying private drive, no trespassing.

"Friendly bunch, those Paynes," Mikeal thought to himself. "You know, Chief; this road would be a good spot for an ambush."

"No kidding, probably should've parked and walked in, but a little late to start second-guessing."

After another couple of minutes, the car cleared the hedge rows, and the house suddenly appeared in a clearing. The house looked like a Thomas Kinkade painting, minus all the lights. Barely any paint remained on the wooden sides, and the tin roof appeared to be original to the home. As the patrol car came to a stop in the clearing, the Chief honked the horn to let them know they had visitors.

"Anybody home?" the Chief shouted.

"Yeah, we're here," a woman's voice answered from the door of the home.

"Mrs. Payne, could you spare a few minutes? We'd like to talk about your boys," the Chief asked.

"I figured as much," she responded. "No other reason the Big Chief would come out this far to talk to a bunch of hillbillies."

"Mrs. Payne, is your husband around? We'd like to speak with both of you if possible."

"Yeah, he's over there in the barn, with his rifle pointed at you." she deadpanned her response.

The Chief turned to face the barn. "Ed, we're not here to cause any trouble, we're just trying to figure out a good way to get your boys back in custody without anyone getting hurt."

"Why do guys always pick on a poor bunch of rednecks whose only crime is trying to make a living?" a weak, elderly-sounding voice answered back from the barn.

"Ed, I don't make the laws, I just try to keep the peace and enforce them." the Chief replied. "Come on out and let's talk this through, Ed."

"Alright, but I'm not putting my rifle down!"

"Do what feels best, Ed. I'm not here to take your guns," replied the Chief.

Slowly, Ed appeared from the shadows of the barn, and Mikeal, who had been scanning the surroundings ever since they got out of the car, was surprised when he saw Mr. Payne. Having never met the man, his image was based on what he had heard in town about Ed Payne—a short-tempered, mean S.O.B. who would start a fight if he thought you were looking at him the wrong way! What emerged from the barn was a skinny, hunched-back, weathered old man who may have been five foot four if he was wearing platform shoes.

"Let's go inside; my back's been bothering me," Ed said as he walked by both the Chief and Mikeal without looking at either.

"Whatever you say," the Chief replied.

Once inside, they all took a seat in the front room. The inside of the home was appropriate based on its exterior appearance. Dark wood paneling hinted at a potential late '60s, early '70s remodel. The fireplace looked original, except for the wood-burning stove which had been stuffed into the hearth at some point during the last twenty years.

The Chief opened the conversation with "Ed, I'm not here to judge your boys, but they have been charged with making and distributing meth and need to stand trial. If they're innocent, they'll be set free and can restart their lives again."

"What if those picked for the jury are out to get me and the boys? What guarantee can you give us it'll be fair?" Ed replied.

"Mr. Payne," Mikeal asked, "do you still have that old Sears and Roebuck double-barrel twelve-gauge shotgun I've heard so many people talk about?"

The Chief looked at Mikeal with a puzzled look. "You've been here the whole time, not opened your mouth, and now you want to look at an old shotgun."

"Let the boy be," responded Ed. "Yes, son, I still have my old Betsy. Would you like to see her?"

"Yes, sir, I would love to see her," Mikeal responded.

"It's in the back bedroom; let's all go take a look."

Mikeal and the Chief followed Ed to the back bedroom. "Here she is, my father ordered her from the catalog about 1921 or maybe 22, I don't really remember, to tell you the truth. My Pa didn't have much to hand down when he died, but I gladly took this gun for my inheritance. I've killed many a squirrel, rabbit, and turkey over the years with this gun."

"What other guns do you have?" Mikeal asked.

"Nothing of note; they're all fairly new. I have a 9MM Glock under my pillow and a couple of can-popping .22 rifles. Can't really see anymore; haven't hunted anything in the past five years," Ed exclaimed.

As they turned to walk back to the front room, the Chief asked, "Ed, when was the last time you saw Billy and Tommy?"

"The day we were in town at the hardware store, Chief! But you know that because that's when they were arrested!"

Any goodwill generated by the gun discussion was now gone, as Ed glared at the Chief. "So, Ed, you're telling me you haven't seen or spoken with your boys since they escaped?"

"Chief, I'm not telling you anything about my boys, other than I haven't seen them or spoken to them since they were arrested."

"Alright then, Mikeal, anymore guns you'd like to see, or can we go?" John asked.

"I'm good," he responded. "Ed, we'll be in touch." and with that, both the Chief and Mikeal walked out the front door and returned to the car.

As they drove away, the Chief looked over at Mikeal. "So, what was the deal asking about this old shotgun you heard about in town?"

Mikeal responded, "Well, honestly, your conversation with him was going nowhere. I took a chance on him owning an old gun, maybe leading to us getting a better view of the house."

"Wait a minute, that was just a guess that he had that gun?"

"Chief, the majority of the families in this area are living on the same land their families homesteaded over a hundred years ago; of course, they all have old guns. It was an educated guess he would also have one."

"Alright, detective, what did you learn from inspecting the gun?"

"Not a damn thing! However, walking to the back room, I noticed the door was shut to one room, but there was a light on inside. Another room had its door open, and I could see someone had been sleeping in the bed."

"Alright, Mikeal, so what are you implying? Are you trying to tell me those boys are staying with Ma and Pa because a room had a light on and another room had a slept-in bed?"

"Well, yes, that, coupled with the fact that when we first pulled up, I saw someone on the roof with a gun and what looked like another boy hiding at the end of the hedgerow. Yeah, I guess that's what I'm telling you, Chief."

CHAPTER 4

It was almost midnight when the deputy dropped Emma off
at the apartment the night before. Even in a four-wheel-
drive, the trip home was treacherous, but slow and steady
wins the race, and that was how Deputy Devin Bordeaux
played it. The combination of a white-knuckled ride and
brutally frozen air hitting her face had her fully awake by the
time she turned the key to enter the apartment.

She spent the next two hours reliving the day with her
roommate, Rebecca. They shared a two-bedroom apartment
about thirty miles south of Emma's work, only a couple of
streets off the main highway connecting Bozeman, the
Resorts of Big Sky, and the Northern Entrance of
Yellowstone National Park. Ironically, Rebecca came to
Montana from Florida about three months before Emma.
They attended the same college but never met until Emma
answered an ad on Craigslist for a roommate.

Rebecca had more questions than Emma had answers. They
talked for almost two hours before Emma could feel her body
trying to shut down. As she tried to exit the downstairs
sitting area more than once, she was pulled back by another
question from Rebecca.

"Doesn't the front of the coffee shop face the parking lot?"
Rebecca asked, hopefully her last question.

"Yeah, but what's your point?" Emma replied.

"Wouldn't you have seen her leave?" Rebecca followed.

"Jesus, I was swamped with customers!" Emma barked back. "Rebecca, I gotta get some sleep. Can we pick this back up in the morning?" Rebecca nodded they could. Emma then proceeded up the stairs to the second floor to finally grab some sleep.

After brushing her teeth and washing her face, she set the alarm for 9:30 and crawled into bed a couple of minutes before 3:00 AM. She was out immediately.

Only a few hours later, she was awakened from her deep sleep by a loud knock on the downstairs door. "What the hell," she thought, "who's banging on the door this early?" She strained to see her clock, and it was 6:30 AM. She maybe had gotten three good hours of sleep.

"Must be for Rebecca. I'll let her deal with this," she thought, as she rolled back over and pulled the covers over her head. Bang, Bang! "Shit, Rebecca, will you see who's at the door?" she yelled.

"Alright," Rebecca yelled back to her. A few minutes later, Emma heard Rebecca open her bedroom door. "Emma," Rebecca called out, attempting to keep her voice low.

"What, Rebecca?" Emma answered, with no attempt to disguise the irritability in her voice.

"The Sheriff is downstairs asking for you," she asked in an even quieter voice.

"Oh, Jesus, why is he here so early? I don't even start work until eleven," Emma muttered. "Alright, tell him I need about ten minutes to look human; and I'll come down."

After about fifteen minutes, Emma finally made her way downstairs. Before she reached the bottom step, she realized it wasn't the Sheriff, but the deputy who brought her home last night.

"Any reason why you're here so early?" she tried to calmly ask.

"The Sheriff wanted to go over your statement again." he answered.

"Well, Deputy, we have an issue. I don't start work until eleven today."

"Well, I'm sorry about that, but the Sheriff wanted to do a walkthrough of all your and Sammie's steps early before too many people started to arrive."

After letting out a large sigh, Emma said, "Let me grab my coat, and we can go."

The drive back to the resort was quiet for the first fifteen minutes before Emma asked, "Did you not sleep?"

Devin laughed. "I didn't start my shift until 6:00 yesterday afternoon. Normally I'd be finishing at 6:00 a.m., but I took a few hours off earlier in the week, so I'm finishing at 10:00 today." The remainder of the trip, Devin explained, he had the weekend off before reporting back on day shift the following Monday.

They finally arrived back at the resort around 6:45 a.m.. They drove past her Honda Civic still sitting in the parking lot from the prior day, parking up close to the main building. She could see other officers going back and forth from the different buildings. It appeared they had the area behind the coffee shop blocked from any traffic going through.

"Officer Devin, or should I call you Deputy Devin?" Emma asked.

"Just Devin is fine, Miss."

"Okay, Devin, what do you want me to do now? I don't start work until eleven, so I'm still a little lost as to why I'm here so early."

"As I told you earlier, the Sheriff wanted to walk through the scene with you," he responded.

"Okay, it's back to a scene? Last night, the sheriff indicated to me that she probably just took off." Emma shook her head, confused by the whole situation.

"I shouldn't have said 'scene,' sorry, it just comes out automatically sometimes," Devin replied. "Let me go find the sheriff. If you want to go hang out in the restaurant, I'll send the sheriff that way when I find him."

"Alright, fine by me. I'm starving," Emma said as she walked away.

"Morning, Emma," Terry yelled from the kitchen as she walked through the front door of the restaurant.

"Terry, don't you ever leave this place?"

"Only to sleep, shit, and shower. Other than that, I never leave," he jokingly responded.

"Wow, TMI, Terry, please don't share," was the only reply Emma could muster. She walked over to the drink area, grabbed herself a cup, filled it with ice, and proceeded to top it off with diet coke. Even though she had been working as a barista for a couple of years, she never touched coffee. She then made her way to one of the tables in the back of the dining area.

The Sheriff's Tahoe pulled into the resort's parking lot next to Devin, around 7:15 A.M.. The resort buildings were on the East side of the ski slopes, receiving sun several hours before it made its way up the mountain. In another thirty minutes or less, the resort would be covered with full daylight, and the snow would begin melting quickly.

Deputy Devin was the first to greet the sheriff as he stepped out of the Tahoe. "Good morning, Sheriff! Looks like the start of a beautiful day."

"Yeah, let's hope so, Devin. Christ, it's June; we should be done with snow," the sheriff replied as he walked past the deputy.

"Ah, Sheriff, we had a little issue overnight," Devin said in a mumbled voice.

The Sheriff stopped in his tracks and without turning around replied. "Really?"

"Afraid so, we had a couple of bears show up last night. They really made a mess of the scene."

Mikeal started to second-guess his decision of not bringing in a crew overnight to process the scene. However, he was acting on guidance from superiors. At the start of spring, after the tourist ski season was over, the County Commission had put in place measures to save on expenses. At the top of the list was no overtime, unless there was some type of natural disaster. He still had doubts this was anything more than someone walking off the job, but if he was wrong, this would be a major setback. In typical fashion, he handled it with humor.

"What, I didn't know we had a crime scene," Mikeal said sarcastically.

"You know what I mean, Sheriff, the area around the dumpster."

"Devin, would you ride out and pick Emma up? I promised we would get her to work this morning."

"Sheriff, I've already picked her up, she's waiting for you in the restaurant."

Mikeal looked confused before replying, "I thought she didn't start until eleven?"

"I believe you left that part out! She wasn't very pleased to see me," Devin replied. "Sheriff, I hope this isn't inappropriate, but have you been feeling alright?"

"Not sure what you're getting at, Deputy," Mikeal responded in a stern voice.

"We've worked together for a couple of years. You've always been two steps ahead of me, but lately..."

"But lately what?" Mikeal stared directly into Devin's eyes.

"Well, all I'm saying is lately you've been very forgetful," Devin finished.

Mikeal continued to look directly at Devin. Without saying a word, he knew his deputy was correct. He couldn't remember the first time he noticed, but at least over the past few months, Mikeal's body had sometimes felt disconnected from his mind. Things he normally recited from memory were forgotten or missed. He thought he had been doing a good job of concealing, but maybe not.

Both men awkwardly stood silent within feet of each other. After a few minutes, the Sheriff turned and walked towards the back of the building. Turning the corner, he could see the dumpsters in the distance. The sun continued its march to full daylight; however, it hadn't reached the dumpster area, which was still covered in the shadow of early morning. Even in the shadows, he could make out trash disturbing what otherwise was a clean blanket of snow covering the ground.

"Fucking bears," he murmured under his breath. Stopping at what appeared to be the shop's back door, he could see a single line of human footprints headed towards the two dumpsters at the back of the lot. Easily placing his size twelve boot into the first few tracks, he quickly envisioned Emma walking back and forth to the dumpsters, attempting to place each return step in one already made. Further scanning the area, there were no signs of anyone else being back in the area. As he approached closer to the dumpsters, he started to see scattered trash consistent with what you would expect coming out of a coffee shop. Coffee grounds, paper filters, cups, and plates littered the ground along with the remains of dark trash bags. "Looks like the bears cleaned out any leftover pastries thrown in the trash," he thought to himself.

The temperature overnight had bottomed out in the low twenties, resulting in no snowmelt. However, over to his right was a depression slightly larger than half of a basketball. Mikeal assumed this resulted from a trash bag covering the location during most of the snowfall. He knelt down next to it to get a better view. The lack of sun cast a gray hue over the area, but even then, he could see the dark coloration, which Emma took to be blood.

"Maybe, one way to find out," he thought to himself. He quickly felt through his jacket pocket for something to collect a sample. His pockets were empty, except for a few sandwich bags, his notebook, and a pen. Feeling the sun now touching the back of his neck, he probably had less than fifteen minutes before the snow would start to melt quickly. He looked back towards the coffee shop, hoping another officer was around, but no one was in sight. He stood and started to walk back when Deputy Allison Lightjack appeared. "Allison," the Sheriff barked through the air! "Come here and bring a forensic kit with you."

Allison covered the ground between the shop and dumpsters in half the time it took Mikeal to traverse the same ground. The Sheriff was always surprised by how quick, she was, considering her short stature and being a little on the heavy side. Allison was Lakota or Teton Sioux, growing up in Western South Dakota before moving to Bozeman when she enrolled at Montana State University.

"I'd like to know what this stain in the snow is, get a sample and get it down to the lab as fast as you can," Mikeal asked.

"Yes sir!" Allison replied before dropping to a knee. Without taking any action, she slowly examined the depression. Eventually, she brushed back a little of the snow on top before deciding to dig another hole a couple of feet away from the stain.

"Sheriff, look, the bottom inch or so touching the pavement is ice," Allison remarked.

"Well, it had been reaching the low sixties the last couple of weeks, so what made contact with the ground probably immediately started to melt," Mikeal added.

"Exactly, so if we can get a picture of how deep this stain goes, we can estimate the time it ended up here," Allison finished.

"That's why you're the expert, Allison."

She removed more snow closer to the stain before pulling out a camera and taking multiple photos from different angles. Then, removing a trowel from her backpack, she scooped up a portion of the stained snow and proceeded to place it in an evidence bag. "I've got a cooler back in the car. I'll get it on ice and head back to the station."

"Let me know what you find," the Sheriff uttered as she was already walking away.

With the sun fully up and little cloud cover, it was quickly starting to warm. On the trip in this morning, the radio indicated highs were expected to creep into the low sixties. By noon, the snow and any remaining evidence would be gone.

Now in full daylight, he scanned the area behind the shop when something caught his eye at the tree line, located about twenty yards behind the dumpster. As he walked past the dumpster, he could feel the pavement give way to land hidden under the snow.

Walking across the short clearing, the bear tracks were clearly visible in the snow. They were on the smaller side, so probably black bears rather than grizzlies. Regardless of type, either would be large enough to take down a human. Once he made it to the tree line, he could clearly see what caught his eye. On the left side entrance of what appeared to be a trail heading into the woods, entangled in the thorns of a Prickly Rose, was a red piece of fabric blowing in the wind.

"Ok, how did this get here?" he thought to himself. "Blown by the wind or did someone pass this way?" He quickly put on a pair of gloves and started to examine the piece of cloth held tightly by the plant's thorns. He could tell it hadn't been cut by scissors; jagged lines and dangling threads indicated it had been ripped.

Scanning the surroundings, he could see the trail continued deeper into the woods. Retrieving his phone from his jacket pocket, he quickly snapped off a couple of pictures before removing the cloth and placing it in a plastic sandwich bag. He then proceeded to follow the path deeper into the woods. The trail quickly started to descend the ridge-line, forcing him to hold on to anything firmly attached to the ground or risk having his feet slide out from under him. The path eventually bottomed out, running parallel with a gravel road. After about fifty yards, the trail started to edge back into the woods as the road veered off to the right. Mikeal thought to himself, "Alright, which one do I follow? I can easily cover more ground in the car on the road, so back into the woods it is."

The trail immediately started to climb. Having spent most of his life in the woods, this shouldn't have been an issue for him, but the last five years had not been kind to his waistline nor his conditioning. After what seemed like only a few hundred feet up the mountain, his heart was pounding, he was out of breath, and his head was starting to feel dizzy.

"Wow, I've really let myself go these last few years," he thought as he stopped to take a break. He scooped up a handful of undisturbed snow, which he immediately shoved in his mouth. Feeling the temperature of his body continuing to climb, he unzipped both his outer vest and fleece jacket. After a few minutes, his heart rate slowed down, and he proceeded on his journey up the ridge-line. Eventually, he came to a clearing with a four-by-four area completely void of snow. The smell of burnt wood permeated the air. A small but visible stream of black smoke climbed its way up into the treetops. Littered with beer cans and other assorted pieces of trash, this spot was occupied by someone within the last twelve hours.

Mikeal pondered whether this could be associated with the disappearance or just a place where local kids met up. As he reached for his notebook, the snap of someone or something stepping onto a dry tree branch broke the silence.

"Who's there!" the Sheriff instinctively yelled. He quickly pivoted around attempting to identify the direction from which the sound came. "This is Sheriff Mikeal Lancaster, I'll ask again, who's there," but still no response. "Look, I'm not here to bust anyone for underage drinking or smoking pot, just trying to locate someone who is missing. Sammy, if that's you, please show yourself so I know you're not here to do me any harm."

Normally, Mikeal wasn't easily spooked by sounds in the woods. However, a few weeks earlier, he had a nasty encounter while investigating a report of a stolen vehicle. On the other side of the county, in the middle of nowhere, someone snuck up from behind, placing the muzzle of their weapon against the back of his head. Luckily, he had backup who were quickly able to disarm the assailant. He had been having recurring flashbacks ever since.

Still without any response, he pulled his service revolver from its holster. "I've asked nicely, unfortunately your lack of response has raised the seriousness level. My gun is drawn, please identify yourself or I'm..." Before he could finish his sentence, he heard the sound of another breaking twig.

This time he had a fix on where the sound came from. After hiking up to the clearing, the trail descended back down another ridge. It sounded like the noise was below his feet on the downslope of the trail.

"I'm in trouble," he thought to himself. "If I start down the trail, they'll see me way before I see them." His only thought was "I need to get low to the ground." The Sheriff quickly dropped to his knees and then belly as he dragged his body towards the edge of the clearing and the start of the trail's descent down the ridge. As he crept closer to the edge, he kept scanning the horizon looking for the source of the sound. Finally, at the edge, he had a good view of the open hollow below. The snow hadn't penetrated this side of the mountain as well as the other. The base of snow only appeared to be four or so inches deep, with the green ferns and other vegetation remaining visible. This didn't give him the clear view he had hoped. Mikeal quickly got to his knees and in a crouched position slowly made his way down the trail. It had been several minutes since he heard any sound other than birds calling out to each other, warning the others of the impending gun battle about to take place. "Crack," the sound of a breaking twig resonated just a few feet behind him. Mikeal's heart dropped to the bottom of his chest.

Mikeal could literally feel the hair stand up on the back of his neck. He knew he needed to turn around and confront the situation he was in; however, his body was frozen in place. "Shit, I don't have a clue as to what I need to do."

His mind was racing. Should he throw up his hands, admit defeat and hope they don't execute him, or turn and go out in a blaze of glory? "Fuck this, I'm no coward," he thought as he quickly pulled his pistol and turned to confront this unknown enemy! In what seemed like a fraction of a second, he whipped around and fired off a shot waist high, ensuring he would hit something.

As the echo of the shot reverberated through the valley below, he was in full view of his assailant. His jaw dropped as a coyote took off through the brush attempting to get away from this madman. The Sheriff took a firm seat as his butt hit the ground.

"Jesus, a damn coyote," he muttered to himself!

Mikeal looked down at his hand, still holding the pistol; it was still shaking. "I'm getting too old for this," he thought as he looked around, making sure no one else witnessed the spectacle that just unfolded. After what seemed like fifteen minutes, he had composed himself and not even realizing it, had started to follow the trail back to the resort. Walking past the clearing down to the roadside, before he knew it, he was coming out of the woods behind the dumpsters.

"Sheriff," Devin yelled upon seeing him.

Mikeal didn't answer but continued walking back towards the cordoned-off area around the dumpsters.

Devin continued to call out, "Sheriff" with no return response.

Finally, with the Sheriff ten feet away, Devin tried to get the attention. "Sheriff," but before he could get out another word, the Mikeal responded.

"Devin, I heard you the first time, what do you want?"

Mikeal and Devin were now literally three feet apart. Devin quickly surveyed the Sheriff from head to toe. His jacket was open, shirt pulled out of his pants with the ends appearing to be soaked, "Sheriff what happened to you?"

"Long story, simple ending, I tripped over a tree root and face-planted."

"What were you doing in the woods," Devin asked.

The Sheriff, still embarrassed by getting spooked in the woods, started to walk away before turning around to ask Devin what time his shift ended.

"Technically about an hour ago, but I can stay longer if needed," Devin replied.

"No need," the Sheriff pulled the plastic evidence bag containing the piece of cloth from his pocket. "Can you take this back to Allison? Probably nothing, but you never know."

"Sheriff, what about Emma? She's still waiting for you in the restaurant," Devin stated.

"Yeah, I know, but I'm not finished at the coffee shop," Mikeal replied before walking away.

The sun was fully up in the sky, and the snow was rapidly melting, creating one big pile of slush in the parking lot. Mikeal paused by the side door of the coffee shop, looking down at the now-exposed pavement; it was littered with cigarette butts. "Designated smoking area," he remarked before walking around to the front.

Through the front window, Mikeal could see two employees behind the counter. One was a big lady in both width and height; "wouldn't want to mess with her," he thought to himself. Her partner was a more normally sized lady with long black hair.

Inside, a few customers had already taken root on the couch, drinking coffee and reading the morning paper. Walking through the front door, it appeared all eyes turned to him.

"Morning, Sheriff," a voice from the couch broke the silence.

"Good morning," he replied.

Once inside, he had a clearer vision of the two women behind the counter. The larger woman had very manly features, hidden under a deep base of makeup. Looking at her hands, they weren't well-manicured. Her nails were unpolished, short, and it appeared she may be a nail biter. As described by Terry, the dark-haired lady, whom he assumed was Larissa, was very attractive, although she had way too much makeup on.

"Sheriff," the dark-haired, normal-sized lady spoke up; "what can I get you?"

"What's your name?" he asked.

"I'm Larissa," she politely responded.

Before he could ask another question, the front door opened.

"Can someone tell me what's going on?" The man said in a loud voice.

Mikeal turned to answer, but before getting a word out, the man was in his face.

"I'm assuming you're in charge."

"Maybe I am," the Sheriff answered, "but who the hell are you?"

"Steve Taylor, I run food and beverage at the resort. Can you please tell me why we have all these police cars in the parking lot and access to the back of the building blocked?"

"I don't see why not," Mikeal answered. "Late yesterday afternoon we received word one of your employees went out on break and never came back. Nightfall was setting in when we arrived, so we blocked off the area where she was last seen. We're back this morning to figure out where she went."

Steve, looking towards the counter, asked; "Larissa, you worked yesterday, who's missing, Emma?"

"Mister Steve, I don't know who's missing."

"It's Sammy." the Sheriff answered. "Evidently, Larissa called out sick yesterday; it got busy, feeling overworked, she took a break and never came back."

As Mikeal was speaking, Steve stared at Larissa, shaking his head as if to say, "I can't believe you called out sick again."

Returning his attention to the Sheriff, Steve replied, "Well, she's not the first employee to walk off the job mid-shift and not return. I've been at this resort for over twenty-five years; we usually get one or two a year. Sometimes, they'll show up a week or two later to collect their last paycheck, but most just disappear into the wind."

"That's what we're thinking," Mikeal responded; "However, we did find something else that may say otherwise."

"What was that, Sheriff?"

"It's probably nothing, but until we're a little farther along in our investigation, we will not be able to share."

"If you would excuse me, I need to head over to the restaurant to speak with Emma, so she can walk me through what she saw last night. Do you mind if I walk through your shop to the back door?"

"No, go ahead," Steve answered.

Emma looked up just in time to see the Sheriff walk through the front door. She grabbed her coat and proceeded to meet him halfway.

"How's it going?" Mikeal asked.

"Other than being awakened and brought here several hours before my shift, I'm doing great, Sheriff."

"Yeah, sorry about that, should've verified when you started, but oh well, things happen."

"Yes, Sheriff, things happen; you just try your best not to step in it," Emma responded.

They both walked out of the restaurant and headed to the coffee shop.

"Okay, Emma, I don't need all the details of yesterday, so let's start when Sammy was about to go to lunch."

As they walked through the front door of the coffee shop, Henrietta was the first one to greet them; "Hi, Emma," she shouted. Emma quickly replied but then walked past Larissa without a sound or making eye contact.

After she had passed, Larissa commented; "Emma, Steve wants to talk to you."

"Well, Steve will have to wait; can't you see I'm helping the Sheriff?"

They both proceeded to the back room of the shop, stopping by the back door. "Okay, Sheriff, this is the last place I saw Sammy."

Mikeal quickly glanced around the ten-by-ten room with his eyes stopping by the trash next to the back door. "So this is where the trash stays until you take it to the dumpster? How many bags are here by the end of a typical day?"

"Usually, we end the day with three or four bags; it depends on how busy it's been," Emma responded.

"What's normally in the trash bags?" he asked?

"Well, duh, Sheriff, trash; what else would you expect in the bag?"

"Emma, no one likes a smart-ass!"

"Not trying to be an ass, but evidently I don't understand what you're asking."

"Alright, let me ask you another way; is it mainly solids, liquids, or a combination of both?"

"Mainly solids, maybe a little bit of liquid, but not much."

"So how many bags were here when you started to close up yesterday?"

"I believe there were four from the prior day, and we added another four, so eight total," Emma answered.

"When you and Sammy were standing here, before she left for a break, what was her temperament?"

"Temperament? She was pissed! It was an extremely busy morning; we had to clean up from the night shift; neither of us were happy campers!"

"Did she give you any indication she might not come back?" Mikeal asked?

"I don't know," Emma responded in a tiresome voice. "Now that I'm thinking about it, maybe she did, but at the time, I thought she was just blowing off steam."

"So when she left, did she take any of the trash bags with her?"

"I don't think she did, but I'm not one hundred percent positive she didn't."

"No problem, Emma. When you have a minute to think, I'd appreciate it if you would try to remember."

The Sheriff gave Emma a couple of minutes to think before stating, "Let's walk outside." Mikeal and Emma opened the back door to stand on the patio, which was now completely free from snow. "I'm assuming this is where you guys go for a smoke?"

"Yeah, I don't," Emma replied, "but just about everyone else does."

"Does Sammy smoke?"

"Occasionally, I've seen her light one up, but not often."

"I've noticed from this patio you can see the dumpsters in the distance. When you started to bring the trash out last night, did you see the other bags already sitting by the dumpster?"

"I guess I never looked up, Sheriff. It was a long day; I worked the afternoon by myself. I just wanted to finish and get home. I guess I was on autopilot; I didn't notice the bags until I was at the dumpster."

"Let's walk towards the dumpster, and you let me know when you realized there were already two bags there." They both silently walked towards the dumpster at the back of the lot.

About thirty yards from the dumpster, Emma said, "Here! Right about here! I guess I looked up for the first time and saw them."

"Is it normal to leave trash bags outside the bin?"

"Not at all," Emma replied. "When we were going through our new employee training, they stressed trash had to go in the dumpster and to make sure it was closed properly, or the bears would get into it and make a mess. If not, we would then have to clean up. I'm not a garbage man, Sheriff, so I always make sure it's in the dumpster."

"Except last night," Mikeal laughed.

"Well, yeah, except last night," she answered.

Suddenly, like a light switch was turned on, Mikeal's face became serious. "Emma, do you usually dump ashtrays into the trash?"

"No, Sheriff, the shop is smoke-free. Why are you asking?"

"Hold on a second," he said as he walked a few feet away, kneeling. He pulled a plastic bag from his coat and picked up something off the ground and placed it in the bag.

"Sorry about the dramatics, I just had a thought about something. There are only a few cigarette butts by the dumpster; I'm guessing they should match those up by the patio." Mikeal didn't share what he was really thinking - that if they didn't match, someone else was back here. "Well, anyways, I think that should cover it, for now. Emma, you've been a big help; we will find your friend. I have a good feeling she's going to be okay."

"But what about the blood?" Emma asked.

"We've got a sample of it to test, but frankly, there wasn't enough blood to be concerned about. The bears tore open the trash bags, and we didn't find any body parts, so I'm not thinking this is a murder scene. I'll walk you back to the shop; I need to pick up some of the cigarette butts from the patio to test against those at the dumpster."

CHAPTER 5

The phone rang the first time around 6:00 a.m., but Mikeal hardly noticed it as he turned over and put the pillow over his head. Approximately fifteen minutes later, it rang again. Still not fully awake, he reached for his phone. He didn't recognize the number but knew the area code, 828. "Who's calling me from North Carolina this early on a Saturday morning?" he thought. Before he could answer, the caller hung up.

Slowly, he rolled his feet out of bed and onto the floor. He sat on the edge for a few minutes before getting up to head into the kitchen to make the day's first cup of coffee. A few minutes later, he heard his phone go off again. "Shit, phones in the bedroom," he muttered. He quickly raced back and retrieved it. "Hello," he answered.

"Is this Mikeal," a lady's voice pleasantly asked?

"Yes, it is. Are you a robot?"

"What? A robot? What do you mean?" she asked, her tone less pleasant than before.

"I'm sorry, I thought you might be one of those robocalling things. I once talked to a lady for ten minutes before I realized it was a recorded message."

"No, I'm not calling to sell anything."

"Okay, then why are you calling?" he asked.

"I don't know if you remember me, but you knew my daddy well. I'm Sky, Sky Wolf."

"Wow, John's little girl! What's it been, about twenty years?"

"Yeah, it's been a while. I'm twenty-eight now."

"That's crazy; I can still picture you as a little girl. How's the old man doing? I still think about him often, but we probably haven't spoken in about five years."

"Well, that's why I'm calling. He passed away yesterday morning."

"Oh no, I'm so sorry for your loss. Your father was a great man; I learned a lot from him."

"He also spoke highly of you, Mikeal," Sky replied.

"Your dad and I found ourselves in a lot of crazy situations back in the day. He was the calmest man I have ever known. We were never in a situation where he didn't know what to do. If you don't mind me asking, how did he die?"

"Cancer. It had been eating at him for the last couple of years. Started in his kidneys, spread to his lungs, and then to his brain. He had been in hospice care for the last six months."

"Wow, I am really sorry to hear this about your father, but thanks for thinking about me and letting me know."

"That's just it," Sky responded, "I wasn't thinking about you. We were going through dad's things, and he had your name and number in his wallet. I just assumed you guys were still in regular contact and that he would want us to let you know."

After hanging up the phone and grabbing a quick shower, Mikeal made one more cup of coffee before heading out the door. Normally, he wouldn't go into the office on the weekends but decided this Saturday he would make an exception. After stopping by the diner to grab a quick bite to eat, he made it to the office before 9:00 a.m.

"Good morning, everyone! Lovely way to spend a Saturday, isn't it?"

"Good morning, Sheriff. What are you doing here?" Allison asked.

"What, because I'm the boss, you don't expect me to come in on Saturday?"

"No, it's just you never come in on Saturdays," a confused Allison answered.

"Well, I'm here today. Who else is here?"

"I'm here," came a voice from the back room.

"Is that you, Jordan?" Mikeal asked.

"Yep, it's me," she replied.

"Did you get the results back from the evidence we gathered at the resort yesterday?" Mikeal asked Allison.

"Not yet. Hopefully, by tomorrow, the lab will be finished."

"Alright, I'll be in my office if you need me."

The Sheriff loved his job but not the paperwork that came with it. Entering his office, he was reminded by the two stacks of files on his desk. He would often wait until the very last minute before completing something. In this case, the County District Attorney, who was up for re-election the following year, had sent over twenty old cold case files that she had asked the Sheriff to review two months ago. Her office had been calling regularly over the last two weeks to see what progress, if any, he had made.

Over the next twenty minutes, Mikeal alternated between staring at the files on the corner of his desk and thinking about his old friend, Chief John Wolf. He felt bad knowing his friend had his number with him up until the day he died. He honestly couldn't remember the last time they spoke. Several years ago, Mikeal had helped save a family who had driven into a flooded area, where their car was almost swept away by the raging river. Sometime during the rescue, Mikeal had slipped and was washed several hundred yards downstream before grabbing hold of a tree. Several hours later, rescuers in a chopper were able to lower a basket and pull him to safety. The water immersion had destroyed his cell phone and all its data, including Chief Wolf's number. "That must have been five or six years ago," he thought to himself.

Shortly after bringing the Payne Brothers in, Chief Wolf offered Mikeal a permanent job in the sheriff's department. It wasn't a deputy position but it came with a promise. If Mikeal would study and take the G.E.D. test and pass, the Chief would promote him to an officer as soon as a position opened up. Mikeal upheld his end of the deal; after studying for three months, he passed his G.E.D. on the first try. Over the next ten years, Mikeal learned everything he could about being a police officer from Chief Wolf. Eventually, Mikeal tired of the constant drug issues in the area. Dealing with Meth heads was a weekly occurrence. He eventually decided to move west, settling in the Big Sky area of Montana. Based on his law experience in the mountains of North Carolina, he quickly got a job with the Gallatin County Sheriff's Department. With his sense of humor and southern twang, he quickly became popular in his new territory. After a couple of years, the Sheriff retired, and on a bet, Mikeal decided to actively pursue the job. Within five years of moving to the area, Mikeal was now the Sheriff.

"Sheriff... Sheriff... Sheriff!" Allison finally shouted.

"What? Oh, I'm sorry, Allison, I must have zoned out for a moment."

"No worries, but I'm headed out for lunch. You need me to pick you up anything?"

"No, I'm good. I'll probably only be here another hour or so."

"Suit yourself; I'll see you when I get back." "Alright, Mikeal," he said to himself, "I guess it's now or never on these files." He reached over and pulled the first file off the top of the stack. Written on the cover was the date July 17th, 1978. Okay, old but not an ancient file. Flipping through the first few pages, he realized it's an abduction case. No time for this one, and he set it to the side and pulled another file. This one also dated in the seventies; a stolen 1972 Corvette. Why would the DA want me to look into this? It's just a car. Okay, now I'm starting to see why; this car belonged to the Munson family." The Munson family had built their wealth on lumber and cattle and was well known in the area with plenty of political connections.

The next hour or so, he spent alternating between looking at files and news on his phone, before eventually losing interest in both. Looking at his watch, he guessed Allison should be back from lunch. "Allison, do you have a second?" he called out. After a few minutes, she appeared in his doorway.

"Yes, Sheriff, you called."

"Yeah, come on in and sit down. I know you said it might be another day or so before we get any lab results back, but what's your gut feeling?" he asked.

"I'm not sure, still trying to process what we have. Yeah, I know, but surely you're leaning one way or another. If I said I needed an answer right now, what would you tell me?" Mikeal pressed.

"If you needed an answer right now, I would say she left on her own."

"You feel a hundred percent positive about that?"

"Sheriff, you put me on the spot. No, I'm not one hundred percent positive, more like eighty-five," Allison responded.

"Fair enough, let's see what the lab results tell us and go from there."

"Wait a minute, Sheriff, your turn! What do you think happened to Sammy?"

"I'm leaning towards job abandonment. Outside of potential blood by the dumpster, there's no other evidence of foul play. Anyway, that's not why I called you; I need your help on something else."

"Okay, what have you got?"

"The DA wants us to look through some cold case files to determine if any may relate to what we're currently working on."

"Sure, I'll be glad to help, Sheriff."

"Great, I'll give you half and keep the rest. Let me know by next Friday if anything looks interesting or familiar." Allison grabbed the files and headed back to her desk. "Oh, and Allison, please let me know as soon as the lab work comes back."

Over the next several hours, Mikeal finally developed a rhythm looking through the files on his desk, mainly looking for any type of present-day connection. After an hour or so, he decided to get up and stretch his legs.

The building housing the sheriff's office was a single story, but it also had a full basement which contained the dispatch area, storage, and a large conference room. On the main floor were the Sheriff's personal office and an open room which contained eight desks. A hallway ran out of this room down the front of the building, with a break room followed by two interview rooms.

Stepping out of his office, the big room was empty, but he could hear female voices down the hallway. "Hey, Sheriff," Jordan, who was facing the door, answered when Mikeal suddenly appeared in the doorway.

"How was lunch?" he asked.

"Good," Jordan responded. "I have some fries left. Would you like them?"

"No, I'm good, but thanks for the offer. It's been a quiet day since I've been here. You guys get any calls?" Both Jordan and Allison shook their heads to indicate no calls had been received. "Alright, I'm heading back to my office to wrap things up and head home. I'll see you both on Monday."

Once back in his office, as he was putting things away, he noticed a wad of paper in the back of his top desk drawer. "Damn, I really need to clean this desk out one day." He started to go through the papers which mainly consisted of old receipts. "When was the last time I filled out an expense report?" he thought to himself. Most of the receipts were six months or older. As he went through gas and food receipts, he came across a folded post-it note. On the note was written "Chief Wolf" and a phone number. Mikeal stared at the note for a couple of minutes; it wasn't in his handwriting. "Allison and Jordan," he called out, "can you guys come here for a minute."

"Sure," he heard Allison respond.

"Take a look at this note, do either of you recognize this handwriting?"

"Yeah, it looks like mine," Jordan answered. The Sheriff started to open his mouth, and the phone rang.

"I'll get it," responded Allison as she started to run back to her desk.

After a momentary pause, Mikeal asked Jordan, "Do you remember when he called?"

"Sheriff, I know we don't get a lot of calls, but I can't remember a call from a few weeks ago. Why was it important?"

"Nah, I guess not, was just curious if you remembered when."

"Sorry, I can't help, but now you found his number, call him back."

"I wish I could, but that's impossible to do now."

"What do you mean impossible? Pick up the phone and call him," she responded with an amused look on her face.

Mikeal looked up from staring at the post-it note. "I received a call from his daughter this morning. Chief John Wolf passed away yesterday morning."

"Oh, Sheriff, I'm sorry to hear that! Isn't he the one that got you started in law enforcement?"

"Yep, he pulled me out of my trailer, made me get my G.E.D., and gave me a job. I owed a lot to John Wolf; it's a shame I didn't have the time to return his last call."

"It's kind of crazy; of all days, today was when you found the note."

"Just a coincidence, Jordan. I don't believe in any of that ghost mumbo jumbo," Mikeal replied. "I guess indirectly his death made me come in to work on a Saturday. Kind of feeling nostalgic, so probably subconsciously, I decided my office would remind me of him."

"Hey, guys," suddenly Allison was back at his door. "That was Gary Weaver calling."

"The dog-wolf guy?" Jordan asked?

"Yep, I think he calls them wolf dogs."

"What's going on?" the Sheriff asked.

"One of his dogs went missing but finally returned with a large bone in its mouth. He thought it might be human."

"Well, I guess we need to go take a look," Mikeal stated. "Come on, Allison, you can ride with me; Jordan, you've got the fort while we're gone?" "Yep, I got it," she replied."

CHAPTER 6

Mikeal and Allison started out heading towards the Weaver Farm near Hebgen Lake. Like everything else in Montana, nothing is near. Even in the same county, the ride from Bozeman to the lake would take almost two hours.

"Did Jordan remember taking the call you were asking us about?" Allison attempted to make small talk on the journey.

The Sheriff continued to stare at the road ahead before answering, "No, figured it would be a long shot, probably came in about six months or more back."

"I'm not familiar with the name; he's not a local?"

"No," Mikeal answered, "he's back in North Carolina."

"Oh, is that who you worked with before moving west?"

"Yep, Chief John Wolf gave me my first job, many many moons ago."

"I'd like to meet him, would love to hear some stories from when you were starting out," Allison replied. "I would be interested to hear if you made the same silly mistakes I'm making while learning the job."

"Yeah, I'd like to see him again, but I waited too long. His daughter called me this morning, he died yesterday."

"Oh, Sheriff, I'm sorry to hear that. Do you know what happened?"

"Yeah, Cancer ate him up from the inside."

"You going back east for the funeral?"

"What's the point? He's the only one who knew me. Won't do him any good now to see my sorry face."

"Yeah, but it might give you closure, Sheriff."

"Maybe, maybe not. Well anyway, this is rather depressing, let's talk about something else. So what do you know about the guy that called this in?"

"Not much, Sheriff. I've gone out there a couple of times with the vet when they had new pups. You know, to verify the dog is properly tattooed."

"Yeah, what is it, fifteen days from when they're born?" Mikeal asked.

"Yep, fifteen days. We've never had an issue, and from what the vet's told me, he's a much-respected breeder."

Over the next hour, as the miles passed by, little to nothing was said. Allison could tell the Sheriff was in deep thought and left him to it. Mikeal kept playing an endless loop of memories through his head, mostly of his time in North Carolina with Chief Wolf.

Allison passed the time looking at the beautiful mountains, once again covered in snow from the prior day's storm. After not seeing another vehicle in the last hour, suddenly a few appeared parked on the roadside. "Must be near a river," she thought, as they passed a gentleman carrying a long fly rod.

Finally, the silence was broken when Mikeal asked, "What type of dogs is he mating with the wolves?"

"German Shepherds," Allison replied.

"Interesting, that could be one tough dog," Mikeal thought.

"Another ten or so miles, Sheriff, and we'll need to turn off the highway." After about ten minutes, Allison told Mikeal, "Around this turn, there'll be a dirt road on the left we'll need to take."

"Got it," Mikeal turned the Tahoe onto the dirt road and proceeded deeper and deeper into the woods. At first, they were passing normal fenced-in pastures with your typical three rows of barbed wire. While the snow had completely left the road, patches broke up the green grass of the pastures. Passing an intersection with another dirt road, Mikeal noticed the street sign was now marked as a private drive, and the fence line changed from barbed wire to an eight-foot-high chain-gate fence. "I know everyone in Montana lives in the sticks, but this guy really lives back in the woods," he told himself. Eventually, they reached a gate across the road.

"Now what?" Mikeal asked.

"He said to call him when we reached the gate." Allison already had his number keyed into her phone. "Mr. Weaver, this is Allison with the Gallatin County Sheriff's office; we spoke earlier. Yes, we're at the gate. Okay, thank you," and Allison hung up the phone. "He'll be here in about five minutes to let us in."

Within minutes, they could see a four-wheeler approaching from the other side of the gate. A young twenty-something man jumped off and proceeded to unlock and swing open the gate. "When you get to the end of the road, go left towards the barn," he instructed. "Mr. Weaver will be waiting for you."

With those instructions, Mikeal put the truck back in gear and proceeded down the road. After about five hundred yards, the woods gave way to a large clearing. Straight back was a nice, but not overly large home, but to the left was a massive steel building.

"I'm guessing that's the barn," Allison responded.

"I reckon," Mikeal answered.

As they were exiting the Tahoe, the young man on the four-wheeler also pulled up. "Come on, I'll take you both inside to Mr. Weaver." The boy led them to one end of the barn where a massive sliding door was open, revealing the inner workings and layout of the building. As they walked inside, a middle corridor with large cages the size of a horse stall on both sides appeared.

"How many animals do you have at a time here?" Allison asked.

"It depends on the time of the year. In the summer, we normally have about fifteen to twenty. Mainly our core breeding wolves and Shepherds. We can hold up to a hundred animals if needed," the young man replied.

"Doesn't sound like you have many, I don't hear a sound," Mikeal replied.

"Well, if you're expecting to hear barking or howling, you'll never know they're around," the young man answered. Halfway through the building, another large sliding door on the right opened up to the outside. "Go through this door and hang a left, and you'll run into Mr. Weaver," the boy says, before turning around and retracing his steps back out of the building.

As they exited the building, the bright glare of the sun temporarily blinded their view, but they quickly hear a voice: "Sheriff, thanks for coming all the way out here." Placing his hand across his forehead, Mikeal was able to make the outline of a man.

"Thanks, Mr. Weaver, I assume."

"Yes, but call me Gary. Mr. Weaver makes me sound like an old man."

Finally, with his eyesight adjusted to the sun, Mikeal was surprised by what Mr. Weaver was wearing. Expecting someone with dirty coveralls and dirty hands, Mr. Weaver, instead, was wearing a crisp collared button-down shirt and khakis.

"Pretty large operation you have here," Allison chirped in.

"Yeah, we have a couple hundred acres. You guys have time to see some of the property?"

"Two hours out here, we might as well stay for a little while," Mikeal answered.

"You saw our kennel; nothing more really to see in there, mainly used for housing and feeding. In front of you, we have two quarter-acre fenced training sites. The dogs usually spend an hour or two every day in here working with our trainers."

"What are you training them for?" Allison asked.

"Most of our customers are police departments who utilize our dogs in their canine fleet of officers. So we work a lot on installing discipline in the animals, structure, and an understanding of how to take down prey in a non-lethal manner, if you know what I mean."

"Yeah, I guess it's bad for business if your dogs took down a perp by ripping his throat out," Mikeal joked.

"It must cost a fortune to feed these guys. I'm guessing it's not off-the-shelf dog food," Allison asked.

"We try to feed them wild meat as often as we can. During hunting season, we kill Elk and Mule Deer for feed. We also work closely with the state's FWP (Fish, Wildlife & Parks) department to have access to roadkill."

"Why do you call them dogs rather than wolf dogs?" Allison asked with a puzzled look on her face.

"Our animals are more dog than wolf. I won't bore you with a lot of breeder lingo, but our dogs would be classified as an F3. We find, by the time you get to this level, they're not as solitary as animals with a higher wolf DNA percentage."

"Wolves travel in packs, what do you mean by solitary animals?" Mikeal chimed in.

"That's very true, Sheriff, but it's humans that they shy away from, which when your bread and butter is service animals, that's a trait you try to minimize."

"So, Gary, what exactly is an F3," Allison started to ask before Mikeal interrupted.

"Look, Mr. Weaver, no disrespect intended, but I'd like to focus on what you called us about," Mikeal stated.

"Oh yes, sorry. I can talk for hours about our operations. Let's jump in my truck, and we'll drive to the back field," Gary offered. As they proceed to drive to the back of the property, Gary tells them, "this is where we let the dogs run around and get their exercise during the day. We more or less have a hundred acres of pastureland and another fifty acres of wooded area fenced. I'll need to stop for a second and open this first gate."

Looking through the front windshield, the gate system reminded Mikeal of the Jurassic Park movies he had seen in the past. It consisted of two gates: one to enter the perimeter of the field, followed by a holding area and then another gate. Gary jumped back in the truck and proceeded to move forward into the enclosure. Once inside, he jumped back out, closed the first gate, and then pressed a button on the side of the enclosure which started to open the second gate, before climbing back into the truck.

"I know it's a pain, but I haven't figured out a better way to do it."

"Hey, whatever works," Mikeal replied. The truck pulled through the second gate and took off across the pasture. After a couple of minutes, they slowed as they approached the tree line. "There's something up ahead I want to show you." The truck slowly eased to a stop about fifty yards into the woods.

As they all exited the vehicle, Gary started to walk deeper into the woods. "One of our dogs got out a couple of nights ago; luckily for us, she returned this morning."

"Got out," Mikeal replied, "Well, she didn't jump the fence; I'm reckoning they're eight feet tall."

"Close to nine feet to be exact!" Gary answered. "It's pretty rocky back here, but she found soft soil and was able to dig under." Arriving at the base of the fence, Gary points to where the dog had dug out.

"Well, Gary, I'm glad your dog came back, but how does that apply to us?" Mikeal asked.

"Let me show you what she brought back; it's over here in the truck."

They all walk back to the truck, and Gary drops the tailgate before climbing into the bed of the truck. He opens the toolbox, which was mounted to the floor directly behind the rear window. He then proceeds to pull out a well-worn towel, approximately three feet in length, rolled up like a yoga mat. Once he starts to unwrap it, it's the size of a small beach blanket. Even before he's finished unwrapping it, Allison knows it's a human femur bone.

"Okay, Gary, that's a game-changer, that's definitely human," Mikeal responds. The bone had an earthy appearance, with a brownish hue indicating it had been in the ground for a while.

"I'm no expert, but based on the size, that's probably from a female," Allison noted. Allison puts on a pair of blue gloves and took the bone from Mr. Weaver. Allison rubbed her hand along the surface; it felt pitted and rough. "The ends feel a little slippery in my hands," she then holds it up to her nose.

"What are you doing?" Gary asks.

"Just trying to get a feel for the possible age; it could be really old or something more recent."

"Really, how can you tell?"

"Older bones are going to be dry and, depending on age, could be a little brittle. After so many years in the earth, they also lose any smell that was associated with them. Just feeling and smelling this one tells me it's probably been in the ground five years or less."

"Fascinating, just from feeling and smelling the bone, you can tell!" Gary remarked.

"Of course, we'll send it off to the lab for a more scientific approach, but I bet I'm close," Allison said with a smile.

"Allison, can you tell if there had been any trauma to the bone?" Mikeal asked.

"Hard to say, we'll know more once we can get it back to the lab."

Allison carefully wrapped the bone back up in the towel before climbing into the back seat of the truck. Within a few minutes, they're back at the big metal barn. As they exit the vehicle, Gary asks if they would like to see the pups born overnight.

"I would love to," Allison answered before Mikeal could decline.

Mikeal looks down at his watch, eager to get back into town. "I'm sorry, Allison, but we really need to get back to town, maybe next time." Allison and Mikeal then follow Gary out of the building back to Mikeal's Tahoe.

"Well, thanks for showing us around, Mr. Weaver. We'll need to bring a team out here in the morning to locate where your dog found the bone. I hope it will be okay to use this area to stage the search," the Sheriff asked.

"No problem at all, as a matter of fact, I'd like to help. I'll harness Sheila up, and hopefully, she can help lead us back to where she found the bone."

"That would be awesome, thank you, Mr. Weaver."

The drive back to Bozeman was a repeat of the drive out. Very little was said, with Mikeal appearing to be deep in thought, leaving Allison alone to watch the mountains go by. It was approaching 9:00 p.m. when he dropped Allison off at the station; thirty minutes later, he turned into his driveway, finally home. What he thought was going to be only a few hours in the office turned into a long day, with the promise of an even longer day tomorrow. As he walks into the house, it's dark, but repeating the same path over the five years he's lived in the home, he's on autopilot as he walks through the front room into the kitchen to turn on the light.

"Well, what's for dinner tonight?" he says to himself as he's looking into a mostly empty refrigerator. Grabbing the milk and a box of corn flakes from the pantry, he quickly prepares his dinner before walking into the den and taking a seat in his recliner.

As he's sitting there, his mind wandered back to the news of his mentor, Chief John Wolf, passing away. The first few years working for John were not the easiest. A stickler for details, Mikeal's rough and, let's be honest, lackadaisical way of doing things resulted in more than one ass chewing. This culminated towards the end of his second year with the Chief when Mikeal hadn't secured a valuable piece of evidence. Somehow, the defense attorney found out it had been kept in his police cruiser for over a week before being logged in as evidence. The District Attorney protested the evidence was still secure locked in the patrol car. However, once the defense produced a video tape of Mikeal sitting in a cafeteria; followed by the cameraman walking over to his cruiser and opening the unlocked door, it cast doubt on how all evidence was handled, directly contributing to the accused walking out of the courtroom a free man.

It was touch and go for a while if Mikeal would remain on the force. There was a small but vocal fraction of the community's leaders who were never happy a predominantly white man had been allowed to join the force. However, Chief John was so respected in the Snowbird Community, he always had the final say in personal matters.

This wake-up call and specifically the support he received from the Chief convinced Mikeal he really needed to focus on the great opportunity he had been provided. Within months, a new, more focused Mikeal was starting to get noticed for all the right reasons. He made a point to bond with his coworkers, who in turn began to work with him, learning the intricacies of law enforcement.

Over time, all was forgotten regarding his rough start. However, there was always a restlessness to Mikeal, never happy in his current environment, always searching for something different. This eventually led to the painful decision to leave the area and move west. The first couple of years he was gone, it was easy to stay in touch with friends back East. However, over time, those connections slowly faded away and were replaced by new friendships and associates in Montana.

Mikeal finishes his bowl of cereal, not really satisfied with the results, but at least something was in his stomach. He proceeded to take his boots off and turn on the TV for a few minutes to kill some time. With tomorrow's long drive, he'll be getting into bed a little earlier than normal. Flipping through the channels, he quickly finds his favorite subject, animal documentaries. This one was on the wild dogs of Africa, which he had already seen a couple of times.

"Well, at least it'll keep my interest for a few minutes." Before long, with the wild African dogs running around in the background, he was asleep in his recliner.

CHAPTER 7

"Chief, it's about the Payne boys; we just got a call they were spotted over around Dry Creek Campground."

"Alright team, let's roll. Mikeal, come with me," instructed Chief Wolf.

With that, three cruisers pulled out of the lot, headed towards Bryson City. Dry Creek was a campground and tubing site a few miles north of downtown Bryson City. During the summer, it was a popular spot with families who could cheaply rent floats and provide a day of entertainment for kids and adults of all ages tubing down Dry Creek. Word had gotten out the brothers were staying in a friend's trailer parked there. As soon as they cleared downtown Bryson, the Chief came on the radio to instruct everyone to cut their sirens. With only one way in and the Paynes located somewhere near the back, the Chief feared they would be spotted before getting to them. The three patrol cars turned right and headed to the main gate. The park ranger opened the gate to let them pass without stopping. The camp road was one large loop, and the Chief took a right turn as the other two cruisers went to the left.

"Supposedly, it's a white fifth wheel with a red Dodge Ram parked nearby," the Chief stated.

"Chief, fifty yards up on your right," Mikeal spotted the red pickup.

The cruiser quickly came to a stop before making it to the truck; they both jumped out and ran towards the camper. Mikeal could see the other deputies on foot running towards the backside of the camper. The Chief slowed as he got to the truck. As they looked around, there was no one in sight, but Mikeal could see a little trail of smoke rising from a fire pit on the site.

"Alright Mikeal, cover me, I'm going to the door," John said before leaving the cover of the truck and running towards the camper door. Mikeal pulled his service revolver, pointing it at the camper door. He steadied his arm by placing it on the truck bed.

"This is Chief John Wolf; we have a warrant for Billie and Tommie Payne. Please open the door and come out with your hands above your head."

A minute or two passed with no response from anyone inside the camper. The Chief repeated his order once again; still, no response. He looked over at Mikeal and shrugged his shoulders as if to say, 'Well, here goes nothing.' In a split second, Chief Wolf whipped the door open, swung his service revolver inside, and in one fluid motion was standing inside the camper.

"Clear!" everyone heard John yell as he stepped back outside. Mikeal and the other deputies quickly fanned out to cover more ground. Mikeal stopped by the smoldering fire and bent down to get a better feel for the remaining heat.

"Chief, these coals are still red hot, someone recently tried to put this out with water."

As Mikeal surveyed the back of the campsite, he saw what appeared to be a couple of trails heading back into the woods. As he got closer, he decided to follow the first one, which appeared to head deeper into the woods. At first, the trail was pretty clear, with a well-worn dirt trail approximately two feet wide. Following it deeper into the woods, it began to narrow to about six inches with heavy weeds on both sides. Still, he hadn't seen any signs that anyone had been on this trail recently. He was starting to doubt his instincts, "Looks like I picked the wrong trail." After a minute of uncertainty, he decided to press on a little further. The trail had started to climb up along one of the mountain ridges; he could no longer hear the sounds of the campground or any of the families tubing down the creek. Still climbing, he started to hear the sound of rushing water. Knowing there were several small waterfalls in the area, he was expecting to eventually run into one. Further in, he could now see a small creek running down the mountain about twenty feet below the footpath. Up ahead, he could see the path become wider once again. Now, he could definitely hear the sound of the falls, but the side of the trail was heavily forested and overgrown. He pulled away at some of the kudzu to try and locate the falls. After ripping away several vines, he had a better view of the little canyon below. There she is, another beauty of nature. He wasn't sure exactly which fall he was at, but it didn't really matter. At this point, it was obvious the Paynes were tipped off and got the hell out of dodge. After several minutes of watching the water rush over the falls before falling forty-five feet to the canyon floor, he turned to leave and started his descent towards the campground.

"Hello, Deputy," he suddenly hears from behind. "I heard you were looking for me." Mikeal slowly turns around and immediately recognizes Billy Payne.

"I'm impressed, Deputy; I didn't think I left any indication this was the trail I took."

"Where's your brother, Billy?" Mikeal calmly asks.

"My brother's whereabouts are of no concern to you presently. You're dealing with me and Remington," as Billy lifts the barrel of his rifle towards Mikeal.

"Billy, I know you're a lot of things, but you aren't a killer," Mikeal tries to reason with him.

"Well, Deputy, you're right about that. My momma and daddy taught us it was a sin to kill, but I'm starting to lose interest in our little conversation. Time to say goodbye, Deputy."

Suddenly, everything went dark. Mikeal's head was throbbing. He could tell he had been placed in a chair but felt no control over his body. Slowly, his eyes were starting to adjust to the near darkness. The place looked familiar, and actually, it looked a little too familiar. He started to stand but quickly became nauseated and fell back into the chair. "What's going on?" he thought to himself before attempting to stand again. As he continued to shake the cobwebs from his head, it was starting to become apparent he had been having a dream.

He stumbled towards the kitchen, where by the stove clock he could tell it was a little past 2:00 a.m. in the morning. Fumbling through the kitchen cabinet, he found a bottle of Ibuprofen, taking three and chasing it with a glass of water before stumbling off to bed, hoping to salvage a couple of hours of sleep before the alarm went off.

Devin and Allison were the first to arrive Sunday morning at Gary Weaver's farm. Even though it was technically his day off, all hands were required for the search. After passing through the front gate and traveling the short distance to the barn area, Allison spots Mr. Weaver sitting on the front porch, drinking his morning coffee.

"Good morning, Mr. Weaver."

"Good morning, Allison. Where's the Sheriff?" he asked.

"Mister Weaver, I'm Deputy Devin; the Sheriff had a few things to take care of this morning; he should be here in the next thirty minutes or so."

Gary stands up and motions for Devin and Allison to follow, "come on inside, I'll make you a cup of coffee." Devin, who doesn't drink coffee, decides to take the diplomatic way out by pretending he needed something from the Tahoe.

"Sounds good to me," Allison responds and follows Gary inside.

After about fifteen minutes, Devin hears the sound of a vehicle traveling up the gravel driveway. The Sheriff's Tahoe comes to a stop beside Devin's vehicle.

"Good morning, Sheriff!"

"Morning, Devin," he responds in a less than enthusiastic manner.

"Sheriff, you're not looking so great."

"Yeah, tell me about it. I've had a splitting headache all morning." In the background, they both hear the sound of a screen door shutting and turn around in time to see Gary and Allison exiting the house.

"Good morning, Sheriff!"

Mikeal responds with a half-hearted attempt at throwing his hand in the air. "Sheriff," Allison states, "you don't look so good."

"So I've been told," he responds.

They all walk over to the training field where a group of approximately fifteen other officers from the Sheriff's department and other local law enforcement agencies had already assembled. Jumping up into the back of a pickup, Mikeal addresses the crowd.

"Alright, let's get down to business. We're basically going to be looking for a needle in a haystack today. There are thousands of acres on the backside of this property, and these aren't flat pastures. I'm guessing there are hundreds of game trails that we can follow. At this point, we don't have a clue as to the identity, other than we believe the deceased to be female. If we knew how this person died, we could rule out a significant portion of the search area. Unfortunately, we don't have that answer, so we're starting with a large search area. If this was a hiker who got lost and starved to death, they were probably deep into these mountains, and we'll never find the rest of the body. If this was a dumped body, they'll be found closer to a road or other human access point. So, we're going to divide and conquer. Devin, you have the map of the area; I'd like you to direct the officers from the other agencies in identifying access points within a five-mile radius of the farm. Identify the most promising and search. Allison, Mr. Weaver, and I will take the dog and head into the search area first. Give us a good forty minutes before you bring your team in to start searching."

"Well, Mr. Weaver, you ready to get started?"

"Yes, sir. I've already had one of the trainers take Sheila to the back lot where she escaped."

"Sounds good. Let's roll." Jumping in Gary's truck, they go through the same process as the day before, reaching the back lot, meeting up with Sheila and her trainer in about ten minutes.

"Good morning, Dan," Gary greets the gentleman with Sheila.

"Dan, our girl ready to go?" Mr. Weaver asks.

"Oh, yes, she's already been trying to pull my arm out of socket to get going."

This was Mikeal's first chance to set eyes on Sheila. She was larger than he had expected, with a long face, pointed ears, mostly black face, and a gray body. Her dark brown eyes were staring straight at him, studying him, trying to determine if friend or foe. She didn't make much of a sound, but every ten seconds or so, she would look up at her handler as if to say, "I'm ready; let's go! Daylight's a-wasting; let's get through this fence."

Gary walks over to the fence and starts to snip the wire to create an opening, and soon all three men and Sheila are on the outside of the fence.

"Sheriff, it's best if we step back and let Dan and Sheila take the lead," instructs Gary.

"No argument from me. I'm fine staying out of the way and bringing up the rear," Mikeal answers.

Dan pulls out a towel, which Mikeal recognizes from yesterday, and puts it against Sheila's nose. "Alright, girl, this is what we're looking for; let's go find it." Looking around, there is no visible trail leading away from the fence opening. Sheila momentarily sniffs around the tall weeds before something gets her attention, and she is off, pulling, almost dragging Dan behind her. Over the next fifty yards or so, they're on a slight incline, still no visible trail in sight. Through briars, vines, stumps, and tree roots, they continue to make their way another thirty yards before coming to a small clearing. Sheila circles the edge of the clearing, nose to the ground, stopping occasionally to take in the lay of the land. Mikeal also takes in the surrounding landscape, looking for anything that looks like disturbed earth. Within a few minutes, Sheila is off again, dragging Dan behind. After traveling another quarter mile, Mikeal hears Allison's voice on the radio, "Sheriff, come in?"

"Yes, Allison, I read you loud and clear."

"We're ready to start our search. Permission to start?" Allison asked.

"Give us five more minutes and then proceed," Mikeal responded.

"Ten-four," and the radio was silent again. The group continued their march behind Sheila, still with no trail in sight; however, the ground vegetation and tree roots were no longer a concern. They had been replaced with stands of Rocky Mountain Juniper, Lodgepole Pines, and an occasional Quaking Aspen. Soon they were at the top of the summit with a clear view of the valley below. With a view of thousands of acres and acres of trees, Mikeal scanned the area below looking for a possible clearing. In the far distance, his ear picked up the possible sound of autos on a highway.

"Devin, do you copy, over?"

"Copy," Devin replied.

"Devin, see if you can get a fix on our location, over."

"Ten-four, give me a minute," Devin responded.

"I'm hearing highway sounds northeast of where I'm standing," Mikeal added.

"Northeast, that would be Highway 191, Sheriff."

"Any other roads in the area?" Mikeal asked.

"Only Forest Service Road 986 is identified on the map," Devin answered back. "We've already sent a team in that direction as well as Service Road 791, which is west of your current location, Sheriff."

"Great," Mikeal responded. "We'll continue making our way to the northeast." Mikeal and the team continued to press on. Sheila would occasionally stop and have a sniff around, but then she was off again. This process went on for miles and miles.

"Gary, exactly how much ground could this dog cover in a night?" Mikeal asked.

"Easily fifty to sixty miles," he responded.

"So we're basically only getting started?"

"Sheriff, fortunately for us, Sheila wasn't familiar with this territory. My guess is she spent more time smelling than running. If that's the case, she probably only covered half that distance."

"Sheriff, do you copy?" Devin's voice was suddenly heard over the radio.

"Copy, what do you got?" Mikeal replied.

"We've found a ground disturbance about thirty yards from Service Road 986. Instructed the team to mark the perimeter until I can get out there and lay eyes on it."

"Roger," Mikeal replied! "Devin, how far are we away?"

"I was just checking, Sir. Looks like two miles due East; I'll send you the coordinates."

"Alright, looks like a change of plans. We're heading East," Mikeal told the group.

Devin quickly traveled north on Highway 191 before turning off on the fire service road. The road immediately ascended the mountain and down the backside before leveling out. After traveling a short distance, the road made an almost ninety-degree turn to the right. After clearing the turn, Devin could see the police cruiser parked a couple of hundred feet ahead. After parking behind the vehicle, he exited and immediately started to mentally process the area around him.

"Deputy," a voice shouted from the woods. Devin turned and saw the officer waving from about twenty yards inside the tree line. He quickly scurried up the embankment and followed the officer to the site. At first, the scene didn't appear to be out of the ordinary. Situated in a small clearing, with Chokeberry shrubs dotting the landscape, was a small patch of bare earth, maybe ten by ten feet in area. There were obvious signs the earth had recently been disturbed with a slight depression, possibly suggesting where the bone was pulled. With the recent snowmelt, the top layer of dirt was muddy enough to capture the indentation of a dog or possibly wolf footprint. Devin had a good feeling about this being the correct location. However, one thing was bothering him: why did the officer stop here? When he surveyed the area after exiting his vehicle, nothing alerted Devin that this looked like a good place to stop. If he hadn't seen the cruiser, more than likely he would have continued up the road.

"Why'd you stop here?" Devin asked the officer.

"You know, it was the craziest thing, deputy. I made the hard turn down there and started up this stretch of road, and a wolf ran across in front of me."

"A wolf?" Devin replied.

"Yeah, I stopped the car and looked out the side window, and he was just standing up on the bank staring back at me. I waited for a few minutes, but he didn't move until I opened the door and started to get out. So, I followed him into the woods. Once I got to the top of the bank, I could see him standing in this little clearing. Once he saw me, he took off, and that was the last I saw of him."

Devin got back on the radio and called out to the Sheriff.

"Copy, Devin," Mikeal's voice came back. "Are you at the site?"

"Yeah, I am Sheriff. It looks promising, but we've maintained our distance."

"Great, Devin. If these bones are several years old, we'll need the experts on this one."

"That's what I'm thinking," Devin replied.

"Sit tight; we should be there in the next thirty minutes or so," Mikeal called out.

Devin and the officer went back to securing the perimeter of the site. Meanwhile, Allison, who had heard the radio chatter between Mikeal and Devin, called the Sheriff to confirm it was okay to call off her team's search. Just before noon, Mikeal, Gary, Dan, and Sheila cleared the last ridge and were on a downhill march towards Forest Road 986 and the potential crime site. It had been a good while since Sheila last stopped to smell around in an area, almost turning into a spectator rather than an active participant.

"Dan, has Sheila lost interest in what we're doing?" Mikeal asked.

"I'm not sure," he replied back. "She's becoming a little timid. Could be another wolf in the area, and she knows she's trespassing."

Within a couple of minutes, Mikeal could see the road ahead, but no sign of Devin. They cleared the tree line and walked out on the dirt road. "Looks like we came out a little north of where I was aiming," Mikeal shared with the group as they started walking south down the road. Very quickly, they saw the glare of the sun beaming off the cruiser's windshield.

"There you are," Devin shouted at the group.

"Better late than never," Mikeal shouted back. The Sheriff instructed Gary and Dan to stay back by the patrol cars as he followed Devin into the woods. The scene was just as it was described; the ground just wet enough to leave tracks. This squashed any idea Mikeal would have of trying to get a closer look.

"Well, looks like we wait until we can get someone out here from the State's forensic team."

"I'll call and see if they can get here before nightfall," Devin replied.

CHAPTER 8

Monday morning, June fifteenth, started early at the
department. Mikeal arrived shortly before 7:30 a.m.
Entering his office, the first thing he saw was the stack of
folders, right where he left them on Saturday. Mikeal sat
down, staring at the files. He knew they needed to be
reviewed but couldn't find the motivation.

The next thing he knew, he was standing out in the big room,
asking for everyone's attention. Walking towards the back
wall, which held a large whiteboard, he picked up a marker
and started to write. Devin, Jordan, and Allison looked on as
Mikeal started with the name, Sammy Hudson, followed by
the timeline he created based on Emma and Terry's
statement.

"Alright, we've got two cases I want us all to be focused on,"
the Sheriff shared as he turned back to the deputies. "Sammy
Hudson, female, mid-twenties, left for a late lunch and never
returned. I've written out her physical description on the
board. Devin, have you had any luck acquiring an actual
photo?"

"Not yet, but I'm working on it," Devin quickly replied.

"Based on the timeline we've constructed, she was last seen
between 4:30 and 5:00 p.m. last Thursday evening," Mikeal
stated. "Allison, will you give us an update on the evidence
collected?"

Allison stood and walked towards the board before turning and addressing her fellow officers. "A brownish-red stain in the snow was reported near where she could have been. We've sent this off to the lab and are waiting to hear back. Second piece of evidence, cigarette butts taken from the general vicinity of the stain and from the back door of the coffee shop. Final and third piece of evidence, a fragment of red cloth, located about twenty yards behind the location of our first piece of evidence."

"The board lists what she was wearing as a blue t-shirt and blue yoga pants. Why would you think a torn red cloth would be related?" Jordan spoke up to ask.

"It may or may not be related. However, it was at the start of a trail into the woods. If the victim was truly abducted, we can't rule out this may have come from the perp's clothing," Mikeal added. "Finally, I've also spoken to her manager, and he informed us employees walking off and not returning is fairly common at the resort. So, this all may end up being a waste of our time, but until we know that, we're treating this as a potential missing person, so be diligent while out on patrol to locate this individual."

"So that's case one, next, we have a human femur bone found on Saturday out around Hebgen Lake. Subsequently, as many of you know from participating in yesterday's search, we believe we found the location where the remaining body parts are buried. Devin, would you share where we are with the site?" Mikeal added.

"I reached out to a contact I have at the state shortly after we discovered the area. They flew in last night and should be at the site by now," Devin stated.

"I'm assuming the site stayed secure overnight? Last thing we need is another bear incident," Mikeal sarcastically quipped, followed by muted laughter from the group.

"Yes, sir. We assigned two deputies and brought out the bright lights and kept it illuminated overnight. They checked in this morning; everything's fine. Lights did the trick and kept any inquisitive animals away during the night."

"Alright, so that's all we're currently working with. Once the Forensic Team finishes, the site will be turned back over to us, and we'll have more to share," with that final statement, Mikeal headed back towards the office to continue his stare down with the files on his desk.

As he approached his office doorway, he called out, "Allison, you got a minute."

"I'll be there in a second; let me finish this email," was her response.

Mikeal grabbed one of the folders from the corner of his desk, opening it and blindly staring at the police report. He was still on the losing end of a staring contest with the files when Allison poked her head into his office. Before she could say a word, he looked up and asked, "any word from the lab?"

"Nothing yet, but we should have something before end of day."

"Until then, remember, we don't have a crime, just a missing person, so let's not waste a lot of time on this."

"Understood," Allison replied before turning and heading back to her desk. As she was leaving, she heard the Sheriff say, "Devin and I will be heading back out to Hebgen Lake this afternoon. Let me know as soon as you hear anything."

Mikeal returned his attention to the files. Instead of a deep dive into each, he decided to categorize them. He remembered a couple were vehicle thefts; quickly skimming through, he found two additional files, bringing a total of four as auto-related, which he eliminated from his stack. This was followed by segmenting out everything related to theft of property. Before he could get any further, Jordan appeared, sticking only her head in his door, "Got a second, Sheriff?"

"What's up?" Mikeal asked.

"At the briefing, you mentioned employees disappearing at the resorts in Big Sky was common," she stated.

"Well, that's what the manager stated," Mikeal clarified, "and?"

"I decided to do a check in our database on similar cases, and guess what, there's only been one!"

Mikeal sat up in his chair before stating, "I need to see that file." A big smile spread across Jordan's face as she stepped into complete view, with the file in her hand.

Mikeal laid out the folder in front of him. Looking over the police report, Tina Lattimer from Spokane, Washington, hostess at Big Sky Resort, was last seen on June third, nineteen seventy-five. Before her disappearance, she had confided to coworkers that she felt someone had recently been following her. Three days before her disappearance, she showed up at the emergency room, bloody and beaten from what she said was an attempted rape. Flipping through the folder, Mikeal did not detect any information regarding lab work. Unlike today, in the mid-seventies, the development of rape kits was in its infancy. If Tina showed up at the emergency room today, they would have, at their option, a Sexual Offense Evidence Collection (SOEC) kit or PERK (Physical Evidence Recovery Kit). Looking over one of the witness statements, she was last seen getting into a Jeep Wagoneer around 2:00 p.m. on the third of June. Primary suspect: Steve Taylor, but he had an alibi putting him at least fifty miles from the abduction scene on the third. Reviewing officer notes, they felt whoever was responsible for the attempted rape came back and finished the job. After following up with relatives over the next two years with no contact, the case grew cold and faded into the background. "Not really a lot to go on," Mikeal thought to himself. "No description of her original attacker. I wonder if this Steve Taylor is still in the area." "Steve Taylor... wait a minute," Mikeal's mind was racing. That name sounded familiar, but where did he remember it from? He pulled out his notebook and started to quickly skim through the pages. Bingo; the manager of the Coffee shop at Summit Mountain Resort.

"Sheriff," Devin's voice broke his thought process. "Are you ready to go?"

Mikeal looked up without speaking, sitting silent for a few seconds before standing. "Go start the vehicle. I'll be out in five minutes tops," he instructed Devin. He handed Jordan the file and motioned for her to follow. Leaving his office, they walked towards Allison's desk, with Jordan right behind.

Stopping at her desk, Mikeal looked down at his watch, which read 12:05 p.m. Realizing the day was slipping away, he proceeded to instruct Allison and Jordan to go pick up Steve Taylor, the manager of the coffee shop, and bring him in for questioning.

Once again, he looked back at his watch.

"What is it?" Allison asked.

"I'm trying to figure out how to be in two places at once," Mikeal stated. "Get him here around 6:00 p.m.. I should be back from Hebgen Lake by then."

"But I thought we weren't doing anything regarding the disappearance until we heard back from the lab," a confused Allison asked.

Without directly answering, he headed towards the door, only replying, "Jordan will fill in the details."

Anxious to find out what was going on at the site, Devin drove with a heavy foot most of the way, arriving in a little less than two hours to the site just off Forest Road 986. Along the way, Mikeal had repeated several times that they had to be back at base no later than 6:00 p.m.

The quiet secluded scene from yesterday was alive with activity as people moved back and forth like a colony of ants. The fire road was now lined with patrol cars, ATVs, a coroner's van, and two large twelve-passenger vans with the Montana State Seal on both front doors.

As they headed up the berm and into the woods, they passed a couple of uniformed officers milling around the tree line, securing the perimeter. Farther back in the woods, a dozen or so individuals, all dressed in white, were low to the ground, as though they were children in a sandbox. Even with all this activity, the area was as quiet as a church on Sunday.

"Excuse me," a voice from one of the officers guarding the perimeter broke the silence. "We need you to put these booties over your boots before you head back there. You wouldn't want to contaminate any potential evidence, would you?"

"No, of course not. We were just looking for who's in charge," Mikeal replied as he slipped the bluish-green booties over his boots.

"That's Dr. Baldwin; he's the silver-haired gentleman."

"Thanks. Is it okay for us to go in now?" Mikeal asked.

"You're good to go."

As they approached the clearing, they could see it had been gridded out, and there were five technicians in white bio suits hovering over the site. Another older gentleman with silver hair was typing notes into his tablet.

"Dr. Baldwin, I'm Sheriff Mikeal Lancaster. Thanks for getting out here so quick."

The doctor looked and nodded, returning to entering notes into the tablet. "Okay, I understand you're busy, but do you have anything you can share?" Mikeal asked. Without taking his eyes off the tablet, the doctor responded by asking the Sheriff for thirty more minutes, and then he would have something to talk about.

"Fair enough." Devin and Mikeal stepped back and returned to watching the technicians inspect the site. From what Devin could observe, it looked like they had only dug about a foot below the surface. He could tell one of the technicians was close to uncovering something by putting down the trowel and switching over to what looked like a paintbrush to slowly start brushing away dirt. Devin soon could see the outline of a bone emerging from the dirt. After another few minutes, another bone appeared. Dr. Baldwin had walked over and bent down next to the tech; he could tell they were discussing something but Devin couldn't hear what they were saying. After a few minutes, the doctor stood up and walked over towards Mikeal and Devin.

"Sorry about earlier," the doctor replied. "The older I get, the harder it is to focus. Didn't mean to sound rude."

"No problem, doc. We've all been there," Mikeal answered.

"Well, you guys were correct. It is a female buried here, probably ten, maybe fifteen years ago. She's been in the dirt a while."

"Any guess as to the age of the victim?" asked Devin.

"We're not sure at this time, but probably in her twenties," replied Dr. Baldwin. "We'll know more when we get the bones to the lab and processed."

"Anything else you can share at this time, doctor?"

"Yeah, it's what we haven't found. So far, no evidence of the victim being clothed, and we haven't been able to locate the skull."

"Wait, the victim was decapitated?" Mikeal asked?

"Well, not necessarily. It could have been dragged away at a later time by animals."

"It looked like she was buried fairly shallow," Devin added to the conversation.

"Correct, young man. Little time was spent digging this grave," answered the doctor. "The next step will be expanding our search radius to see if the skull can be located somewhere in the surrounding area."

"When do you think you'll have more intel, doc?" asked Mikeal.

"Once we get all this back to the lab, cleaned, and processed, probably a week more or less."

Mikeal looked down at his watch; it was getting close to 3:30 p.m., and he was finally starting to feel confident they could get back to base with time to spare before interviewing Mr. Taylor.

"Doc, we have the femur bone out in the cruiser. Will one of your crew follow us out and pick it up?" the Sheriff shared as he started down the path back to the road.

"Certainly, Troy, will you follow these officers back to their car and pick up the evidence they have?"

After turning the bone over to Dr. Baldwin's technician, they were quickly on the highway heading back to Bozeman. Within minutes of leaving, they started to encounter a light rain.

"So, Sheriff, what's your gut telling you based on what the doc said?"

"Well, Devin, still hard to say, but it looks like this wasn't anything premeditated. Otherwise, they would have had time to dig a proper grave. Another three feet or more, and we would have never found Jane Doe. She would have been lost to eternity."

"What about the missing skull? That's weird."

"Yeah, but like the doc said, shallow grave, could've been dragged off by an animal."

"What about Satanists, could it have been a ritual killing?"

"Devin, we're in Montana. How many Satanists have you come across since living here?" Mikeal asked.

"Well, none, but that doesn't mean they're not here."

"Man, your wife needs to stop you from watching all those horror movies you enjoy. It's starting to affect your reasoning!"

"Sheriff, all I'm saying is you can't rule anything out."

"I agree with you on that. We're looking for a perp who committed this crime ten to fifteen years ago. It could be anyone, and they could be anywhere by now."

Devin started to make a comment about the rain intensity picking up when Mikeal's phone started to ring. "Hey, Allison, what have you got?" he replied on speaker.

"Just wanted to let you know, we picked up Steve Taylor. We should be back at base in another hour," Allison stated.

"Alright, we're probably another fifteen minutes behind you," the Sheriff stated before hanging up.

Over the next fifteen minutes, the rain continued to intensify. The wipers on the Tahoe were at full speed, struggling to keep up with the downpour slamming against the windshield. Another ten minutes passed before the rain started to let up, giving Devin a clear view of the red lights from the vehicles out in front starting to break.

"What now?" Mikeal said in an anxious voice, looking down at his watch now reading 5:15 p.m. They were only thirty minutes from base, but traffic was at a standstill. Both officers exited the Tahoe, walking towards the front of the stationary line of vehicles. A pickup pulling a fifth-wheel trailer had jackknifed, blocking both lanes of the highway.

"Damn it!" Mikeal could see the broken axle on the trailer, realizing they wouldn't be able to clear the road on their own. Devin walked back to the Tahoe and called in the accident. They were going to be here for a little while.

CHAPTER 9

In Montana, once you leave a city, it takes at least an hour to get anywhere. This time was no exception; the first wrecker arrived about an hour after Devin called in to dispatch. They both remained at the accident site until the highway had been cleared, finally arriving back at base a few minutes before 8:00 p.m.

Jordan met both officers at the front door, instructing the Sheriff that Mr. Taylor was in interview room one. "He's pretty pissed about waiting," she added. She wasn't positive he was listening as Mikeal urgently walked past her on his way to the interview room.

"Sheriff, we also received the lab results; the blood found at Summit Mountain was human," Jordan quickly stated.

This statement immediately stopped Mikeal in his tracks. Turning back to Jordan, she added, "It was a small amount of blood, definitely non-fatal blood loss, but obviously, they couldn't rule out the victim could have been moved elsewhere and died."

Mikeal paused to think for a minute, "So unless we can find additional evidence or details, we'll have to continue to treat this only as a potential missing person case."

"Well, I still think we need to check out where she was living and contact relatives to see if she's shown up anywhere," Devin added.

"Devin, you're right. We still need to do a little follow-up."

"Will you handle that for me?" the Sheriff asked.

"Be glad to, Sheriff."

"Jordan, where's the Lattimer file?" Mikeal asked, not noticing she had been holding it in her hand. Taking the file, he retreated towards his office, instructing Jordan to inform Mr. Taylor he would be there in about fifteen minutes.

Mikeal closed the door to his office and took a seat behind his desk. He needed to clear his head of Sammy Hudson and focus on Tina. He quickly studied the three pages of case notes at the beginning of her file. Suddenly, he was interrupted by Allison knocking on his door. He motioned for her to enter before asking, "Where have you been?"

"I've been babysitting Mr. Taylor, where do you think I've been, sir?"

"Right, stupid question," Mikeal acknowledged. "Any observations you'd like to share?"

"Well, to start with, he's a pretty arrogant bastard!" she immediately shared. "Other than that, he was pretty calm for the first thirty minutes or so. He asked a couple of times if he needed a lawyer."

"What did you tell him?" Mikeal asked.

"Our normal script; just a routine interview, free to go at any time, but if he felt the need for an attorney, by all means get one."

After a slight pause, she continued, "It did get a little interesting after I left the room and started to observe him through the glass. At first, he sat there motionless, with his arms crossed, slouched in the chair. After about ten minutes, he started to tap the fingers of his right hand on the table. The last hour, he's been on his feet pacing around the room like a caged animal."

Mikeal learned from Chief Wolf the technique of unsettling an interviewee before questioning. Adding a little bit of anxiety often created doubt and second-guessing as they attempted to recite pre-rehearsed answers. He waited an additional ten minutes before grabbing the file off his desk and heading to the interrogation room. "Sorry to keep you waiting, Mr. Taylor. I was stuck on a call that didn't want to end," Mikeal recited his normal script as he entered the room, sitting across the table from Mr. Taylor.

Steve Taylor then went into a five-minute rant regarding his treatment. Mikeal sat back in his chair, observing and taking mental notes on the man across from him. Although they briefly met at the resort, nothing had stood out. As Steve's angry words continued, his extremely white teeth flashed like a wild animal feeling threatened. His eyes were focused on the Sheriff, who also took note of how dark his blue eyes were, followed by noticing his manicured nails. Short in stature with blond hair, a three-piece suit rounded out his appearance.

Mikeal could feel his tirade starting to slow before speaking up, "The sooner you let me start, the quicker you'll be out of here."

Trying to control the interview, Steve started by asking, "I'm guessing by the fact I'm here Sammy hasn't been found?"

"Well, yes and no," Mikeal replied.

"I'm not following," Mr. Taylor countered.

"Yes, you are correct Sammy hasn't been found, but no as to why you're here," Mikeal added before taking back over the interview, "Mr. Taylor, does the name Tina Lattimer mean anything to you?"

"Tina Lattimer," Steve restated before quickly answering, "No."

"Maybe if I put this in the context of time, you'll remember who she is from 1975?" Mikeal responded.

"Sheriff, that's over forty years ago. You expect me to remember someone from that far back?" Steve replied.

Mikeal leaned across the table and stared directly at Mr. Taylor. "Yeah, I would expect you to remember the name if you were a suspect in her disappearance!"

This sets Steve off, who stands shaking his finger at the Sheriff, "Wait a minute, I didn't come here to talk about the past. I thought you wanted to discuss Sammy's disappearance. I'm out of here," he angrily shouts before turning towards the door. Mikeal briefly looks over at Alison sitting next to him with a satisfied look on her face. Jordan, who's been behind the glass since the start of the interview, presses the button locking down the room. Steve vigorously shakes the motionless door handle before kicking the door. "I'm not saying another word until I have an attorney present," Steve angrily shouts.

Mikeal looks down at his watch, reading 8:45 p.m.. Satisfied he's pushed enough to get a truer feel for the man, he attempts to deescalate the situation, "Mr. Taylor, you can call your lawyer if you would like, but you'll end up sitting here another hour before he'll arrive. We're not leveling any charges against you. However, you made a statement the first time we met, that it was commonplace for employees to just walk off the job. Do you remember telling me that?" the Sheriff asked.

"Yes, I recall."

"So please, sit back down," Mikeal pleaded.

Steve took a couple of deep breaths before returning to his chair.

"In doing our due diligence, we looked for similar cases of people reported missing in the past. You know how many we found?" Mikeal followed.

Steve, once again sitting with arms crossed, replied, "I'm sure there were probably a dozen or more."

"Actually, we only found one. Dating all the way back to the seventies, a lady you knew," Mikeal added. "Look, we're just checking out anything that could be related. I can easily add a write-up to the file saying you were uncooperative and wouldn't discuss the case, and we'll move forward with or without your cooperation."

"Wait a minute, Sheriff; I never said that," Steve answered.

"Well then, Steve, why are you claiming you never heard the name?"

"Listen, Sheriff, I was a young stupid kid back then, who had a crush on Tina. I followed her around like a dog. She was the first girl I really liked. I didn't realize when she kept saying no to my advances she meant no! I just thought she was playing hard to get."

"So when she told your co-workers how creepy you were, you got mad and beat her up," Mikeal replied in a stern voice.

"Sheriff, I've never struck a woman in my life. Yes, I was embarrassed by what she said, but I didn't hurt anyone as a result. I found another job and moved on with my life. I had already left the company when Tina disappeared. I gave my statement to the police back then, and they cleared me. I don't understand why I'm being asked about something that happened forty-plus years ago!"

"Mr. Taylor, you've been acting like a caged animal this whole interview, you're quick-tempered, and repeatedly show very aggressive body language. Now you expect me to believe if someone humiliated you, your response would be to just walk away? Something doesn't add up."

"It's nothing personal," Mikeal tries to reassure Steve, "but we only have a limited amount of names in this file, and frankly, you were convenient to discuss the case with. We only have a few more questions and we'll be finished."

"Steve, will you be okay answering only a couple more?" Mikeal asked.

"I'm here, let's finish this, and I hope this will be the last time I have to discuss Tina."

After not saying a word for most of the interview, Allison spoke up.

"Mr. Taylor, that's one of the most hateful things I've ever heard. Tina had parents; she had family who were never given closure in this case. Please show a little respect!"

Steve just looked at Allison and shook his head, as though at this point he was just numb to the whole process.

"What type of car did you drive in 1975, Steve?" Mikeal continued the questioning.

"Finally, an easy question," Steve thought to himself. "In seventy-five, I was driving a 1969 Chevy Camaro, wish I still had it, today it's a very collectible auto!"

"Second question, did you know anyone who drove a Jeep Wagoneer?"

"A Wagoneer, no, I don't recall anyone I knew having one, but I probably saw one or two in the area back then."

"Great," Mikeal responded, "Do you remember where you saw these vehicles or what the driver looked like?"

"Well, back in those days, I was constantly working at one of the resorts in Big Sky, so more than likely it was at one of the resorts. I don't remember anything about the driver, but I'm assuming it was a man."

"Any physical description of the vehicle you can remember, such as color or if it had been modified with bigger tires?"

"I'm not sure, maybe blue or red, probably standard-size tires," Steve replied.

"See, that wasn't so bad," Mikeal said while leaning back in his chair. "I appreciate you taking the time to discuss this with us. In regard to your employee Sammy, we're not going to be opening a case regarding her disappearance. The lab confirmed it was human blood found by the dumpster, but the amount was so small it probably came from a small cut. We believe she got fed up with the job and left."

"Well, as I said, she wouldn't be the first employee we've had quit mid-shift. Regardless of what your records show, it's been fairly common over the years. This Friday is payday; she'll probably show up to get what we owe her," Steve replied.

"Well, if she does show up, please let us know so we have a record of her being seen. Alright, Steve, I'm sorry we got off to such a bad start, but we appreciate you coming in; you're free to go. Allison, will you walk Mr. Taylor to the front door?"

Mikeal gathered up the file and retired to his office. A few minutes later, Allison appeared in his doorway.

"So, what do you think," Allison asked, "are you buying his story?" Before Mikeal could answer, Allison shared her thoughts, "It doesn't add up. You saw how angry he got. At a minimum, he raped and beat the shit out of Tina, sending her to the hospital!"

"He's definitely quick-tempered, but that's a big leap to rape and assault," Mikeal stated. "Did you look at his hands, manicured with polish for Christ's sakes," he added. "If he was involved, someone else did the dirty work."

Mikeal used his computer to look up Steve Taylor in their database. No flags on his record, not even a mention he was a suspect in the Lattimer case. "Look, the reality is unless he were to confess, between the passage of time and lack of evidence, we're fooling ourselves thinking we'll get any farther than the original investigation."

As they continued their conversation, they could hear the ring of an incoming call, which was quickly answered by Devin.

"So, what's next, Sheriff? Focus on the vehicle? I can look through the vehicle database to see how many of these vehicles are still registered in the area?"

"Don't spend too much time, but take a look and let me know what you find," Mikeal added.

"Excuse me, Sheriff," Devin's voice interrupted the conversation. Both Mikeal and Allison turned towards Devin. "That was the state forensic team. While searching for the Jane Doe skull, they came across two more burial sites in that area!"

CHAPTER 10

The almost two-hour drive out to Hebgen Lake was starting to become routine for Mikeal and Devin. Each time they traversed the route, Devin's foot got heavier and heavier.

"New record: one hour twenty-five minutes," Devin boasted as the Tahoe came to a stop on the gravel road. After climbing the embankment and putting on their blue booties, they both went in search of Dr. Baldwin. The original site where Jane Doe was found had been completely cleared of ground cover out to a radius of about fifty feet. The depression where the first body was found appeared to be at a uniform depth of about two feet. Another fifty feet slightly to the left was another set of stakes and rope creating a two-by-two grid. Mikeal continued to look around but had not seen the third site.

"Devin, didn't you say they had found two additional bodies?"

"Yeah, that's what they said on the phone, but I don't see the third either."

"Excuse me, where can we find Dr. Baldwin?" Devin asked one of the technicians who happened to walk by.

"He's about twenty yards behind you." Devin and Mikeal turned simultaneously to look back in the other direction. In a small clearing, partially obstructed by a few Chokeberry Shrubs, stood the doctor and a couple of his forensic technicians. As they both cleared the shrubs, they could see where another section of ground had been cleared of all vegetation and a two-by-two grid outlined the site. As they approached, Dr. Baldwin looked up from his discussion with the techs, motioning for Mikeal and Devin to join them.

"Doc, looks like you've been busy," Mikeal replied.

"Yes, we've been very busy," he answered. "Looking for the skull, we had cleared out the majority of the area behind where we found Jane Doe. We brought in the ground-penetrating radar and found Jane Doe number two fairly quickly, maybe on our third pass or so of the area. We mapped the rest of the cleared area without finding anything else. We thought we were finished but found Jane Doe number three on pure dumb luck. Troy, pointing towards one of the techs, had to take a piss, wandered over here, and luckily noticed a bone lying on the surface before relieving himself."

"These all have to be related; we're in the middle of freaking nowhere," Devin calmly stated.

"Yes, this is definitely not a coincidence," the doctor replied. "All three have been here maybe twenty or so years. We found nothing else with the bodies, so they were all probably naked when dumped, and like Jane Doe one; all three are missing the skull."

"Decapitated?" Mikeal asked.

"Looks that way, but we'll know for sure once we get this all back to the lab and can examine the top of the spine in greater detail."

"Sheriff, looks like we've got a serial killer in our midst," Devin proudly stated.

"Unfortunately, it appears that way, Devin." "Doc, do you think this is everything that's here, could there be more bodies?" Mikeal asked.

"Sheriff, I wouldn't rule out anything. That's why we've requested a little help from the National Guard. They have ground-penetrating radar units which are a little more heavy-duty than ours. Plus, additional manpower, we expect them here in two days, and then we'll expand our search area." "Sheriff, I'm not a betting man, but I'm pretty sure we're going to find more bodies."

"Yeah, that's what my gut's telling me as well," Mikeal answered.

Mikeal and Devin were soon on the highway traveling back to Bozeman.

"Devin, let's take the turn and head back to Big Sky."

"Summit Resort I'm assuming?"

"You're a smart kid, yep, Summit Resort."

About thirty minutes later, they were pulling into the resort's parking lot. As they were exiting the vehicle, a man Mikeal recognized but couldn't place appeared walking towards them.

"Sheriff, any update on Sammy?" the man asked. Seeing a puzzled look on the Sheriff's face, he identified himself. "You interviewed me the day she disappeared; I'm Terry, the chef over at the bistro."

"Oh, yeah, sorry about that, too many new faces recently. Well, Terry, yes, we have an update, based on the little evidence found at the scene, we're unable to determine if a crime may have been committed."

"So that's it, nothing else is going to be done," Terry angrily replied.

"Well, our hands are tied," Devin interjected.

"A missing person isn't a crime; therefore, we have no authority to proceed. I would recommend you reach out to the national missing person hotline if you're still concerned," Mikeal calmly replied.

"That just doesn't sit right with me, Sheriff; you should be doing something," Terry stated as he walks away towards his truck.

Mikeal watches as Terry climbs into his truck, an early eighties Chevrolet Silverado with what looked like about an eight-inch lift added. "Always wanted a four-wheel drive with a big lift on it," Mikeal mentioned. "Now I'm too damn old to be able to climb into the thing. Let's go see if we can find Emma." As they walk into the shop, they see Emma conversing with a customer. They decide to take a seat on the sofa and wait till she's finished. A few minutes later, Emma walks over to the couch.

"Do I even want to hear what you're going to tell me?" she asks?

"Well, first of all," Mikeal says, "it's not bad, but probably not what you want to hear."

"So she's probably not dead, but you haven't found her," Emma blurts out?

"Correct," Devin replied.

"So what's next, Sheriff, some kind of investigation?"

"Well, not exactly. From our end, a missing person isn't a criminal case; therefore, it's limited in what we can do."

"So the stain in the snow wasn't blood?" she asked.

"Yes, it was confirmed to be human blood, but definitely not enough to have come from a serious wound, maybe a small cut of some sort."

"Can you at least get in contact with her parents or talk to her roommate?" Emma pleaded with the officers.

"We need to at least find out if she's safe."

"We wish we could do more, but ever since these efforts to defund law enforcement have taken hold, we just don't have the extra resources. This is a large county, and we have to prioritize how we use the resources we have left. I'll tell you what I told your coworker, Terry, in the parking lot. Call the National Missing Person Hotline and give them as much detail as possible; maybe they can help." Mikeal can tell that Emma is starting to get upset about the situation, but there's really nothing they can do. Both he and Devin stand before walking to the front door. He briefly turns back towards Emma, before realizing nothing he said would make a difference, so he turns back and silently exits the front door. Once outside, Devin asks, "Would you happen to have her address or a number for her parents?"

"Unfortunately, no, but you can call Steve tomorrow; he has all the employee records."

"Great, I'll do that first thing tomorrow morning," the deputy replies.

"Emma, you okay?" Henrietta asks?

"Just peachy, why would you ask?"

"Well, ever since you finished speaking with the Sheriff, you haven't really said a word."

"I'm sorry, Henrietta, I guess my mind's been in overdrive trying to figure out what I can do to help Sammy."

"I thought the Sheriff indicated she was probably fine."

"He doesn't know; he's just guessing," a clearly agitated Emma responds. "The Sheriff thinks she's probably alright, but he doesn't have any proof. All I know is that blood was found by the dumpster, and my guess is it's Sammy's!"

"I've got an idea! Henrietta, can you hold the fort down for a few minutes; I need to run over to the office!"

"Yeah, it's dead this afternoon, shouldn't be an issue, but don't be gone for a couple of hours."

"I'll be back in thirty minutes tops," Emma responded as she went out the back door. The resort's corporate offices were on the other side of the parking lot directly above the bistro. There was no direct access from inside the restaurant, but a set of stairs on the backside led up to a nondescript door at the top. As she entered, there was a small open area with what looked like a receptionist desk, followed by a long corridor with offices on both sides, ending at what looked like a conference room. She had been here once before to drop off paperwork before starting work at the resort. Since there was no one at the reception desk, she continued down the hall till she heard Steve's voice on the phone. Tentatively standing in his doorway, she waited for him to acknowledge she was there. After about thirty seconds, he looked up and noticed Emma standing in the doorway. He put his hand up in the air and gave her the "give me a minute" sign before returning to his call.

"Alright, I understand sometimes we can't help equipment failures, but this has been twice this month. I've got a business to run and can't be running out of supplies." "George, we've known each other for twenty years, done business for ten. I need a commitment or you're going to force me to look for another supplier." "Yeah, yeah, I'll give you one more chance, but that's it. George, I've got to go; we have some sort of issue at the coffee shop." As Steve was hanging up the phone, Emma took one step into his office. "If you're here about being short on supplies, you heard the call. George needs to spend a few dollars on something more than his wife. His trucks are all over ten years old, and I doubt they're properly maintained; that's why they are constantly breaking down and delaying our deliveries."

"No, Mr. Taylor, I'm not here regarding supplies, but wanted to ask you a favor regarding Sammy," Emma responded.

"Sammy," Steve replied back. "I'm sorry, Emma, today has been extremely hectic. I had meant to come over and tell you guys I had spoken with the Sheriff. He said that more than likely she just walked off the job, got in her car, and probably high-tailed it back to California."

"When did you speak with the Sheriff?" Emma asked with a surprised voice.

"He asked me to stop by the station last night, said he had good news and asked me to share it with the team."

"He was just over at the shop and didn't say anything about speaking with you," she responded.

"Well, I'm not sure what else I can say. You heard my call, it's been hectic today, and I just haven't had the time to tell you."

Emma thought something doesn't sound right about this but decided she would ask Steve a few more questions. "So what exactly did the Sheriff tell you, Mr. Taylor?"

"Well, not really a lot. The blood they found was human, but in such small quantities it would have probably come from a small cut."

"They could have told you that over the phone; sounds odd for them to ask you to come into the station for that," Emma replied. She could see her last response rattled Steve slightly. He started to fidget in his seat.

"Well, Emma, if the Sheriff asks you to come to the station, what would you do, ask questions, or comply with the police?"

"I would start asking questions; they don't have the right to call you up and demand you come in."

"What are you, Emma, one of those defund the police supporters? I thought you were chummy with the Sheriff," Steve angrily responded back.

"Not in the least! My sister's a cop, but that doesn't mean you have unlimited rights to demand people do this and that," she fired back. At this point, Steve's face was slightly reddish, with a few beads of sweat dripping down the side of his forehead. He sat quiet for a couple of seconds, taking a few deep breaths.

"Well, Emma, I'm not saying you're right or I'm right. I guess it's just the generation gap. When I was growing up, you just complied with whatever the police asked. Evidently that's not the case anymore. Anyways, that's all I know; wish I could tell you more, but that's all they shared with me."

"You mentioned a favor," he asked?

"The Sheriff said it would be a good idea to call the National Missing Person hotline and let them know about Sammy. I was hoping you could give me Sammy's info so I could share it with them?" Emma asked.

"If I could, I would gladly give you that info, but there are laws limiting what I can share on employees. It's definitely against the law to share personal info with other employees."

"Well, she's no longer an employee, so that shouldn't apply, Mr. Taylor!"

"Emma," he responds, "Even when you leave, I'm not allowed to share that info. The Sheriff would have to produce a court order before I could even provide it to law enforcement."

"Well, alright, thanks for nothing," Emma responds before storming out of the room.

A few minutes later, Emma was back in the coffee shop.

"Well, you look even madder than when you left; I'm assuming the visit to the office didn't go as expected," Henrietta stated.

"I saw Steve; he spoke to the police last night about Sammy, but something tells me he wasn't telling the truth. Well, at least not everything; some of what he shared matched what the Sheriff told me this afternoon."

"Emma, that guy's a creeper. I wouldn't believe half of what he was saying," Henrietta replied. "You shouldn't spend any time alone with him; I've heard stories; he's got a thing for young women."

"Stories or no stories, he's hiding something about Sammy. Henrietta, you wouldn't happen to have Sammy's phone number or address?"

"Nope, I only worked with her a couple of times, not enough to be chummy. Plus, Emma, look at me, most people only see a freak; they're not lining up to be my friend." Emma walks over and gives Henrietta a big hug.

The next morning, Emma is on the early shift with Larissa at the shop. The normal breakfast crowd shuffles in throughout the morning, picking up their coffee, pastries, and croissants. After a lull between 10:30 and 11:00 a.m., the normal lunch crowd passes through, picking up iced coffee and Paninis. After the lunch crowd has exited, Emma takes off her apron and tells Larissa she's heading to lunch. Larissa responds in her broken English, "but I go first!" Her point was moot because Emma had already cleared the back door.

The resort crew is allowed to have lunch in the restaurant, but it has to be after members and guests are mostly finished, and they're only allowed to sit at the tables in the back. "Hey, Emma," Terry yells from the kitchen, "you having the burger combo?" he followed. The combo in this instance was a diet coke, hamburger, and french fries. Emma wasn't sure how many times she had lunch in the restaurant in her short tenure at the resort, but one hundred percent of the time she ordered the combo. However, before last week, she had never had any interaction with Terry, so how would he know this? She thought about this for a second or two before responding, "You got it."

In short order, the waiter brought her a diet coke and a few condiments. Another ten minutes passed before Terry showed up with the burger and fries.

"Wow, should I feel special, the chef hand-delivered my meal," Emma sarcastically responded.

"I guess the Sheriff told you the same rubbish he told me yesterday about Sammy just walking off the job," Terry interjects as he takes a seat across the table from Emma. "You're not buying that, are you, Emma?"

"What do you think; of course I'm not buying the BS, Terry! We need to do something, but I'm not quite sure what yet," Emma replied. After a bite of her burger, she stated, "Maybe we should start our own investigation."

"Start our own investigation? What are you talking about, Emma, you're no detective," Terry chuckled.

"I've watched detective shows; I know just enough to be dangerous."

"Okay, then Emma, where do we start?"

She wasn't expecting Terry to volunteer to look for Sammy. She once again remembered Sammy's warning about staying away from this guy, but he'd been nice, and she didn't really have anyone else to ask. "I need to get a hold of her personal information, you know address, emergency contact, phone number, those types of things," Emma answered. "I spoke with Steve, but he said he wasn't legally able to share the info. I need to find a way to sneak into his office and take a peek at his files."

"Well, I know during the day he doesn't lock his door when he steps out. He's normally only out fifteen or so minutes, but that may give you enough time to get in and out," Terry answered.

"That would be great except what about the receptionist; her desk is right by the door. I'd never get by her if Steve wasn't in his office."

"Well, I guess it's your lucky day, Evelyn is on vacation this week, and Steve's the only one in the office."

"That's wonderful, Terry. Will you help get him out of the office for me?" Emma pleaded.

"I guess, what do you have in mind?" Terry asked.

"When I was up there earlier, he was on the phone with one of our suppliers. Make up something about missing supplies or something; I don't know, just something to get him out of the office for about fifteen minutes."

Terry sat quietly thinking for a few minutes. "Okay, I think I know how to get him over here for a few minutes. Finish your lunch, and let's do this. I'm heading back to the kitchen; when you're ready, I'll give him a call, and you sneak out the back door, get in and out quick. I'm not sure how long I can keep him, but I'll text you as soon as he's heading back."

"Terry, I owe you big time for this!"

"You're damn right, and I always collect my debts."

Emma quickly inhales the burger and fries. She's starting to feel her anxiety build and starts to doubt whether she can go through with the plan. Mentally she tells herself over and over, "you can do this, Emma." Alright, enough thinking, time for action; she leaves the table and finds Terry back in the kitchen. Terry quickly gets Steve on the phone.

"Steve, we've got an issue over here with our inventory count. If we don't get a shipment in tonight, we're going to run out of eggs tomorrow morning." "Yeah, I've counted them twice; we've got twelve dozen less than what the computer says. You're probably right; math isn't my strong suit. Could you come over and recount? Great, I'll see you in a couple of minutes." Terry puts his phone back in his pocket and looks at Emma, "He's on his way, get ready." Emma takes up a position by the kitchen's back door while Terry walks to the front to spot Steve. After a few minutes, she hears Terry say, "Steve, thanks for coming over." She quickly slides out the back door, running to the stairs at the back of the building. Up the stairs, through the front door, she's quickly at the doorway of Steve's office. Just as Terry indicated, the door was wide open. The desk was centered in the room but pushed to the far wall. There was a couch placed directly in front of the desk. Against the back wall were two large vertical filing cabinets with four drawers each. Behind the desk was a credenza, which appeared to have two lateral files in the middle. Emma guessed the personnel files would be in one of the two vertical filing cabinets. She walked over and attempted to open the top drawer, but it didn't budge. She tried to open the top drawer in the other cabinet; the same thing, it didn't budge. "Damn it, they're both locked," she muttered to herself. She moved over to the desk, slipping into the chair, she pulled out the middle lap drawer. Finally, something that's unlocked. She shuffled through the papers, pens, staples, and post-it notes but found no keys. She proceeded to go through each drawer in the desk but still found no keys. She pulled out her phone to see if Terry had texted. "Great, nothing from Terry," she put her phone down on the desk and slumped defeated in the chair. "All this work and nothing to show for it," she said to herself. As she stared out across the desk, she noticed a coffee cup in the corner of the desk by the monitor filled with pens. She remembered her father had kept change and sometimes keys in a coffee cup on his desk. Sitting up in the chair, she reached over, grabbing the mug, and dumped the contents out on the desk. Bingo, a set of small copper-looking keys was lying right in front of her.

"You're right, Terry; the inventory count is off in the computer."

"Shouldn't have doubted you," Steve replied. "Let me get back over to my office and place an order; shouldn't be a problem to have them delivered early tomorrow morning."

"Great, thanks for handling this for me," Terry replied. As soon as Steve walked to the front, Terry sent Emma a text, informing her he was heading back. Emma had gotten the first cabinet opened, gone through all four drawers, coming up empty with no personnel files. Quickly moving to the other cabinet, she finally located the files. Flipping through the names, she came to Samantha Hudson. "Sammy, I found you!" She pulled the file and moved back to the desk to take a picture of the data she needed. She picked up her phone and saw the text from Terry. "Shit!" Emma went into full panic mode; the text was from a couple of minutes ago. Quickly, she opened the file and started taking pictures of the two pages; she wasn't sure if they were in focus or not, but there was no time for a retake. As she put the files back in the cabinet, Steve was ascending the stairs, returning to his office. Emma's hands were trembling as she tried to lock the cabinet back and return the keys to the coffee cup. She heard the front door opening; her hands were now shaking almost uncontrollably as she tried to return all the contents to the mug. Her anxiety had built to a fevered pitch, and she started to feel lightheaded. Instead of the pens going back into the cup, they were still scattered over the desk surface.

Suddenly, a voice snapped her back to reality. "Emma, what are you doing in my office?" Steve asked angrily.

The only word Emma could get out was, "ah."

"I'll ask you again, why the hell are you in my office?"

All of a sudden, she got a moment of clarity. "Mister Taylor, I came to apologize."

"Apologize for what?" Steve, still angry, asked.

"You know, earlier, after thinking about it, I should have been more respectful to you." Steve, still not necessarily buying her answer, looked at the pens scattered across his desk.

"What's all this? I didn't leave my office looking like this."

"No sir, you didn't. I was reaching for a pen to leave you a note when the door opened. It scared the crap out of me, and I guess I knocked over the cup holding your pens."

"Well, clean it up and get out of my office!"

"Yes sir." Emma picked up the pens, placing them in the cup, and quickly exited the office. Steve followed her out and watched her walk down the hall to the front door. "Emma," he called as she reached for the door handle.

"Yes, sir?"

"If I ever catch you in this office again, you're finished. You hear me?"

"Yes, sir, loud and clear."

As Emma started to descend the stairs, her legs felt as though they were about to buckle, and her heart was ready to explode through her shirt. She had never been so scared in her life, yet at the same time, she was starting to feel alive again. As she continued her descent, the adrenaline that had been making her lightheaded and her heart pound was turning into an energy she hadn't felt in years. Clearing the last step, she had finally regained a normal heart rate and, before she realized it, was walking into the back of the coffee shop.

"Where have you been?" Larissa's annoyed voice asked. Emma, still in a trance, didn't hear Larissa, walking right past her to grab her apron.

"Emma, where have you been?" she asked again.

"What?" Emma finally acknowledged. "I told you I was going to lunch."

"You were gone too long and left me here by myself."

"Larissa, you're a big girl, you'll survive. It's not like you've never shown up late or called in sick, leaving me out to dry," Emma snapped back.

"I don't do that!"

"You most certainly do, and if you don't realize that, you're dumber than you look."

"You're bullying me!" Larissa shouted back.

"You're damn right, and if you don't get out of my face, I'm going to kick your ass!" Emma had never been in a fight in her life and didn't have a clue if Larissa would accept her challenge. The adrenaline still flowing through her body had taken over her thought process. Before the tension between the ladies could escalate further, Henrietta walked through the door.

"Good afternoon, ladies!"

"Thank goodness you're here, Henrietta. Emma was very mean to me," Larissa stated.

"I'm sure it's nothing you didn't deserve," Henrietta responded.

Over the next hour, the three ladies were able to work together until Larissa's shift ended, and she left.

"So what was the deal between you two when I came in?" Henrietta asked.

"She was upset because my lunch break went a little long."

"Wow, that's the pot calling the kettle black," she replied, shaking her head in disbelief.

"Henrietta, can you keep a secret?"

"Oh yes, I love secrets. What have you got?"

"I snuck into Mr. Taylor's office this afternoon and made copies of Sammy's file," Emma proudly stated.

CHAPTER 11

As soon as Emma made it home, she made a beeline straight up the stairs and into her room. Quickly plugging her phone into the computer, she downloaded the pictures from Steve's office and brought them up on her computer screen. Looking through her employment application, she came across Sammy's address: 611 South 14th Avenue, Bozeman, Montana, 59715. Emma was somewhat familiar with this area, which was close to Montana State University. Scanning the app, she found that her previous job had been in Twin Falls, Idaho, and before that, Spokane, Washington. Her emergency contact was listed as her mother, Delores Hudson.

"Alright, I've got to start somewhere," Emma said to herself. Taking a deep breath and then exhaling, she dialed the number listed on the application. After the third ring, Emma realized that, with what was probably showing up as an unknown number, she was letting it go to voicemail. She quickly tried to think up something clever but non-alarming to say. However, she never got the chance. After the fifth ring, she was informed the intended recipient's mailbox was full before being disconnected.

"Fudge!" Emma shouted at the phone. Rubbing her hand on her forehead, she let out another sigh. This day had been draining, but she wasn't ready to throw in the towel yet. She decided to put Sammy's address into Google Earth and look at the street view. Okay, nothing great but only a couple of streets over from the university. Before leaving Florida, she had looked in that area for a place to stay. She knew many of these homes were rented out to multiple college students or seasonal workers. She decided to go to the county's Treasurer site to find out who owned this property. After a few clicks, she was able to enter the property address and obtain the registered deed holder: a Virginia Madison.

Emma then decided to look into this Missing Persons Hotline the Sheriff had discussed. She found a site tied to the National Forensic Science Technology Center at Florida International University, better known as FIU. They had a website, NamUs.gov, which housed the National Missing and Unidentified Persons System database. Wow, they have a lot of information; Emma hadn't realized that there were over 100,000 active missing persons' cases and more than 40,000 sets of human remains that have not been identified in this database. The site would even help print missing person posters. "I'm going to need to write this all down to have constant access," she thought to herself. She remembered her stepmother had given her a journal before leaving Florida; this would be perfect to keep her notes and other thoughts. She quickly jotted down the info and put the journal in her backpack.

The following day, Emma was back on the closing shift at the coffee shop. It had been a steady but fairly low volume day by the time she was due her lunch break around two in the afternoon.

"All right, Henrietta, you okay with me taking lunch?" Emma asked.

"Go for it, girl, I got this," she replied.

Emma grabbed her backpack and made her way to the restaurant, taking her normal seat in the back of the room. She placed her order before pulling out her journal to look over what she had written down the night before. As she started to write out a little to-do list, Terry showed up with her food. "Here you go, burger and fries," he said before placing the plate in front of Emma and then sliding into the bench on the opposite side of the table. Leaning over the table, he whispered, "Did you get what you needed from Steve's office?" Emma looked up at Terry as her mind raced, attempting to formulate a response. Should she tell him how close she came to getting busted or tell a more simplified story?

"Yeah, I found her file and got out before he saw me," was her final response.

"So what's next?" Terry pressed.

"I've got her address and the name of her landlord; I'll probably stop by on my off day and see what they know."

"Have you tried calling her parents?" he asked.

"Tried to leave a message last night, but her mother's mailbox was full."

As Terry was standing up to head back to the kitchen, he told Emma: "If there's anything I can do to help, please let me know."

Still aware of Sammy's warning, she hesitantly replied, "Yeah, thanks, I'll let you know."

Emma normally was off two days during the middle of the week, however, with the recent influx of summer guests at the resort, this had been cut down to only a Thursday. On a typical schedule, she normally tried to do an outing with friends, however, with only one day off, half of it was spent driving to and from Bozeman to pick up groceries and other supplies from Walmart. This Thursday she would also be playing detective while in town.

She got up earlier than normal and was on the road to Bozeman before 7:00 a.m., hoping to stop by Sammy's address before everyone had left to start their day. It was a little after eight when she arrived at 611 South 14th Avenue. As she came to a stop in front of the house, she could see a single car in the driveway. "Great," she thought, "somebody was home." As she sat in the car, she could feel the anxiety start to build inside her. "Come on, Emma, pull yourself together, you're only going to ask about your friend." "You can do this, no time for a panic attack today," she told herself over and over. After a couple of deep inhales and exhales, she exited her vehicle. As she walked the short distance from the street to the front door, the anxiety was slowly easing away, replaced by a calmness sensation rarely felt. Ringing the doorbell, she stood and waited, hoping it would be Sammy answering the door. After a couple of minutes, a young lady wearing scrubs opened the front door.

"Good morning," Emma greeted her. "I'm hoping you can help me; I have an employee who had to leave work sick a couple of days ago. She hadn't checked back in, so we were becoming concerned. Is Sammy Hudson here?"

"Sammy? I'm not familiar with a Sammy," the lady replied.

"Yes, Samantha Hudson; she listed this address on her employment application. Would you happen to be Virginia Madison?"

"Oh no, that's the lady who owns this house. I'm just renting. There are other renters in the basement, but I don't know any of their names." Emma must have had a puzzled look on her face, but before she could ponder what she just heard, the lady in the scrubs told her there was a separate entrance on the side of the house to enter the basement.

"I'm sorry I can't be more helpful, but we never see them."

"Thanks, I'll go around the side and see if they're in," Emma replied.

"Would you like Virginia's number? She may be able to give you a little more info on your employee?"

"Thanks, that would be great."

After obtaining the landlord's number, Emma walked around to the side of the house. There was a covered stairwell leading down to the basement, which she descended to the door. She knocked on the door for several minutes before assuming no one was home. "Looks like it's on to plan B", she told herself after returning to her automobile.

While sitting in her car outside Sammy's rental, Emma called the number the lady in the scrubs had provided. A lady's voice answered on the second ring. "Is this Virginia Madison?" Emma asked.

"Yes, it is. May I ask who is calling?" she responded.

"Yes, Mrs. Madison, this is Emma from Summit Mountain Resort. I'm calling regarding one of your renters, an employee of mine, Samantha Hudson."

"Oh yes, Sammy is at one of my properties over on 14th Avenue. Is she okay? Did she get hurt at work?" Virginia responded.

"No, but she left work several days ago feeling sick, and we haven't heard from her since. We were a little concerned, so I stopped by her address on file, but no one's home."

"Sammy's in the basement unit. Did you try the side door?" Virginia asked.

"Yes, I had spoken to a lady upstairs, and she directed me in that direction. I knocked on the door, but there was no answer."

"I haven't seen or heard from Sammy, but that's normal with most of my renters. I live a few miles outside Bozeman."

"So, as far as you know, she hasn't moved out?" Emma asked.

"No, she hasn't given me any indication she was planning on moving out early. Matter of fact, her rent has been paid through the end of August."

Having ended the call with Virginia, Emma realized her investigation was quickly going nowhere. "How can someone be so insignificant they could disappear, and no one would miss them?" she asked herself. Emma could feel the sadness she had been fighting over the last several years start to creep back into her mind. She had often discussed this with her therapist; dark, sad thoughts would often start and quickly get out of hand, and Emma would spend whole weekends in her room with no desire to even get out of bed.

As she continued to sit in the car, she noticed the lady in scrubs had left the house. Emma decided to go back to the basement door and try again before leaving. She quickly returned, knocking a little harder on the basement door. Still, no one came to the door. Emma reached down to turn the doorknob, expecting it to be locked, but it wasn't. She slowly opened the door, "Sammy, it's Emma, are you in here?" With no response, she proceeded to shut the door and look around.

The front part of the basement was nothing special, a couple of old couches facing the television, which was beside the front door. Behind the couches were the kitchen area and a laundry. In the middle of the basement was the stairs leading back to the main level. On her right was an opening leading to a hallway where there were four doors. Only one was open, and she could see it was the bathroom. She went up to each of the closed doors and in a low voice called out, "Sammy, are you in there?" With no response from the first two closed rooms, Emma turned her attention to the last room at the end of the hall. As she approached, she heard the whining of what she believed to be a small dog. "Sammy, are you in there?" she whispered through the door. No response, only the continued whining of the dog.

She decided to backtrack and see if the prior two bedroom doors were locked. As she walked towards the back bedroom, she heard the upstairs door open and shut. "Shit," Emma muttered to herself as she froze in her tracks. After a few seconds, she finished making her way to the other bedroom and attempted to turn the doorknob. It didn't budge, so she turned her attention to the remaining door, which was directly across from the opening leading back into the living and kitchen area. Bingo, this door was unlocked. Emma slowly opened the door and started to peek inside when she heard the basement door open. Her heartbeat went into overdrive as she slid into this unknown room and quickly closed the door. As she tried to calm her nerves, she looked around the room for anything that looked like or reminded her of Sammy. Nothing, but she could now hear that something was scratching at the door behind her. "Muffin, come to mommy, let's get you some water," a woman's voice rang out. Emma could hear her footsteps approaching the door she was standing behind. Her mind was going into overdrive thinking of a way to explain her presence in this lady's house. The footsteps stopped right outside the door. Emma wondered if whoever was on the other side of this door knew a stranger was less than three feet away; they would be shocked. Emma was starting to feel lightheaded, like she was about to pass out from the stress when she heard additional footsteps coming down the stairs.

"Linda, is that you?" came another woman's voice.

"Hey, what's up?" she responded.

"Great," Emma thought. "Now there were two people about to find an intruder in their home. Could the day get any better?"

"Linda, there's something up with the washer. Have you been having any issues?"

"None that I'm aware of, but it's been a while since I ran a load."

Emma felt the voices were sounding a little farther away than before. She slowly opened the door but didn't see the ladies. However, at her feet was a little teacup-sized poodle. Emma put her finger across her lips to tell the dog, "don't give me away to mama." She slowly crept out of the room, making her way towards the stairs. She could now see both ladies in the back laundry room and decided to make her escape up the stairs. She slowly and deliberately tried to step as quietly as possible ascending the stairs, but the wood seemed to crack and moan louder and louder with each step. She could see the door at the top of the stairs was open, but before she could reach the top, a man stepped into the opening.

"Who the hell are you?" a deep, angry male voice reverberated down the stairs, freezing Emma in her tracks.

Emma couldn't speak, she couldn't move; she just wanted to be able to become invisible.

The man descended down the stairs, grabbing Emma tightly by the wrist. "Linda, who is this?" The man called out to one of the ladies in the laundry. A large lady, probably in her early thirties with pink hair and a septum piercing, stepped out. Eyeing Emma, she replied, "Never seen her before."

Finally unable to stand the pain she was experiencing in her wrist, Emma called out, "You're hurting me!"

This prompted the other lady out of the laundry room. She seemed noticeably older than the other two. "Mark, let the girl go now," she growled at the man.

"But..." he started to say before being interrupted.

"I said let her go!" the older lady commanded.

"Alright," Mark let go of her wrist and backed away.

Emma instinctively started to back away towards the door she originally entered.

"Hold on, you're not going anywhere until I understand what you're doing in our house," the older lady shouted at Emma.

Pointing to the couch closest to the door, she instructed Emma to take a seat. At this point, tears are freely flowing down Emma's face. She tries to speak, but no sound comes out. "Get her a tissue and some water," the older lady instructs the man. He quickly returns with a glass and a tissue. Emma takes the half-full glass in her shaking hands, downing it quickly. Taking the tissue from his hand, she's finally able to get out the words. "Thank you."

"I work with Sammy," she finally manages to say.

"Well, Sammy's not here," the septum-pierced woman states.

"She left work early last week and never came back. I was hoping she would be here," Emma stated. The three housemates looked at each other, determining how to proceed. Emma noticed the man shaking his head no, as if to be telling the others not to say what he thought they were going to say. The older lady, ignoring his plea, spoke for all, "She hasn't been here for a couple of weeks." The pink-haired septum lady then added, "I walked in one evening and she and Mark were having one hell of a screaming contest. She then disappeared into her bedroom for a minute before reappearing a few minutes later. Next thing I know, she stormed past me and left. I haven't seen her since."

Emma looked up at the man with contempt in her eyes before he tried to explain to all that it was just a misunderstanding.

Sensing the group was becoming a little less hostile, Emma asked if it would be possible to look around Sammy's room. The two ladies looked at each other before agreeing, "It's all the way in the back," the older lady stated.

"It's locked," Emma stated, remembering her earlier attempt to enter.

"Check above the door. If there's not one there, you're probably out of luck," the older lady stated before climbing the stairs up to the ground floor.

"I can get you in if it's locked," the pink-haired lady informed Emma as they both approached Sammy's room. Standing on the tip of her toes, Emma felt unsuccessfully for an additional key. Taking a step back, the pink lady grabbed the handle while inserting what looked like thin metal rods into its center, opening the door in seconds.

The pink-haired lady then quickly disappeared back to the front of the house. Emma slowly entered the room; clothes were thrown across the floor, and the twin-size bed was unmade. Emma could picture her friend retreating to this room every evening, just as she did every night, finished with having to interact with people. Next to the head of the bed, which was pushed against the front wall, was a little desk with several notebooks laying across its top. She opened one and started to flip through the pages. There were a couple of sketches of birds, what looked like song lyrics, and some rambling thoughts about the world. She quickly lost interest and started to inspect the other side of the room.

A little one by two-foot window at the top of the back wall let in the only natural light. She opened what had to be a closet door and found a jacket hanging on the back of it. She felt through the outside pockets, locating a couple of coins, some chapstick, and hopefully what was an unused tissue. She then felt through the inside pockets, finding a folded piece of paper. Unfolding it, she read the writing, "I miss you! When can we see each other again?" It was signed "Steve."

A sick feeling started to overtake Emma. While Steve was a fairly common name, she knew it had to be Steve Taylor. She made her way back to the desk, taking a seat in its chair. Staring at the brown carpeting, while her mind replayed the last month, she couldn't recall any interaction between Steve and Sammy. This was when she noticed the small trash can under the desk. She picked it up, and started to examine its contents. Mainly dirty tissues, lunch receipts, and some clothing tags, before seeing something she didn't expect. At the very bottom was a home pregnancy test with two pink lines clearly visible. As she held it in her hand, a voice broke the silence in the room.

"That's what we were arguing about," Mark's voice filled the room. Emma looked up to see him in the doorway. As he started to walk towards her, she became very uncomfortable. Stopping before he reached her, he sat down on the bed, explaining further.

"We'd gone out a couple of times. She made it clear up front she wasn't looking for anything serious, but you know, it seemed like there was chemistry between us," he explained. "The evening started out normal; she came in from work, and I was sitting on the couch watching TV. She asked about my day before she disappeared into her room. After a couple of minutes, I heard the fan running in the bathroom, you know, just normal things you do when you get home from work. Maybe twenty minutes later, she came out and sat down on the couch. She was white as a ghost. I asked her what was wrong, but she just sat there. I guess I should have just shut my mouth, but I had to ask again. That's when she blew up at me."

"So you're the...?" Emma started to ask.

"No, we'd never had sex," Mark calmly stated.

"Do you know who will be the father?" she followed.

"She never mentioned a name, but said it wasn't someone she wanted to be with long-term."

Emma stood up, dropping the pregnancy test back in the trash, before proceeding to the door. Turning back, the aggressive man who had grabbed her by the wrist earlier was still sitting motionless on the bed.

"Did she ever mention the name Steve Taylor?"

CHAPTER 12

Mikeal woke up covered in sweat. He could tell it was still early by the blackness he saw between the window curtains. The night before, he woke at 2:00 a.m., completely drenched in his own sweat, and it appeared tonight would be a repeat. As he sat on the edge of the bed, waiting for his eyesight to adjust to the darkness, he could see by the alarm clock that he had almost made it till 5:00 a.m.

Throughout the week, he had been plagued by persistent headaches that typically greeted him on his return home in the evening. Attributing them to seasonal allergies, he soldiered on. During the past week, the excitement of discovering the three graves had given way to a mundane routine of paperwork, with the team patiently awaiting the forensics' results. Mikeal also suspected that his constant scrutiny of the computer monitor had taken a toll on his eyes, contributing to his discomfort. After a quick shower and a change into a fresh uniform, he made his way to the kitchen, thirsting for a simple glass of water.

As he spent the week combing through the D.A. cold files, he had tasked Jordan with delving into the archives in search of any long-forgotten female missing person cases from the seventies. There had to be a connection with the three graves in the woods. Sitting on his kitchen table were the results of her search.

He sat down at the table and started to go through the files. The first was an unsolved murder from nineteen seventy.

Nancy Hulligan was last seen alive on August fourth, leaving her house to go for a run. Witness statements placed her two miles from her home around 9:00 a.m. that morning, running in the opposite direction from where she lived. Mikeal wasn't sure why this file was included, but decided to read further. Okay where did they find the body, Mikeal thought as he searched through the file for an answer. Interesting, he thought as he reviewed a document that had been folded and placed in an envelope. A drifter named David Miller had confessed to killing her about five miles from her home. However, when he took the police to where he had supposedly disposed of the body, nothing was found.

Mikeal got excited, thinking now they have bodies, could they be in the general vicinity of where Miller had taken the investigation. He quickly flipped through the pages looking for details of the location. When he found the information, his excitement quickly exited his body. Miller had taken the team to the far Northeast section of the county, in the exact opposite direction of where the bodies were found.

Further reading into the file, he learned Miller was eventually found mentally incompetent to stand trial. The paperwork listed various mental facilities where he was housed, but nothing was listed after 1979.

Looking at the clock on the stove, it was now approaching 6:30 a.m. Maybe there were a few things he could follow up on this one. After grabbing his keys, he picked up Nancy's file as he headed out the door.

"Any word from the state on the bodies recovered?" Mikeal asked Devin once arriving at the station.

"Nothing yet, I'm thinking early next week," he responded. He continued making his way towards his office where he shut the door and quickly fired up his computer. While still fresh in his memory, he was keen on doing a little research into the Nancy Hulligan case. His first stop was checking to see if she still had relatives in town. "Well, I'll be damned, it looks like the family never moved." An Oliver Hulligan was listed as the home's owner at the address listed in the file.

Turning his focus to David Miller, he murmured, "Let's uncover the post-1979 story of Mr. Miller." The database yielded numerous entries under that name, prompting Mikeal to backtrack through the file in hopes of finding a distinctive identifier for this particular individual. Yet, his search yielded nothing of significance. Determined to narrow down the results, he opted to filter them based on the mental facility where David had been sent due to his mental incompetence to stand trial. This refinement swiftly reduced the list to fewer than ten candidates.

Four of the ten were in mental facilities post-1979, with two other individuals listed as deceased. Mikeal buzzed Allison's number.

"Good morning, Sheriff," she answered.

"Allison, I'll be sending you information on four individuals bearing the name David Miller. One of them was a suspect in a case from the seventies that I'm currently revisiting. He was discharged from a mental facility in early 1979. I understand it might be a stretch, but please do your best to track him down."

"Yes, sir. I'll get right on it," she responded.

Leaving his office, the Sheriff looked over in Devin's direction, "Come on, Devin, we're going for a little ride."

Within a few minutes, the Tahoe was traveling North on nineteenth avenue before making a right onto Highway one ninety-one.

"Sheriff, where are we headed?" Devin asked.

"A neighborhood off of Highland Boulevard," he responded. "Jordan had pulled a few missing person cases files for me; I believe the victim still has family there." As they pulled into the driveway at 1140 North Spruce, Mikeal had no idea how this conversation was going to go. As they rang the doorbell, waiting for an answer, a lone jogger ran by, throwing up a hand to wave. Mikeal thought about the irony; over forty years ago, a lady left this house to go for a run and never returned. He wondered if anyone remained in the neighborhood who remembered Nancy. Soon a young lady answered the door.

"Good afternoon, we're looking for an Oliver Hulligan, would he happen to be home?" the Sheriff asked.

The young lady had a puzzled look on her face but responded, "No, he was at work. Oliver's my husband, can I help you?"

"Well, maybe you can. We're looking into the disappearance of a lady from this address back in the seventies."

"Nancy," she responded in a very excited voice!

"So, you knew Nancy Hulligan?" Mikeal responded.

"Well, yes, I mean no... I didn't personally know her, but she was my husband's mother. Let me call him; he'll want to speak with you."

"That would be wonderful, but let me set expectations; we haven't found Nancy, but we may have new evidence," the Sheriff replied. "We're putting a fresh set of eyes on the case and would appreciate it if your husband would discuss what he remembers."

The lady remained quiet for a few minutes, digesting the Sheriff's comments before telling the officers she would grab her phone and call her husband.

While the lady was calling, Devin whispered to the Sheriff, "Care to fill me in on what's going on?"

In a low tone, Mikeal gave Devin the basics: drifter confessed to killing her, found mentally incompetent to stand trial, never found a body.

"You're thinking the bodies...," Devin started to say when the woman returned.

"My husband said he would be here in ten minutes. Would you officers like something to drink while we wait?"

Almost exactly ten minutes later, Oliver Hudson walked through the door. He appeared to be almost twenty years older than his wife, probably in his mid-fifties with salt and pepper hair. After exchanging pleasantries, he asked the officers to have a seat.

"So, my wife tells me you're reopening my mother's case."

"Yes, Mr. Hulligan, we're taking a look at several cases from the early seventies. What do you remember about the day your mother disappeared?" Mikeal asked.

"From what I can remember, it was a typical day, nothing out of the ordinary. I was eight, my mother would always get me up for school, make breakfast, and take me to the bus stop. Every other day, she would go back home, change into her running gear, and go for a jog. When I got on the bus that morning, I had no idea that would be the last time I ever saw my mother."

Mikeal could see a tear forming in the edge of Oliver's eyes. No doubt internally, his mind was probably being flooded with memories of his mother. "I'm sorry to bring these memories back up, but we need to understand what was going on in your mom's life around the time of her disappearance."

"No, it's alright," Oliver responded. "I'm more upset with myself than your questions; this is probably the first time I've thought about my mother in a long time."

"Do you remember how far your mom normally ran?" Devin asked.

"Yes, I do," responded Oliver. "She had a ten-mile loop she would always run on weekdays."

"How did her disappearance affect your father?" Mikeal asked.

"Her disappearance devastated my father; he became a different man after we found out she had been killed."

"How did he change?" Devin followed.

"My father had always been outgoing, quick with a joke, but that all changed. I remember coming home from school, and he would just be sitting there in his recliner, lights off, curtains closed, staring at my mom's picture on the wall. I remember asking him about my mother. At first, he would talk a little about what happened, but as I got into my teens, he would always change the subject or leave the room if anyone brought up my mother."

"Is your father still alive?" Devin inquired.

"Yes, but I don't think he could add much. He's been suffering from dementia for the last decade. Some days are better than others, but his memory is shot."

"Does he still live in town?" Mikeal asked.

"Yes, he's over at the Bozeman Lodge; I can call and give them a heads up you're coming to see him," Oliver offered. Mikeal nodded in the affirmative.

"What do you know about David Miller?" Mikeal continued.

Oliver let out a big sigh before beginning, "David Miller confessed to killing my mother, but he was deemed mentally unfit to stand trial. I must have been ten years old at the time, and I couldn't grasp the full gravity of the situation. What sticks with me is my father's unwavering belief that David Miller wasn't the one who took my mother's life. I vaguely recall my father locking horns with the police after Miller led them to where he claimed to have buried her. Dad's argument was that Miller probably read about the disappearance in the paper and, in his drug-out state, hallucinated the whole gruesome act."

"Do you remember what the police said?" Mikeal asked.

"They were pretty confident they had the killer," he quickly responded.

"Alright, we'll thank you both for taking the time to relive some very unpleasant times," Mikeal replied as he stood to leave. "We'll head over to speak with your dad next."

"Sheriff, thank you for caring enough about my mother to revisit the case, it means a lot."

"One last question, Mr. Hulligan, do you remember anyone in the neighborhood back then owning a Jeep Wagoneer?" Mikeal asked.

Oliver thought for a moment, "No, I don't; our neighbors were more of the station wagon crowd."

Within a few minutes, they were pulling into the parking lot at the Bozeman Lodge, an assisted living center right down the road from the sheriff's station. "We're here to see Wendell Hulligan," Mikeal told the lady at the front desk.

Without looking up at either of them, she replied, "One minute, let me contact the nurse in charge of that wing." While she waited for a response, another line rang; "Thank you for calling Bozeman Lodge Assisted Living Center, how may I direct your call," she answered. "Yes, sir, they're actually standing in front of me, I'll let the nurse in charge know." Finally looking up at the Sheriff, the lady smiled and told them that was Mr. Hulligan's son. Before Mikeal or Devin could reply, her phone started buzzing. "Yes, the Sheriff would like to speak with Wendell. I just spoke with his son, and he said it was alright." Hanging up the phone, she returned her attention to the two officers. "The nurse will be up here in a minute, if you would like to take a seat."

A few minutes later, she arrived and took them to Wendell's room. "Sheriff, just so you know, Wendell doesn't really speak in sentences anymore. If you're lucky, maybe a word or two, but nothing else. Don't expect to carry on a conversation with him."

"Does he ever mention anyone's name?" Mikeal asked.

"Yes, he always asks for Nancy."

"What about his son, does he ever speak about Oliver?" Mikeal pressed.

"His eyes light up when we tell him Oliver is coming to visit, but I've never heard him say the name. Alright, here we are," Mikeal nodded as the nurse opened the door. "Wendell, you have visitors from the sheriff's office. Alright, I'm going to leave you boys alone. Sheriff, if you need me, you can press the red button on the wall, and someone will respond."

"Thanks, nurse, but we should be good."

The room exuded an aura of minimalism, featuring a solitary hospital bed nestled against one wall, with Wendell comfortably ensconced in a recliner nearby. The room's only window held a view of a sprawling grassy field, stretching toward a serene tree-line. A nightstand, a modest anchor of personal belongings in this sterile space, cradled a lone photograph capturing his son, Oliver, and wife.

Wendell, a frail elder, bore the weight of time on his withered frame. His hair had surrendered to the passage of years, now a sea of silver, while two days' worth of unshaven stubble adorned his weathered face. In his present condition, he seemed scarcely to tip the scales beyond a mere hundred and twenty pounds. A closer inspection revealed his blue eyes had lost their luster, clouded over with a distant gaze, as though he were traversing the corridors of his own history.

Without any other seats in the room, Mikeal sat down on his bed where he had a direct view of Wendell. Attempting to start a dialogue, Mikeal asked Wendell how his day has been going. No response, just a steady look back at the Sheriff. Over the next few minutes, Mikeal tries to get a word out of Wendell, failing each time.

Finally, Devin, who had remained standing, leans over towards Mikeal and whispers, "We're wasting our time; his mind is gone."

Almost immediately, without any change in facial expression, Wendell clearly says, "Nancy."

"Yes, Mr. Wendell, we're here regarding your wife Nancy," the Sheriff followed. "Do you remember when she disappeared?"

No verbal response from Wendell, just a continuous stare back towards the Sheriff.

"We're revisiting the case; we spoke with your son Oliver earlier. We were hoping you may be able to provide something possibly overlooked in the original investigation."

"1970," Wendell answered out of the blue.

"That's right; your wife disappeared in 1970. What else would you like to tell us, Mr. Hulligan?"

Silence once again returned to the room.

"David Miller," Devin spoke aloud.

Wendell's stare quickly moved away from the Sheriff towards Devin.

"Alright, Devin, you have his attention, now what?" Mikeal asked.

Devin stated again, "David Miller." Wendell's face was quickly turning from pale to red, while his eyes remained firmly fixed on Devin. Devin once again started to say, "David," but before he could say Miller, Wendell sternly replied, "No!" Which he then repeated.

Mikeal moved closer to Wendell. "David Miller didn't kill your wife, did he?"

Wendell turned his attention back towards the Sheriff. Nothing was said over the next couple of minutes. "We don't think David had anything to do with your wife's disappearance either," Mikeal finally broke the silence.

In a sudden and somewhat surprising turn, Wendell, whose frail body seemed to hover on the brink of its limits, made a determined effort to rise out of his chair. Devin, his face a portrait of astonishment, couldn't help but blurt out, "Is he supposed to be doing that?"

The Sheriff, in a calm yet slightly exasperated tone, responded, "How should I know, Devin? I'm not his doctor. But let's not panic. Just press the button and get someone in here, so we don't end up taking the blame for any mishap."

After successfully standing, Wendell shuffled his feet toward the nightstand beside his bed, carefully retrieving the framed picture of Oliver and his wife. He then returned to his seat and handed it to the Sheriff, whispering softly, "Nancy."

Mikeal, initially puzzled, felt compelled to correct the apparent confusion. "No, that's your son and his wife," he gently offered, before a realization dawned upon him. Mikeal remembered his mother's habit of swapping pictures within frames. She would replace older photos with newer ones, while leaving the old still in the frame. The Sheriff flipped over the frame, quickly manipulating the clips securing the back. As the backing was removed, another photograph lay hidden within.

Mikeal's eyes fixated on the photograph, capturing a man and a woman in what appeared to be the front yard of a residence. The resemblance between the man in the picture and Wendell was striking, and he couldn't help but feel the weight of the moment. Tentatively, he asked, "Is this you and your wife?" But Wendell remained lost in the depths of his own memories, offering no response.

Even though Wendell grappled with dementia, Mikeal couldn't bring himself to take a photo of something so sentimental without permission. He approached the situation delicately, saying, "Wendell, I'm going to make a copy of this photo and put your original back in the frame." He swiftly captured a few copies with his phone.

"June 1970," Mikeal mused, his voice tinged with a hint of nostalgia. "This could very well be the last photograph of Nancy."

"Thank you for your time, Wendell," Mikeal continued, preparing to leave. "I'll place the frame back on your nightstand." As they turned to depart, the room was filled with Wendell's voice once more, a soft plea that couldn't be ignored. "Find Nancy."

Mikeal turned back to face Wendell, offering a reassuring response, "Sir, we'll do everything in our power to find your wife."

Mikeal let Devin drive back to the station while he looked at the picture on his phone.

"Well, Sheriff, any of this info useful or did we waste a half day?"

"I'm not sure, Devin; the file seemed to indicate an open and shut case with the killer identified, but the family seems to have their doubts."

"You mean an old man with dementia who can't really communicate."

"Well, yeah now, but you heard his son; he argued with the police back then, saying he wasn't the guy. I've asked Allison to track down this David Miller. If he's still alive, we'll see what he can remember. I'd also like to see if we can enlarge this picture. My guess is it was taken in their neighborhood."

CHAPTER 13

"I'm headed to lunch, Larissa. See you in an hour," Emma said as she walked out the back door of the shop. Foot traffic had been extremely light in the shop, and the day had been flying by. Emma was on autopilot as she headed to the restaurant, took her seat in the back, and ordered her burger combo.

After infiltrating Mr. Taylor's office, she elevated her game and formally began documenting her thoughts, meticulously taking notes in a journal. She jotted down two new findings: first, the discovery of the note from Steve, and second, the revelation of the positive pregnancy test. She also deemed it crucial to record details about her roommate, Mark, and the heated argument that had led Sammy to storm out of their shared home.

The vanishing act of Sammy had to be connected to the pregnancy; Emma felt certain of it. She toyed with the idea of contacting the Sheriff with this newfound information but hesitated, convinced they wouldn't pursue a deeper investigation.

As she sat there, contemplating her next steps, her thoughts kept gravitating back to her boss, Steve Taylor. An instinctual unease lingered within her; she couldn't shake the suspicion that he wasn't revealing everything he knew. Whenever she was in his presence, an unsettling feeling enveloped her due to his peculiar mannerisms. He exuded an off-putting arrogance, especially when interacting with women. His behavior grew progressively more unsettling with younger individuals. Emma couldn't fathom how Sammy had become entangled with such a man; it simply didn't add up.

As Emma continued to deliberate her next move, Terry materialized, carrying her burger combo. His eyes, however, honed in on the notebook she had laid out on the table. "What's this?" he inquired, his tone laced with unsettling curiosity. Before Emma could formulate a response, he callously seized the notebook from the table.

"Give that back!" Emma's demand cut through the tension in the air.

"Hold on," Terry retorted with unnerving speed, swiftly flipping through the notebook's initial pages before carelessly dropping it back onto the table. "Oh, do we have an undercover detective among us?" he sneered, his words laced with mocking sarcasm that sent shivers down Emma's spine.

This marked the first time Terry had displayed such a sinister side. Emma's memory instantly conjured Sammy's warning, urging her to steer clear of him, but her overwhelming urge to confide in someone about Sammy's pregnancy was consuming her. "I'm just trying to unravel what happened to my friend," she replied, her voice tinged with caution as she attempted to tread lightly around Terry's ominous demeanor.

As if a switch had been flipped in an instant, Terry returned to his previous demeanor and took a seat at the table, his old, seemingly benign personality back in place. He politely inquired about what Emma had uncovered, his tone now remarkably congenial.

Emma contemplated grabbing her notebook and making a hasty exit, leaving her food behind to put distance between herself and Terry. Yet, an inexplicable force kept her rooted to her seat.

Terry, his expression softer and more reassuring, began to backtrack. "Look, I was only joking around," he admitted, his voice genuinely apologetic. "I didn't mean to startle you. Honestly, I'd like to understand the progress you've made," he added, attempting to cover up any hint of his previous sinister disposition.

Emma, with a lingering sense of unease, found herself on the precipice of divulging Sammy's pregnancy news to Terry.

"No way, and you suspect Steve Taylor might be the father?" Terry reacted, his response swift and animated. After a brief pause to process the revelation, he asked, "So, what's your next move?"

"I can't shake the feeling that Steve had something to do with Sammy's disappearance," Emma admitted.

Terry probed further, "Do you have any concrete evidence?"

"Nothing solid," Emma admitted, "but when he talked about his conversation with the Sheriff, it just didn't sit right with me."

"That's Steve for you," Terry responded. "I've personally never had any issues with him, but the women in the kitchen say he's unsettling to be around."

"I know exactly what they mean," Emma added, shuddering at the memory of her interactions with Steve.

Terry hesitated, then continued, "I shouldn't gossip, but I've heard stories from years ago, rumors linking him to a co-worker's disappearance."

Emma was taken aback, unable to conceal her astonishment. "You're kidding me."

Emma contemplated the situation and proposed, "So, do we inform the Sheriff then?"

"Emma, I don't know. It might have been just talk, but maybe," Terry pondered.

"We need to tell the Sheriff; he needs to know," Emma insisted, growing increasingly agitated.

Terry tried to temper her urgency. "Let's take it slow, Emma. First, I need to keep my job, so the last thing I want is to anger Steve. Besides, this might have been mere gossip. I'm sure if he were a suspect, they would have investigated him thoroughly."

"So, we just let him go on his way?" Emma responded, her frustration evident.

"No, that's not what I'm saying at all. We need to dig a bit into his past, maybe keep an eye on him to see if anything suspicious comes up," Terry suggested.

"So who's the wanna-be detective now," Emma, feeling a little more at ease around Terry, stated.

"Sammy was my friend too, I can help you if you'd like?"

Still harboring suspicions about Terry based on Sammy's words, Emma hesitated before reluctantly allowing the words to slip out, "Thanks, Terry. I'd appreciate your help."

With just two tasks remaining on her original list—another attempt to contact Sammy's mother and the printing of missing person posters, Emma couldn't shake the nagging feeling that Terry might have other motives.

"Well, next up, I have a template for a missing person flyer," she explained, trying to maintain a semblance of control in the situation. "I'll need access to a printer, some paper, and assistance with distribution."

Terry's enthusiastic response heightened her guard even higher. "Emma, I'd be delighted to assist you with printing the posters. I've got a high-speed printer at home that can churn out fifty in about five minutes."

Emma hesitated briefly before handing over her pen and a piece of paper, asking Terry to jot down his phone number and address. "Could you come to my place on Friday?" he inquired. "We can print out your posters and discuss what we need to do about Steve."

"Great, I'll be there," Emma agreed, trying to ignore the creeping sense of unease that threatened to consume her.

With Emma's discomfort around Terry still lingering, Friday soon arrived. She had the lunch shift, which she figured could always be used as an excuse to leave if the situation turned awkward. Typing the address Terry had given her into her phone, she discovered it was only a twenty-minute drive from her apartment, situated along the highway leading to the North entrance of Yellowstone.

After spending ten minutes on the main road, Emma took a turn onto a gravel road that led deeper into the woods. As she followed the winding path, her phone's GPS chimed in, announcing, "You have arrived." Emma came to a stop and glanced around, but there was no home in sight. To her left, the land sloped downward into a hollow, while on her right, a pasture stretched out with a few cows grazing by the fence, seemingly unperturbed by the presence of her car. "Damn GPS, not worth a dime in the rural Montana mountains," she muttered in frustration.

Resolving to find Terry's place, Emma continued driving for another quarter of a mile before finally spotting a mailbox with the number Terry had provided.

She proceeded up a gentle rise and came to a halt in front of a single-wide trailer. It sat perched on a level lot, carved into the mountainside terrain. Further up the mountainside, a grand but weathered house stood, its paint seemingly surrendered to the elements over the years. With its enduring metal roof still standing firm, Emma couldn't help but wonder if anyone still inhabited the place. Scattered across the landscape, she noticed half a dozen or more old vehicles, each bearing the patina of time. One truck, in particular, drew her attention, its engine bay now home to a young tree, its roots boldly reaching into the past.

"Emma, you made it," Terry's voice broke the silence as he greeted her. "Any trouble finding the place?" he asked.

"No, it was a pretty straightforward drive," Emma replied, her eyes taking in the surroundings. "You own all this?"

"Yeah, it's all been mine since my dad passed away," Terry admitted, a hint of nostalgia in his tone.

Curiosity compelled Emma to ask, "Is this where you grew up?"

Terry nodded. "Yep, the house up there on the hill was the only place I ever called home until we put this trailer in. Come on inside, Emma; I'll get you something to drink."

Emma stepped into the trailer, her cautious anticipation giving way to surprise as she observed its pristine cleanliness, devoid of any clutter. "Why did you move out of the big house, Terry? It looks like you'd have more room there."

Terry explained, "My dad gave me this trailer for my twenty-first birthday. It had just been him and me in the house; my mother left when I was young. After he passed, I guess I could've moved back, but I didn't see the need. It's just me, and this trailer suits me fine. I'm guessing you'd like a diet coke?"

"Yeah, that would be great," Emma accepted his offer. "I hope you have a USB port on your computer."

Terry returned with her drink and assured her, "Here's your drink; let me grab the computer from the back room."

Moments later, he reappeared carrying his laptop, which he placed on the coffee table before pulling out the drawer under the television; revealing his printer.

"While these posters are printing, would you like me to show you around the property?" Terry offered.

Emma, feeling a mix of curiosity and caution, replied, "Yeah, that would be nice." They stepped out of the trailer, and as they walked, Emma couldn't help but inquire, "What's the story with all these vehicles scattered everywhere?"

Terry explained, "My dad was a carpenter. Most of these were his work vehicles. He'd drive them until rust ate away at them, almost falling apart. Then he'd salvage the engine and put it in a better body. He'd get about five winters out of each vehicle."

Emma probed further, "Any of them worth any money?"

Terry shook his head, a wry smile playing on his lips. "No, they're all too far gone. I can't even give them away for scrap."

As they made their way up the mountainside, drawing closer to the main house, Emma's eye caught a small building tucked behind it. She pointed and asked, "What's that?"

Terry chuckled, "That, Emma, is the outhouse."

Emma's surprise was palpable. "What?"

Terry laughed heartily, "Yep, I grew up without indoor plumbing. If you needed to go, you had to head outside."

Emma was astounded. "I thought that went away in the 1800s."

Terry teased, "Wow, Emma, you really are a city girl."

Eager to explore, the caution she had initially clung to had all but vanished. She inquired about entering, but Terry clarified, "You could, but I'd need to retrieve the keys first."

Perplexed, she asked, "It's locked? Why would you lock it up?"

Terry clarified, "The floor in that building could give way at any time. It's safer this way."

Emma shrugged, conceding, "Well, I guess I don't want to see it that bad. Maybe next time. What about the house? Can we go in there?"

Terry hesitated before answering, "I'd rather you not."

Emma was intrigued. "Another bad floor?"

Terry's reply carried an air of caution, "No, the floor's actually in great shape for a house of that age. It's the uninvited house guests I'm more concerned with. Last time I was in there, about a month ago, I had to deal with a couple of rattlesnakes. I don't think you want to mess with them."

"Printing's probably done; let's head back and map out our next plan of attack."

Once back inside the trailer, they gravitated toward the circular kitchen table. The relaxed atmosphere they'd enjoyed outdoors had dissipated, replaced by an unspoken tension that lingered in the confined space. As they settled in, Emma couldn't help but ponder whether Terry sensed the palpable strain that had woven itself into their collaboration.

Emma initiated the conversation by addressing their first issue, her voice carrying the weight of their mission. "Steve's days off are usually Saturday and Sunday. I'm rarely off on weekends. Terry, can you follow him?"

Terry, his reluctance thinly veiled, replied, "Well, I happen to be off this weekend, but this isn't exactly how I'd planned to spend it."

Emma met his hesitation with a determined gaze, her voice laced with conviction. "Remember, Terry, it's not about you; it's about Sammy."

Terry couldn't help but crack a wry smile, acknowledging, "Wow, you wasted no time playing the guilt card."

With a resigned nod, Terry conceded, "Alright, I'll follow him around this weekend and see what I can learn."

"Great," Emma said, leaning forward. "I'm on the late shift both Saturday and Sunday, so I'll start putting up the posters before work each day."

"Alright," Terry agreed, his earlier reluctance giving way to a shared determination. "Sounds like we have a plan."

Sitting in his truck on a chilly Saturday morning, Terry couldn't shake the feeling that Emma had used his own words to maneuver him into sacrificing his weekend. However, one thing about him was unwavering: when he committed to something, he followed through.

He had stationed his truck inconspicuously, three blocks away from Steve's house, and patiently waited for what felt like an eternity. It was another full hour before he watched Steve finally emerge from the house, slide into his car, and back out of the driveway. Terry engaged the truck's gears and discreetly began tailing Steve, maintaining a cautious distance between the two vehicles.

After a tense ten-minute drive, Steve pulled into the parking lot of ACE Hardware. Terry followed suit, parking at a safe remove from Steve's vehicle, his senses on high alert.

After thirty minutes later, Steve reappeared, clutching a box as he strode back to his car. He made a right turn onto Highway 191, heading west out of town. At the Four Corners junction, where the main highway veered left, becoming the Gallatin Highway, Steve bucked the trend, continuing straight onto Highway 84. Terry maintained a safe distance, following him for about an hour until Steve made an unexpected exit.

As they approached the Harrison Hills area, Steve made a left turn off the highway, traveling a brief distance before pulling into the driveway of what appeared to be a nondescript metal commercial building. Terry had no choice but to keep driving past the structure until he found an opportunity to turn around. Once heading back towards the building, he pulled over at the roadside and retrieved his binoculars from the passenger seat.

It seemed that Steve had ventured inside the building by this point, and Terry glanced at his watch, realizing it was already 10:30. The first hour crept by, feeling like an eternity. The second hour dragged on, seemingly twice as long. "Damn, this is like watching paint dry," Terry muttered to himself.

Another hour came and went, and finally, Steve emerged from the building. Terry's mind raced with speculation about what had taken so long inside. Steve turned his car around in the yard and soon retraced his path in the opposite direction.

Terry bided his time for another agonizing thirty minutes, ensuring that Steve wouldn't double back before he cautiously approached the building. Parking his truck, he closed the distance, and as he drew near, he realized the doors and windows at the front of the structure were obscured by a dark tint, rendering it impossible to see what lay within.

Undaunted, he continued his circling to the back of the building where more windows and a door presented themselves. Terry tested the door handle, confirming it was securely locked. The windows here shared the same covering as those at the front. He pressed his ear to the door, straining to detect any hint of sound emanating from inside. Suddenly, a compressor roared to life, jolting Terry. For a split second, fear gripped him as he considered the possibility that Steve hadn't left for good.

"Why would he go off and leave the air running?" Terry wondered aloud, his heart pounding. With a surge of trepidation, he turned and sprinted back to his truck. Fumbling with his keys for a moment, he managed to start the truck and hastily exited the property.

On his way back home, Terry called Emma's number. "Hey, Emma, do you have a moment?"

"Hold on, let me see if I can step out for a minute," she replied. A few moments later, she returned to the line. "What's up, Terry? Did you find out anything?"

"Yeah," Terry began, "I found out Steve sleeps in on his day off. I parked outside his house for a couple of hours this morning before he finally left."

Emma asked for more details. "Did you uncover anything useful?"

Terry pondered the question before responding, "Possibly. I followed him to an ACE Hardware where he picked up something before heading out towards Harrison Mills. He stopped at what seemed like a small commercial building. He stayed inside for hours before finally emerging. After he left,

I tried to take a peek inside, but all the windows were heavily covered with tint. One thing struck me as odd, though – he left the air conditioning running."

Emma offered a possible explanation, saying, "Maybe he just forgot."

Terry shook his head. "Steve's a penny-pincher; I bet he left it on for a reason. Either he planned to return later, or something inside needed to stay cool."

Emma's voice carried a hint of concern. "Something or someone," she speculated.

Terry continued, "I'm not sure. I listened for a couple of minutes, and I didn't hear any noise coming from inside."

Emma couldn't help but wonder, "Could someone possibly be in there?"

Terry replied cautiously, "Anything's possible, but I'm not willing to make that bet just yet."

Emma shifted the focus. "So, what's your plan, Terry?"

Terry considered their next steps. "I think I'll drive back out there tomorrow afternoon and take another look."

CHAPTER 14

Once back at the office, Mikeal promptly sent the photo to Devin's computer. The image had weathered over the years, but its essence remained intact. Wendell and Nancy stood side by side, framed by a tree on one side and a street view on the other, with mountains looming in the background.

"I could be wrong," Devin mused, "but I think this was taken in their driveway."

Mikeal nodded in agreement. "I'm thinking the same thing, but to be certain, we'll need to pay Oliver another visit." He leaned closer to Devin's computer. "Zoom in on the street behind them."

Devin attempted to enhance the image, but it only resulted in a blurry mess. "Can you make out any of those vehicles parked on the street?" Mikeal asked.

Devin shook his head. "No, I see the same blur you're seeing. Not enough pixels to enlarge it like this. Give me some time; I'll try some Photoshop magic."

Mikeal agreed. "Alright, but let me know as soon as you have something to look at."

Mikeal retreated to his office to tackle the growing pile of emails awaiting his attention. Nearly two weeks had elapsed since the resort employee's disappearance. With a sense of urgency, he entered "Hudson" into the search bar of Outlook, hoping for any leads. The search algorithm rapidly combed through the 200 unopened emails, but it returned empty-handed.

Undeterred, he expanded his search to include "Sammy" and then "Samantha," but the results remained frustratingly elusive. Little did the Sheriff know that Emma now possessed crucial information that, if shared with him, could potentially prompt a more robust and resourceful approach to the investigation.

Another hour passed, and then Devin appeared at the door. "I've got something," he announced proudly.

Mikeal followed him to his desk. "Let's take a look."

Devin showed him the enhanced photo. "It's not much bigger than the original, but take a look at the vehicle on the street."

Mikeal's eyes widened in surprise. "Well, I'll be damned. Is that what I think it is?"

Devin confirmed, "Yep, a Jeep Wagoneer parked about four houses down from where the photo was taken."

"Pull up Oliver's house on Google Earth," Mikeal instructed.

Devin did so swiftly. "Got it."

"What's the address where we think the Jeep is parked?"

Devin found the address and quickly typed it in before Mikeal could ask.

"Let's do a search on property owners."

"I'm way ahead of you, Sheriff."

"Alright, hotshot, who owned the house in 1970?"

Devin's brows furrowed as he checked the records. "That's odd. The earliest record for this property is 1971. It must have been in the early stages of being built when this photo was taken."

Mikeal pressed further, "Who built the home?"

Devin provided the information. "The original deed shows it was purchased from Lynn Brothers Construction."

"Search for that business," Mikeal urged.

Devin's quick fingers danced across the keyboard. "Looks like they went under during the housing crisis, closed in 2007."

"Who were the owners?"

"A Roy and Gary Lynn," Devin replied. "I'm assuming they're brothers, given the company name."

Mikeal wasted no time. "Allison!"

"Yes, Sheriff?"

"See what you can find out about Roy and Gary Lynn. They owned a construction company for several years, Lynn Brothers Construction. It looks like they were building a home near where Nancy Hulligan disappeared back in 1970."

"Devin, we're hitting the road again. Let's head back to Oliver's place and confirm this location. You give the Hulligan's a call to let them know we're on our way," Mikeal instructed Devin.

Fifteen minutes later, their vehicle pulled into Oliver's driveway, where both Oliver and his wife were anxiously waiting at the front door. Mikeal stepped out of the vehicle and moved to the center of the front yard. "Oliver, come over here for a moment and take a look at this photo. I believe someone captured your parents standing in this very spot," Mikeal said.

Oliver scrutinized the image and nodded. "Yeah, that's our driveway, same tree but much bigger now," he confirmed.

"See that vehicle parked down the road? It's a Jeep Wagoneer," Mikeal pointed out.

Oliver squinted at the distant vehicle. "Is that the same one you asked me about the other day? I don't recall anyone in the neighborhood owning one like that. Perhaps they were just visiting someone around here."

"Or maybe they were part of a construction crew," Mikeal suggested.

Oliver considered the possibility. "Could be," he replied. "We were one of the first houses on this street, and it seems like something was always being built when I was a kid. Oliver's face held a mix of hope and uncertainty as he posed his question, "Do you think that vehicle might be connected to my mom's disappearance?"

Mikeal met Oliver's gaze with empathy. "I'm not certain, Oliver," he began. "This photo was not part of the original investigation. Right now, we're focused on uncovering any new leads or missed evidence that could potentially push your mother's case forward," he explained, emphasizing their commitment to discovering the truth.

"Oliver, I realize this might be a long shot, but do you think your father might have kept anything else belonging to your mother, aside from photographs?" Mikeal inquired.

Oliver thought about the question a moment before replying, "I vaguely recall about a year after she disappeared, my father asked me to help him store a couple of boxes in the attic. When I asked what was inside, he explained that he had cleared out her bedroom and bathroom, gathering her belongings. He said we'd keep them until we found her. I believe those boxes might still be up there."

"Can we go take a look?" Devin asked, breaking the silence that hung in the air. Without waiting for a response, both Oliver and Devin disappeared into the house, leaving Mikeal and Oliver's wife standing alone on the front lawn. During their previous visit, Mikeal and Devin had barely ventured beyond the threshold, keeping their conversations within a mere ten feet of the front door of the two-story home.

With a determined sense of purpose, Oliver swiftly bounded through the front door, and Devin followed closely behind. Inside, they navigated through the house, making their way to the center where the staircase awaited. With quick strides, they ascended the stairs, arriving at the second-story landing, which featured four doors. Three of them led to bedrooms, while the fourth served as the entrance to the bathroom area.

Oliver reached up, pulling down the hanging rope that concealed the attic access in the landing. As he prepared to ascend the collapsible ladder, Devin offered a flashlight, anticipating the need for additional light. Oliver declined. Once he reached the attic's entrance, he flipped on a light switch that bathed the space in illumination. Without hesitation, he disappeared into the attic while Devin waited anxiously below.

Normally, Oliver only ventured into this part of his home twice a year when retrieving or storing Halloween and Christmas decorations. It had been over four decades since he had helped his father move his mother's belongings to a remote corner of the attic. Hunched over to avoid the protruding nails in the ceiling, he carefully shifted boxes as he navigated toward the place where his mother's physical mementos had been stowed. Suddenly, his path was bathed in light, surprising him. Turning back towards the entrance, he saw Devin at the attic's entrance, providing much-needed illumination with his flashlight.

Oliver resumed his slow march toward the far left rear of the attic, finally arriving at his destination. He took a seat on a nearby box and began to open a container filled with his mother's possessions. Devin watched silently as Oliver uncovered the box of memories, his gaze fixed on its contents. After a few minutes, Devin, concerned, asked if Oliver was alright.

Breaking the silence, Oliver replied, "Sorry, Devin. This isn't the box."

Oliver rubbed the back of his neck, frustration evident on his face, as he continued to scan the attic, determined to find where he had left his mother's items. "Hold on," he said, sliding off the box where he had been sitting. He dropped to a crawl and disappeared behind a wall of boxes. Moments later, he reemerged, pushing a box toward Devin, before disappearing again to retrieve another.

Returning with the second box, both men gathered around the two brown cardboard boxes, each adorned with a heavy layer of dust. Opening the first box, Devin immediately spotted a pair of old Puma running shoes. Oliver carefully retrieved them and ran his fingers over every imperfection, while Devin remarked on how small they appeared.

"When you're a child," Oliver spoke, "your parents seem like giants. I guess this is my first realization of how small she was."

Sensing the emotional weight pressing on Oliver, Devin suggested they take the boxes downstairs and transport them to the lab. There, he hoped, modern technology would work its magic and provide valuable data to advance his mother's case.

About thirty minutes after they had entered the home, they reemerged, each carefully carrying a dusty cardboard box. Mikeal couldn't help but notice a faint marker outline on the side of the box, bearing the initials N.H.

"Thanks, Oliver," Mikeal said appreciatively, acknowledging their host's cooperation. "We'll return this once we've had a chance to go through it and catalog anything that might be useful. Your assistance means a lot."

Oliver nodded, visibly affected by the emotions stirred within him as he clutched his mother's shoes. "Sheriff, it's been untouched in the attic for over forty years. Take your time. Honestly, I'm not sure I want any of it back."

Minutes later, Mikeal and Devin were back on the highway heading toward the station. "Sheriff, what should I be looking for going through this box?" Devin asked.

"Look for anything that could possibly contain DNA."

"Sheriff, are you thinking one of the three Jane Does could be Nancy?"

"I'm not ruling anything out, but Dr. Baldwin did indicate bones could have been from the seventies. It's worth a shot."

Soon they were walking back inside the station, where they were greeted by Allison. "Sheriff, I have the information you were looking for on Roy and Gary Lynn."

"Great, what have you got?" Mikeal replied.

"First of all, they weren't brothers. Roy was Gary's father."

"Well, that's stupid. Why did they call it Lynn Brothers Construction?" Devin sarcastically answered.

"From what I could find, Roy originally started the company with his brother Henry. Henry died in 1965."

"Are either Roy or Gary still in the area?" Mikeal asked.

"Unfortunately, both are deceased. Roy died in 1979, and Gary passed in 2004," Allison answered.

"Wonderful," Devin replied, shaking his head.

"Is that it?" Mikeal pressed.

"Yeah, they're both dead. I'm not sure what else you're looking to learn," Allison replied.

"What about the vehicles they owned? Can you identify what vehicles were registered in their names from 1969 through '75?"
"Yeah, I can check with DMV," Allison dejectedly responded as she headed back towards her desk.

"Devin, I'm headed to my office. Let me know when you have all this cataloged, and we can review."
"Got it, I'll let you know," he responded.

Mikeal had been in his office for approximately thirty minutes when the phone rang, displaying the 406 area code from Billings. He answered with a brisk, "Hello, Gallatin County Sheriff Lancaster."

"Sheriff, Dr. Baldwin calling," came the voice on the other end.

Mikeal leaned forward, a glimmer of anticipation in his eyes. "Doctor, I hope you're calling to tell me about the three bodies we found."

"Indeed, Sheriff. We have some new information today."

"Let's hear it," Mikeal prompted.

"We believe Jane Doe one and two were killed within a few months of each other, possibly between 1975 and 1978. Jane Doe three's death was earlier, possibly five years prior. All three victims were Caucasian, and it appears they had their heads removed by a single, sharp object. There were no signs of repeated blows to the top of the spine."

"Does that mean they were decapitated postmortem?" Mikeal inquired.

"Yes, Sheriff. It's likely that this was done after death to make it easier to sever the heads," Dr. Baldwin explained.

Mikeal grunted in agreement, "Sounds like a sick individual."

"Perhaps," Dr. Baldwin replied, "but it's also possible they were trying to conceal the cause of death."

"You're right. A bullet to the brain would still leave evidence all these years later," Mikeal acknowledged.

"What about the victims' ages?" he continued.

"We ran their DNA through our databases, but there were no matches," the doctor replied. "Based on our analysis, Jane Does one and two were in their early twenties, while Jane Doe three was older, possibly around thirty."

"Doc, we're working on a disappearance from 1970 and might have something that matches. The missing woman was thirty-one years old at the time. We'd appreciate it if you could take a look," Mikeal requested.

"Send it over; we'll gladly examine it. We'll also continue searching other databases nationwide to see if we can find a match," Dr. Baldwin assured him.

"Great, thanks Doc, we'll talk soon." As he was hanging up the phone, he noticed Devin outside his office door and waved him to come in.
"I didn't want to disturb you while you were on the phone, but I've completed inventorying the box."

Mikeal followed Devin as they descended the stairs into the basement of the building, each step tinged with anticipation. The atmosphere was stifling in the dimly lit room, devoid of natural light, where shadows seemed to swallow everything, leaving only a solitary metal table bathed in the harsh glow of a single light source. Upon this table lay the meticulously arranged contents of both boxes, as if they were artifacts of a long-lost civilization, waiting to unveil their long-guarded secrets. Devin commenced his recounting of the discoveries from the first box.

"It appears that Wendell gathered everything from the bathroom into this box," he explained. "We've got her hairbrush, toothbrush, face cream, and even a hairnet."

Although Devin had placed each item into individual evidence bags, Mikeal decided it was best to glove up before any further examination. His gaze fixated on the hairbrush, now sealed within an airtight evidence bag. Strands of dark hair were still visible, looking delicate and brittle after four decades apart from its owner. He wondered if the DNA within those fragile strands could still be salvaged, holding the potential to unlock long-buried secrets.

The room's heavy silence was shattered by the creaking of the door as Deputy Allison Lightjack joined the proceedings. Mikeal's attention was then drawn to the old, weathered Puma running shoes, each carefully encased in its own evidence bag. He couldn't help but wonder how many miles Nancy had logged in those shoes before consigning them to a remote corner of her closet. The painful truth gnawed at him – these were not the shoes she had worn during her fateful last run.

Devin scrutinized the second Puma shoe, bringing it closer to the light. "The heel of this shoe is completely worn out," he observed, giving it a gentle shake, eliciting a faint rattling sound from within. Curious, Allison asked, "Rocks?" Both Mikeal and Devin nodded in agreement before resuming their examination of the other items.

Mikeal suggested, "Let's send the hairbrush and shoes over to Dr. Baldwin; I promised him we'd be sending something soon."

Devin promptly responded, "I'll take care of it before I leave."

CHAPTER 15

Even though it was one of her few off days, Emma decided to get up early. Her plan was to put up the missing posters of Sammy around Big Sky and Bozeman, hoping someone would come forth with information. She still felt Steve knew more than he was letting on, but she had no concrete information she could take to the police. With nothing concrete of her own regarding Steve, all her hopes were on Terry finding out what was in the building Steve had visited yesterday.

Around noon, Emma decided to take a break after hanging nearly half of the missing person posters. She stepped into a nearby diner, located just around the corner from the empty storefront where she had placed her last poster. The diner was bustling with patrons, making it a challenge to find an available table. Finally, she spotted one tucked away in the far corner of the crowded room.

A waitress approached, carrying a tray of food for the adjacent table. The lively chatter between the patrons and the waitress drew Emma's attention. Her gaze landed on four men dressed in the distinctive uniforms of Montana Forestry Commission firefighters, their shirt sleeves adorned with patches indicating their affiliation. After taking the neighboring table's order, the waitress turned her attention to Emma, promptly jotting down her order for a burger, fries, and a Coke before heading back toward the front of the restaurant.

Emma returned her focus to the group of firefighters, inadvertently eavesdropping as they discussed their recent work. They had been tasked with clearing ground cover in a remote area, and Emma couldn't help but overhear one of them pose a grim question to his companions, "Do you think they're going to find any more bones?"

Another firefighter sought clarification, "How many bodies have they found so far?"

The first man responded with a somber tone, "Three."

The men then turned their attention to the food in front of them, and all conversation abruptly ceased.

Turning her attention back to Sammy, she briefly pondered a potential connection to the firefighters' story. She decided to call Terry to check on any progress.

"What's up, Emma?" he answered.

"I was hoping you could tell me!"

"Well, I've been parked on the side of the road for the last two hours, Steve hasn't left the house," Terry responded.

"Terry, have you heard anything about bones recently being discovered in the woods?"

Terry's normally playful voice turned serious as he asked, "Where? What woods?"

"I don't know, that's just what I overheard these firefighters talking about in the diner," Emma responded.

"Listen, this is very important," Terry stated in a very agitated tone, "We need to know exactly where they're talking about."

As he asked the question, Terry felt a chemical change going on in his body; his pulse was increasing, and his body heating up. This was a familiar sensation that he never could quite grasp. He had always been adept at masking his true emotions.

Even though the firefighters were still at the adjacent table, feeling uncomfortable asking them the question, she lied to Terry, indicating they had already left.

A silence lingered between them, leaving Emma with time to reflect on Sammy's earlier warning about Terry's supposed dark side. The memory sent shivers down her spine, and she couldn't help but question Terry's motives.

Before she could ponder further, Terry's voice broke the silence once more. "Never mind."

Emma couldn't restrain herself, and the words tumbled out, "Terry, what the hell was that about?"

She could hear Terry taking a couple of deep breaths before responding, his tone filled with uncertainty. "I wish I knew.

Have you ever experienced an overwhelming, uncontrollable feeling deep inside, as if your mind goes on auto-pilot?"

Terry went on to explain that he had struggled with this issue throughout his life, comparing it to Tourette's syndrome. He confided that it was one of the primary reasons why he had difficulty maintaining friendships.

Empathizing with Terry's admission and reflecting on her own struggles with anxiety, Emma's demeanor softened as she began to understand the depth of his personal challenges.

Terry shifted the conversation back to their surveillance of Steve Taylor's home. "Emma, I'm starting to think this is getting us nowhere. I'm planning to head back out to the building we tracked him to yesterday."

Emma, determined to assist in any way possible, replied, "I'll meet you there, just text me the address."

Terry hesitated, then spoke with a hint of concern. "Emma, I'm not sure it's a great idea. If Steve were to suddenly show up, I'd need to make a quick exit, and having you there might slow things down, no offense."

Emma felt a pang of frustration. "Terry, that's not fair. She's my friend, and I want to help."

Terry sighed, realizing the tension between them. "Okay, Emma. If you really want to help, here's what you can do. Drive over to Steve's place and keep an eye on him for the rest of the evening. If he leaves, follow him discreetly. But please, let me know immediately if he starts heading in my direction. I need to know so I can get out of there fast."

Emma reluctantly agreed, recognizing the importance of their mission. "Alright, I'll do that," she replied, her determination unwavering.

As Emma drove toward Steve's house, her emotions were on a rollercoaster ride. One moment, she'd be filled with hope, believing they were close to finding Sammy, only to be plunged into the depths of despair and anxiety minutes later. The thought of Terry discovering Sammy's lifeless body in that mysterious building haunted her. Was she wrong to suspect Steve's involvement? Could he be nothing more than a socially awkward individual with no malicious intent, just searching for companionship? Emma questioned herself, wondering if she had unfairly judged him, desperately seeking someone to blame for Sammy's disappearance. Doubt crept in, making her question whether she was creating connections that didn't truly exist.

She parked her car a block away from Steve's house, keeping a discreet distance. His car was in the driveway, and a few lights illuminated the windows of the house. Emma decided to text Terry, informing him that Steve was still at home. Then, she reclined her seat slightly and attempted to relax as the afternoon slowly unfolded, a sense of anticipation and uncertainty hanging heavily in the air.

Terry retraced his steps from the previous day, arriving once again at the ominous metal building Steve had led him to. His truck rolled to a slow stop in the gravel parking area, and he emerged from the vehicle, scanning his surroundings with caution. The building stood about thirty yards from the lonely two-lane road that cut through the desolate landscape. It appeared as though this lot had once been part of the sprawling pasture that now enveloped it, separated only by a weathered three-strand barbed-wire fence. The metal structure's walls had been originally painted a foreboding red, which time had faded, and the front was devoid of windows, with a solitary black door serving as its enigmatic entrance.

As Terry drew nearer to the building, a knot of unease tightened in his stomach, threatening to double him over. He fought to regain his composure, his heart pounding in his chest. Approaching the front entrance, he realized that his plan had a critical oversight—he hadn't considered how he would gain access to the building. Unperturbed, he quietly made his way to the rear, desperately hoping to find an unlocked window that would grant him entry.

Suddenly, Emma jolted awake, her senses heightened as she heard the unmistakable screech of tires. She instinctively looked up, just in time to witness Steve's car tear down the road with an urgency that sent alarm bells ringing in her mind. "What the hell," she muttered to herself, her heart racing as she watched him disappear into the distance. Something was definitely amiss.

Without wasting a moment, she fumbled for her phone and dialed Terry's number. "Hey, are you there?" she asked urgently.

"Yeah, what's up?" came Terry's voice on the other end.

"Steve just bolted like a bat out of hell," Emma reported, her voice trembling with concern.

"Shit," Terry cursed under his breath. "I must have triggered a silent alarm."

"You're in the building?" Emma exclaimed, her surprise evident.

"No, but I'm about to make a hasty exit before the cops show up," Terry replied with urgency. "I'll catch up with you later."

Steve arrived at the building within thirty minutes, his face betraying little emotion as he parked his car. He circled the perimeter, his movements deliberate, waiting for the Sheriff to show up. Everything seemed normal on the outside – no broken windows, and the door remained securely locked. Fifteen minutes later, Deputy Devin pulled up.

"It took you long enough," Steve snapped as Devin emerged from his patrol vehicle.

"I left within minutes of getting the call, not sure how I could have been here any quicker. Have you touched anything since you've been here?" the deputy inquired.

"Deputy, do I look stupid? Of course, I haven't touched anything!" Steve retorted, his tone defensive.

"Sir, I'm just trying to verify the scene hasn't been compromised. No one's calling you stupid. However, if you continue with this attitude, there will be consequences," Devin responded sternly.

"Are you threatening me, deputy?" Steve challenged.

"No, sir, just stating facts. At this time, I'd like you to take a seat in your car while I check the outside of the building," Devin calmly instructed.

Reluctantly, Steve retreated to his car, eying Devin with a mixture of frustration and suspicion. Meanwhile, Devin approached the building, his steps methodical. He inspected the front door, still locked, running his gloved hand along the doorframe. He found no signs of forced entry. He proceeded to the back of the building, meticulously examining each window along the way, repeating his inspection technique at the back door with no notable findings. As Devin rounded the corner and came back into Steve's view, the latter couldn't contain his impatience.

"Anything?" Steve inquired.

"No signs of forced entry," Devin replied. "What kind of alarm system do you have?"

"Motion sensors. You have thirty seconds to disarm the alarm after entering," Steve explained.

"Well, if someone entered through the door, they either picked the lock or you've got some rats in the building that set off the alarm," Devin observed.

"Deputy, look around you. See all these fields? Of course, we get rats from time to time. Motion sensors are designed not to pick up anything below two feet from the ground. I'm thinking someone must have picked the lock."

"Alright, as soon as my backup arrives, we'll take a look inside," Devin stated.

Another five minutes passed before Deputies Allison and Jordan arrived. Steve couldn't hide his impatience as he asked, "Where's the Sheriff?"

"Sheriff's busy," Allison replied sternly. "Looks like you'll have to work with the B team."

"Mr. Taylor, is there any type of hazard we need to be aware of before we go into the building?" Deputy Devin inquired.

"No, Deputy, only supplies," Steve replied.

"What type of supplies?" Devin pressed.

"Oh, mainly related to running the resort – alcohol, coffee, and other nonperishable items. The resort doesn't allocate a lot of space for storage, so I have to be creative," Steve explained.

"Well, let's get started. Sir, please unlock the door and turn off the alarm," Deputy Allison directed Steve.

Steve complied, disarming the alarm system, and the three of them entered the building. It wasn't a very large structure, allowing for a quick scan of the layout. In the back right corner, they found a small windowed office. Opposite the office was a much smaller, non-windowed room.

"Is that a bathroom?" Allison asked.

"Yes, the bathroom and cleaning supplies are also stored there," Steve replied.

"Steve, does it appear if anything is missing?" Allison inquired.

"Nothing obvious, but I wouldn't have an exact count of inventory in my head," Steve admitted.

"Alright, we'll take it from here, Mr. Taylor. If you would please return to your car while we look around and take notes," Allison instructed, her tone conveying a subtle sense of skepticism.

"No, It's my property; I think I'll stay," Steve quickly replied. He took a step in the direction of the office, where his face wore an uneasy expression. "Besides, I haven't really had a good look at everything. Let me go check my office; that's where I'm afraid someone may have attempted to steal something."

Steve started toward the office, but before he could reach the door, Devin swiftly grabbed him by the arm. The tension in the air became palpable as a brief skirmish ensued, Steve struggling to break free from Devin's grasp. Deputy Jordan stepped in to assist, and in the midst of the struggle, she received an accidental elbow to the face. She dropped to one knee briefly, her determination unshaken, and then rebounded by deploying pepper spray with precision, scoring a direct hit to Steve's face.

"You little..." Steve's agonized yell was cut short by the blinding pain. Allison, seizing control of the situation, acted swiftly. With a well-placed kick to the back of Steve's knees, she brought him to the ground. Devin, a victim of collateral damage, had been too close to Steve's face when the pepper spray was unleashed. Coughing and choking, he staggered out the front door in search of relief, leaving the scene momentarily chaotic and charged with suspense.

Jordan, still in a slight daze from the hit to the face, stumbled her way out to the patrol vehicle. She hastily grabbed several bottles of water, her immediate focus on providing relief for Devin's stinging eyes, which were still recovering from the pepper spray. The cool water proved to be a soothing antidote to the burning sensation, and Devin let out a sigh of relief as his vision gradually cleared.

During this time, Allison efficiently handcuffed Steve, securing his hands behind his back. With Steve now subdued and unable to see due to the lingering effects of the pepper spray, she guided him toward the backseat of the patrol vehicle. Steve's protests and threats continued, his anger unabated.

"I'm going to sue this county for everything it has, and each one of you individually!" he raged, his voice reverberating through the tense scene.

Aware that little could be done to calm him down at this moment, Allison placed a bottle of water in Steve's trembling hand. She then deftly lifted his feet and maneuvered them inside the vehicle before swiftly closing the door. The action not only secured Steve but also served to muffle his continued verbal outburst, providing a brief respite from the chaotic situation.

The three deputies gathered at the front of the building, a subdued tension hanging in the air. Devin's eyes were still a fiery red from the pepper spray, the irritation refusing to abate, while Jordan's nose had swelled noticeably, bearing the aftermath of the skirmish as a testament to their encounter with Steve.

Unfazed by the confrontation, Allison took charge of the investigation. "We need to file an incident report. Are you okay with me calling for backup to complete the search of the building?" she inquired.

Devin understood the importance of filing the report but expressed his reluctance to bring in additional personnel to conclude their initial efforts. Jordan also agreed that she was physically capable of continuing.

Allison nodded in agreement as they resumed their investigation. "I'm not convinced he's storing supplies for the resort," Jordan chimed in.

"Most likely pilfering and selling on the side, but let's uncover the truth," Devin added.

"Devin, you and Jordan check this area, while I take a closer look at the office he seemed so eager to visit before us," Allison instructed.

The office was fairly minimal, with no computer but an adding machine. There was a desk with two locked drawers, and an ashtray on the desk with a couple of cigarette butts, one of which appeared to have lipstick on it. Allison carefully placed the butts into an evidence bag. She continued to scan through the papers on the desk before noticing the office had a dropped ceiling. She stepped onto the desk chair and onto the desk itself, flashlight in hand, and pushed up on a corner of the ceiling tile, peering into the cavity. Nothing but insulation and what appeared to be a combination of chewed-up paper and insulation, likely a rat's nest.

Meanwhile, as Allison checked out the office, Devin and Jordan had been busy going through the rows of metal shelving. Just as Steve had explained, there were multiple cases of wine, tequila, and other hard liquors lining the shelves. In addition, there were large boxes of coffee beans, non-dairy creamer, and artificial sweeteners. Finally, he made his way to the back corner where the bathroom was located. He opened the door and was surprised to see in addition to a toilet and sink, there was also a walk-in shower.

He opened the door to the cabinet under the sink. It was filled with what you would have expected: extra rolls of toilet paper and bathroom cleaning supplies.

"Devin, what are you doing?" Allison's voice suddenly appeared.

"Just finishing checking out the bathroom, you find anything?" he asked.

"In the office, there were two buds in the ashtray. One looks like it may have lipstick on it. I'm willing to bet you if we ask if he's been here with anyone, he'll deny it."

"Is that what he was so eager to hide from us?" Jordan asked.

"Well, one way to find out, let's go ask him," Devin said as he started walking towards the door.

"Hey, did you check up in the bathroom ceiling?"

"No, I didn't," Devin replied.

"Will you?" Allison asked nicely.

Devin walked back to the bathroom and stood up on the sink to reach the ceiling. Pushing up on one of the ceiling tiles, he shined his flashlight into the dark cavity. "See anything?" Allison asked.

"I can't tell. It looks like there's something in the back corner, but maybe it's only a shadow." He hopped down from the sink vanity. "It's over here in the corner of the shower. Did you see a ladder anywhere out there?"

Allison turned around and looked around the building. "Yeah, hold on, I see a ladder." She brought the ladder to the bathroom and set it up in the shower. "I'm already gloved up. I'll check it out," as she climbed the ladder. Pushing up the corner tile, she could feel the weight of something on top of it. She reached her hand up into the cavity. "It feels like a plastic bag." She slowly slid the tile to the side, exposing more of the bag. "Yep, definitely a plastic bag, Devin, let me hand it down to you."

Devin took the bag from Allison and lowered it to the floor. "It's light, probably some old clothes or rags."

"Yeah, probably, but why put it in the ceiling?" Allison replied. "Let's take it out into a more open area to take a look inside."

Allison untied the knot and opened up the bag. "Yep, told you it was clothes," Devin stated. They pulled each piece of clothing out and laid them on the ground. They both looked up at each other at once with a surprised look on their faces. In front of them were a women's blouse, bra, panties, and blue jeans.

"Why would there be women's outfits hidden in the ceiling of this building?" Allison whispered to Devin.

"Maybe it's related to the lipstick on the bud you found in the office."

"I don't think so. Look at that blouse; it's been out of style for a while," Allison replied.

"I'll follow your lead. What do you want to do?" Devin asked.

"Let's go ask Mr. Taylor a couple of questions, and then we'll go from there."

Allison and Devin emerged from the building and approached the patrol vehicle where Mr. Taylor was detained. Despite the subsiding effects of the pepper spray, its impact on Steve's face was unmistakable. His eyes were nearly swollen shut, leaving only a small slit visible, and the whites of his eyes were bloodshot and fiery red. The once defiant and aggressive demeanor had transformed into a meek and subdued state.

"Can I go now?" a humbled Steve pleaded.

"Unfortunately what happened earlier is going to make it impossible to release you tonight," Allison calmly informed. "Now how you cooperate going forward will either help you or hurt you. So please keep that in mind when you're answering our questions." With the full impact of the earlier confrontation finally settling in on Steve, he dropped his head to his chest and sat there quietly.

"Who's normally with you when you come out here?" Allison started the conversation.

"No one. I come out here to work, not socialize, officer."

"There were two cigarette butts in the office ashtray; one appears to have lipstick on it."

"Would you like to revise your answer to my question?" a non-amused Allison asked.

"Well, ah, oh yeah, last time I was here, one of my employees from the resort came with me."

"Does that employee have a name?" Devin asked.

"Larissa, she works for me in the coffee shop."

"Second question, we found something hidden above the ceiling tile in the bathroom. Care to explain what it is and why it was placed there?" Allison asked.

"Officer, I don't have a clue what you're talking about," Steve responded.

"Well, unfortunately, Mr. Taylor, since you already lied on my first question, why do you expect us to believe you now?"

"I'm telling the truth," Steve with a slight bit of anger in his voice responded. "We're going to need to get the Sheriff out here to sort this out."

"I don't have time for this, I want to go home," an angry Steve responded.

Allison walked away from Steve and Devin before she called the situation into Mikeal, "Sheriff, we've got a situation out here on Steve Taylor's property, request your presence." After a few seconds of radio silence, Mikeal's voice appears over the radio.

"Allison, what's going on?"

Allison proceeded to brief the Sheriff on the incident that necessitated the use of pepper spray and then transitioned to the discovery of potential evidence. "Sheriff, we've had an incident that led to the use of pepper spray, but that's not all.

We stumbled upon something unusual - women's clothing hidden in the ceiling of the building. Mr. Taylor has already been caught in one lie during our questioning, and it's starting to seem like there's more to this situation than meets the eye."

"Got it, send me the address, and I'll get there as soon as I can."

Allison walked back towards the group, "Alright, Mr. Taylor. The Sheriff's on his way, and we'll get this sorted out."

After what felt like an eternity, though it had only been about forty minutes, Mikeal finally arrived at the scene around 5:00 p.m. Stepping out of his vehicle, he couldn't help but notice the unmistakable effects of the pepper spray on Steve Taylor's face as he was handcuffed in the patrol car. The three deputies hurriedly converged on him before he could approach the building.

Allison was the first to acknowledge his arrival, "Evening, Sheriff."

From left to right, Mikeal quickly surveyed the trio before him. Devin's eyes were swollen, bloodshot orbs, while Allison, positioned in the center, appeared unharmed. However, when Mikeal's gaze landed on Jordan, he couldn't help but wince. Her nose had ballooned to twice its usual size, with dried blood marring the edges of her nostrils, and her upper lip seemed strangely inflated, as if it had overdosed on botox.

"Allison, it appears you're none the worse for wear. I'll need you to complete the incident report," Mikeal stated before continuing, his tone tense, "Will there be anything in the report I'll need to be concerned about?"

Allison quickly replied, "No, sir."

"What charges will you be filing?" the Sheriff inquired, his voice laced with anticipation.

The three deputies exchanged glances before Devin answered, "Hindering an investigation, at a minimum!"

Satisfied that there would be no repercussions, he turned his attention back to the investigation. "Show me what you found!"

Allison walked the Sheriff to the back of the building, showing him where the bag was pulled from the bathroom ceiling.

"Sheriff, I can understand having a bag of old clothes to use as shop rags, but to be hidden in the ceiling is a little odd. Plus, we have this," Allison pointed to the clothes laid out on the floor.

Mikeal stared for about a minute, taking in the scene before commenting, "This isn't a random bag of clothes, is it?"

"No, sir, it's as though someone entered the building dressed before leaving without their clothes."

"What does Mr. Taylor say about this?"

"We only shared with him that items were found suspiciously tucked away in the bathroom's ceiling, which he claims to have no knowledge of, but I'm having a hard time believing him."

"Why is that, Allison?"

"Sir, the whole altercation started when he attempted to get into the office before us. Subsequently, during our inspection, we found some cigarette butts in an ashtray in the office. One appears to have lipstick stains on it. We didn't tell him what we had found but asked if he ever brought anyone out here. He emphatically said no. After mentioning the evidence, his story changed; he brought one of his workers from the resort with him. Sir, we both know this guy is a creep."

"Yeah, that's what I've heard, but still, we can't arrest him for just being creepy. Do you think the cigarette remnants were what he was trying to conceal?" Mikeal asked.

"We didn't find anything else in the office, so I'm guessing so," Allison responded.

"Let's get the clothes and cigarette butts bagged and to the lab. I'll go talk with Mr. Taylor."

Mikeal exited the building and began his approach to the patrol vehicle, his anticipation of a tense conversation weighing heavily on him. Steve Taylor remained secured in the back seat, his hands cuffed behind his back. As Mikeal opened the back door, he readied himself for a torrent of angry words. To his surprise, Steve seemed seething yet measured in his words, carefully plotting his revenge against the Sheriff and his deputies, vowing to use every legal means to destroy their law enforcement careers. Mikeal patiently listened until Steve had vented his frustration, offering to assist him out of the vehicle once he had finished.

As Steve stood, he motioned for Mikeal to remove the handcuffs. The Sheriff paid no heed to the request, instead diving straight into questioning the suspect.

"Any particular reason why you were hesitant to inform my deputies about bringing women out here, Mr. Taylor?" Mikeal inquired, his tone unwavering.

Steve met the Sheriff's gaze with a look of disdain before responding. "Sheriff, your deputies were summoned here because my alarm went off. When they started interrogating me as though I'd committed a crime, it got under my skin. Maybe I didn't think clearly, but I assure you, I have no knowledge of anything illicit being hidden in this building."

"How long have you owned this building?" Mikeal asked.

"I've had it since 1980. Why do you ask?"

"Was it laid out this way when you bought it?"

"Haven't changed a thing," Steve replied.

Feeling that any chance for further meaningful discussion had withered away, Mikeal placed Steve back to the unforgiving confines of the patrol vehicle. As he turned his gaze back toward the metal building, the three deputies closed in on him like a shadowy specter.

"How did it go?" Allison ventured to ask, her voice tinged with unease.

"He was surprisingly calm," Mikeal responded, but there was a heavy weight to his words.

"Well, that's good, right?" Jordan attempted to inject some optimism.

Mikeal, however, couldn't share in her optimism. He cast a distant, foreboding stare toward the looming mountain range on the horizon before he answered, "I'm afraid not this time. He's promised to unleash a storm of vengeance upon us."

"Sheriff, everything we did was by the book," Devin protested firmly.

"I have no doubt," Mikeal acknowledged, his tone resolute. "But regardless, I want every detail of what transpired, both the commendable and the regrettable, documented in this incident report."

CHAPTER 16

The past week had mercilessly deprived Mikeal of precious sleep. For the fourth consecutive night, he found himself jolting awake, drenched in cold sweat and grappling with a relentless headache. Initially, he attributed it to his troublesome sinuses, a recurring issue he thought he could easily handle with medication. Yet, it lingered, defying his attempts at relief. If only his work didn't demand every ounce of his energy, he might have sought medical advice by now. Regrettably, he couldn't recall the last time he had visited a doctor. It had been years, he surmised, but the exact count eluded him. Despite his role requiring an annual physical, it seemed that no one in the administration had enforced this stipulation. As he lay there, tossing and turning, he contemplated, "Perhaps if this continues into next week, I'll finally make that doctor's appointment," silently reassuring himself.

As he continued to lay in bed, Mikeal's mind wrestled with the intricate puzzle that had been steadily taking shape over the past few weeks. Three lifeless bodies unearthed, possibly interred in the earth since the late sixties or early seventies, paired with the unsettling backdrop of two mysterious disappearances from a similar era. One of those disappearances, deemed a murder, still lacked a body, making identification of the victim all the more challenging due to the severed heads—a macabre detail that further obscured the truth. Additional threads wove through this chilling tapestry: a suspicious Jeep Wagoneer, potentially linked to one of the abductions; a piece of evidence sent for

DNA analysis; and the findings at Steve Taylor's building that may or may not be connected to the buried remains. Mikeal felt the weight of the investigation pressing on him. "I need to find the common thread," he muttered to himself. The critical turning point hinged on Nancy Hulligan's DNA, and the prospect of it matching one of the unearthed bodies. "Without a match, I've got nothing," he silently admitted. His head throbbed relentlessly, and he suspected that mentally retracing the evidence hadn't helped. Nevertheless, he knew that regardless of how terrible he felt, duty beckoned. Glancing at his alarm clock, which displayed a little past six in the morning, he decided to rise, swallow some aspirin, and seek solace in a hot shower.

Mikeal arrived at the station a little after seven; it was dark and quiet. "Looks like I'm the first one in today," he thought after disabling the alarm and heading to his office. It had only been a couple of days since they had sent the hair samples to Billings for identification, but he was still hoping to get an answer back today. Checking his emails, there was nothing from the state. He was copied on an email Allison had sent last night to the local lab, regarding the clothes found at Steve's. Her email indicated this should take top priority in their queue, and if they had questions, to call the Sheriff. Mikeal chuckled at how Allison used him to push through her request. "Well, I guess I would have done the same."

Slowly throughout the morning, the station began to fill with employees. Devin was the next to arrive, followed shortly afterwards by Allison. Mikeal's headache had disappeared, but he could feel it still lurking in the back of his brain. As he waited on word from the state and local lab, he tried to get caught up on his email. After several hours staring at the computer, he decided to get up and take a walk to stretch his legs. "Hey Allison, have you heard anything from the lab?"

"Nothing yet, sir. I was planning to call them around four if they haven't reached out first."

"Great, let me know when you hear something. I'm taking a little walk; I'll be back in about thirty minutes."

Before he knew it, Mikeal had already been walking for about fifteen minutes and was approaching the old downtown area of Bozeman. This section stretched through maybe four traffic signals. Both sides of the street were lined with bars, restaurants, an art gallery, and several clothing stores.

"Good morning, Sheriff," an elderly man who had just come out of a restaurant says as he passes Mikeal on the sidewalk.

"Morning, sir," he replies. As Mikeal approaches the end of the strip, he realizes he's close to the city's administrative annex, which houses the crime lab.

"Good morning, Sheriff. What brings you over to our building?" the lady at the front desk politely asks?

"Just stopping by the crime lab to check on some items we sent over last night."

"Alright, I'll buzz you in. Do you need directions?"

"Thanks, but I think I remember how to get there, straight ahead and make a left at the end of the hallway."

"You got it, Sheriff. Have a great day."

Mikeal was quickly at the end of the first hallway where he made a left, which took him to the backside of the building where the crime lab was located.

"Well, look here, Tim, we're in the presence of royalty today," Roberto, the lab manager, blurts out as he sees the Sheriff enter.

"Sheriff, I've worked here at least five years, and I believe this is only the second time you've visited. I'm assuming this is about the bag of clothes we received last night?"

"That would be a correct assumption on your part," Mikeal responds.

"Well, Tim logged it in as evidence about an hour ago; we were just about to check it for traces of blood. You're welcome to watch if you have time," Roberto offers.

Mikeal nodded. "Thanks, I would like to watch."

Roberto led Mikeal to a side room, motioning to turn off the lights. "Before we can test, we need as dark of a room as possible. Next, we're going to cut off a section of the blouse to test."

Mikeal pointed at the neckline. "Can you take it from the neck area?"

Tim carefully cut a two-inch by two-inch square from the blouse's neckline. "Alright, the next step is to spray it with Fluorescein," he explained as he coated the cloth with its contents.

Roberto switched on a handheld fluorescent light, illuminating the cloth with blue dots.

"Bingo," Tim blurted out, "we have something."

"Does this mean there's blood on the blouse?" Mikeal inquired.

Roberto replied, "Not necessarily, but it is highly likely. There are a few other things that would create a false positive, but my guess is this is blood."

Mikeal pressed further, "Great, when can we pull DNA from it?"

Roberto cautioned, "Slow down, Sheriff. There are still some processes that need to be completed. First, we need to confirm if it's blood, specifically human blood. Then we can consider extracting DNA. Unfortunately, we do not have this technology in our lab; we'll have to send this to the state for further analysis."

Mikeal's frustration showed. "Well, how long will that take?"

"I'm not sure," Roberto replied. "The state lab will have to confirm that, but I'm guessing it could take up to fifteen days."

Mikeal's anticipation turned into impatience; this was not what he wanted to hear.

Mikeal's phone suddenly disrupted the quiet of the lab. "Sheriff, where are you?" Allison's concerned voice greeted him on the other end.

He quickly responded, "I just walked over to the lab. What's going on?" Allison proceeded to tell him that the District Attorney had just shown up and was causing quite a commotion. "Looks like Steve Taylor followed through on his threat."

Mikeal was completely out of breath by the time he re-entered the Sheriff's office. What normally took twenty minutes to walk, Mikeal accomplished in less than ten. Despite the mid-sixty-degree summer day, his back was covered in sweat, though it quickly dried. Panting, he managed to ask, "Where is she?"

Shaking her head in disbelief at what she was witnessing, Allison replied, "She's in your office."

Mikeal took a deep breath before entering; he had been on the wrong side of Courtney Weber a couple of times, and it never ended well for the sheriff's department. The DA, Courtney Weber, was an imposing lady, almost six feet tall even without heels. She had blond hair, blue eyes, and was always immaculately dressed in a power suit. Before Mikeal could get a word out, she looked up from her phone as he entered his office, her calm demeanor adding to the tension. She calmly stated, "Do you know why I'm here?"

Already in fight-or-flight mode, her calmness caught him off guard, and he stumbled with his words, "I believe so..."

As she stood, her voice took on a more urgent tone, "Are we still holding Steve Taylor?" She asked, coming to a stop just a foot away from the Sheriff. Mikeal nodded in the affirmative. "Well then, I hope we have a solid case against him, otherwise, and I quote from his attorney, he will sue us for harassment and false arrest. Do you understand what that will mean for you and your deputies involved!" Without waiting for an answer, she continued, "It will mean your out of a job!"

Everything was spiraling out of control, and Mikeal wasn't even sure if a crime had been committed. Steve Taylor's aggressive behavior had forced his hand. Even if it was accidental, Taylor had struck an officer, leaving them with no choice but to arrest him.

With rising anger in his voice, Mikeal fired back, "He struck a deputy; that's why he's locked up downstairs. Come on, give me a break," catching the DA off guard this time. Mentally, Mikeal's sudden outburst of anger had put Courtney on her heels. But twenty years of experience in the DA's office, listening to husbands who beat their wives and calmly claimed they had no choice, or murderers who insisted it was a robbery gone wrong and they had been cornered, left her unfazed. She came out swinging.

"If you think you never have a choice, then maybe I've badly overestimated your confidence level," she shouted back at Mikeal.

"Well, thank God I'm elected by the people, not you, so I couldn't care less about your opinion of me!" The words flew out of the Sheriff's mouth like high-velocity arrows fired from a compound bow, aimed directly at the DA's heart. Unfortunately, his aim was off, and the words passed straight through her, missing all vital organs.

Regrettably for Mikeal, Courtney was unfazed in her response. "Well, that may be true, but here's another fun fact: the deputy who discharged her pepper spray is now immediately suspended, pending an investigation of this incident." She briefly looked down at her watch, mentally noting that it was 10:35 a.m., before continuing, "And when I say immediately, she needs to be off this property by 11:00 a.m."

Courtney turned back towards the Sheriff's desk, collected her purse, and coldly walked past Mikeal into the larger room housing the deputies. She turned back as though she had forgotten something, locking eyes with Mikeal and delivering a menacing ultimatum, "Either charge him with a crime, or I want him released within the hour! Do you understand me?" With that, she left the building as quickly as she had entered, leaving an air of tension in her wake.

Returning to his now empty office, Mikeal slumped back in his chair, urgency gnawing at his thoughts. Time was running out, and they needed to extract whatever information they could from Steve Taylor before he walked free. With each passing moment, the case against him grew weaker.

Mikeal knew they had to make Steve sweat, to push him to the brink and see if he would crack. He couldn't afford to waste a single minute. Rising from his chair, he walked out to address the deputies.

"Devin, go get Mr. Taylor and put him in interview room one," he instructed with a sense of determination.

Turning to Allison, he continued, "Allison, I talked to the guys at the lab, and it appears there were traces of blood on the blouse you found, but it will be several days before they have anything concrete. Have you heard back from the state lab?"

"Nothing," she replied.

"I need you to become a nuisance with them," Mikeal urged, his voice tense. "Call them two, three times a day asking for an update. Push them to move us to the front of the line, or continue with your robo-calling. Do whatever it takes, got it?"

"Will do," Allison answered, determination in her eyes.

Mikeal then motioned for Allison to follow him as they hurried towards the interview room, where the fate of their case and Steve Taylor hung in the balance.

Passing Jordan in the hallway, the Sheriff's heart suddenly felt heavier. He knew that eventually, he would have to inform the young deputy of her suspension, but that matter would have to wait for now. Mikeal briefly halted to make a request. He asked if she could perform a property lookup to find information on the previous owners of Steve's warehouse. Mikeal recalled that Steve mentioned he had bought it in 1980. He further instructed Jordan to bring any relevant findings to the interview room as soon as possible.

"I won't say a word until my lawyer arrives," Steve declared with unwavering confidence, a smug look firmly etched on his face as Mikeal entered the interview room.

The interview room was a cramped, windowless space, scarcely measuring ten by ten feet. Its minimalist furnishings included a plain table positioned in the center, topped with a recording device. Around it stood four utilitarian folding metal chairs, one already occupied by Devin, while Steve Taylor sat directly across from him. The sterile white walls bore no artwork, and a lone camera, its red recording light blinking incessantly, dangled from the ceiling's corner.

Mikeal settled into the chair adjacent to Devin, while Allison opted to remain standing, claiming her place in one of the room's corners. Devin notated that others had entered the room. With the DA's words still ringing in his ears and Steve Taylor's ominous threat hanging in the air, Mikeal decided not to take any risks. He instructed Allison to recite Mr. Taylor's Miranda rights before engaging in any dialogue.

"Do you understand why you're here?" Mikeal initiated the conversation. Steve met the question with stubborn silence, crossing his arms and turning his attention toward one of the barren walls, clearly indicating his reluctance to engage with the officers. Sensing this, Mikeal decided to press on with the limited information they had, hoping that the right choice of words could breach Steve's fortress of silence.

"You're here with us this morning because, whether intentional or deliberate, you injected yourself into a crime scene after being specifically told to wait outside," Mikeal began, his voice carrying an undercurrent of tension. He paused, letting the weight of his words hang in the air before continuing, "Now, I understand it was your property, but until we clear a potential crime scene, all the liability is on the State to ensure it's a safe environment to re-enter."

As the silence grew more oppressive, Mikeal pressed forward, the room's atmosphere becoming charged with uncertainty. Steve remained frustratingly silent, his demeanor a mask of disinterest. "All we currently know is that you've made several false statements, which we need to clear up and understand the 'why' behind them."

Allison's voice cut through the stillness, her words echoing ominously from the corner of the room. "If you're so innocent, why can't you explain who you were with in that building?" Her question caused Steve to briefly shift his gaze, and Mikeal shot an irritated glance over his shoulder at Allison, silently conveying that her interjection wasn't helping the situation and only added to the growing tension.

Mikeal knew time was running out; it was foolish to believe that once Steve's lawyer arrived, he would become any more forthcoming with details. The stakes were high, and the room felt like a pressure cooker ready to burst.

"We found items that appeared to have been deliberately hidden in the ceiling of your building," Mikeal pressed on, his voice carrying the weight of the investigation. "We've tested these items, and there were traces of human blood. These items are consistent with a time period we're investigating related to another case."

Yet Steve's silence persisted, a palpable unease settling over the room. It was as if they were playing a high-stakes game of cat and mouse, each word or silence potentially holding the key to unraveling the mystery.

A sudden knock on the door finally rattled Steve, his body jerking slightly in his seat as though he had been pulled from a trance. Allison answered the door and motioned for Mikeal to join her outside the room. Devin and Steve remained locked in a staring contest, tension rising with each passing moment.

As Mikeal and Allison re-entered the room, resuming their positions, the sense of time running out grew more pronounced.

"Has my lawyer arrived?" Steve asked in a stern voice, his impatience and anxiety palpable.

Ignoring the question, Mikeal resumed his questioning, well aware that the room's atmosphere was becoming increasingly charged with suspense. He believed that coaxing Steve into breaking his silence might be their only chance at unraveling the truth.

"We've just found out that the item in question can be dated back to the early seventies," Mikeal pressed, his voice unwavering. "When did you take ownership of the building, Mr. Taylor?" Steve remained steadfast in his resolve to remain quiet, but Mikeal could sense the crack in his armor, the vulnerability beneath the silence.

Steve fidgeted in his seat, torn between his desire for release and his reluctance to speak. "Well, there you have it," he finally broke his silence, his voice revealing the strain he was under. "If this so-called evidence is from the seventies, I didn't own the building until the mid-eighties."

The room hung in suspense, the fragile balance of power shifting. Mikeal knew that every word counted, every revelation could lead to the truth they desperately sought. Yet, just as it seemed Steve might start talking, the door suddenly flew open, and a man in a brown suit entered, immediately instructing his client not to say another word. The room held its breath as the tension reached its peak.

Glancing at Steve before speaking, the lawyer declared firmly, "My client will not be answering any more questions."

Mikeal was overcome by a crushing sense of defeat, realizing that the breakthrough they had painstakingly approached had been ruthlessly snatched away. The room's atmosphere grew denser with suspense, and though it was still early in the afternoon, it felt as if the clock was about to strike midnight in their quest to keep Steve in custody any longer.

"Steve, you know we're going to get DNA from the cigarette butt in your office," Mikeal pleaded, desperation seeping into his voice. "We'll then test it against your employees to find out who it was. You can save us a lot of time by just telling us."

Steve looked to his lawyer for approval, the tension in the room reaching a fever pitch. "Look, I'm in a relationship with one of my employees, but that's it!" he finally admitted, the words tumbling out. "If this gets out, I could lose my job."

"Is it Sammy Hudson?" Mikeal inquired, pushing for more answers in the dwindling moments they had.

"My client won't utter another syllable; you must either press charges or set him free!" The brown-suited lawyer's voice spiked with palpable urgency. Mikeal folded his arms and clenched his jaw, conveying his finality. In perfect unison, Steve and his lawyer stood and briskly exited the room.

CHAPTER 17

Jordan's conversation with Mikeal went just as poorly as he had anticipated. Despite his assurance that it was a suspension with pay, the mere notion of this stain on her budding career left her teetering on the brink of submitting her resignation. While Mikeal wholeheartedly agreed that, in his opinion, she had done nothing wrong, he acknowledged the stringent rules governing law enforcement that demanded unwavering adherence. Among these rules was the mandate for an investigation or review each time an officer deployed any type of weapon, whether lethal or non-lethal – in this particular case, pepper spray.

Mikeal added with a heavy sigh, elaborating on the excruciating process, "These internal investigations typically drag on for a torturous seven to fourteen days." A somber silence hung in the air as he continued, "In the meantime, I'm afraid you'll have to relinquish your gun and badge." Jordan, teetering on the verge of tears, reluctantly accepted her fate. She carefully unholstered her pistol, placing it with a heavy heart on the Sheriff's desk. The most agonizing moment, however, was yet to come – the painful surrender of her badge, a symbol of her dedication and commitment to the force.

With a heavy heart, Mikeal followed Jordan out of the office. He couldn't help but watch as the young, dejected deputy trudged back to her desk, knowing that she was shutting down her computer, possibly for the last time in her career. With each click and keystroke, the weight of uncertainty pressed upon her. She gathered a few personal items, her every movement tinged with a foreboding finality, before quietly exiting the building.

As Mikeal returned to his office, a wave of memories from his own past engulfed him. Remembering himself in a similar predicament, suspended for mishandling evidence and letting a guilty party slip through the cracks. In that moment, a torrent of recollections rushed through his mind, like a condensed lifetime of memories compressed into ten seconds. The entirety of his relationship and friendship with Chief John Wolf seemed to unravel before him in a whirlwind of visuals. Shaken, Mikeal steadied himself against the corner of his desk, his thoughts a turbulent storm, before finally collapsing into his chair, overwhelmed by the weight of his own past.

As he struggled to disentangle his thoughts from the weight of the past and concentrate on the pressing matters at hand, a sensation of relief washed over him. His sinuses, which had been a persistent nuisance for the past week, finally began to clear. He leaned across his cluttered desk, searching for the box of tissues Jordan had requisitioned earlier. In his haste, he could sense beads of sinus drainage fall onto the scattered papers below. Wiping at his nose, he was startled to discover that it wasn't mucus but blood that now marred the tissue. A creeping unease gripped him as he realized that the majority of the tissue was now soaked in crimson. With a quick, anxious motion, he reached for another tissue, noticing the blood splatter had dripped across the paperwork strewn across his desk.

Clutching the tissue firmly against his bleeding nose, he rushed towards the restroom, his footsteps echoing with urgency. As he reached the bathroom, he positioned himself before the mirror, his heart pounding in anticipation. With deliberate care, he peeled the tissue away from his face, revealing the extent of the damage. He still sensed a faint trickle of blood lingering in his sinuses, but now, only a mere trace escaped his nostrils. It had been at least three days since he'd last wielded a razor, and, as he leaned closer to the mirror, the dried blood clinging to the bristly stubble above his lip and on his chin came into stark, unflinching view.

He turned the faucet, letting the water cascade into his open palms, forming a delicate pool. Swiftly, he brought the cool liquid to his face, flinging it across the crimson-stained area like a cleansing torrent. After a few minutes of diligent scrubbing, he gingerly resumed scrutinizing his reflection in the mirror. The once-vivid flow of blood had mercifully ceased, and his efforts had succeeded in fairly erasing the stubborn traces of what had already dried.

As he retraced his steps toward his office, a sudden, vivid onslaught of memories, even darker and more haunting than before, swept through his mind like a relentless tempest. These recollections, which he had convinced himself were securely interred in the depths of his brain years ago, now clawed their way to the surface with unnerving clarity. These were not the fond or flattering memories he once held of Chief John Wolf, but rather the ones that had festered deep within him, driving a wedge between them and ultimately causing Mikeal to lose touch with the Chief after departing North Carolina.

It all began with the profound loss of John Wolf Sr., a devastating blow that struck his son with the force of a thousand storms. Mikeal, who had come to rely on the Chief as both a mentor and a guiding force, had witnessed the Chief's daily pilgrimage to his father for invaluable advice and spiritual solace. The sudden passing of John Wolf Sr. in his early seventies left a gaping void that plunged his son into a harrowing descent, a descent that would culminate in the seismic event that shattered the unbreakable bond between Mikeal and the Chief.

Haunted by an agonizing absence of closure with his father, Chief John Wolf Jr. embarked on a journey into the realms of foreign faiths and unfamiliar spiritual practitioners, venturing beyond the confines of the Cherokee Nation. This exploration sent shockwaves of disapproval rippling through the tight-knit Snowbird Community, casting shadows of doubt over the Chief's actions. Mikeal, consumed by genuine concern, repeatedly attempted to engage the Chief in earnest conversations, only to be met with rapid dismissal and the assertion that he simply couldn't comprehend.

Nevertheless, as Chief John Wolf Jr. found no solace outside the bounds of the Nation, he gradually began to rekindle his former self—a glimmer of hope amid the encroaching darkness. Regrettably, that hope was cruelly extinguished with the arrival of a stranger to the community. Dawn Ross, hailing from Oklahoma, claimed lineage from the legendary Cherokee Chief John Ross. In her early thirties, she exuded an undeniable allure; her slender frame adorned with sleek, ebony-black hair cascaded down her back.

Initially, Mikeal extended a hand of friendship to the enigmatic young woman. However, their exchanges soon took an unsettling turn, delving into her purported ability to communicate with the deceased. A nagging suspicion gnawed at Mikeal as she recounted a vision that had rudely awakened her from slumber one fateful night—a vision that declared her gift was urgently required by a great man residing somewhere within the original Cherokee Nation.

Determined to shield the Chief from a perilous path, Mikeal endeavored to caution him about this newcomer. Regrettably, his warnings only piqued the Chief's curiosity, rather than deterring it. Over the ensuing months, Chief John Wolf Jr. became increasingly ensnared by this enigmatic woman. Though all could see the toll it exacted on his work, his unwavering faith in her promise of connecting him with his departed father remained unshaken—a glimmer of hope for the elusive closure he yearned for.

Sensing an impending catastrophe that threatened to obliterate the career of a remarkable man, Mikeal summoned his last reserves of determination to convince Miss Ross to put an end to her misguided endeavors. On a sweltering summer evening, he arrived unannounced at her residence, apprehension weighing heavy on his chest. Even before reaching the doorstep, he was greeted by a haunting symphony of low, echoing moans that emanated through the open windows of her home. He strained his ears, desperately trying to discern whether these sounds were born of pleasure or agony.

With cautious and deliberate strides, Mikeal circled around to the side of the house, navigating the dimly lit exterior. The moans had escalated in volume, now unmistakably audible as they reverberated through the still night air. A faint wisp of smoke curled from a far window, teasing his senses as he drew nearer to the source of this disconcerting spectacle. He inched his way closer to the opening, where the moans were now recognizable as pleasurable.

With painstaking care, he inched one eye above the window's lower threshold. In that fleeting moment, an irreversible truth dawned upon him: he was about to witness something that would forever be seared into his consciousness. There, amidst the dimly lit room, John Wolf lay sprawled flat on his back, completely bare of clothes, his large frame spread across the bed. On top, riding him like a stallion, was diminutive Miss Ross, her voice weaving an eerie, mystic incantation into the air, in-between her moans of pleasure. Mikeal hastily retreated back to his vehicle, no longer making any effort to conceal his presence.

Finally, Mikeal regained his connection with the present, sitting amidst the blood-splattered Nancy Hulligan file strewn across his desk. Just as the room seemed to settle into an oppressive silence, his phone pierced the air with its shrill ring. He knew this number, picking it up with a sigh, his voice tinged with exhaustion as he answered, "Doctor Baldwin, it's been a long hard day, please tell me you're calling with some good news."

The voice on the other end replied, "Well, Sheriff, I do have some good news, but I'm afraid there's also some bad. Which would you prefer to hear first?"

"Let's start with the bad," Mikeal replied wearily, "and end with the good."

"Very well then," the doctor continued, "the hair fibers you sent over were just too old to yield any DNA. So, unfortunately, that's a dead end. However, regarding the blouse we received last night, we were able to confirm that it contained human blood. At one point, it was heavily stained with blood. We also found traces of detergent residue, indicating that someone had attempted to clean the garment."

Mikeal's mind raced with the realization that if they had known this information earlier in the day, they could have kept Steve Taylor in his cell. He asked, "Would the amount of blood on the blouse have been fatal?"

"We can't say with absolute certainty," the doctor responded, "but it's highly likely that the individual would have died."

"That's encouraging to hear," Mikeal replied, "now if only we had a body, we could press charges."

"Actually, Sheriff, there's more," the doctor interjected.

"What do you mean, more?" Mikeal questioned.

"We were able to extract DNA from the blouse, and it's a match with Jane Doe number two," the doctor revealed.

Mikeal sat in stunned silence for a few moments, the visions of smug looks fading on both Steve Taylor's and the DA's faces. "Do we have a name for the victim?" he finally asked.

"We didn't get a hit when we ran it against our database," the doctor explained. "However, we weren't expecting to either. In the seventies, when this victim perished, DNA testing was in its infancy at best. So, unfortunately, we do not have a name."

The Sheriff ended the call with the doctor, hanging up the phone and leaning back in his chair. He replayed the conversation in his head, alternating between rewinding and fast-forwarding. On one hand, they had crucial evidence to advance the case against Steve Taylor, but Mikeal had hoped to provide closure to the Hulligan family as well.

Desperately craving a positive end to the day, Mikeal powered down his computer, gathered his belongings, and headed towards his vehicle. Although late afternoon had arrived, there was still ample daylight left to bask in. As he settled into his car, his thoughts drifted towards the prospect of yard work—a welcome distraction from the engulfing darkness of the building unsolved cases that had begun to suffocate his life.

Just as he pulled out of the parking lot, a familiar sensation coursed through him, his nose giving way to an unsettling opening. With one eye cautiously trained on the road, he rifled through the front of the vehicle, frantic for a tissue. None appeared, leaving him with no choice but to employ his sleeve as a makeshift barrier to prevent the relentless flow. A quick glance downward revealed the evidence of his battle—a large swath of maroon intermingled with the brown of his shirt sleeve, a grotesque tapestry of bloodstains.

Mikeal's free hand found its way to the bridge of his nose, a desperate attempt to stanch the bleeding. Breathing through his mouth and with blood beginning to pool in the back of his throat, he coughed violently, sending a macabre spray of crimson across the interior of his windshield. It was no mere sinus infection, but something far more sinister that eluded his understanding. With a 24-hour urgent care facility just blocks away, he navigated the streets with an urgent haste.

Approaching the check-in counter, Mikeal was keenly aware of his disheveled appearance. Yet, as he observed the sudden pallor that washed over the receptionist's face, he realized that his condition must be even graver than he had feared.

Rapidly, he was whisked away to a back room, the sterile scent of antiseptic hanging heavily in the air. With a quick adjustment of the examination table, they positioned him at a slight incline to ensure he wasn't lying flat on his back. A nurse, her face etched with urgency, promptly stuffed his nostril cavities with gauze in an effort to slow the relentless bleeding until a doctor could attend to him.

Within minutes, the doctor entered the room, taking in the palpable fear that gripped his patient. The nurse and receptionist had briefed him on the situation, but they had omitted the critical details—namely, that this was a law enforcement officer, and the front of his uniform was drenched in a disconcerting amount of blood. The doctor, his voice tinged with concern, wasted no time in asking, "Were you struck by someone or something?"

Despite the growing lightheadedness, Mikeal managed to respond, his voice strained. He explained that he had initially thought it was a simple sinus infection, but the bleeding had intensified and refused to cease.

The doctor worked methodically, gently extracting the gauze from Mikeal's left nostril. With a deft touch, he tilted the tip of Mikeal's nose back, directing a focused beam of light into the nasal cavity. The procedure was repeated on the other nostril, as the doctor meticulously examined every detail.

"It appears that the bleeding has subsided," the doctor
attempted to reassure his patient, but his gaze then shifted to
the nurse, whom Mikeal was now noticing for the first time.
Addressing her, he instructed, "Let's prepare a saline
solution to cleanse his nasal passages, and I'll make the
necessary preparations for cauterization." He then turned his
attention back to Mikeal, seeking confirmation that he
understood the impending procedure. Mikeal nodded in
affirmation before reclining his head against the inclined
examination table once more.

The entire process took another agonizing thirty minutes.
Before departing the room, the doctor instructed the nurse to
complete the necessary paperwork, assuring Mikeal that he
would return in approximately ten minutes.

While the doctor was gone, the nurse quickly filled out the
necessary paperwork. Another nurse entered the room
instructing Mikeal, she was there to get him cleaned up. They
also offered him a clear see-through bag to take his blood-
covered shirt off and not damage his other clothing. The
documentation nurse then went over what he could and
couldn't do over the next five days, as his nose recuperated
from the cauterization procedure.

After an agonizing thirty-minute wait, the doctor returned
with a grave expression. "We've managed to halt the bleeding
for now, but this isn't a permanent solution. I strongly
recommend that you allow us to transfer you to the hospital,

where they can conduct tests to pinpoint the root cause of your issue."

Mikeal, attempting to swing his feet off the examination table and sit up, responded with determination, "Well, Doc, that's not going to happen."

Having encountered his fair share of determined law enforcement officers in the past, the doctor realized the futility of further argument. He conceded, albeit with a hint of exasperation, "Do what you have to do, but you're not leaving here until we can collect some blood from you for further analysis."

Mikeal, beginning to regain his composure, couldn't resist a touch of humor. He quipped, "Will this blood-drenched shirt be enough?" The doctor, unamused, rose from his seat and exited the room, leaving Mikeal to his thoughts.

CHAPTER 18

The following morning, Mikeal returned to the station. After arriving home from the urgent care the previous night, he had promptly taken a much-needed shower and gone straight to bed. Fatigue had embraced him tightly, and he had slumbered undisturbed until the relentless 5:00 a.m. alarm jolted him awake. Feeling remarkably refreshed after weeks of minimal sleep, he arrived at the station just in time to greet and check in with a few of the deputies from the night shift, who were concluding their duties for the day.

In the ordinary world of Bozeman, life continued, oblivious to the lingering specters of crimes that had unfolded over four decades ago, now reemerging to haunt a select few. Jordan had been the first casualty in a series of events that Mikeal feared might ensnare others before the mysteries of the past could be unraveled and laid to rest.

Mikeal's initial task that morning was to brief Devin and Allison on the events of the previous night. With the intention of sparing Jordan from any additional distress about her suspension, he had tactfully waited until both Devin and Allison had left before delivering the news to her. He aimed to balance the unsettling update with a glimmer of hope, commencing with the details of his conversation with Dr. Baldwin from the state lab.

Maybe another ten or so minutes passed before he heard the unmistakable voices of Devin and Allison entering the building together. He called out for both to join him in his office once they were logged in for the day. They soon both appeared, and he motioned for both of them to have a seat.

Unaware he was giving anything away, Allison looked at him before asking, "What are you smiling about, Sheriff?"

His smile spread even farther across his face before he started, "I received a call from Dr. Baldwin last night with news." Devin quickly interrupted, "Hold on, Jordan will want to hear this as well." Starting to rise from his seat, Mikeal motioned for him to sit back down before stating, "Jordan's not going to be available this morning."

Both Devin and Allison sat upright in their chairs, their attention laser-focused, an air of anticipation thick between them as they leaned forward, awaiting the information that hung in the balance.

Mikeal took a moment, letting the tension build, before delivering the news. "Well, there's a bit of a mixed bag. Unfortunately, the hair sample we provided to the state had deteriorated too much to yield a usable DNA strand. So, we won't be able to directly connect the crime with a specific individual. However, we still have that image of what looks like a Wagoneer at the construction site on their street."

Allison seized the opportunity to contribute, her voice laced with determination. "As for Lynn Brothers Construction, their office was just a block off Main Street here in Bozeman. After checking DMV records, it appears that neither the company nor the brothers themselves owned a Jeep Wagoneer."

Mikeal leaned forward, pressing further. "What about employees? Any chance that someone who worked for them might have been involved?"

Allison's response was tinged with regret. "Unfortunately, both Gary and Henry have passed, so I'm not sure if those records still exist."

Devin, ever the strategic thinker, chimed in with a new angle. "What about family members? Wives, children, anyone who might have been associated with the company?"

Allison's brow furrowed in thought, and she nodded. "You bring up a good point, Devin. I'll look into that and let you know what I find."

Devin couldn't help but voice his curiosity, his eyes fixed on Mikeal as he asked, "Well then, where's the good news?"

In a calculated move to electrify his weary team, Mikeal played with their expectations, drawing out the moment before delivering the exciting revelation. With a slight hesitation, he finally disclosed, "The clothing found at Steve Taylor's building has been confirmed to contain human blood!" He watched as both deputies leaned in even further, sensing that the time was ripe for the bombshell. "And," he continued, "they were able to link it to Jane Doe #2 from Hebgen Lake."

Devin, usually the epitome of composure, suddenly leaped to his feet, unable to contain his excitement. "Yes! We have a match!" he exclaimed.

Allison, caught completely off guard by the thrilling news, sat in stunned silence, her mouth agape.

Mikeal confirmed, "Yes, Devin, we finally have a match."

Once her voice returned, Allison eagerly inquired, "So, how are we going to play this?"

Devin, his determination unwavering, outlined their next steps. "Well, we found the evidence hidden in Steve Taylor's storage building. He lied when first confronted about taking someone there, and he was a suspect back in the seventies for another disappearance. You know what they say, 'Three strikes and you're out.' We've got enough to get him off the streets."

Tension hung in the air as Allison interjected, her voice edged with doubt. "You heard the DA yesterday, I'm thinking he's untouchable now."

Mikeal, however, halted any further discussion with a firm tone. "Leave the DA to me."

Repeating most of what Devin said previously, he swiftly ran through the mounting evidence against Steve Taylor: First, he was an original suspect in a disappearance that aligned with the timeline and age of the bones linked to Jane Doe #2. Second, he had access to the location during the period when clothing contaminated with blood matching Jane Doe #2 was discovered. Third, there was a trail of documented lies and deliberate efforts to obstruct the investigation. Lastly, there was the ominous sense of urgency—Taylor had been accompanied at the building, and now one of his current employees was missing, a situation that raised concerns about her safety.

"We need to collect samples from all the current employees at the coffee shop," Mikeal declared, his voice filled with urgency. "If none of them matches the saliva from the lipstick-covered cigarette butt, then my guess is it belongs to Samantha Hudson."

Both Allison and Devin shared the Sheriff's conviction but understood that they now had to somehow persuade the DA to retract her support for Taylor.

"In order to keep this as discreet as possible, we'll aim to make the arrest at his home," Mikeal proposed.

Allison immediately stepped up, her determination clear. "Great, I'll grab Jordan and head that way."

In the midst of the excitement, Mikeal momentarily forgot about delivering the news of Jordan's suspension. Eager to maintain the momentum they were building, he chose to be less than honest. "Jordan's busy with an assignment I gave her," he instructed, deflecting her involvement for now and assigning Stevenson to the task.

"I'll call the DA's office right now," Mikeal replied, the tension in his voice palpable. "Devin, once I'm finished, let's head back out to the resort and talk to Sammy's co-workers again. We'll collect saliva samples from each of them and see if they noticed any interactions between Sammy and Steve."

Devin waited anxiously at his desk, envisioning the Sheriff's struggle to plead their case with the DA. His vantage point offered a clear view through the windows into the Sheriff's office. While he couldn't hear their conversation, he could only imagine the fervor based on Mikeal's animated gestures. After about fifteen minutes, it seemed to be over. Mikeal's arms were no longer flailing in desperation; instead, he appeared deep in thought, engrossed in his computer screen.

Allison's touch on Devin's shoulder broke his intense focus on the Sheriff's actions. A few minutes later, the silence in the nearly vacant office was shattered by the sound of the dot matrix printer coming to life. Both watched with bated breath as Mikeal emerged from his office, waving a set of papers that granted a warrant to search Mr. Taylor's home and arrest him for the murder of Jane Doe #2.

"Allison, keep it quiet, no sirens," he instructed, the gravity of the situation weighing on him. "We're a small town, but gossip spreads like wildfire around here. Get in and out as quickly as you can."

"Yes, sir, quick and quiet," Allison affirmed.

Devin, ready to take action, was handed the keys by Mikeal. The urgency of the moment was palpable as they prepared to confront Steve Taylor.

They had been on the road for about thirty minutes when Mikeal's phone rang, and Allison's voice came through urgently. "Sir, he's not at his residence. What should we do?"

Mikeal took a moment to think before responding, his voice tinged with concern. "Alright, fall back a couple of streets and wait. We're about thirty minutes out from the resort. If he's there, we'll let you know."

Shortly before noon, Mikeal and Devin arrived at the resort. As they entered the front door, Mikeal greeted the two women behind the counter, trying to keep a sense of normalcy despite the growing tension. "Good afternoon, ladies."

"Afternoon, Sheriff," Henrietta replied.

"Well, hello, Sheriff," Emma said as she walked around the counter to join them in the front lobby.

"How can we help you?" Henrietta asked, her tone polite but curious. Mikeal took a deep breath before posing his questions.

"Have either of you ever been asked to travel off-site by Mr. Taylor?" he inquired, a sense of urgency in his voice.

Emma's response was immediate and adamant. "I wouldn't go anywhere with that creep!"

Mikeal clarified, "That's not what I'm asking, only if you were asked."

Emma took a moment to collect herself. "No, Sheriff, he has not asked me to travel with him. But if he did, the answer would be no."

Devin directed his question to Henrietta, "What about you?"

Henrietta shook her head. "No, I'm afraid he hasn't asked me either."

Mikeal continued his line of inquiry, now focused on Sammy. "What about your co-worker Sammy?"

Emma's face registered surprise and anxiety. She could feel her pulse quicken and her anxiety surge as she wondered if the Sheriff had uncovered her suspicions regarding the pregnancy involving Steve Taylor and Sammy. Her voice trembled as she said, "I need to sit down."

As Emma staggered back, Devin reached out and steadied her by grabbing her forearm. Henrietta quickly brought a glass of water as the entire coffee shop fell silent, with all eyes fixed on Emma.

"Emma, are you alright?" Mikeal knelt down, his voice filled with concern. Emma stared blankly at the ground, her expression devoid of emotion. Mikeal attempted to ask again, but before he could continue, he stopped mid-sentence when he saw Steve Taylor entering the coffee shop through the back door, a chilling presence that sent shivers through the room.

When Steve Taylor saw the officers, he froze in his tracks. A tense silence hung in the air as both sides exchanged hostile glares, their contempt for each other palpable. Finally, Mikeal decided to break the silence.

"Mr. Taylor, can you step back outside with me for a minute?" Mikeal's tone was calm, but there was an underlying seriousness to his request. He turned to Devin and instructed, "Devin, wait inside with the ladies, please."

Out on the sidewalk, Steve was seething with anger. He couldn't contain his fury. "The gall of you to show your face at my employer again. Obviously, you don't give a damn about your career, which is about to be over. But to end the young deputy's career you brought with you? You should be ashamed of your actions!"

Mikeal remained composed, allowing Steve's verbal barrage to wash over him. He knew the truth was on his side. Once Steve had finished venting his anger, Mikeal calmly delivered the news.

"Sir, we found evidence during our search of your building," Mikeal began. "That evidence was sent to the lab, which confirmed it contained traces of blood. It was also identified that a strong and deliberate effort had been made to rid this evidence of the blood. Furthermore, another lab was able to match DNA obtained from your building with that of a body we recently recovered."

Mikeal watched as the color drained from Steve's face. What had started as a slight reddish tint turned to a pale, ghostly white. The smugness and arrogance that had characterized Steve's demeanor moments ago vanished, replaced by a stunned and muted tone.

"You're here to arrest me?" Steve asked, his voice trembling.

"I'm afraid so," Mikeal confirmed.

Steve glanced around, clearly concerned about the public spectacle. "Is there any way this can be done out of sight of my staff and resort guests?" he inquired, a hint of desperation in his voice.

Mikeal's response was measured. "Well, that depends on you, sir. As long as you're cooperating, I'm willing to accommodate."

Steve appeared to have aged ten years in only the last few minutes. The fire and angst that Mikeal had witnessed during their previous encounters had now disappeared. In its place was a realization that after all these years of getting away with murder, the end was finally in sight.

"Sheriff, I need to tell my team I'll be out of pocket for a few days," Steve muttered, his voice filled with resignation. He turned and walked back into the coffee shop, with Mikeal closely following behind. Devin, who had been standing nearby, watching over Emma as she struggled with her emotions, snapped to attention, awaiting the Sheriff's guidance. Mikeal shot Devin a reassuring look, indicating that everything was under control.

As the day's events solidified in Emma's mind, confirming a physical relationship between her friend Sammy and Steve, she became physically ill. She abruptly emptied the contents of her recently finished lunch onto the coffee shop's floor, the splatter reaching Steve Taylor's shoes and the lower part of his pants. Additional patrons rushed to Emma's aid, creating a chaotic scene.

Seizing the opportunity, Mikeal motioned to Devin to quickly escort Steve through the front door and into their awaiting vehicle. The impending sense of doom hung heavy in the air as they prepared to take Steve into custody, bringing him one step closer to facing the consequences of his actions.

Both officers were now in the vehicle heading back towards town, with Steve Taylor in tow. "Allison, your team can stand down, we made contact with Mr. Taylor," Mikeal broadcasted across the radio.

"Roger, so you have him in custody?" Allison replied.

"Affirmative, we're in route back to base."

Shortly after two in the afternoon, Steve Taylor arrived at the Gallatin County Sheriff's Office. Devin escorted him to the booking area, where he would undergo processing.

"Sheriff, they'll be finished with him in another thirty or so minutes," Devin, appearing in Mikeal's doorway, explained.

"Great, we'll need to give him the opportunity to reach out to his attorney. Once he's arrived, we'll get this show on the road."

Another hour passed before Mr. Taylor's attorney finally made it to the station. Devin informed the Sheriff, "Sir, they're set up in room one. I'm ready when you are."

Mikeal picked up a file from his desk that he had been reviewing over the last hour and made his way over to room one. He walked in, followed by Devin, and sat down. He proceeded to open the file and place it on the table, then crossed his arms, alternating between looking at the defendant and the open file in front of him. An awkward quietness began to envelop the room before Mr. Taylor's lawyer broke the silence.

"My client would like to know who he is being charged with murdering."

"Fair question. Unfortunately, we do not have an answer at this time," Mikeal replied before continuing, "I believe one of us in this room knows the answer, but they're not sitting on my side of the table. Here is what we do know: during this investigation, your client has provided several false or misleading answers to simple questions. We found physical evidence in a property that he has had access to since the sixties. Large traces of blood were found on that evidence, from which we were then able to pull DNA. This DNA matched a set of remains found in the Hebgen Lake area. Based on this information, we have booked your client under suspicion of murder."

"Sheriff, I have never hurt anyone in my life," Steve blurted out before his lawyer could stop him.

"Alright, you'll get your chance to prove it in court. In the meantime, if you're not the killer, you can start cooperating and help us catch the real killer," Mikeal sternly responded. "Let's try this again; the first question my officers asked was whose lipstick was on the cigarette butt found in your office?"

"My client previously provided you with details. It was an employee of the resort."

Showing a little bit of frustration, Mikeal lashed out, "Do you not understand the seriousness of the charges facing your client!"

"Alright, Devin, let's lock him up until we can get a team back out to the resort to collect a saliva sample from every employee in the coffee shop. I'm willing to bet money it's not anyone we can test," Mikeal stated.

As both officers stood to leave, in a soft, defeated voice, Steve uttered the word, "Wait."

"We're stepping out for a few minutes. Mr. Taylor, I suggest you have a good long talk with your attorney. You can either work with us or against us, but frankly, we're done playing your games," Mikeal stated before he and Devin exited the room.

"Sheriff, remember the cigarette butts we picked up by the dumpsters during the Sammy Hudson disappearance?" Allison quickly stated after they entered the hallway.

"Yeah... and?" Mikeal waited.

"They match what was found in Steve's office."

"Let's see if he comes clean when we go back in. If not, we'll need to get saliva samples from the female employees at the resort."

"Great work, Allison," Mikeal smiled as he walked off to his office.

Mikeal and Devin returned to the room after the fifteen minutes were up. "Alright, before we get started, I'm going to share with you a piece of evidence we just obtained," Mikeal offered. "Please consider it before answering any of my questions. The cigarette butt found in your office is a saliva match to a cigarette butt found at the resort near the dumpsters. Take that nugget in, digest it slowly, and then answer my question. Mr. Taylor, who were you smoking with in your office?"

Steve sat in silence for a moment, then looked over at his attorney, who nodded his head in agreement. "Steve, I'll ask again, who was in the building with you?"

Steve cleared his throat and answered, "Samantha Hudson."

CHAPTER 19

"Well, that was just downright odd," Henrietta said with a perplexed look on her face.

"Odd indeed, Henrietta," Emma responded.

"He looked like he had seen a ghost after speaking with the Sheriff. What do you think's going on?" Henrietta asked.

Emma didn't answer, but she knew this related to Sammy's disappearance. She excused herself, indicating the need for a trip to the restroom to clean herself up after her vomiting incident. The half bath, tucked away behind the customer counter, was a small room with a toilet, but at least it had a door. Behind it, Emma hid in solitude, gathering her thoughts. As she took a seat, the events of the last thirty minutes rushed through her mind.

She hoped the police were finally taking Sammy's disappearance seriously, but would it be too late? After all, Sammy had been missing for almost a month. It all seemed to be connected to her pregnancy; Emma was sure of it. She regretted keeping that information to herself; perhaps if she had shared it with the Sheriff, Steve Taylor would have been arrested sooner. Too many thoughts, all flooding her mind at once. She needed to talk to someone, and Terry was just across the parking lot. She had to get over there to see what he thought they should do next.

Exiting the bathroom she examined the customer area, noticing it was empty. "I'm going to take a break, will you cover until I get back?" She shouted over to Henrietta.

"Sure, no problem," she responded.

Emma walked over to the restaurant and took her seat in the usual location. However, this time when the waitress stopped to confirm her normal order, she only asked if Terry could step out for a moment to speak with her.

"What's up? You sick? Why aren't you ordering lunch today?" Terry asked upon his arrival.

"Just not hungry today, I guess."

"Jennifer said you needed to speak with me?"

"Yeah, we just had an interesting visit from the Sheriff, and he left with Steve," Emma responded.

"What happened?" Terry eagerly asked, his anticipation almost palpable.

"At first, I thought it was odd. He was asking us if we had ever traveled off-site with Steve. Henrietta and I both told him we hadn't. But then he started asking about Sammy, that's when I connected the dots. I think they learned about her pregnancy."

"It happened so fast. One minute I was speaking with the Sheriff, the next Steve appeared at the back door, and the Sheriff immediately walked him back out," Emma rapidly described before slowing down to a pause. Continuing, she described how they returned about five minutes later, and Steve's face was white as a ghost.

"Then what?" Terry clamored, his eagerness like a starving animal waiting to be fed.

"I threw up everywhere," Emma shamefully started to describe.

Terry fell back in his seat, a disgusted look on his face, as though learning the grand meal he was about to eat was rotted.

A heavy silence hung between them, growing increasingly uncomfortable until Terry broke it. He leaned forward, his curiosity getting the better of him. "Do you think they found anything when they investigated the break-in at his building?"

Emma was about to respond when a voice from the kitchen area called out to Terry, informing him of an important phone call from a supplier. He rose from his seat, his tone regretful as he addressed Emma. "I'll have to take this call, but let's continue our discussion tonight. Can you give me a ring later?"

After completing her shift at the coffee shop, Emma headed home. She was nearly within a fifteen-minute of her apartment when her cell phone rang. "Hello?" she answered.

"Emma, this is Deputy Allison from the Gallatin County Sheriff's Office. We've had a development regarding your co-worker," Allison began, but Emma couldn't contain her excitement and interjected, "You found Sammy?"

"Well, no, we haven't found her, but there's been a significant development, and we're launching an investigation into her disappearance."

"I knew it!" Emma exclaimed, the volume of her voice resonating through the phone and taking Allison by surprise.

"Pardon?" Allison responded, moving the receiver slightly away from her ear.

"Oh, sorry," Emma apologized, "When the Sheriff stopped by today, I found it odd that he was asking about Sammy. This involves my boss, Steve Taylor, doesn't it?"

"I can't answer that at this time," Allison replied, "but we would like you to come to the office and go over the events of the day Sammy disappeared. When can you make it?"

"I can come down there tonight!" an energetic Emma responded.

Allison hung up the phone and turned to the Sheriff, saying, "She's on her way and should be here in about an hour and a half."

"Perfect, now we've got to head back in there and squeeze the truth out of Steve before his lawyer shuts him down," Mikeal responded with an air of determination. "Were you able to gather every piece of evidence we have on the Samantha Hudson case?"

Allison picked up a file from her desk and handed it to Mikeal. "Everything we have is contained in this folder." Mikeal swiftly flipped through the contents of the folder, most of which he still remembered. "Great, well, wish us luck. Hopefully, we can extract a confession and bring this to a close tonight."

Mikeal and Devin returned to room one. A little over an hour ago, Steve Taylor had admitted to being alone with Sammy Hudson at his storage building. They had collectively agreed to break for dinner before resuming the interrogation. During this pause, besides compiling all their findings on Sammy's disappearance, they had also alerted the District Attorney about the new development. She insisted on being present before they proceeded. The DA arrived promptly and settled beside Allison in a secluded room, ready to scrutinize the interrogation video.

"Gentlemen, are we ready to recommence?" Mikeal inquired rhetorically. "Very well then, Mr. Taylor, let's pick up where we left off. You confessed to being offsite with an employee, Miss Samantha Hudson. Please educate us on why you initially deceived my investigators about your companion."

"Sheriff, my client was scared and didn't use the best judgment when confronted by your deputies," Steve's lawyer interjected. "Let's say, hypothetically, that it was possible. However, we asked on multiple occasions, why did he continue to tell the same lie?" Mikeal wanted to know.

"Listen, Sheriff," Steve finally spoke up, his voice shaky. "With Sammy's recent disappearance, when they asked, I panicked, thinking if I told the truth, they would think I was somehow involved in her disappearance."

"Well, your lie certainly made you the prime suspect," Devin interjected, his eyes locked onto Steve. "I know now how stupid it was to lie, but no more secrets. I'll tell you anything you want to know. I just want to get this nightmare behind me and resume my life."

"I would also like to interject that my client had no motive to wish harm on Ms. Hudson. They were in a purely casual relationship," his lawyer added, the suspense thickening.

"Let's start with you truthfully walking us through the steps leading up to you and Sammy ending up in your office," Mikeal responded in a no-nonsense tone, the room heavy with anticipation.

Steve paused, his gaze fixed on the floor as though he was trying to piece together a puzzle of memories. "Shortly after Sammy started working for me, she began visiting my office almost every day, just to chat. She seemed genuinely interested in what I did. After about a week of her visits, I asked if she'd be interested in a mentorship. She agreed, and she started coming to my office almost every day after her shift ended. The first couple of weeks were great. I thought we were developing a strong professional relationship, but I also was starting to feel like maybe there was some chemistry on a personal level developing. So I decided to put all my cards on the table and asked if she would ride out to my warehouse to discuss how to manage inventory. She agreed, and we went."

Mikeal could sense Steve's growing discomfort with the direction his story was taking, but he pressed on, the room thick with an escalating suspense that seemed to drain the air of moisture, constricting it around them and causing Steve to struggle with each word.

"Once we arrived, I showed her how everything was organized and invited her into my office to show the inventory system I had created. We talked shop for maybe another ten or so minutes, and then I told her I had some weed and asked if she would like to partake. Everything seemed fine; the weed was calming my nerves, so I decided to make my move. I put my arms around her waist and pulled her close."

"How did she react to your advance?" Mikeal interrupted, the anticipation hanging in the air like a storm about to break.

Steve sat quietly for a moment, the temperature in the room feeling stifling. Steve reached for the water bottle he had left on the table from dinner, quickly finishing off what was left. "She pushed me back and asked what the hell I was doing."

"How did you respond to this rejection, Mr. Taylor?" the Sheriff asked, the suspense building with every word.

"Well, I was embarrassed. I tried to explain that I thought she was sending signals that she was interested in more than just work. She yelled at me and told me I was crazy, that the thought of her being interested in someone like me was ridiculous."

"Did that make you angry, Mr. Taylor?" Mikeal responded, the suspense reaching its peak.

"Hell yeah, it did. What did she mean, someone like me?"

Mikeal could see Steve was starting to get worked up, and he decided to press further, intensifying the suspense. "So, what did you do, Mr. Taylor, with all this anger building inside you?"

Steve gave Mikeal a very menacing look, but before he could say anything, his lawyer intervened. "Alright, Sheriff, I think my client and I need to discuss a few things before we continue. May we have thirty minutes?" Mikeal picked up his file from the table and walked out of the room, leaving the suspense-filled atmosphere behind.

Mikeal and Devin entered the room where Courtney and Allison had been watching the interrogation unfold. "What do you think?" Mikeal asked them, his voice tinged with anticipation.

"Well, his attorney is correct," Courtney responded, her voice carrying a sense of unease. "I'm not seeing a motive, at least in regards to his missing employee. But my bigger question is, why did you start with that? I was sure you were going to press him on the evidence found in his possession, the evidence we can actually trace back to a body, or at least what is left of it."

"Right now, we still have nothing, except a pending lawsuit and one pissed off DA," Courtney stated, her frustration simmering beneath the surface. "Without a confession, there's not enough here to prosecute. We have better odds with the bloody clothes and corpse you dug out of the ground. However, there are still quite a few dots you'll need to connect before we can take it to trial."

"Understood," Mikeal answered, the suspense hanging heavily in the room. "But do we have enough to keep holding him?"

"Yeah, probably we have enough," Courtney replied reluctantly, the suspense lingering in the air like a dark cloud.

After a thirty-minute break, the pair returned to the room. Mikeal glanced down at his watch; it was already seven in the evening. The tension in the room was continuing to build, and he knew they had reached a critical juncture.

"Alright, let's pick back up on your story," Mikeal began, his voice measured and deliberate. "Sammy had just rejected you, you were embarrassed, she made a comment you didn't like, and you became very angry toward her." He leaned in, the suspense growing heavier with each word. "What happened next?"

Steve's response was calm, almost unnervingly so. "She demanded I take her home."

Mikeal refused to let up. "Where did all your anger go, Steve? I'm sure it didn't just magically disappear. She just called your manhood into question. Come on, did you let her have it?" His words were calculated to provoke a response, but Steve remained composed.

"Listen, in the heat of the moment, you're angry, a little high, not thinking straight," Mikeal continued to press, the suspense in the room intensifying. "I'm not condoning it, but did things get a little physical?"

"Listen, Sheriff," Steve's lawyer interjected, his tone authoritative, "my client has indicated that nothing happened. She only asked to be taken home. I would appreciate it if you would stop trying to provoke my client."

Mikeal's patience was wearing thin, and he lashed out, his frustration evident. "Listen here, Mr. Cheap Suit. A young lady is missing, and all I'm trying to do is get to the bottom of what happened to her. Your client has lied to us repeatedly. So excuse the hell out of me if I'm not showing enough empathy for your client!" The suspense in the room was now a relentless force, pushing everyone to the brink.

"So what did you do after she asked to be taken home?" Mikeal's voice was taut, charged with the unspoken tension in the room.

"I'm not going to lie, Sheriff," Steve began, his words carefully measured, "yes, I was angry and pissed off as a result of her actions, but I didn't touch her. I left the office and went outside to cool down." The silence hung heavy as Steve paused for a few seconds, the suspense building like a storm on the horizon. "When I returned to the office, she was on the phone with a friend, trying to get a ride back home. I told her it wasn't necessary, and she hung up the phone."

"Did you get the name of the friend she called?" Devin asked, the suspense in the room reaching a crescendo.

"No," Steve replied, his voice holding an edge of frustration, "she didn't say, and I didn't ask."

"What happened on the drive home?" Mikeal's question sliced through the thick atmosphere of anticipation.

Steve hesitated, the suspense now almost unbearable. "Well, I guess I apologized what seemed like a thousand times. I tried to tell her I was sorry, but she wouldn't even speak to me. When we arrived at her house, she jumped out and ran inside. That was the last time I saw her."

"What night did this happen?" Devin's inquiry hung in the air like a weight.

"I believe it was June ninth," Steve answered, the room's tension reaching its zenith. Devin and Mikeal exchanged a significant glance simultaneously, the suspense thickening with each passing moment.

"This happened the day before she disappeared?" Mikeal's voice was heavy with implication as he sought confirmation.

Steve put his forehead in his hand and breathed a deep sigh, the room now a pressure cooker of suspense. Trying to justify his actions, Steve said, "Now, can you see why I originally lied to your officers? I know this doesn't look good, but I swear I did not harm Samantha." The suspense in the room was now a suffocating force, leaving everyone gasping for answers.

Shortly after Mikeal and Devin had left to resume their interview, Courtney and Allison, settled in their seats, ready to observe the next chapter in this unfolding interview, were interrupted by a firm knock on the door. Allison sprang to her feet with a sense of urgency, responding to the unexpected visitor. Courtney strained to hear the muffled conversation taking place, but the details remained frustratingly out of reach. After a brief exchange, Allison left the door slightly ajar as she turned to address Courtney. She relayed the news that Emma had arrived and needed to alert the Sheriff.

Without a moment's hesitation, Courtney leaped to her feet, her voice laced with determination as she redirected Allison's course of action. She firmly instructed Allison to refrain from notifying anyone else and emphasized that both Allison and the DA would conduct the interview with Emma. Courtney also instructed Allison to find a replacement for monitoring the ongoing interview's video feed and to usher Emma into the adjacent interview room without further delay.

Allison went to the front of the station finding Emma sitting alone in a chair outside the Sheriff's office. "Emma, follow me; we'll be with you in a few minutes. Can I get you anything to drink while you wait?"

"No, I'm good," Emma responded, her nerves beginning to fray as Allison left her alone in the room. As she waited, her eyes wandered around the unfamiliar surroundings. This was her first time this deep inside a police station, and the room held an air of mystery. A table with two chairs on each side, a large dark window that she assumed concealed recording equipment, and a wavering wave at what she believed to be observers on the other side—all contributed to the mounting tension.

After a few minutes, Courtney Weber, accompanied by Allison, entered the room and took seats opposite Emma. Confusion gnawed at Emma as she voiced her expectation to speak with the Sheriff. Courtney, without missing a beat, initiated the dialogue, her authoritative presence sending shivers down Emma's spine.

"As I'm sure the deputy discussed with you, we have now opened an investigation into the disappearance of your co-worker, Samantha Hudson, or Sammy as she is commonly called. I've reviewed your original statement and would like to ask you a few more questions based on some recent information we've obtained. Are you ready to start?" Courtney took charge, and Emma felt the mounting pressure, her nervousness growing with every passing moment. The tall, imposing figure of Courtney Weber across the table only added to her unease, setting the stage for a daunting encounter.

Courtney carefully laid out her copy of Emma's statement across the table, her eyes briefly scanning it before she began her inquiry. "On the day Sammy disappeared, you mentioned she was agitated or upset before she left for her break. Please, walk us through that morning again."

Emma hesitated, uncertainty gnawing at her. Should she divulge the truth about the pregnancy? Her thoughts raced until the impatient DA, Weber, interjected, her tone a sharp reminder of the urgency of the situation. "Emma, do I need to repeat the question?"

"Alright," Emma began, her voice quivering slightly, "as I mentioned before, when we opened that morning, it was immediately noticeable that the prior closing crew didn't clean up before leaving. That put us both in a bad mood."

Courtney probed further. "Could she have been conversing with someone from the resort, which put her in a bad mood? Who arrived first that morning?"

"I was there first," Emma replied, "and Sammy came in maybe fifteen minutes later."

"So, if you were there first, you witnessed all her movements and saw everyone she spoke to?" DA Weber pressed, a sense of urgency in her tone.

Emma mumbled her response. "I guess so..."

"Well, you either did or you didn't. Think, Emma, this is really important," the DA urged.

Feeling the anxiety build rapidly, Emma struggled to find her words. Fortunately, Allison, who understood Emma's sensitivity from prior interactions, stepped in to help. "When she first arrived, did you see her come in from the parking lot?" Allison asked, offering Emma a supportive glance.

Emma looked up at Allison gratefully before answering, "Well, I guess I didn't see her pull into the parking lot."

Allison paused, then continued gently, "So when did you first see her?"

"When she started to unlock the front door, I was in the back, but knew the sound," Emma replied, her tension easing slightly with Allison's understanding approach.

Attempting to regain control of the conversation, DA Weber softened her tone before posing another question. "Emma, would you agree, then, she could have had a conversation with someone before you ever saw her, is that fair?"

Emma nodded in agreement, her anxiety subsiding a bit.

Courtney proceeded with her inquiry. "Did she mention anything that morning about a co-worker?"

"Well, yeah," Emma responded, a hint of frustration in her voice. "We were both pretty upset with Larissa. She always half-asses things, leaving us to clean up after her."

"Besides Larissa, did you discuss any other co-workers?" Courtney probed further.

"If you're specifically asking about Steve Taylor, let me save you the trouble," Emma replied, her voice carrying a hint of smugness. "Unfortunately, she didn't mention his name."

With those words, Steve's ominous presence hung heavily in the room, casting a shadow over everyone. Emma had been biding her time, waiting for the opportune moment to reveal her trump card, and now it had arrived. In an abrupt and audacious revelation, she shattered the oppressive silence, her words landing like a lead weight. "Did you know Sammy was pregnant? I believe Steve's the father!"

The revelation sent shockwaves rippling through the room, each wave carrying a sense of foreboding that seemed to grow with every passing second. For an instant, the silence was so profound that you could almost hear the collective gasp of those present.

Emma's gaze shifted from the stunned faces of both the DA and the deputy. In that fleeting moment, a victorious smile crept across her face, like an arrow finding its mark. For the first time, it felt like someone was truly hearing her words and grasping their significance. However, that smile slowly faded, replaced by an undercurrent of anger. The inaction of the Sheriff's office may have cost her friend her life, and the weight of that realization hung heavily in the room, casting a pall of despair over them all.

CHAPTER 20

Mikeal's mind churned, replaying Steve Taylor's last comment over and over like a broken record. The layers of deception that had unfolded during the interview made it challenging to discern if this was the genuine truth. Why would Steve intentionally place himself with Sammy the night before her disappearance? The room's growing silence began to press on them all, an unspoken tension settling in like a dense fog. Devin cast a sidelong glance at the Sheriff, searching for any sign of direction, but Mikeal appeared lost in thought.

Sensing the discomfort enveloping the room, Mikeal squirmed in his chair, the unease mounting with each passing moment. He eventually let out a long, heavy sigh. The DA's admonition to focus on hard evidence of a crime rather than a potential disappearance weighed heavily on his mind.

"Mr. Taylor, the evidence found hidden in your ceiling, what can you tell us about them?" the Sheriff finally broke the silence.

"As I've stated before, until a couple of nights ago, I had no idea there was anything hidden in the ceiling of my building," Steve replied.

"Assuming that's true, how did they get there? In a building your family has owned since 1965?" Mikeal pressed.

"I don't have a clue, Sheriff. That's the God's honest truth."

"They didn't just magically appear there, did they? Who utilized that building before it came under your ownership?"

"My father did, but he was pretty sick the last six years of his life. I doubt he set foot in the building after 1975," Steve explained.

"What was the building's purpose?"

"My father was a picker. He couldn't pass up a yard sale or flea market without stopping. I remember my mother telling him he was turning the house into a junkyard, and his 'treasures' needed to go. Dad never wanted to get rid of anything, so he built the building and moved his stuff into it sometime before I graduated high school, around '67 or '68."

"What did you do with his stuff when he passed?" Devin inquired.

Steve's tense demeanor softened slightly, a faint smile crossing his face as he reminisced about his father. "He had that place so packed with stuff you couldn't move around in there. We probably hauled out two dump trucks full of what he called his treasures. A few old signs and a couple of gas pumps we were able to sell for a decent price, but the majority, we couldn't give away."

"Did you find anything unusual?" Mikeal probed.

Steve blinked, momentarily perplexed. "Unusual, Sheriff? I'm not sure what you mean."

"You know, something that didn't align with your father's collecting habits. Perhaps items typically associated with a woman?"

"Well, Sheriff, I can tell you for certain there were no clothes, for men or women, in that building. My father did have several collections of dishes, but I doubt that's what you're interested in," Steve responded.

Steve's attorney, more astute than the Sheriff had realized, picked up on the surprise in Devin's eyes when clothes were mentioned. "So this evidence consists of clothing?" he asked, his curiosity piqued.

Before Mikeal could answer the question, the door swung open, revealing Allison's presence. She spoke urgently, her tone conveying the gravity of the situation. "Sir, can you step out for a minute?" Mikeal nodded, his curiosity piqued, and left the room, with Devin staying behind.

As Mikeal emerged into the hallway, he anticipated a brief sidebar with Allison. However, to his surprise, he found DA Courtney Weber standing there, her arms crossed and a worried expression etched on her face. Their eyes locked, and she wasted no time in delivering her bombshell. "Sammy was pregnant," she stated flatly.

A chill raced up Mikeal's spine, causing him to lean back against the opposite wall for support. In that moment, a profound sense of guilt washed over him, and he began to doubt every decision he had made from the very beginning. The weight of his inaction bore down on him, and the haunting thought that he might have contributed to someone losing their life filled his mind.

Allison, recognizing the palpable tension in the hallway, attempted to break the icy silence that had settled over them. "I guess we have our potential motive," she interjected, her words hanging in the air like an uneasy promise.

As Mikeal turned toward the door, ready to reenter the interview room, Allison's voice hesitated, causing him to pause. "Sir..."

"Earlier today, I was reviewing Jordan's file notes and emails," Allison began carefully. "She had tracked down a relative of Tina Lattimer, a sister who lives in Wyoming."

Mikeal's interest sparked, and he leaned in. "Had she spoken with her?" he asked eagerly.

"Not that I could tell. It seems she located her on the very day she was suspended," Allison replied.

A flash of contempt crossed Mikeal's face as he glanced in the direction of the DA. The suspension of Jordan had not only left them short-staffed but had also cost them valuable time in pursuing this crucial lead.

"I spoke to her this afternoon," Allison continued, attempting to ease the tension building between her boss and the DA. "She's willing to submit to a DNA swab."

Mikeal's expression softened, and a glimmer of relief shone in his eyes. "That's the best news I've heard in a while," he remarked, cutting his contemptuous gaze from the DA and heading back into the interview room to resume questioning.

Returning to the interview, Mikeal picked up where he had left off, his tone determined and relentless. "So you're still claiming you have no idea where this evidence came from, even though they were found in a building owned by your family since it was built?"

"Isn't it obvious," the lawyer finally spoke up, his voice laced with frustration, "the clothes were planted there by someone."

"Planted? How, when, and why?" Mikeal pressed, his patience wearing thin.

"That's not my job, Sheriff. You're the investigator," the lawyer retorted, his eyes locked onto Mikeal. "But someone is attempting to frame my client!"

Mikeal leaned forward, his gaze unwavering. "Well, this is what I think. I think your client abducted Tina Lattimer in 1975, killed her in this building, stripped her naked, and took her out towards Hebgen Lake to bury her body. Upon returning, he cleaned up the scene, took the clothes home in an attempt to wash the blood out before hiding them in the ceiling and forgetting about them. That's what I think," Mikeal declared, his arms crossed as he sat back in his chair.

Steve's voice shook as he responded, his eyes pleading with sincerity. "So that's what this is about. Sheriff, I was cleared of having anything to do with her disappearance in the original investigation, but you won't let it go. I've said this until I'm blue in the face—I've never harmed anyone. I honestly don't know how those clothes got to my property."

"Sheriff," the lawyer interjected once more, "are you confirming the body found was Tina's?"

"We're about to confirm it. We've located a family member who will be giving us a DNA sample," Mikeal replied tersely.

Steve spoke up, his voice filled with a somber sense of regret. "I hope it is Tina. She was a good girl, very funny, always telling jokes. Her family deserves closure. Unfortunately, I was not involved, so her killer, if they're still alive, is still out there."

As Emma approached the turnoff to her apartment, she made another attempt to call Terry, but once again, her call rolled over to voicemail. Frustration and anxiety began to swell within her. "I'm going to be useless unless I can share this information with someone," she thought. She passed the turn to her apartment, deciding to head toward Terry's place. Maybe it was for the best that he hadn't answered his phone. Emma was bursting at the seams with the need to share her encounter with the DA, and the only way to manage her anxiety was to speak with someone face to face.

When she arrived at Terry's, the driveway was empty, but she knocked on the trailer door anyway. Peering through a window, she saw that the interior was dark and devoid of any signs of life. She tried calling Terry again, but the call immediately went to voicemail. "Hey, this is Emma again. Are you on your way home? I'm at your house. Give me a call as soon as you can."

She returned to her car and sat waiting for Terry's response. After thirty minutes passed with no word from him, she began to contemplate leaving. "Just my luck, I'll leave and pass him on the road. Surely he's received my message by now." She thought about taking a walk around his property while waiting.

As she walked, the discarded vehicles scattered across the property held no interest for her. Instead, she was drawn to the house Terry had grown up in, which stood on the mountainside approximately a hundred yards away from the trailer. The house had a front porch that stretched the length of the building.

Weaving her way through the abandoned vehicles, Emma reached the front of the house. The aged wood creaked and moaned with every step she took as she ascended the stairs to the landing. The view from the porch was breathtaking. Emma could see for miles into the valley below, even though the trees obstructed most of the view. The distant sounds of vehicles passing up and down the highway reached her ears. She took a deep breath and enjoyed this rare moment of complete relaxation. It was a calmness she hadn't experienced in recent memory, and for the first time in a while, she felt at ease in both body and mind. "Where could Terry be?" she wondered before glancing at her phone, only to realize it no longer had any service. "That's why he hasn't called me back."

Emma shifted her attention toward the house. Two windows flanked each side of the front door, both of which were covered with faded newspapers. There was a screen door followed by the main wooden door, which had a squared window in the top half. It reminded her of her grandmother's house back in Alabama. Every summer, when they'd visit her, one of the kids—her, her sister, or her brother—would inevitably manage to get their fingers smashed in a similar screen door. On this one, the bottom screen was missing, and the top part was pulled away from the wood around the door handle. Emma peered through the window into the house without opening the screen, curious about what she might find inside.

The front room was a dimly lit, roughly ten by twelve-foot rectangle with a fireplace at one end and devoid of any furniture. The wood floor and paneling gave the room a shadowy, almost eerie atmosphere, even in broad daylight. Emma decided to investigate further. She opened the screen door and reached for the doorknob, only to find it locked. "Damn it, it's locked," she muttered to herself in frustration. She thought maybe it was just stuck, so she gave it another try, putting her shoulder into it for extra force. But once again, the door refused to budge.

Undeterred, Emma decided to explore the back of the house. She descended the stairs, taking a right turn toward the rear of the building. The backside of the house was relatively level with the mountainside, and she noticed a screened-in porch on the far left that seemed to lead into the main house. As she entered the porch, her eyes fell on a white freezer located against the side of the house beneath a window. Although it was plugged into an electrical outlet, there was no audible hum of a working unit. Emma placed her hand on top of it and confirmed that it was no longer functional. At some point, someone had bolted a locking hinge to the top, securing its contents with a keyed lock.

Like the windows at the front of the house, the window above the freezer was covered with yellowed newspaper. However, without direct sunlight, the writing on the newspaper remained visible. Emma examined it closely and found a date: October 12, 1972. She couldn't recall exactly, but Terry had mentioned that his father had lived in this house well past 1972. The question gnawed at her: Why would someone tape up their windows like this?

Gathering her courage, Emma turned the doorknob and cautiously pushed the door open, revealing the kitchen beyond. She hesitated for a moment, her uncertainty about entering without an invitation gnawing at her.

As Emma cautiously stepped inside, she couldn't shake the eerie feeling that had settled over her. The kitchen, frozen in time like the rest of the house, appeared as though it had been pulled from a museum. An ancient wood-burning stove stood as a testament to a bygone era. Oddly, the presence of an electrical outlet on the back porch and a refrigerator indicated that this house had once enjoyed the comforts of modernity. The unanswered question hung in the air: Why had the stove never been replaced?

Empty white cabinets with clear glass lined the walls, and a window above the sink hinted at what must have been a breathtaking view. However, that view, like the others, was concealed behind layers of old newspapers. Emma's gaze fell to the yellowed linoleum floor beneath her feet. Her curiosity led her to the refrigerator, but a nagging fear held her back. Opening it might unleash the foul stench of long-forgotten food, but her reflexes overcame her hesitation. To her great relief, the refrigerator held only bottled water and a few Gatorades.

Leaving the kitchen, Emma entered the room visible from the front door. The space was even darker than before, and she used her phone to activate a flashlight. The fireplace, now on her right side, revealed a hallway to her left, likely leading to the bedrooms. As she moved further into the room, her flashlight revealed something surprising. In the firebox, remnants of burnt logs hinted at a recent fire. She picked up one of the logs and inhaled its scent, confirming her suspicion that the fire had not occurred long ago.

Still crouched on the floor, she examined the wooden floor and discovered dark stains scattered across it. The largest stain covered an area of almost four by four feet in the middle of the room. Her eyes drifted upward, searching for any signs of a roof leak, but the ceiling appeared intact with no visible indications of water damage. Puzzled, she muttered to herself before deciding to explore the rest of the house.

Her flashlight pierced the darkness as she stood before a hallway, its four closed doors silently beckoning her. Emma's heart raced as she selected the first door to her right, pushing it open cautiously. The room within had walls adorned with the same dark wood paneling as the front room, and its emptiness initially suggested it was like the rest of the house. Yet, in a corner, an armoire stood silently, and when she opened it, she found herself face to face with an array of dated light jackets, all sized for women. A chill ran down her spine, unsettling thoughts racing through her mind.

"These must have belonged to Terry's mother," she tried to rationalize, but a nagging unease clung to her.

Across the hallway and slightly down, she entered the bathroom. Its appearance mirrored that of the kitchen. A clawfoot tub commanded the space, and an exposed plumbing system ran beneath the sink. Emma marveled at the absence of a shower, a stark contrast to her own modern upbringing. While her reflexes had driven her actions earlier, this time both her mind and body agreed: there was no reason, absolutely none, to open the toilet seat and peer inside.

She moved on to the next bedroom, crossing the hallway to find a considerably larger room than the previous one. Against the far wall, an iron-spindled bed frame remained, holding only box springs and a stained mattress. Emma couldn't shake the unsettling image that flashed through her mind, causing her to grimace at the thought of what might have transpired on that bed. Opposite the foot of the bed was a built-in closet with sliding doors, and once again, she discovered a few articles of clothing—a couple of blouses, blue jeans, and assorted hosiery.

The last bedroom she checked contained another small bed, with a couple of posters still clinging to the walls. But what was most notable was the pungent, unpleasant odor that filled the room, a musky, sweaty feet scent that clung to the air. It was revolting, and Emma was torn between her curiosity to explore further and a growing sense that she should leave immediately. Ultimately, the overpowering smell made the decision for her. She hurriedly left the room and firmly closed the door behind her.

As she retraced her steps out of the house, her nerves on edge, she was startled to see Terry standing at the back door, his presence like an unexpected jolt of electricity in the otherwise eerie atmosphere.

Mikeal sat behind his desk, his mind churning with uncertainty about the path ahead. He had failed to extract a confession from Steve Taylor, leaving him with little more than a glimmer of hope that matching the clothing to Tina's sister's DNA would yield a breakthrough. Even with this potential lead, he knew that building a solid case with only circumstantial evidence would be an uphill battle, and securing a conviction far from guaranteed. What troubled Mikeal even more was the nagging doubt—could his relentless pursuit of closure for the families result in the unjust targeting of an innocent man?

Though he had never been particularly religious, Mikeal firmly believed that no single individual had the right to pass judgment on another. His role as a law enforcement officer was to present factual evidence to be weighed by a jury of peers who would ultimately determine the truth and decide upon the appropriate judgment. It was an imperfect system, one in which he had witnessed both the guilty walking free on technicalities and the innocent suffering the consequences of flimsy evidence. Mikeal couldn't deny that this internal struggle had been the source of his sleepless nights and the relentless headaches that tormented him, night after night.

Devin stood silently by the Sheriff's office door, sensing that Mikeal was lost in thought, and waited for the right moment to interject. As Mikeal let out a heavy sigh and finally looked up, his eyes met Devin's.

"I'm sorry, Devin, did you say something?" Mikeal inquired.

"No, Sheriff, I could tell you were deep in thought, so I was just biding my time," Devin replied.

Mikeal let out a weary smile before asking rhetorically, "Yeah, just thinking about this investigation, wondering where we go from here."

"Well, the good news is we'll soon have Tina's sister's DNA," Devin reassured him.

"What are your thoughts? Do you think Steve is the guy?" Mikeal sought Devin's perspective.

Devin hesitated, choosing his words carefully. "Sheriff, that's a difficult question to answer at this point. I'm wrestling with keeping my personal feelings out of the equation. Guilty or not, he's an arrogant son of a bitch."

Mikeal chuckled softly, acknowledging the challenge. "Yeah, I'm grappling with that aspect as well," Devin nodded wearily.

"Well, it's been a long day. Mind if I head home?" Mikeal offered an understanding smile.

"That sounds like an excellent plan," he concurred. "I'll follow your lead."

And so, they both made their way towards the exit, leaving behind the lingering weight of an unresolved case and the unspoken doubts that hung in the air.

CHAPTER 21

Mikeal was beyond exhausted; the days had begun to blur together, and he was desperately in need of some rest. The drive home was relatively short, but it provided him with a chance to catch up on any voicemails left on his phone during the day. With one eye on the road and the other on his phone, he saw that he had three messages. Two were mere five-second voicemails from Allison. However, the third message, unfamiliar and lasting thirty-five seconds, immediately caught his attention.

"Mr. Lancaster, this is Dr. Engram from the Urgent Care you visited a couple of days ago," the voice on the voicemail said. "Your lab results have come back, and there are a couple of things we need to discuss. You really should have this checked out. Please call us back as soon as you can."

The late hour made it impractical to return the call now. Mikeal attempted to put his phone back in his jacket pocket when it slipped from his hand, landing in the narrow gap between the seat and the center console. Struggling to stay focused on the road, he blindly reached down, hoping to retrieve his phone. He could barely feel it, but it remained just out of his grasp. As he saw that the road stretched straight ahead for about a hundred yards, he steadied the wheel and made one last desperate attempt to recover his phone. However, in that split second, his eyes darted away from the road.

When he looked back, a dark blur streaked from left to right, cutting across the road directly in front of him. Panic surged through him, and he instinctively jerked the wheel to the left. But when he tried to regain control and steer the vehicle back onto the road, the high center of gravity caused it to teeter dangerously. The sensation of the right-side wheels losing contact with the ground was unmistakable, and Mikeal knew he was in trouble as the vehicle started to roll.

"Mikeal, Mikeal, wake up!" The voice was familiar, but Mikeal's head throbbed, and darkness enveloped him. Disoriented and panicked, he had no idea where he was. "John, is that you? Where are you? Everything's dark, I can't see a thing." His eyes began to adjust, and he noticed a faint light in the distance. "John, I can't feel my body. Where are we?"

"Mikeal, you have to wake up!" John's voice was urgent. "Mikeal, help me! I can't feel my body. Where am I?" Panic was mounting within Mikeal, and he struggled to make sense of the situation. Something was terribly wrong, but he couldn't grasp what it was.

Then, a strong hand grabbed his, pulling him toward the light. Gradually, the fog lifted, and his surroundings became clearer. "Are you okay, buddy?" John Wolf asked.

"What the hell is going on, Chief?" Mikeal demanded.

"I'm not sure," John replied. "You fell asleep right after we left Townsend. I think you were having a dream, which is surprising considering the intense snoring I've had to endure for the past two hours."

"Why were we in Tennessee?" Mikeal questioned, still disoriented.

"Alright, now you're just messing with me," John chuckled.

"I'm serious as a heart attack; what's happening? You're dead!" Mikeal, with confusion in his voice, added.

"I'm dead?" Was this Mikeal's attempt at humor emerging, the Chief thought, before jokingly replying, "Well, someone forgot to inform me. Does this mean I won't get paid for today?"

"No, I'm serious," Mikeal insisted. "Your daughter called me a couple of weeks ago and told me you had died."

John's confusion deepened. "Wow, that's a shocker. Someone should have let me in on that secret. But wait a minute, my daughter's only five; she couldn't have called you."

"Mikeal Lancaster, I swear, if you hadn't been with me all day, I'd think you were stoned out of your mind," John said sternly. "I've never seen you act like this. Maybe you're not cut out for police work. Come on, quit fooling around. We'll be back at the station in fifteen minutes. You're still a rookie, and if you talk crazy like this around the office, you won't make it through probation."

Mikeal felt the throbbing in his head intensify as the light began to fade. "Mikeal, Mikeal, wake up!"

"No, I need to sleep, leave me alone! You've got to wake up. Come on, Mikeal, you can do it, wake up!" Mikeal was caught in a strange sensation; John's voice had transformed into that of a woman's, with what sounded like a German accent. The darkness persisted, but the voice remained consistent. "Mikeal, Mikeal, please wake up!"

Once again, he saw the distant light. Gradually, his eyes began to focus, but he couldn't discern where he was. Somewhere behind him, a constant beeping sound persisted, and he started to realize that this must be a dream. Another familiar voice called out, "Sheriff, we're all here; you need to wake up."

Now, it seemed as though the light was pouring into the room. "Allison, is that you?" he inquired. Still unable to see through the blinding light, he added, "Allison, where are we?"

"You're in the hospital, Sheriff," she replied.

"What? Why am I in the hospital?"

"You were in an accident," the lady with the German accent said. "Alright, Sheriff, let's not worry about asking any more questions until we can get you stabilized."

As feeling began to return to his hands and feet, Mikeal's panic lessened. Sight returned to both eyes, although everything remained blurry, and the throbbing in his head grew more intense. He tried to use his hands and arms to position himself more upright in the bed. The doctor noticed his struggles and intervened. "Hold on a second, Sheriff; we can raise the head of the bed if you're trying to sit up."

As the bed adjusted, Mikeal finally took in his surroundings, understanding that this was indeed real and not a dream. He found himself in a fairly large, open room with multiple beds. Some were plainly visible, while others had curtains drawn, indicating they were occupied. "I'm in the emergency room?" he asked the doctor.

"Yes, you were brought in about an hour ago," she confirmed.

With his vision gradually returning to normal, Mikeal felt some relief. "Your blood pressure is starting to drop back into a more normal range. How are you feeling, Mikeal?" the doctor inquired.

"Like my head had been bounced around like a basketball."

"You took a severe blow to the head," the doctor explained. "It'll take a few days, maybe a week, for it to return to normal."

"Doctor, does he have a concussion?" Allison asked.

"Without a doubt," the doctor replied. "We'll be running some tests throughout the night to make sure nothing outside of normal is going on inside."

Mikeal, starting to feel a little better, decided to make light of the situation. "Doctor, I've never been good at tests. Can I at least have a tutor to help me prepare?"

"You'll do fine," she reassured him. "In addition to X-rays, we'll be doing a CT scan. It's nothing major, but we'll need to inject you with a dye to check for any internal bleeding."

"Needles? I hate needles," Mikeal groaned.

"Most people do, but in our case, it's a necessary evil. You'll do fine, don't worry," the doctor assured him.

"Your accent, is that German?" Mikeal asked.

"No, I'm Dutch."

"I'm sorry; I hope that didn't offend you. I'm just a country boy from North Carolina; you're the first person I've met from Holland."

"No offense taken," the doctor replied.

"Doc, when can I get out of here?" Mikeal inquired.

"Well, definitely not tonight," the doctor responded. "Let me see when we can schedule these tests, and we'll go from there."

The doctor left the room, and Mikeal turned his attention to Allison. "What the hell happened, Allison? I don't remember a thing!"

"We're not sure, Sheriff," she explained. "There were no skid marks on the road. It looks like you just left the road, and the ditch stopped you from hitting the trees."

"Could I have possibly passed out?" Mikeal wondered aloud.

"Maybe," Allison suggested. "It's strange; I remember leaving work, but nothing else."

"When they unloaded you from the ambulance, you mentioned the name John a couple of times. Do you remember?" Allison asked.

"Yeah, I thought I was having a dream. I was back in North Carolina or something."

"Was this the friend who just passed away?"

"Yes, John Wolf, who gave me my start. I was trying to tell him he was dead, but he didn't believe me."

The doctor returned briefly to inform Mikeal that it would be an hour or so before they would take him for the tests. "Sheriff, I would suggest you try to get some sleep. After we've completed the tests, we'll move you to a private room."

"I'm going to leave as well," Allison added.

"Mr. Lancaster, you need to wake up. Come on, Mikeal, let's wake up." A still groggy Mikeal asked if it was time to go back for the test. "No, sir, you've already done that; I'm just bringing your breakfast," the nurse answered. "It's eight fifteen; you need to eat. Let me raise your bed." As Mikeal rubbed the cobwebs from his eyes, he realized he was now in a completely different area of the hospital. "What time did you say?"

"It's eight fifteen," she replied. "I don't remember a thing after the doctor left last night. I really need to get out of here and back to work," Mikeal pleaded.

"Sir, the doctor will go over everything with you when he stops by this morning."

"Where's the female doctor I had last night?"

"I'm not sure, sir; I only started at seven this morning. Let me look at your chart. Oh, you had Dr. Vermeulen; I'm surprised she was working the emergency room."

"Why is that a surprise?"

"Well, she's the Chief of Staff at the hospital. Normally, she wouldn't be here that late."

"When do you expect this doctor to stop by?" The nurse looked down at her wristwatch. "Oh, probably before ten, would be my guess."

"So I'll be lucky to get out of here by noon, is what you're saying?"

"Mr. Lancaster, I'm not saying anything officially, but if I were you, I wouldn't expect to be out of here until later today."

"Excuse me, nurse," a voice from the hallway is heard, "is this gentleman giving you a hard time?" A very uncomfortable expression comes across the nurse's face. Mikeal, seeing this, explains, "That's my Deputy Allison, never mind her."

"You're the Sheriff," she asks in a very skeptical voice?

"Yes, I am, unless I was replaced last night. Allison, I am still Sheriff, right?"

"Yes, unfortunately, you're still Sheriff."

"You're putting me behind on my rounds," the nurse replies before scurrying out of the room. "Wow, she's stiff," Allison comments as she finally walks into the room. "Either that or she's got outstanding tickets," Mikeal joked. "Looks like I'm going to be in here at least through lunch; anything new happening with the case?"

"Not yet," Allison replied. "Hopefully, by the end of the day, we'll have the Lattimer DNA results back from the lab."

"Looks like insurance will total out the Tahoe."

"I thought I just hit a ditch," Mikeal asked?

"Yeah, evidently you rolled it several times before hitting the ditch hard enough it bent the frame. You still have no clue what happened?"

"I remember leaving the station and waking up in the emergency room, nothing in-between."

"Other than your dream, you mean," Allison clarified?

"I don't know, maybe. I'm starting to doubt having a dream."

"You were having something; your shoulders were moving like you were trying to get out of something, and you kept saying John. Yeah, it seemed very real, but who knows."

"Excuse me, I don't mean to interrupt," came a voice from the doorway. "Mr. Lancaster, I'm Dr. Harvey, how are you feeling this morning?"

"Doc, I feel like I was hit by a truck, other than that I'm doing alright."

"Do you have a moment we could talk?"

"Sure, no time like the present," Mikeal responded.

"I mean privately," Dr. Harvey clarified.

"I'm just leaving," Allison politely offered. "I'll see you back at the office, hopefully this afternoon. So, Doc, am I going to live, and most importantly, will I be out of here by this afternoon?"

"I'm not certain at this time," the doctor answered.

"You do know I was just joking about the first part?"

"Mr. Lancaster, we found a spot on your brain when we reviewed the MRI."

"What do you mean a spot?"

"We found a small mass near your cerebral cortex, which is possibly affecting your limbic system."

"Doc, you're going to have to dumb this down; other than 'small mass,' I haven't a clue as to what you just said!"

"Understandable, Mr. Lancaster. The limbic system controls your memory, emotion, and motivation. Have you been having headaches or issues with sleeping?"

"Yes, I have been," Mikeal answered. "How long would you estimate you have been dealing with these issues?"

"I'd say no more than a couple of months at the max."

"Well, good. Based on that and the current size, we think we've caught it early enough to effectively treat."

"So what's the next step, Doc, go in and cut it out?"

"If only it was that simple," the doc replied. "Cutting it out would potentially cause more issues than it would solve; we'll need to shrink the tumor."

"When you say shrink, you mean chemo?"

"Yes, your treatment will involve chemo," Dr. Harvey replied. "Hair loss, vomiting, constant fatigue, I'm assuming I should expect," Mikeal asked.

"Each patient experiences different reactions to the treatment. Mr. Lancaster, you appear very fit, so my guess is your effects would be mild."

"I'm in the middle of something right now at work; do we have time before the treatments need to start?"

"Unfortunately, Mr. Lancaster, waiting is not a good idea," replied the doctor. "Call my office on Monday, and we'll work out the details. In the meantime, there's no reason we can't release you today, so I'll stop by the Nursing station and get the paperwork rolling to get you out this afternoon." As the doctor left the room, he turned back once more. "Mr. Lancaster, don't take this lightly. I believe we've caught this early enough to avoid any long-term issues. However, if you wait or delay treatment, all bets are off."

"Doctor, I promise I'll call on Monday," Mikeal responded.

Later that afternoon, Mikeal was released and picked up by Devin to return to the station. As they drove through the town, the weight of the unresolved case hung heavy in the air, creating an atmosphere of tension.

"Any new developments since I've been out of action?" Mikeal finally broke the silence.

"No, sir, nothing new to report. We're still waiting on the Lattimer DNA results to come back," Devin answered, his voice reflecting the anticipation and uncertainty surrounding the case.

The two men continued in silence until arriving at the station. Upon entering the building, they were greeted by Allison, who wore a solemn expression.

"How are you feeling, Sheriff?" she asked, her tone laced with concern.

"I feel fit for duty," Mikeal responded, trying to muster confidence despite the growing unease.

"Great because there's someone you should see in room one."

"Who?" Mikeal asked, his curiosity piqued.

"You won't believe me until you see it with your own eyes, Sheriff."

With a sense of foreboding, Mikeal walked towards exam room one. Opening the door, he couldn't believe what he was seeing.

"Sheriff, I'm Samantha Hudson. I believe you've been searching for me," her arrival lending an eerie air of suspense to the room.

CHAPTER 22

"Mikeal, caught completely off guard, just stared at the young lady standing across the table from them. His heart raced, and a feeling of unease settled over the room. He couldn't recall if he had ever seen an actual photo of Sammy before, but over the last thirty days, he had built a mental image of her, and this wasn't it. The height was about right, but expecting a redhead, her blond curly locks were completely unexpected.

After an awkward start, Mikeal finally responded, his voice laced with tension, 'Well, I'll be damned.'

Mikeal motioned for her to take a seat while he and Devin sat on the other side of the table. The room felt charged with uncertainty, and the air was thick with unspoken questions.

Quickly glancing over the written statement she had provided earlier to Allison, Mikeal noted it lacked any details, a factor that only added to the growing tension in the room.

"According to the statement you provided Deputy Allison, you were feeling overworked and decided to walk away, going back to California."

"Yeah, that's pretty much it," Sammy replied, her words seemingly incongruent with the gravity of the situation. The tension in the room tightened another notch.

"Why was the decision to leave so abrupt?" Devin asked, his voice probing for hidden answers.

Sammy hesitated, her eyes darting between the two men as if weighing her options in a high-stakes poker game. Mikeal studied her face, noting the visible conflict regarding what answer and how much detail she should provide. He took this as a sign she was reluctant to bring up her pregnancy, but the air grew heavier with unspoken truths.

"We understand there was an incident the night before between you and your boss, Steve Taylor," Mikeal decided to ask, hoping to unravel the enigmatic puzzle that was Sammy.

Sammy's face quickly turned pale like a ghost. 'How do you know that?' she replied, her voice quivering with a mixture of fear and confusion.

"We have a statement from Mr. Taylor with his explanation of what happened," Mikeal stated, his tone firm and relentless.

"What did he say?" Sammy asked, her voice betraying her anxiety.

"Sammy, what he said in his statement is irrelevant. We would like your version of what happened." Mikeal's words hung in the air, like a promise of revelation.

Sammy slumped back in her chair, her discomfort palpable. She was caught between a rock and a hard place, and it was clear she had secrets she was reluctant to share.

'I can see this is making you very uncomfortable,' Mikeal noted, his voice softening. 'I'm very sorry to make you relive this incident. However, there's a number of things going on which your statement will be able to confirm or deny. It's very important, Sammy; your cooperation may help others.'

Reluctantly, Sammy agreed, her voice trembling, 'Alright, exactly what would you like to hear?'

"Walk us through from the beginning through the end of the time you spent with Steve Taylor," Mikeal urged, the tension in the room reaching its peak.

She painstakingly recounted the genesis of her relationship with Mr. Taylor, and Mikeal followed along, mentally comparing each detail to Steve's statement.

'So that brings us to the evening you visited the storage building,' Mikeal continued, his voice almost a whisper. 'We understand this will be painful, but please provide as much detail as you can remember.'

The silence that followed was deafening, and the room seemed to hold its breath as Sammy hesitated, her eyes distant, reliving the painful memories. It was as though the entire world hung on her next words, and the tension was nearly unbearable.

'The first fifteen minutes we were there, everything was normal,' she began, her voice quivering slightly. 'Steve seemed very excited to be showing off his place and his inventory system. He was explaining everything he did in painful detail, and I was starting to lose interest.' The air in the room grew thick with anticipation.

'I asked if he had a bathroom and he pointed towards the far back corner.'

Mikeal leaned forward, his eyes locked onto her as he pressed, 'Then what happened?'

She hesitated, and the room seemed to hold its breath, waiting for her next words. 'Well, after using the restroom, I could see he was still focused on checking his inventory,' she continued, her voice trembling. 'I kind of wandered over to the other side of the building.'

'Did you ever go in the office?' Devin asked, breaking the silence with a sense of urgency."

Hesitating once more, she answered in the affirmative, and the room seemed to hold its breath again, waiting for the impending revelation. Mikeal remained silent, his gaze intense, urging her to continue.

"I smelled weed in the office, so I went looking for it," she finally admitted, her voice barely above a whisper. "After a few minutes, I found a sandwich bag containing a number of joints, took one out, and lit it up. I turned to face the door, and Steve was standing there, staring back at me." A shiver of suspense ran through the room as her story unfolded. "What are you doing with my weed?" he asked. "I didn't know what to say, so I just shrugged my shoulders and offered him a hit. We shared it until it was down to a small roach. Lit up another one and smoked it down. We were both feeling pretty buzzed when he grabbed me and planted a big kiss on my lips!"

The room held its breath as her words hung in the air, and tension mounted. "I shoved him away and said some very unflattering things about his manhood before demanding to be taken home."

As Sammy recounted her story, everything aligned perfectly with what Steve had previously stated, almost too perfectly. Mikeal's mind raced ahead, searching for answers. Why would Sammy be trying to protect Steve? The pieces of the puzzle still didn't quite fit, and an unsettling feeling gnawed at him. He was deep in thought when Sammy's voice broke through the haze, bringing him back to the present.

"Sheriff, you're bleeding," she pointed out.

Instinctively, Mikeal reached for his nose, examining his hand. A light film of blood covered the back of his index finger. He felt a hint of embarrassment and a growing fear that the bleeding might escalate, much like it had the previous day, overwhelming the tissue Sammy had offered.

Devin, sensing the Sheriff's struggle, decided to take over the interview. "How did you get home?" he asked, attempting to steer the conversation in a different direction.

Sammy continued, her voice laced with frustration. "He drove me home, apologizing the whole time. But I didn't want to hear anything coming out of his mouth. I thought we had a very professional relationship, and he was really trying to help out my career. But in the end, he was just another man trying to get in my pants. I couldn't sleep all night, went into work very agitated. Then the dumb woman who closed the night before half-assed cleaning the place. It was too much, and after eating lunch, I said, 'Screw it, I'm leaving.'"

Mikeal examined the tissue firmly pressed against his bleeding nostril while Devin continued with the interview. To his relief, it only held a slight discoloration from the blood. Mikeal nodded to Devin, indicating that he was ready to proceed with the interview.

"The following day, the day you left, did you see Mr. Taylor at work?" Mikeal asked.

"I was afraid of running into him, so I had kept an eye out for his vehicle, but never saw it. He may have come in after I left, but to answer your question, no, I didn't see him the day I left."

"Anything else, Sheriff?" Sammy asked. "Reliving this has made me nauseous, and I'd very much like to leave now." Mikeal and Devin quickly glanced at each other, both acknowledging she wasn't going to mention the pregnancy on her own.

"Sammy, thank you for your candor, but I only have a few more questions," Mikeal continued. "On the day you disappeared, walk us through what happened after you left the restaurant."

Sammy thought for a moment before answering, "Before I had left on break, I promised Emma I'd take some of the trash out. I'd forgotten about the trash bags until I walked back from lunch, and they were still sitting where I left them by the back door. At that time, there was probably about three inches of snow on the ground, so it was pretty easy to drag the bags to the dumpster."

"When you arrived at the dumpsters, did you notice anything odd or out of place?" Mikeal pressed.

"Not that I recall, well except I saw Terry's truck come around the corner, stopping once he reached the dumpster."

"What was odd about that?" Devin asked.

"Aside from the scheduled garbage pickups on Tuesday and Friday, there is typically little to no traffic around the rear of the building due to the pavement ending at the dumpsters. Sometimes he's taken trash from the restaurant to the dumpsters in the back of the truck, but not this time. He pulled up next to me with his passenger side facing me. I'm sure if you've seen his truck, it's been lifted, and I'm not the tallest person in the world. But I saw his passenger window roll down, so I dropped the garbage bags, put my foot on his step bar, and attempted to pull myself up by grabbing the bottom of his window. Quickly, I felt a stinging sensation before dropping back to the ground. I could see a large gash on my left hand."

"Were you bleeding like my nose earlier?" Mikeal asked.

"Hell no, this was a gusher; I bled like a pig for about thirty seconds before I could get it to stop!" She energetically stated.

"Then what happened?" Mikeal pressed.

"Well, Terry had gotten out of his truck and helped with stopping the bleeding, before then offering to drive me home."

"Did he drive you home?" Devin asked.

Sammy nodded, confirming that he had indeed given her a ride home. Mikeal, curious for more details, inquired about the conversation during the trip.

"Nothing significant," she replied, her thoughts drifting. Mikeal leaned in closer, clearly sensing something more to the story. "You remember something, don't you?" he pressed.

Sammy hesitated before opening up, "I've never really been comfortable around Terry. There's something about him that always makes me nervous. Once I was in his vehicle, I regretted my decision before we even left the resort."

Devin chimed in, seeking clarification, "What exactly about him creeps you out?"

Sammy tried to explain, "It's not any particular action, but more his personality shifts from Mr. Nice Guy to Mr. Mean."

Mikeal probed further, "So, Sammy, are we talking Dr. Jekyll and Mr. Hyde here?"

Sammy considered, "I wouldn't take it that far, but about five minutes into the trip, he started insisting on taking me to his place. He said I didn't need to leave and a few days of rest at his place would be all I needed. I finally gave him a firm 'no' and told him it was the end of the discussion. That's when his personality changed, and he became aggressive."

Devin sought clarification, "In a physical way?"

Sammy clarified, "No, he never touched me, but he made unsettling statements, like maybe he would take me to his place anyway. He started talking about how remote his place was and how he could make people disappear, as if it were some skill passed down from his father. At that point, I desperately wanted him to stop the car and let me out, but the harsh reality struck me—we were already about ten miles away from the resort, in the middle of nowhere. Strangely, he then fell into an eerie silence, not uttering a single word until we finally reached my apartment."

As Mikeal thought about Sammy's last statement, his mind was revisiting his conversation with Terry. Now knowing Terry deliberately withheld information on Sammy's whereabouts, with no crime committed, he needed to understand why he lied.

"I'm a little troubled by this statement about making people disappear. Can you be more specific about what he said?" Mikeal asked.

Sammy hesitated, her mind racing back to a memory from over a month ago. She replied cautiously, "Well, he started talking about me needing to be cautious about who I associated with. He mentioned that over the years, there had been several individuals who just vanished, without a trace, never to be seen again. They lived in an area with thousands of acres of forest, more populated by animals than permanent residents. He even mentioned that the woods could be hiding bodies that would never be found."

Mikeal's eyebrows shot up as he pressed for clarification, "Wait a minute, that last sentence, is that what he actually said?"

"I believe so," Sammy replied with uncertainty in her voice.

Mikeal and Devin exchanged a significant glance at each other.

"You mentioned he went silent for the rest of the trip, but spoke again once reaching your apartment. How did the conversation end?" Mikeal inquired.

Sammy's eyes darted nervously as she recalled, "He asked if there was anything he could do to change my mind. I told him no, that I had made my decision and would be heading back to California in the morning."

Mikeal pressed further, seeking absolute clarity, "So, without a doubt, Terry knew you weren't coming back?"

Sammy's response was quick and uneasy, "Yes, without a doubt." Her voice held a hint of discomfort as she continued, "Look, I don't want to get him in trouble over this. I understand now that I should've been upfront with everyone, but I had some issues I needed to take care of."

What Mikeal had just heard planted a seed of doubt in his mind about Steve Taylor's involvement in the graves found in the woods. Yet, there were still two major puzzles that refused to fit together. Terry couldn't have been responsible for the graves found in the forest, given his age, and there was undeniable evidence tying Steve Taylor to the grisly discoveries at his building. The unspoken question lingered: why hadn't Sammy disclosed her pregnancy?

Mikeal understood that he couldn't beat around the bush any longer. With a sense of urgency, he leaned forward and asked, "This matter you've alluded to repeatedly, the reason you had to leave... You're pregnant, aren't you?" Mikeal stated bluntly.

Sammy's eyes welled up with tears, and they began streaming down her cheeks. After a few moments and after emptying any remaining tissues she had in her purse, she sadly replied, "I was pregnant." The weight of her admission hung heavily in the room.

Over the next thirty minutes, Sammy opened up about a two-week affair with a married man who had a condo on the resort property. Upon learning of her pregnancy, he had callously cast her aside, making it clear that he already had a family and didn't want another one. Mikeal and Devin obtained his personal details, informing Sammy that they would need to verify the information.

As Devin walked in somber silence alongside the Sheriff back to his office, both men engaged in mental gymnastics, desperately trying to fit the new information into the intricate puzzle they were attempting to unravel.

Upon entering the Sheriff's office, Mikeal settled into his chair behind his desk, while Devin remained standing, anticipation etched across his face. The Sheriff, however, seemed lost in thought, his gaze fixed on some invisible point on his desk. Devin recognized this contemplative look all too well; he knew Mikeal was entrenched in deep thought, and it was best to remain silent. Yet, the growing tension inside him felt unbearable as he waited for the Sheriff to break the silence.

As Devin's eyes bore into the Sheriff, Mikeal suddenly looked up, sensing the unspoken urgency. "Yes, Devin, is there something on your mind?" he asked.

Devin, unable to contain it any longer, finally let his words spill out, easing the tension that had been building within him. "So, none of this matters, Sammy's disappearance, the pregnancy – it's all just white noise, with no actual crime committed," he confessed.

Mikeal leaned back in his chair, considering Devin's words. "Well, not necessarily. We could potentially charge Terry with impeding an investigation," he replied.

Devin offered another perspective. "Perhaps Terry believed he was trying to protect her. After all, if the situation had gone public, it would have been extremely embarrassing for Sammy."

"Could be, but I think we need to get that answer directly from Terry," Mikeal responded thoughtfully.

"Sheriff, I don't see why that would even be relevant anymore."

"Not sure, Devin, but let's be thorough nonetheless and follow it out to the end," Mikeal insisted, his determination unwavering. "I'll need you to ride out to Terry's place and check him and it out. Also, I'd be curious to know the distance between his place and where the graves were found."

Devin turned and walked out of Mikeal's office, formulating his plan, when Allison's voice boomed across the room, "Sheriff Dr. Baldwin is holding on your line."

Mikeal acknowledged and picked up his phone. With curiosity piqued, Allison quickly joined Devin at Mikeal's door, straining to hear any hints of the conversation taking place.

Mikeal's voice resonated with anticipation, "Afternoon Dr. Baldwin, hope you have some good news for us." His responses on the phone were mostly indecipherable, leaving his colleagues in suspense.

Finally, Mikeal asked, his tone shifting, "So you're one hundred percent certain on this? Alright, well thanks, Doctor," and with that, he hung up the phone.

"Well?" Allison inquired eagerly.

Mikeal's expression showed a mix of relief and a faint grin. "We've found Tina Lattimer," he finally shared. A collective sigh of relief swept over all three, even though they were far from securing a conviction in her murder. At least their work had provided a glimmer of closure for one family.

"Allison, I'm thinking we need to let her sister know we have a positive match. Will you drive down to Wyoming tomorrow and tell her in person?" Mikeal requested.

"I'm on it," she replied, disappearing to make arrangements.

Devin's voice quivered with concern as he asked, "Where does this leave us with Mr. Taylor?" The weight of uncertainty hung heavily in the room.

Mikeal's face reflected the inner turmoil he felt. "Great question," he admitted with a sigh. "Unfortunately, I'm not sure. We can still go to trial, with a fifty-fifty chance of conviction based on DNA and where we found the clothes. However, with today's developments, I'm not as certain of his guilt as I was yesterday."

A heavy silence settled over the room once more, and Devin turned to leave, thinking their conversation had come to an end. But then, Mikeal broke the silence with a surprising suggestion, "What if we release him?"

Devin halted in his tracks, his eyes locked on the Sheriff as if the idea was preposterous. "Release him?" he repeated incredulously.

Mikeal's eyes twinkled with a hint of mischief as he explained, "Hold on, hear me out on this. We don't have to tell him that we have a DNA match with Tina's. Let him go, and maybe he'll think he's free, letting his guard down."

Devin's brows furrowed with doubt. "So, we'll have someone watching him around the clock?" he questioned. "I think this is a mistake. We have no other suspects, and you yourself mentioned Terry would have been too young to be involved in these killings."

Mikeal nodded, acknowledging the valid points Devin raised. "True, I did say that," he conceded. "But when Sammy spoke earlier, there was something she mentioned, more of an implication than a direct quote from Terry. It had to do with his father, something about his dad that keeps bothering me. What if Terry witnessed his father do something? His dad was definitely around when these murders took place."

Devin countered, skepticism in his voice, "Sheriff, I'm sorry, but that seems like a huge leap."

Mikeal didn't falter. "Probably," he admitted, "but that's why I need you to talk to Terry and investigate the property, pronto."

Devin understood that the conversation was concluded and turned to leave the room.

Mikeal knew that he needed the District Attorney's approval before releasing Mr. Taylor. Without hesitation, he picked up the phone and informed her of the new information and his plan. He expected a barrage of questions, but to his surprise, she only had a couple, which he quickly answered. Once he secured her approval, he alerted Allison to contact Steve's attorney and prepare for another round of interviews. The tension in the room was palpable as they navigated a precarious path between doubt and the pursuit of justice.

Approaching early evening, the sun casting a warm glow, Allison returned to Mikeal's office to deliver the news that Mr. Taylor and his attorney had arrived in interview room one. Mikeal, with the case file in hand, made his way to the interview room, preparing himself for the conversation ahead.

"Gentlemen, good evening," Mikeal greeted as he entered the room. "We have both good news and bad news; shall we begin with the good?"

Mr. Taylor's attorney responded with a wry smile, "Your rodeo, Sheriff."

Mikeal's voice remained steady as he continued, "We had an unexpected visit from none other than our missing person, Samantha Hudson." Steve immediately sat up in his chair, concern etched across his face. "She's very much alive and well, Mr. Taylor," Mikeal reassured. "Even more interesting, her account of the events that transpired mirrors yours almost identically. I hope you take this as a valuable lesson, Mr. Taylor. The truth always comes to light eventually; whether right or wrong, honesty is the best path to follow."

The attorney, sensing there was more to come, asked, "You mentioned bad news as well?"

Mikeal nodded solemnly. "Unfortunately, we haven't been able to extract viable DNA from the clothes found in your bathroom. Therefore, we can't conclusively rule out whether a crime has been committed. However, the District Attorney insists that we must release you."

"Are you saying my client is free to go?" the attorney pressed.

"Yes, Mr. Taylor, you're free to go," Mikeal confirmed. Allison concealed her inner turmoil, even though she was seething inside over the decision to release him.

Steve and his attorney swiftly gathered their belongings and left the room, leaving Mikeal and Allison behind. It had been a grueling day, and Mikeal was ready to head home, but he knew he had to discuss the plan with Allison. However, before he could speak, Allison voiced her frustration, "I can't believe she made you release him."

Mikeal promptly filled her in, including a detail he had neglected to share with Devin: the District Attorney believed that Mr. Taylor would drop his charges after his release, which would pave the way for Jordan to return from her suspension. He instructed Allison to coordinate with Jordan to maintain 24/7 surveillance on Steve Taylor, a move that was both cautious and strategic.

CHAPTER 23

Terry's sudden appearance startled Emma. She stammered, "Terry, you scared the crap out of me. Why didn't you let me know you were here?"

In an eerie calmness, Terry replied, "Why are you in the house, Emma?"

Emma hesitated before reluctantly confessing, "Oh... I was looking for you."

Terry's demeanor took on a more ominous tone as he warned, "Well, Emma, I live in the trailer below; you know that! I don't appreciate you snooping around like this. I have nothing to hide, but I do value my privacy, which you have now violated." With those words, he turned and walked back into the yard, a sense of doom lingering in the air.

Emma followed him out into the yard, desperately chasing him down the hill after a long silence. She reached out and grabbed his arm to stop him. "Listen, I'm sorry, but at the police station this morning, they told me something was going on between Sammy and Mr. Taylor. I thought you would want to know; that's why I came looking for you."

As if breaking a dark trance, Terry's demeanor abruptly reverted to its usual playfulness, the sense of foreboding giving way to an eerie calm. "Well, why didn't you say that in the first place?" he replied. "Look, I'm sorry; I just don't like people nosing around my stuff. Come on in, and I'll fix you a drink. You can tell me everything that happened at the station."

Inside the trailer, Terry motioned for Emma to sit while he went to the kitchen, which occupied the center of the trailer. Emma watched as he fetched two glasses and a bottle of Coke from the refrigerator. Terry briefly glanced up, locking eyes with Emma, casting an unsettling shadow over the moment. Unease crept over her, and she shifted her attention to a magazine on the coffee table in front of the couch.

A few minutes later, Terry returned to the room, placing her drink beside her on a side table. Emma, feeling parched, hastily consumed half of the drink, only to realize that alcohol had been added. Panicked, she questioned, "Terry, how much rum did you put in my drink?"

With a sinister edge, he retorted, "Don't be a lightweight."

Emma protested, "Lightweight? I need to drive back home! Another one of these, and I'll be under the table."

Emma's unease grew, and she placed the remaining drink back on the table before hastily walking to the front door and exiting the trailer. Terry followed her outside, the sense of discomfort lingering in the cool air.

"Wait a second, Emma," Terry implored, his voice filled with unsettling eagerness. "I'm sorry I got upset with you for being in the house earlier. Let me make it up to you and show you something fascinating we have on the farm."

Emma hesitated, her apprehension deepening. "I'd love to, but I really need to get going," she replied, her voice quivering.

Terry's grip tightened as he took her by the hand, leading her to the passenger side of his truck. "I'm not taking no for an answer," he insisted, his tone growing more forceful. "Just thirty minutes tops, plus it'll give you time to sober up."

Reluctantly, Emma climbed into the truck, and they sped off up the mountain. In just a short distance, the road widened, leading to a large graveled lot encircled by a few desolate outbuildings and one imposing, looming barn. Emma, struggling to regain her balance, felt her head spinning as she stepped out of the truck, her unease growing more palpable by the moment. She tried to stand her ground near the vehicle, but Terry's vice-like grip on her arm left her feeling powerless, as he led her through the barn toward a cavernous opening in the far back. The ominous darkness of the cave swallowed them both, and a sense of dread continued to clutch at Emma's heart.

They paused briefly at the cave entrance, where Terry retrieved a helmet with an integrated light from the wall, and they proceeded further into the cavern. As they ventured deeper into the tunnel, an oppressive darkness enveloped them, and the headlamp became their sole guide through the abyss. Emma's right foot inadvertently caught on an unseen obstacle, causing her to stumble and fall to the ground. Terry, relentless in his grip on her arm, swiftly hoisted her back to her feet, but not without a sharp, searing pain radiating through her shoulder.

"Come on, Emma, just a little farther," Terry muttered, his voice taking on an ominous edge as he urged them forward. Eventually, they reached a chamber that housed what appeared to be a crude elevator. Leading her toward it, he flung open the elevator door and forcibly pushed Emma inside.

"Emma, do you like to play games?" he inquired, his tone taking on a sinister edge. "I'm going to lower you down."

Emma's head throbbed with anxiety, and she desperately wished to resist, to escape this pit of doom. But her body felt uncooperative, like wobbly Jell-O, rendering her powerless as Terry shut the elevator's screen.

Gradually, Emma began to regain consciousness. Her eyes fluttered open, revealing a pitch-black environment, sporadically interrupted by a sickly, yellowish glow emanating from somewhere across the room. Struggling to awaken fully, she tried to shift into an upright position but found that her legs refused to obey, leaving her trapped in a nightmarish limbo.

"Where am I?" Emma's thoughts raced, her initial sense of solitude shattered when Terry's voice abruptly sliced through the eerie silence. "Don't worry about it; you're somewhere safe," he murmured in a calm, unsettling tone. Straining her eyes toward the source of the voice, Emma's vision slowly adapted to the dimly lit surroundings. Across the room, she discerned Terry's face, his posture implying he held a candle at chest level. The feeble illumination cast sinister shadows across his features, reminiscent of a scene from a nightmarish horror tale. She could discern a sinister grin enveloping his face as he began to speak.

"Do you like to play games, Emma?" he inquired, his words echoing with an ominous weight. Emma vaguely recalled his mention of games earlier but remained baffled by their meaning. "Whatever you're doing, Terry, this isn't funny," she protested, her voice barely rising above a faint whisper.

"Oh, this isn't a game about fun. This game is more about life," he paused for a harrowing moment, his sinister countenance transforming into unbridled delight as he concluded, "...and death."

"Terry, I don't understand any of this, and you're starting to scare the hell out of me!" Emma finally gathered the courage to raise her voice.

Terry took a step closer to Emma, sinking to a knee, now mere feet away from her prone form. He scrutinized her from head to toe, then placed the candle on the ground and extended both arms toward her. Instinctively, Emma attempted to block him, but her bound wrists left her defenseless. Her hope dwindled rapidly as Terry's outstretched hands homed in on an unexpected target, one that wasn't her neck. With swiftness and force, Terry seized her by the shoulders, lifting her into a sitting position before gently guiding her back against the room's cold, unforgiving stone wall.

The cold, clammy embrace of the stone wall sent relentless shivers coursing through Emma's trembling body.

Emma, unable to confront the horrors she believed awaited her, had closed her eyes tightly, a futile attempt to escape her grim reality. Slowly, the lids lifted, revealing Terry's face lurking ominously in front of her.

"I'm going to leave for a few days, but I promise I'll be back," he calmly stated, his words a disconcerting whisper in the oppressive silence.

"What? You're not going to leave me down here?" Emma's voice quivered with fear.

"Don't you want to know how the game is played before I leave?" he remarked, his voice dripping with sinister intent.

"This is a game my father taught me. My father and grandfather were predators, hunting the weak and unwanted. It was a game to them, one with a twisted scoreboard. That was the life I was born into, the life that was supposed to feel normal. Around the age of ten, my father started grooming me for our true family business of killing. Like a cat stalking its prey, he'd study their routines, finding the perfect site for an ambush. We'd sit for hours in the Jeep as he detailed what was about to happen. Later, I was locked in a closet, forced to watch as he took lives."

Emma felt like she was having an out-of-body experience. She observed the unfolding scene as if she were a voyeur, not an active participant, while Terry outlined the sinister rules of the game. It was a twisted variation of hide and seek, one where the stakes were terrifyingly high, and only one participant would emerge alive.

"Terry, how did they get away with this? Didn't the families notify the police?" Emma asked.

Terry laughed condescendingly. "You were just like most of their victims—naive and unaware," he sneered. Emma's confusion was evident. "They preyed on the transient workers at the resorts! You work there. Everyone has issues, most are running from something. Do you think their families even know where they are? No, they don't. That's why they're not missed; most are forgotten!"

"Now that you know about my messed-up family, any more questions?" Terry smirked.

"How's Steve Taylor involved in all this?" Emma pressed.

"Taylor was an opportunity you provided, through your hatred of the man," Terry responded.

"Wait, you can't blame me for this," Emma protested.

"Blame? No one's blaming you. I'm giving credit where credit's due. Your insistence on my following Taylor gave me the idea and opportunity to plant evidence in his storage unit. I'd worked with him for years and never knew he had an offsite location."

Terry continued to explain that he had provided Emma with enough sustenance in the form of Gatorade and tins of sardines to last about five days. During that time, he would seamlessly return to his daily routine, patiently awaiting the inevitable search led by the relentless Sheriff. After approximately seven days, if he remained uncaught, he would come back and release her from her nightmarish captivity.

"But if you've only left me with five days of food and drink, how will I survive if you don't return until after seven days?" Emma questioned, her voice trembling with desperation.

Terry chuckled darkly before responding, "Emma, I can't have you simply lounging around, consuming resources while I do all the work. You'll have to figure it out."

As Terry rose to leave, Emma's heart sank. The realization struck her like a heavy blow — he wasn't coming back. It was a final, cruel twist in this sadistic game, giving her a glimmer of hope only to snatch it away, typical of the Lynn family's malevolence.

Devin, sensing the urgency in the Sheriff's voice, had left immediately toward the resorts of Big Sky in search of an answer from Terry on why he failed to let authorities know Sammy wasn't really missing. The drive to Big Sky seemed shorter than normal as late afternoon approached. After the snowstorm early in the month, June quickly bloomed into a typical summer day in Big Sky. With the summer, sunset pushed back to after nine in the evening, the outdoors were fully open to one and all. The typical spots alongside the highway where kayakers put into the river were covered, but very little traffic on the road. Turning off the main highway onto the road leading up to the resorts, passing the golf course littered with carts moving golfers from tee to green, human activity continued to increase as the day wore on.

Approaching six, he finally pulled into the resort parking lot. Exiting his vehicle and entering the restaurant, there was a flurry of staff activity crisscrossing a dining room area with very few customers. "Excuse me, miss, is Terry here?"

"Haven't seen him," she responded as she continued to walk towards the kitchen. Finally, Devin decided to grab the closest person he could find by the arm. "Miss, I'm looking for Terry. Is he working today?"

"We're all supposed to be working today; we had a wedding at four today, but he no-showed," she responded as she walked away.

"Well, this is going nowhere," he thought to himself as he returned to the parking lot. Since he was already out here, he decided to walk over to the coffee shop to see if Sammy had notified her coworkers she was safe. Entering the front door, he only saw Henrietta working behind the counter. He waited until she finished with the only customer in line. "You working solo today?" he asked.

"No, Larissa just left for a break about ten minutes ago," she replied.

"Not sure how to bring it up," Devin paused for a second to gather his thoughts. However, before saying a word, Henrietta acknowledged knowing Sammy was alright. "So she did stop by to let you know everything was fine," Devin confirmed.

"Yep, she stopped by a couple of hours ago. I was in shock when she walked through the front door," Henrietta exclaimed with a smile.

"Awesome to hear. I'm assuming Emma was really relieved," he replied.

"Well, now that you mentioned it, I'm not sure she's aware Sammy is back. Wow, I didn't even think about letting Emma know; I was just so relieved she was alright," Henrietta continued, with a look of angst for letting down her friend. Seeing a look of confusion on the officer's face, she explained that Emma had been off for the past two days.

Devin left the coffee shop and returned to his vehicle, still with an open item on his agenda. He scrolled through the notes on his phone and quickly confirmed Terry Lynn's address. While at the resort, his phone had internet access, so he quickly studied the map, committing the directions to memory. Devin signed off, cranked up the cruiser, and headed south.

After a brisk drive, much shorter by Big Sky standards, taking only thirty-five minutes, Devin found himself at Terry's property. In front of him stood a single trailer, the property behind the trailer sloped upwards with an old farmhouse appearing in the distance. The land between them was a patchwork of rusting cars and trucks, left to decay. With no signs of any vehicles in working condition, Devin was convinced that no one was currently present. However, he felt obligated to knock on the trailer door before embarking on a search of the property. As anticipated, after knocking repeatedly, there was no response.

Devin proceeded around the back of the trailer and made his way up the hill through the auto graveyard. Even amidst the corrosion and encroaching vegetation, he could discern that these vehicles had led a hard life. Among the relics was a 1966 International Harvester pickup, its engine removed and replaced with a tree that had grown to nearly two feet in diameter, reaching skyward. The bed of the truck displayed countless dents, with the wheel wells completely rusted out. Continuing his ascent up the hill towards the house, a vehicle caught his eye. On the driver's door, the faint lettering of "Lynn Brothers Construction" was still discernible. Walking around to the back of the vehicle, Devin found the identifying evidence he needed. Just above the bottom trim on the far-right side of the tailgate, the word "Wagoneer" was still visible.

Suddenly, a voice startled Devin, who had been so engrossed in the auto graveyard that he hadn't heard Terry's truck approaching. Quickly regaining his composure, he explained, "I knocked on the door of the trailer, and no one answered. I was on my way to the house but got distracted by your collection of vehicles."

Terry responded bluntly, "Well, I'm here now, no need to continue to the house."

Devin concurred, saying, "I guess you're right."

Terry inquired, "How can I help you, officer?" Pointing back at the rusty Jeep, Devin asked, "Was this your vehicle?"

Terry replied, "It was my father's vehicle, but it's not for sale."

Devin continued the conversation, saying, "That's a shame. It's a '72, isn't it?"

Terry confirmed, "It's a '72. But why are you here, Deputy? We both know you didn't drive all this way looking for car parts."

Devin decided to be straightforward, saying, "Of course not. I just happen to have a friend with a '71 who's always looking for parts. However, I do owe you an explanation for why I'm here. Earlier, I had stopped by your workplace to let you know Sammy had been found alive."

Terry interrupted, his voice filled with relief, "You found her?"

Devin clarified, "Actually, word had reached her in California, and she returned to clear up the situation."

Terry expressed his amazement, "That's unbelievable, what a relief. Did she explain why she just left without informing anyone?"

Devin carefully phrased his response, knowing that Sammy had indicated Terry was fully aware of her departure. "That is strange," he agreed. "So you didn't have any inkling that she was thinking about leaving?"

Terry responded, "Officer, the last time I saw her was in the cafeteria. It was obvious she was having a rough day, but there was no indication she was going to run off."

As Devin listened, a lump formed in his throat, and the hairs on the back of his neck began to prickle. He was now certain that the Sheriff's hunch was correct. Why else would Terry blatantly lie about his knowledge of Sammy's whereabouts? However, he found himself in the middle of nowhere without backup. His revolver was holstered at his hip, but he hesitated to openly challenge Terry's honesty.

Deciding to exit the situation for now, Devin said, "Fair enough. Well, I've taken up enough of your time, Mr. Lynn. Good day."

Devin walked back down the hill and headed towards town. Once he was back on the highway, where the reception was better, he tried calling Mikeal. The phone quickly went to voicemail. He then attempted the office line but had no luck. Worry gnawed at him as he wondered, "Sheriff, where are you?"

After settling Allison down, by enlightening her with his plan, Mikeal left the office and returned home. Entering his home, he removed his gun belt and placed his phone on the counter. He needed to clear his head of all the thoughts and new revelations the day had brought.

The forest had served as his sanctuary throughout his entire life. Regardless of the difficulties he faced at home or the challenges of work, a weekend in the woods unfailingly revived his spirit and honed his mind. With increasing age and responsibilities, this escape had grown more elusive. Stepping from his deck onto the earth below, he struggled to recall the last time he had truly immersed himself in the wilderness. As he ventured through the cleared expanse of his yard, memories from his youth cascaded over him, briefly replacing his thoughts of seeking justice for the forgotten graves left within the forest.

Upon reaching the edge of the woods, he meticulously surveyed the ground and spotted a small tuft of fur about ten feet away. Kneeling down to investigate, he discerned the remains of an unfortunate rabbit, its fate sealed by a larger predator, likely a coyote, but possibly something larger. Mikeal proceeded deeper into the woods, the journey taking him closer to the rushing water he could hear up ahead. Several streams originating from the mountains behind his home meandered through the woods, though this time of year, they were more a gentle trickle than the swift-flowing water that echoed in front of him.

The forest floor gradually transformed, with vegetation increasing as he approached the source of the sound. Lush ferns and other shrubs seemed to thrive in the damp soil. The stream was as narrow as it was deep, measuring approximately two feet across and from surface to bottom. The water, clear as crystal, was icy cold to the touch. Mikeal traced the water's course as it descended into the valley, entranced by the soothing sounds.

However, his tranquility was disrupted by the sharp snap of a twig, the sound originating from above. Having bent over to scoop water from the creek, he was concealed by the ferns as he scanned the area. A hushed exclamation escaped his lips as he spotted the source of the noise. Crossing the ridge about twenty-five yards above him was a substantial-sized gray wolf. Raised in the South, he was well-versed in distinguishing coyotes, and this creature was notably larger. Mikeal remained hidden until the wolf disappeared from view. Before rising, he checked his watch; it was nearly eight in the evening. He hadn't ventured deep into the woods, but he knew he needed to start heading home, as the sun was approaching the horizon and starting to cast long shadows through the trees.

Upon returning home, the first thing that caught his attention was the blinking light on his phone. "I can never escape work," he muttered to himself as he rummaged through the refrigerator in search of a meal. However, this time, work would have to wait. His brief sojourn in the forest had provided a moment of respite, reconnecting him with his true passion: nature. With a clearer mind and a growing rumble in his stomach, he acknowledged that he hadn't eaten all day. He retrieved sandwich ingredients from the refrigerator and settled at the table.

Unfortunately, the promise of a peaceful dinner was shattered by a knock on the front door. "Damn," Mikeal muttered, "I can't catch a break." The knocking persisted. "Hold on," he called out, "I'll be there in a minute." He returned the cold cuts to the refrigerator and then made his way to the front door. Opening it, he was greeted by Allison.

"Sheriff, are you alright?"

"Am I alright? What do you mean, am I alright?" Mikeal replied, somewhat taken aback.

"Sir, Devin had been trying to call you, and I've been trying to call you, but no one answered. With the accident, we were worried you might have passed out again!"

Mikeal could see the genuine concern in her eyes. In this remote corner of Big Sky country, Allison and Devin were the closest things to family he had. He should be grateful that at least someone cared about his well-being. "I'm fine, Allison. I went out into the woods without my phone. I just got back about fifteen minutes ago and haven't had a chance to check my messages. What's going on that's so urgent it couldn't wait?" Mikeal inquired.

"Devin said he found something out at Terry Lynn's place we needed to investigate further."
"What's it?" Mikeal asked.
"An early seventies Jeep Wagoneer!" Allison exclaimed.

Mikeal locked up the house and jumped in the cruiser with Allison. Within fifteen minutes they were pulling into the station's parking lot where they were immediately encountered by Devin before having a chance to enter the building.

"Sir, I'm pretty sure I've found the Jeep from the photo; it's out at the old Lynn family farm," Devin almost shouted barely able to contain his excitement.

"Excellent work, Devin," the Sheriff commended.

"He's definitely hiding something Sheriff! He's still claiming he didn't know Sammy had left."

"Even after you told him she identified him as knowing in her statement?" Allison inquired.

"I decided not to share that info with him," Devin replied.

"Did you ask Terry about the Jeep?" Mikeal asked.

"Yeah, he admitted it was his father's company vehicle, but wasn't willing to say much else," Devin explained.

"We probably need to get a forensic team over there before he tries to move it. I'll call the DA to get approval," Mikeal stated as he entered the station.

"Sir, I don't think he could move it if he wanted to. The hillside is littered with old abandoned vehicles. The vehicle probably hasn't moved in twenty years," Devin noted.

"Good to know. I'll still call the DA. Devin, organize a team to head back out there tonight. If there's any carpet remaining, let's pull it and get it to the lab," Mikeal ordered.

"Sir, there's what looks like the old family farmhouse. Should we search it as well?" Devin asked.

"I'll ask and see what the DA allows," Mikeal replied.

Mikeal retreated to his office and dialed DA Weber's home number. After a brief hold, Courtney answered. "Sheriff, why are you calling me this late? Don't you ever take a break?"

"Believe me, Mrs. Weber, this is the last thing I had planned for today. However, we may have caught a break in our investigation of the skeletons found at Hebgen Lake. Deputy Devin believes he's found a vehicle matching the description of a Jeep sighted in two of the three disappearances. We'd like to search the vehicle and remove the carpet for testing."

"You have evidence that this vehicle was potentially involved in the abductions?" she inquired.

"Yes, written documentation in one case and a photo in another," Mikeal confirmed.

"Alright, seems reasonable enough. When do you need this, Sheriff?"

"Now," Mikeal urgently replied.

"Consider it done, Sheriff."

"Great. One other favor; there's also an old abandoned house on the property we'd like to search it as well."

"Any evidence suggesting a crime took place in the house?" she asked.

"No, not at this time, but since we're there?"

"No, Sheriff, I think it's best to stick with the vehicle. If you find something there, then I'll give you permission to search the home."

"Fair enough. We'll start with the vehicle and go from there." Mikeal walked out of his office. "We're good to go, Devin do you have a Team put together?"

Devin acknowledged the team was in place, before asking if they had authority to also search the house.

"No, our primary focus will be the Jeep. Let's take a flatbed and pull it out of there. I'll feel better if we take complete control of the vehicle."

CHAPTER 24

Mikeal printed the seizure notice that the District Attorney had emailed before grabbing his jacket and heading out the door to join Devin. The day had been beautiful, but heading up into the mountains, the temperature was expected to drop to the mid-forties within hours of the sun going down.

"You have our paperwork?" Devin asked. Mikeal nodded that he did, and Devin continued, "The flatbed will meet us out at the Lynn farm around ten."

"Well, let's quit jabbing and start moving; it's not a short drive," Mikeal responded, eager to get the show on the road. Sensing that the Sheriff was becoming a little irritable, Devin put the vehicle in drive, and they quietly pulled out of the parking lot, headed towards the highway that would take them back up into the mountains.

Over the next thirty minutes, they traveled in silence. It was dark by now, and as Mikeal sat staring out the passenger window into complete darkness, his mind had switched to focusing on the news he was given after his auto accident. He felt like he needed to share with someone, but even though Devin and Allison were the closest thing he had to family, he was concerned that sharing would make him vulnerable in their eyes. However, Mikeal realized he would never have a better opportunity to privately discuss his situation with Devin.

"Devin, you've probably wondered what caused my accident," Mikeal began.

"I assumed you dozed off for a second, but that's about it," Devin responded. "I figured if there was more to it, you'd eventually let us know."

"Devin, I have a brain tumor," Mikeal bluntly declared.

"Jesus, a brain tumor!" a shocked Devin replied.

Seeing the look of horror on his face, Mikeal quickly tried to downplay the situation. "It's small, and the doc believes it was caught early, so there shouldn't be any long-term effects," Mikeal added.

"Will they go in and remove it?" Devin asked.

"No, we're going the chemo route," the Sheriff replied.

"So you'll..." Devin began.

"Well, maybe. The doc says each patient reacts differently to the treatment. I'm sure there may be some hair loss, plenty of vomiting, and fatigue, but nothing more than that," Mikeal tried to reassure his deputy.

"When does this start?"

"Next Friday," the Sheriff responded. "How long will all this go on?"

"Every Friday for four weeks; the doctor said this was called a cycle. He would reevaluate the results versus the dosage, make any necessary adjustments, followed by another four weeks of treatments."

"Then it's over?" Devin asked.

"Unfortunately, no. The doc said I would need to complete what he called a course of treatments. Evidently, one course consists of about three to six of these four-week cycles, so I'm looking at about three months at the earliest to finish."

"Well, whatever you need from me, Sheriff, don't hesitate to ask," Devin offered.

"Thanks, Devin. The only thing I would ask right now is, let's keep this between ourselves until we see how these treatments affect my outward appearance."

"You need to let Allison know," Devin stated.

"Yes, Allison deserves to know as well. Let me handle that in my own time. I'll let you know after I have spoken with her. Until that time, Devin, please keep this info to yourself."

"You have my word, Sheriff."

Devin and Mikeal arrived at the Lynn family farm first, parking directly under a telephone pole with a large floodlight perched atop it, illuminating a substantial portion of the area around the trailer. They exited the vehicle and waited for the flatbed truck to arrive. Devin pointed in the direction of the jeep, but even with a crescent moon, complete darkness concealed the hillside auto graveyard.

A few minutes later, the flatbed pulled up just as the duo was approaching the darkened trailer to announce their presence. After knocking on the door without an answer, they both proceeded up the hill to where the Jeep lay. Mikeal and Devin, with flashlights out, led the way, with the driver slowly following in the truck. Devin, knowing the direction, kept his light focused on what lay in front of him, while Mikeal shone his flashlight all around the scene, which reminded him of his native North Carolina.

Backwoods farmers and loggers from back home would squeeze every useful minute out of their equipment. It would break down, and they would repair it, repeating the process over and over until all the life was drained from it. Wherever it took its final breath, it would lay until it rusted back into the earth. Mikeal quickly counted about fifteen vehicles scattered across the side of the mountain slope. All had lived a hard life and were unceremoniously dumped there to rot.

"Here it is!" Devin's excited voice broke the eerie silence. Mikeal circled the vehicle, its remaining paint weathered and faded from decades of exposure to the elements. Fortunately, all its glass was still intact, and the interior, though faded from the sun's relentless onslaught, retained its seats and carpeting. Perhaps, deep within the worn fibers of this material, evidence of a long-forgotten crime still lingered.

Mikeal fought the temptation to open the door, fully aware that one misstep could contaminate a potential crime scene. The experts at the state's lab would handle this with precision, and he needed to exercise patience. "Great job finding this vehicle, Devin. This has to be what we saw in the photo."

"Thanks, I only hope we can find useful evidence inside," Devin remarked. Mikeal could feel the temperature starting to drop as he clenched his exposed hands. His eyes, now somewhat adjusted to the night, could make out the silhouette of a house higher up on the hillside.

"Let's go take a look at this house," Mikeal told Devin as he started the climb, leaving the driver and the flatbed to load the vehicle alone. As tempting as it was to enter the home, haunted by the mental scars of his early days as an officer mishandling evidence, Mikeal was determined to follow the correct procedures to ensure no potential evidence would be dismissed in court.

As the two men continued to advance towards the old house, their conversation continued, "Are we going inside?" Devin asked.

"Devin, I told you the DA said no," Mikeal responded. "Anything we find wouldn't be admissible in court."

"In court?" Devin questioned. "We're never going to trial with this. If your suspicion is correct and Terry's father was somehow involved, he's dead. Any potential punishment ended when he died over a decade ago. Sheriff, this is about closure for the families," Devin emphatically stated. Mikeal knew Devin was correct; hopes of finding a live killer had quickly faded.

"You're right, Devin. But what's the hurry then? No one will be trying to flee town. Let's see what the lab finds and go from there. If they find nothing, we're done. The DA has already indicated she won't prosecute Steve Taylor based on our current evidence, which is probably the correct thing to do. Heck, I even have my doubts he was involved."

Terry was suddenly awakened by the hushed, eerie voices of men that seemed to emanate from outside the home he grew up in. His earlier encounter with the deputy, their discussion revolving around the decaying Jeep, had ignited suspicions that this might be connected to some of the family's long-buried secrets. Understanding that staying in his trailer near the front of the property would leave him with no escape route if the need arose, he had retreated to the farmhouse. Uncertain of what the police might have discovered, Terry had taken precautions, arming himself with a high-powered rifle and a 9mm revolver. The old house around him creaked and groaned in the darkness as he cautiously inched closer to the window, heart pounding. With a mixture of fear and exhilaration, he knew every creaky board in the house and could move quietly. He peeled back the edge of the newspaper and peered through the dusty glass, his breath held.

In the distance, he observed beams of light meandering down the hill and deduced that the officers were engaged in the task of removing the Jeep. The idea of firing upon the two deputies at the house flashed through his mind, but it quickly faded, replaced by the realization that it would leave him stranded uphill, unable to make a swift escape or intervene in the removal of the vehicle.

The situation was growing more intricate by the moment, and Terry's thoughts churned with a flurry of strategic considerations. Most people would have been terrified in Terry's predicament, but for him, this was when he truly came alive. The adrenaline rush of imminent danger was his drug of choice. His senses were heightened, and he felt a surge of determination. The cat and mouse game had begun.

As the two officers continued their perimeter check, their attention eventually shifted to the sole outbuilding that remained standing.

"I'm guessing that's the outhouse," Devin chuckled, glancing at the Sheriff.

"Yep, seems like it," Mikeal affirmed.

"Did you have one of these growing up, Sheriff?" Devin quipped.

Somewhat taken aback, Mikeal retorted, "Devin, how old do I look? I might have grown up in the South, but we had indoor plumbing in the sixties."

"Sheriff, just pulling your leg," Devin chuckled.

Mikeal's interest was piqued as he approached the outhouse. "Well, that's peculiar," he exclaimed. "Look at this lock—it's relatively new. Everything else around here is rusted and begging for maintenance, yet, for some reason, the outhouse is secured with a new lock. Doesn't quite add up, does it?"

Devin shrugged. "Who knows? Maybe they lost the keys to the old one and had to replace it?"

Meanwhile, Terry had stealthily maneuvered from one side of the house to the other, aiming to gain a better view of the outhouse and the officers inspecting it. By the time he managed to peel away a section of newspaper from the window, he lost sight of the officers but could still hear their voices. He swiftly deduced that they must have shifted to the backside. Terry knew his hand was being forced, and he had no choice but to act. If they decided to forcibly enter the small building, he had no doubt they would discover the secret passage leading to the tunnel network created by miners over a hundred years ago, later rediscovered by the Lynn Brothers in the sixties.

"Devin, give me a lift," the Sheriff requested. On the backside of the outhouse, about seven feet above the ground, there was a narrow three-by-ten-inch slit cut out of the wall. "Boost me up here; I want to take a look inside." Devin cupped his hands together and bent at the waist to create a foothold, allowing Mikeal to be hoisted high enough to peer inside. "What do you see?" Devin asked, straining under the weight of Mikeal's 205 pounds.

"Alright, put me back down," Mikeal replied. "Nothing in there but the throne."

All eyes converged downhill as the winch roared to life, yanking the Jeep from its decade-long slumber and splitting the heavy night air with its metallic cry. The flat, stubborn tires, worn and weathered from years of disuse, clung to the ground until the relentless winch wrestled the vehicle onto the inclined trailer platform. Once the Jeep's rear tires finally cleared the flatbed's edge, the operator deftly lowered the platform flush with the truck's frame, continuing to inch the vehicle backward. Terry, still lurking in the shadows, watched both men scuttle down the hillside toward the mechanical symphony.

Meanwhile, Devin scrutinized the vacated spot where the Jeep had been lying, searching for any elusive clues, but found nothing of significance. With the vehicle securely chained down on the flatbed, the driver approached Devin, requesting his signature before they could tow the Jeep away.

"Devin, do you have a copy of the court order to leave at the trailer door?" Mikeal inquired.

"Yes, sir. It's in the Tahoe," Devin replied.

"Perfect. Let's get out of here."

The next several days passed without incident, nor any movement in the case. As the DA, Courtney Weber, had expected, once Steve Taylor had been freed from his incarceration, he quickly dropped the complaint against Jordan and the Sheriff's Department. This allowed her to team with Allison on the twenty-four-hour surveillance in place on Mr. Taylor.

The forensic team had painstakingly disassembled the Jeep, meticulously examining it bolt by bolt. After removing the seats, they swiftly extracted the carpeting, shipping it across the state to Dr. Baldwin's lab. Mikeal couldn't shake the nagging question of how Tina's bloodied clothes ended up in that warehouse. He found himself pondering whether there was a connection between Terry's father and Steve's, and whether they were being ensnared to atone for their fathers' sins.

Over the last two days, Mikeal had made it a point to leave the office at five, go directly home, and eat a semi-healthy dinner before spending the remaining daylight hours in the woods. Throughout his career, he was taught to never show fear, and he felt that was achieved at work. However, as

Friday and the start of his cancer treatments approached, the fear of the unknown was starting to tie his stomach in knots.

Strolling through the woods each evening was a therapeutic escape for Mikeal, a brief respite from the looming specter of chemotherapy that lay ahead. In the serene embrace of nature, he found solace and immersed himself in the captivating beauty of the woods. The relentless march of summer had yielded to the majestic arrival of fall, and by mid-October, the forest had transformed into a kaleidoscope of colors. It was a rekindling of his connection with an old friend, a bond he had inadvertently neglected.

The memories flooded back, washing over him like a warm embrace from the past. During his younger years, from his early twenties well into his forties, every fall season was synonymous with hunting. Mikeal had honed his skills, becoming an expert marksman with a rifle and mastering the art of the compound bow. The opening act was turkey season, where he would rendezvous with his two brothers. Together, they'd spend countless hours, concealed at the edge of a tree line, coaxing turkeys into a fateful encounter with their maker.

In those moments of anticipation and quietude, they'd also traverse the corridors of their shared youth, reliving anecdotes and stories from their Deep South upbringing. It was a time of reflection and bonding, an annual tradition that allowed Mikeal to rediscover his roots and cherish the camaraderie of family, just as the woods around him transformed with the changing seasons.

One particular childhood experience always stood out as the culmination of Mikeal and his brothers leaving childhood behind and entering the adult world. Each passing year, the story, the tale acquired a darker and more perilous hue.

It had been a scorching couple of weeks in Western North Carolina. Mikeal, who was seventeen at the time, decided to take his two younger brothers, aged fourteen and twelve respectively, along with a neighbor boy named Howard Alexander over to Deep Creek, near Bryson City.

Deep Creek, especially in the summer months, never lived up to its name. Its main purpose was an area for families to easily tube down the creek with basically no threat of being injured. The real thrill-seekers headed to the Nantahala River, renting kayaks and rafts. When the floodgates were opened at the dam, it created a thrilling experience, albeit one that required caution. Every year, there were fatalities. The Lancaster boys didn't have the money to participate at that level, but they had learned that if you continued to follow Deep Creek farther back into the mountains, you would eventually reach a deep pool of water.

That was their destination that day. They had quickly climbed from the parking lot up the wide trail running along Deep Creek, reaching the usual trail end in less than twenty minutes. While other visitors were exiting the trail to climb down to the mild water below, the Lancaster boys and their friend continued to climb higher into the mountains. The mountain leveled out, and a well-worn trail emerged, leading off the side of the mountain. The boys quickly scrambled down the rock face, reaching the deep pool located fifty feet below. As they had done countless times before, they spent the afternoon daring each other to climb higher and higher up the rock face and dive into the forty-degree water below.

After several hours, the repeated plunges into the cold water were taking the fun out of their adventure. Mikeal looked over at his youngest brother, who was shivering, with a slight blue tint developing on his lips.

"Alright, time to go," he shouted at the group. His two brothers quickly grabbed their stuff and started to climb out of the canyon. Howard wanted to stay, but Mikeal told him that wouldn't be possible. Dejectedly, he grabbed his stuff and started to climb out, followed by Mikeal. It only took about ten minutes before they reached the trail at the top of the rocks. As they started to make their way down the trail, Mikeal noticed Howard was staring into the canyon below.

"Hey, keep your eyes on the trail," he shouted at Howard. Startled, as if he had been daydreaming, Howard quickly turned back to face Mikeal, but his right foot slipped off the edge of the trail. Instinctively, as Mikeal saw him start to go over the edge, he reached out and grabbed him by his shoulder. Howard's momentum acted like a catapult, shooting Mikeal out from the rocks like a slingshot. Mikeal's gaze fixed on the sky as he felt like he was dropping from the heavens in slow motion. This abruptly ended as he hit the water flat on his back, completely knocking the breath out of his body, before rolling over and sinking to the bottom of the pool.

The sound of running water had returned Mikeal to the present day. He realized he was near the spot where he had seen the wolf a few days earlier. He took a seat against a tree overlooking the stream and tried to relax and distance himself from the dark memories of Deep Creek.

With the uncertainty of his tumor diagnosis, he wished he had stayed closer with his family. Over the years, each of his brothers had married and started their own families. The frequency of the hunts had slowed until they eventually stopped completely. As a lifelong bachelor, Mikeal had quickly lost touch with his family, and he had no one to share his stories from the past. This is when he became closer with Chief John Wolf, who also shared the love of hunting and the outdoors.

Eventually, Mikeal's restlessness pushed him to look for new adventures, ultimately resulting in his decision to move west to Montana. As he sat there in quiet contemplation, it all seemed like a lifetime ago. He hadn't seen his brothers in years, maybe spoke to them once or twice a year by phone, and, in general, had lost touch with everyone from his past. With the chemo treatment just days away, should he call them and at least let them know, or does he wait and see? He didn't want to alarm anyone; after all, the doctor said they caught it early. As he turned and headed back towards the house, he had already decided he would take a wait-and-see attitude regarding the treatment.

CHAPTER 25

"Morning, Sheriff," Allison greeted Mikeal and Devin as they entered the station. Mikeal responded with a warm, "Good morning." "Sir, we received an email from the body shop. They expect your Tahoe to be ready by the middle of next week." Devin couldn't contain his enthusiasm, blurting out, "That's wonderful news!" He quickly turned to gauge Mikeal's reaction. "What's wrong, not pleased with your chauffeur assignment?" Mikeal teased before turning and heading to his office.

Seated behind his desk, Mikeal prepared for what promised to be a long day. It would take at least a week for the lab to process the Jeep, and new developments from Dr. Baldwin had come to a halt a couple of weeks ago. Of course, there were the usual tasks and paperwork that continually found their way to his desk, but nothing substantial to occupy his mind and divert his attention from the looming Friday appointment. As anticipated, the morning inched along with Mikeal answering emails and diligently updating his notes on the Hebgen Lake investigation.

Around ten-thirty, a call was patched through to the Sheriff's office. "This is Sheriff Mikeal Lancaster, can I help you?"

"Sheriff, this is Steve Taylor."

Caught off guard, Mikeal remained silent for a couple of seconds before responding. "Well, Mr. Taylor, this is a surprise. How may I help you?"

"Sheriff, this is my first day back at work since our misunderstanding. Frankly, based on what happened, I've been too depressed and embarrassed to show my face at work. However, like everyone else, I need a paycheck to survive."

"Mr. Taylor, I can understand the difficulty you're having, but we were just doing our job. I'm sorry for your current struggles."

Steve interrupted, "Sheriff, I'm not looking for an apology. Emma has missed her last three shifts, no messages, nothing to her coworkers, just silence."

Mikeal sat up in his chair, a feeling of dread settling in. "When was the last time anyone saw her?"

"I'm not sure, maybe last Friday," Steve responded.

Mikeal tried to remember when Emma was at the station, it was sometime last week, maybe Wednesday, he would check with Allison to confirm. "Alright, sit tight Mr. Taylor; we're leaving now, should be there in about an hour. Don't speak with anyone else about this." Mikeal was quickly out of his office.

"Allison and Devin, grab your jackets; we're heading back out to Big Sky," Mikeal commanded. He continued, "Allison, follow us in your vehicle. I'll explain the call I just received from Steve Taylor on the way."

They were soon on the highway, ascending into the mountains. Mikeal sat in the passenger seat, called Allison, and put the phone on speaker. He began to fill them in on the details of the call from Steve. "Devin, when we arrive, find Terry Lynn and press him hard on Emma's whereabouts," Mikeal instructed. "We know he's deceitful, so we need to analyze his every word. We need to know the last time he saw or spoke with Emma and the location."

"Do you think he knows something?" Allison inquired.

"Without a doubt!" Devin responded with conviction.

"True, but we have nothing to force him to talk," Mikeal added.

This situation felt different to all three of them. Unlike Sammy's disappearance, there was genuine concern that Emma might be in trouble. Turning off the highway, Mikeal issued additional orders, "Allison, you and I will head to the coffee shop and gather individual statements from her coworkers."

Arriving at the resort, Devin quickly made his way to the restaurant. He could see Terry working in the kitchen area. "Mister Lynn, can I speak with you for a moment?" Devin inquired.

"If it's about the truck you took, you'll have to wait until my attorney's present," Terry replied from the back.

Devin, walking towards the kitchen, responded, "With your attorney present, why do you need an attorney?"

"I'm not sure what you need that old truck for, but you guys tore up the ground and grass pulling it out, and I need to be compensated!" Terry argued.

Uncharacteristically breaking from his usual calm demeanor, Devin fired back, "Give me a break. It was overgrown in weeds parked on the mountainside. You're not getting a damn thing back for damages."

Without allowing Terry to answer back, Devin continued, "I need to know the last time you spoke with your co-worker, Emma. I need to know the time, place, and what the discussion was about. We can do it here, or I can drag you back to the station. Your choice."

"Chill, dude," was Terry's response. "No need to get hostile." He turned to another person in the kitchen and said, "Gary, I'm going to step out for a few minutes. You got this."

Gary, without looking up from chopping up vegetables, nodded in the affirmative.

Terry walked out of the kitchen and motioned to Devin to have a seat at one of the tables. "Let's see, it must have been early last week, maybe Monday or Tuesday when I last saw Emma," Terry answered. "She stopped by on her lunch break, but I'm not sure what we talked about."

"Think a little harder, Terry. It may be important," Devin pressed.

"Why? What's going on? Now that I think about it, I haven't seen her in a while," Terry said with concern. "Is she alright?"

"We don't know," Devin reluctantly answered. "We've been informed she's missed a couple of shifts with no calls or explanations. We're just trying to determine when she was last seen and her current state of mind."

Terry sat silently, as if deep in thought for a few seconds, before looking up at Devin. "Definitely last Tuesday. I brought out her lunch, asked how she was doing. Everything was fine, but she was still worried about Sammy. We may have spoken for thirty seconds, and I needed to get back in the kitchen. It was a very busy day; most of it was a blur."

"Don't you have waiters?" Devin asked.

"Of course, we have waiters. That's a pretty stupid question," Terry laughed, responding.

"Alright, let me ask another stupid question. If it was so busy in the kitchen, why were you acting like a waiter?" Devin shot back.

Terry gave Devin a defiant look with his eyes before abruptly standing and retreating back to the kitchen area.

All three officers convened at the cruisers after completing interviews with the staff. As expected, nothing major was uncovered. It appeared that the last time Emma was seen at work was on Thursday. Nothing seemed out of the ordinary, but she was still focused on finding out what happened to Sammy.

"Allison, if you would take a ride over to her apartment and find out when was the last time her roommate saw her," Mikeal instructed. "Devin, let's head back to the station. I've got a couple of calls I need to make."

On the way back to town, Devin shared his experience with Terry, "He's a real cocky asshole, Sheriff! There's just something about him that's not right," Devin elaborated.

"Do you think he knows more than he's saying?" Mikeal asked.

"Without a doubt, just like he knew more about where Sammy went but didn't share."

"That's what I don't understand," Mikeal mused. "What did he have to gain from not letting everyone know Sammy was safe and back home in California? None of this makes any sense. If Emma truly was a friend, why would he put her through that uncertainty?"

"I'm with you, Sheriff. It's not something you would expect a normal friend to do," Devin replied.

Mikeal contemplated this for a moment and then added, "Devin, when we get back to the station, why don't you dig a little deeper into Mr. Lynn's background? Let's find out what kind of relationship he had with his father and grandfather. Let's see if we can figure out what makes this guy tick."

Upon returning to the station, Mikeal went back to his office, shutting the door behind him. He was deeply frustrated with himself for not making contact with Emma to confirm she knew Sammy was safe. If he had, it would have alerted them at least four days earlier that she was possibly in trouble. Instead, he had let his focus return to his struggles with his cancer diagnosis. On the return trip from the mountains, he had decided that his chemo treatments would have to wait until he found Emma.

While at the resort, he had asked Allison if, in her surveillance of Steve, she had noticed anything suspicious. She hadn't, but she revealed that Jordan had covered about seventy-five percent of the surveillance. Mikeal placed a call from his office to Deputy Jordan, who was assigned to keep up with Steve Taylor.

"Hey, I received a call from your boy earlier today; evidently one of his employees hasn't shown up for a couple of shifts," Mikeal explained. He listened intently as the deputy outlined Mr. Taylor's movements since being released from jail.

"You're sure he hasn't been out of your sight, even for a couple of hours?" Mikeal asked, a touch of concern in his voice. The officer reiterated that Taylor had primarily remained at home until heading to work this morning.

"Alright, thanks," Mikeal responded before hanging up the phone.

He then made a call to Allison. "What did the roommate have to say?" the Sheriff inquired.

"Nothing we didn't already know. She hadn't seen Emma since last Thursday morning," Allison replied.

"She didn't think that was odd?" Mikeal questioned further.

"Evidently not, Sheriff. She said Emma would often stay with friends who lived closer to work. Anything else you need me to check out before heading into town?" Allison asked.

"No, we're good. I'll see you when you make it back," Mikeal responded.

After returning to the station, Allison was greeted by Devin, who gestured for her to follow him to Mikeal's office. "Sheriff, Allison's back. Are you ready to talk?" Devin inquired.

"Sure, come on in. What did you find out about Mr. Lynn?" Mikeal asked, looking down at his notes.

Devin responded with a concise list: Terry Gregory Lynn's full name, date of birth (March 4th, 1977, Bozeman,

Montana), his father Gary Henry Lynn's birthdate
(December 1st, 1947), and death date (May 15th, 2004).
Devin mentioned that he could only find a birth date for
Terry's mother, Teresa Henderson, born on June 1st, 1951,
who was listed on Terry's birth certificate, but no further
records were available. He attended Gallatin High School but
didn't graduate, with no adult criminal record, only a couple
of minor traffic offenses. However, he did have a sealed
juvenile record, which might explain his lack of high school
graduation. "I'll reach out to the DA and see if we can get
access," Mikeal suggested.

Allison brought up Terry's grandfather, and Mikeal
commended her for the memory. They discussed the
untimely deaths within the Lynn family. Devin added that
Uncle Henry had also died young.

Mikeal recommended a brief reprieve from the somber
details at hand. They were confronting the discovery of three
bodies in a secluded area near the Lynn family's compound.
Among the remains, Tina Lattimer had been positively
identified, prompting speculation that one of the other
bodies might belong to Nancy Hulligan, who mysteriously
vanished back in 1970. Devin also drew attention to the
compelling evidence linking Lynn Brothers Construction to
the vicinity during the time of Nancy's disappearance.

The conversation shifted to a discussion of the potential
involvement of the father or the grandfather in the crimes,
considering their physical capabilities. Mikeal stood up,

signaling deep contemplation, and began to rub his hand through his beard, a sign that Allison and Devin recognized as an indication of deep thought. They exchanged knowing glances, anticipating an impending silence. After a few minutes, Mikeal turned back to face the two deputies.

He discussed the hypothetical scenarios in which the father or grandfather could have been capable of physically abducting women and forcing them into a vehicle. They also had access to a vehicle that matched the description given by an eyewitness and appeared in a photo near another victim's home. Devin asked about the motive, to which Allison responded that rape could sometimes be a crime of passion, not always premeditated.

Mikeal pointed out that Terry wasn't involved as he hadn't even been born at the time of the 1970 disappearances. They wondered if Terry knew some old family secrets. Mikeal then asked about the connection between the Lynns and Steve Taylor. Devin seemed unsure, and Mikeal clarified that besides the Jeep, their only other physical evidence was Tina's clothes found in Steve's storage building. If either Roy or Gary Lynn was the killer, the latest they could have moved the clothes would have been in 2004. Allison raised the question of whether they should have hidden the clothes shortly after the crimes in 1975.

Inquiring about when Steve took over the building from his father, they weren't sure, so they decided to consult their interview notes. Mikeal retrieved the file and began searching through the pages. After a few minutes, he discovered the information they needed: the transfer occurred in 1975. They contemplated the possible involvement of Steve Taylor's father, although they were uncertain.

Devin volunteered to investigate the connection between the Taylors and Lynns, and Allison was assigned to find Emma's parents to confirm that she hadn't returned home. Mikeal planned to call the DA to request access to Terry Lynn's sealed juvenile records. As Allison left the room, Mikeal asked her to close the door behind her. He then dialed DA Weber's number but was informed that court was currently in session, and he should expect a callback later in the day.

CHAPTER 26

When Mikeal arrived the following morning, he found both Devin and Allison already engrossed in their second cup of coffee. "Allison, I heard back from the DA last night. I need you to run over to the courthouse and pick up the records on Mr. Lynn," Mikeal called across the room before vanishing into his office. Allison exchanged a perplexed glance with Devin, silently questioning the sudden change in Mikeal's demeanor. She swiftly finished her coffee, then made her way out of the room through the side door to carry out the task.

Devin was aware that Mikeal's chemo treatments were commencing the next day, a fact he had yet to disclose to Allison. "Hey, everything okay?" Devin inquired, poking his head into Mikeal's office. Mikeal responded with a somewhat distant tone, "Yeah, I'm fine. Why do you ask?" Devin noticed a change in Mikeal's usual composure and the abruptness in issuing orders.

"Your tone was a bit different, somewhat curt with the orders," Devin explained, showing his understanding. "I get it, the nerves about tomorrow."

Mikeal took a deep breath and reclined in his chair. After a moment of staring vacantly at his desk's surface, he met Devin's gaze. "The chemo's going to have to wait. I couldn't sleep at all last night," Mikeal confessed. "I feel like I let Emma down by focusing on my own concerns instead of my duty to protect the citizens of this county."

Devin exchanged a look of disbelief with Mikeal, but before he could respond, Mikeal redirected the conversation back to the Lynn family. "I was planning to visit the resort later this morning to inquire about Mr. Taylor's father's relationship with the Lynn family," Devin reported.

"Let's try reaching him by phone first. He's been very cautious about how he's perceived at work. If we show up to question him again, he'll lawyer up, and we'll hit a dead end," Mikeal suggested. "See if you can get him on the phone," Devin agreed before returning to his desk.

An hour later, Allison returned from the courthouse with the juvenile records of Terry Lynn. She placed the file on the corner of Mikeal's desk as he glanced up, ready to delve into its contents. She turned to leave, but Mikeal's words made her pause.

"Hold up, Allison," he said, concern etched on his face. "What's in the file?"

"All I know is what the DA's office told me," she replied. "They said you should be the only one to look at it."

Mikeal nodded and gestured for her to take a seat. With a sense of anticipation and foreboding hanging in the room, he began to skim through the file. As he reviewed the documents, his expression turned grave, and he ceased listing the petty crimes Terry Lynn had committed.

"Sheriff, what is it?" Allison inquired, her curiosity mixed with unease.

Mikeal looked up from the file, his eyes locked onto hers. "The young Mr. Lynn was quite a troublemaker, with a rap sheet including vandalism, trespassing, and shoplifting," he began, his voice tense. Then, his tone shifted, and he uttered the words that sent a chill down Allison's spine. "In ninety-three, he was convicted of attempted rape on a Sandy McKinnon."

Allison was taken aback by the revelation. "I know her," she replied, shock and disbelief in her voice. "But she's an older lady."

"According to the file, she was thirty-three when this happened," Mikeal said. "Does she still live in the area?"

"As far as I know, she still does," Allison replied.

"There are no trial transcripts in this file. See if you can track her down, and we'll pay her a visit," Mikeal directed, his mind already racing with the implications.

Both of them left his office, with Allison heading back to her desk while he made his way to the coffee machine. However, Devin's voice halted his progress.

"Sheriff," Devin called out. Mikeal didn't stop walking but responded, showing his eagerness for information.

"Spoke with Steve Taylor," Devin began. "He was unaware if his father knew or had any dealings with the Lynns. He said we shouldn't rule anything out, though, because his dad's picking hobby had him running into hundreds of people and places. He did confirm that the bathroom was original to the building. So it's possible the clothes have been hidden there since seventy-five."

Allison reappeared at that moment with her own news. "I found Sandy McKinnon," she announced.

"Wow, that was quick," Mikeal responded. "Where?"

"She still teaches over at Gallatin High School," Allison replied, her tone filled with a sense of urgency.

Mikeal glanced at his watch and then back at Allison. "If we hurry, we can catch her around the lunch break," he said, the suspense building as they prepared to uncover more answers.

The patrol vehicle pulled up to the high school shortly before noon. The ominous clouds in the sky seemed to foreshadow something, casting a gloomy atmosphere over the scene. Mikeal and Allison, driven by a sense of urgency, proceeded directly to the office. Inside, they were promptly greeted by the school principal, a stern figure who gave them a curious look.

"Good afternoon, Sheriff. What brings you out our way today?" the principal inquired, a subtle tension in the air.

Allison took the lead in responding, her tone serious. "We'd like to speak with one of your teachers, Sandy McKinnon."

A voice from an unseen woman on the other side of the counter chimed in, "Her class should let out at 12:15; she'll be available then."

The principal wasn't satisfied with just that and probed further. "Can I ask what this is about?"

Mikeal, trying to maintain an air of secrecy, replied, "We're just looking for a little info on an incident from several years back. If possible, is there an office or somewhere we could quietly speak with her?"

The principal studied the Sheriff up and down finally responding, "One of our counselors is out today; you can use their office."

She then directed them to come around to the side door and said she'd bring them into the teachers' lounge. As the principal led the way, the two officers followed. Inside the lounge, she pointed out the office they could use and asked them to have a seat while they waited for Sandy to arrive.

As they sat there, Mikeal decided to break the silence. "I take it you know Sandy," he said to Allison.

Her face carried a mix of nostalgia and mischief as she replied, "I wouldn't say I know her, but she taught here when I graduated. Let's just say I was aware of her."

Mikeal raised an eyebrow at her choice of words. "That sounds ominous," he remarked.

Allison tried to backtrack a little, "No, nothing like that. Let's just say she was the fancy of every high school boy."

Mikeal's curiosity piqued. "So she was a looker," he prodded.

Allison responded, "She was a looker who knew it. Some of the clothes she would wear definitely didn't pass the dress code the female students had to adhere to."

Mikeal pressed further, "When was the last time you saw her?"

Allison's memories resurfaced. "It's easily been a decade, maybe fifteen years."

With a teasing tone, Mikeal joked, "What if she's now about two hundred pounds?"

Allison was about to respond when the door to the lounge opened, revealing their guest. They both stood up to greet her, and after an awkward silence, Allison finally spoke, "Mrs. McKinnon, I'm Deputy Allison, and this is Sheriff Mikeal Lancaster. We were wondering if you had a few minutes to discuss something from your past that may be relevant to a current case we're working on."

Sandy McKinnon remained silent for a moment, her eyes locked on Mikeal's. Time had indeed been generous to her; in her early fifties, she still had the slim body of a much younger athlete. She wore a striking red V-cut dress, which seemed to captivate Mikeal upon first glance.

"Well, dear, you'll need to be a little more specific," Sandy responded. "I've never claimed to be Mother Teresa; there are several things from my past others might deem scandalous."

Allison's old feelings toward Sandy were rekindled, and she couldn't help herself. "I know I shouldn't, but..." She cleared her throat and continued, "It's about you and Terry Lynn."

Allison had expected satisfaction from knocking Sandy off her pedestal, but instead, she was sorely disappointed. Sandy responded calmly, "What would you like to know?"

Finally breaking free from his trance, Mikeal took the lead. "Ladies, the principal has kindly offered us an office to have this discussion."

They followed Mikeal back to the counselor's office and took their seats. Once everyone was settled, Mikeal began, "Mrs. McKinnon, we're looking into a number of old cold case files. In the notes, there are a few references to the Lynn family.

Researching the family is how we came across your incident with Terry back in ninety-three."

Sandy looked at Mikeal and replied, "Sheriff, please call me Sandy. I've never been married, so the 'Mrs.' doesn't apply. What would you like to know? I still remember it like it happened yesterday; it's not something easily forgotten."

Allison interjected, "I'm not sure you're aware of how this works, but after he turned eighteen, he was able to get these records sealed, so it's as though it never happened."

Sandy's response was unexpected. "Oh, Deputy, I most certainly know how this works." She continued, "Sometime after Terry turned eighteen, his father, Gary, out of the blue, showed up at my house blabbering about what a good boy his son was and how he shouldn't be punished for the rest of his adult life for a silly misunderstanding."

Mikeal asked, "A misunderstanding?"

Sandy's tone shifted, and she replied, "Sheriff, no offense, but I saw how you stared at me when I entered the lounge, and yes, Deputy," she looked in Allison's direction, "I've heard what other women have said as well. Their defense at the trial was that I brought this on myself; the clothes I wore in front of the boys, the way I flirted with them. It was my entire fault. I guess that's why I've never been married; everyone looks at me as a sex toy. I grew up in the middle of nowhere on a farm. I jumped at the chance to go to college and get out of there. Once I started making my own money, I made sure I had nice clothes, hair, and makeup. It made me feel good about myself, unfortunately, others became jealous, and they resorted to telling lies to make themselves feel better at my expense."

Mikeal apologized for his earlier behavior, saying, "Well, I'm sorry about all that, and I apologize for my earlier behavior. You are a beautiful lady, but it was very unprofessional for me to look at you the way I did."

Sandy's cheeks turned slightly red as she showed a bit of modesty. "If you would walk us through what happened between you and Terry," Allison asked.

Sandy began to recount her story, "It was summer; school was out, late June, I believe. I was in the middle of a run, probably about ten miles from home. There had been a slight mist at the start of my run, but now it was starting to really come down hard. Normally, I'd keep running, rain's not really a big deal, but I started to hear thunder in the distance. That's when I heard him call my name."

"I turned towards the road, and there he was, Terry, in a truck with the passenger window rolled down, beckoning me to hop in. At first, I refused, saying, 'Thanks, but I can manage.'"

Sandy remained calm on the outside as she continued her story. Inside she could still hear the rain pounding the truck's roof like a relentless drumbeat, each droplet echoing the gravity of the situation. Her eyes darted back and forth between the Sheriff and deputy, searching for some understanding, for empathy.

Mikeal, trying to unravel the circumstances, inquired, "Did you know Terry prior to that encounter?"

Sandy's gaze shifted to the floor, and her voice quivered as she admitted, "Yes, he was in my English class in the tenth grade."

Allison, sensing there might be more beneath the surface, pressed further, "Did you ever work with him outside of class?"

Sandy hesitated, her memories churning like a storm. "You mean like a tutor or help with an assignment?" she inquired.

Allison confirmed, "Yes, exactly, something like that."

Sandy's brow furrowed as she dug into her recollections. "No, I don't recall seeing him outside of the classroom," she finally responded.

Mikeal, keen on understanding the sequence of events, inquired, "So you originally rebuffed his offer; how did you end up in the vehicle?"

Sandy's voice trembled as she continued, "He continued to follow me. Suddenly, a large bolt of lightning, immediately followed by thunder, struck maybe a mile in front of me. He asked again, 'Are you sure you don't want a ride?' That's when I decided to take him up on his offer."

With each word, Sandy's recounting became more haunting. She remembered shivering in her damp clothing, reliving that fateful night. "So now you're in his truck," Mikeal urged, his eyes locked onto Sandy, "what happened next?"

Sandy felt the weight of that ominous night pressing down upon her as she confessed, "I was soaked, and he had his A/C going. He made some excuse that if he turned it off, the windows would fog. I shut the vents on my side, but I continued to shake. He reached into the back seat and pulled over a blanket. 'Here, wrap up in this till you get warm,' he said. It was so cold; I wrapped the blanket around me, put my head down, and turned my thoughts toward a hot bath when I returned home. He never asked for my address, and frankly, I hadn't thought to provide it."

Sandy's voice grew heavy with the chilling details, and her fear seemed to fill the room. "I'm not sure how much time had passed, but after a couple of turns, we came to a stop. I pulled my head out of the blanket and noticed we were parked up against a large building. 'Where are we?' I asked. 'I can see you're still cold, so I stopped to turn on the heater.' 'Where are we?' I asked, and Terry responded, 'We're only a couple of miles from your house, but I haven't told you where I live.'"

A sense of dread loomed over the room, and Mikeal posed an unsettling statement, "Mrs. McKinnon, we all know where you live."

Puzzled, Sandy questioned, "What do you mean we all know?"

Mikeal's voice grew colder as he recounted Terry's words, "Me and my buddies, we've been to your house," he said, a sinister grin on his face.

"Suddenly, I didn't feel so great about the situation I was in. 'I'm feeling warmer, please take me home; I'd like to get out of these wet clothes,' I demanded."

With chilling precision, Sandy recalled the menacing encounter. "That's when he reached over, pulling the lever to recline my seat, and before I knew it, he was on top of me."

Mikeal couldn't help but get lost in Sandy's eyes once again, though this time, they were filled with a profound emptiness. A tear glistened in the corner of her eye, threatening to spill over.

"Sandy, we can stop if this is becoming too difficult," Mikeal offered, his tone laced with empathy.

Gathering herself, Sandy sat up straight in her chair and resolved to continue. "No, I'm good. Let's finish this conversation."

Mikeal nodded and urged her to go on, "Alright, whenever you're ready."

As Sandy delved deeper into the darkest chapter of her past, suspense hung in the air like a storm cloud about to burst. "I think I was starting to go into shock, knowing what was about to happen. I had a pair of running tights on with my shorts over the top. He was struggling to pull them down; I guess the rain and snug fit had glued them to my body. This was just enough of a delay for my brain to start working again."

Sandy's story was gripping, each word a step deeper into the abyss of that terrifying night. "I saw the seatbelt strap hanging there with a lot of slack. I grabbed it and quickly wrapped it around his neck and pulled it as tight as it would go. He immediately stopped what he was doing and tried to free the belt from his neck."

The room fell into a chilling silence as Sandy's tale reached its darkest moment. Her voice quivered, and fear etched deep lines into her face. "I could see his face was starting to turn purple, and I was expecting him to pass out at any minute, but he never did." Every word hung heavy in the air, and the tension was palpable.

The room felt suffocating as Sandy continued, "Finally, it looked as though his eyes were about to roll back into his head; that's when I tried to push him off me and get out the driver door." Her voice trembled with each word, and she gripped the arms of the chair, reliving the horrors of that night.

"As I moved towards the driver side," Sandy recounted, her voice barely above a whisper, "he grabbed me. With my free leg, I kicked him square in the face." The air seemed to constrict with each passing moment, the fear almost tangible.

In the shadow of her harrowing experience, Sandy's voice grew even softer, trembling with a mix of trauma and resilience. "Finally out of the truck, I was able to run off into the nearby woods and hide."

Allison, her eyes wide with empathy, asked the question that hung heavy in the room, "Did he follow you?"

Sandy had managed to regain some semblance of control over her emotions, but the fear still clung to her like a shadow. She hesitated, her eyes darting around the room as if searching for escape. "No," she replied, her voice tinged with a hint of desperation, "he got out of the truck and briefly looked around before he drove off." Her eyes held the weight of that night, the trauma etched into her very being. "I waited another twenty minutes or so," Sandy continued, her voice gaining a hint of resolve, "to make sure he wasn't returning before running up the road and finding a house with lights on, from which we called the police."

The room seemed to sigh with relief, and the tension, though not entirely lifted, shifted to one of cautious hope. Sandy had survived that terrifying night, but the memory would forever haunt her.

CHAPTER 27

"We headed back to the station?" Allison asked as they returned to the cruiser.

"We're halfway to Big Sky. Let's run out that way and have a word with Mr. Lynn," Mikeal responded. After several minutes on the road, Mikeal asked Allison to call the resort and verify Terry was working.

"He's there, scheduled to work until seven," Allison responded.

They continued their journey towards Big Sky, the landscape around them growing more desolate and remote. A few miles down the road, Allison voiced, "Sheriff, you just missed the turnoff."

Mikeal, eyes fixed on the winding road ahead, had made a calculated decision. "Change of plans. If he's working until seven, we've got plenty of time to snoop around his place."

Doubt crept into Allison's voice as she asked, "What are we looking for?"

"The unexpected," was Mikeal's cryptic response.

After another half an hour of driving, they reached the turnoff to the Lynn farm. Taking the gravel road, they headed uphill, but as they ascended, Allison suddenly cried out, "Sheriff, pay attention!"

"What's wrong, Allison?" Mikeal inquired, the situation growing increasingly mysterious.

"You just blew past the trailer," she exclaimed, her anxiety now tangible. Mikeal scanned the surroundings, desperately seeking a place to turn the vehicle around, but the narrow gravel road was flanked by treacherous ditches. "Damn, hold on," he muttered, his eyes fixed on the road ahead, searching for a way to backtrack.

As they crested a slight rise, the road unexpectedly opened up to reveal a vast clearing. An imposing eight-foot fence encircled the area. To their left loomed a massive, weathered barn-like structure, an ominous presence in the desolation. In front of them, two aging trailers, once bustling with activity, now sat in eerie stillness. To the far right, a smaller building with two garage-like doors lay dormant, casting an unsettling shadow.

"Is this part of the farm?" they both wondered aloud, their curiosity mingling with growing determination. As they faced the compound, the imposing main gate stood locked, a formidable barrier to further investigation. A silent look passed between them, acknowledging that they would have to climb over this obstacle.

Approaching the gate with a competitive spirit, Allison swiftly ascended and gracefully cleared the barrier before Mikeal could attempt his own climb. Mikeal's clunky work boots presented a challenge, making it difficult to find footing on the unforgiving chain-link fence. He struggled, slipping several times before finally conquering the fence and joining Allison inside the compound.

Directly in front of them stood a pair of aging trailers that, in a bygone era, may have served as the site's administrative offices. To their far right loomed a smaller building with two uninviting garage-like doors. As they took in this unsettling sight, Allison couldn't help but express her thoughts. "This looks more like an old mining site than part of the farm," she remarked, her voice betraying a growing unease.

Feeling the weight of their mission, they decided to split up and investigate these structures. Both trailers were sealed shut, their windows offering little more than a stark view of barren interiors, each furnished with only a solitary desk. The true mystery, however, lay beyond the imposing, locked gate, guarding the barn-like structure they could only see from a distance.

Turning their attention to the two-door, windowless garage, the tension in the air thickened. "This one's locked," Allison reported, her words heavy with concern. Mikeal cautiously approached the other door, a lingering sense of dread hanging over their every move. "I think this one's just stuck," he muttered, more to reassure himself than to convince Allison.

Determined, Mikeal made another attempt to open the stubborn door, his efforts met with resistance. "See, it's locked," Allison insisted. However, Mikeal, ever persistent, scanned the ground, realizing he had the perfect tool in the cruiser to address their conundrum. He headed back to the car, leaving Allison puzzled.

Returning with a jimmy stick, typically used for unlocking cars, he wedged it between the door and the door jamb near the handle. A few well-placed maneuvers, and the door surrendered to their relentless determination. "That door was locked," Allison reiterated, her voice tinged with disbelief, as Mikeal managed to pry it open. With an air of confidence, he simply responded, "No, it wasn't locked. I opened it without a key."

Stepping into the two-bay garage, a shiver ran down their spines as they noticed its emptiness on the side they entered. However, the ominous outline of a vehicle, shrouded beneath a massive, eerily green tarp, loomed ominously on the other side. Mikeal, feeling a sense of dread in the pit of his stomach, couldn't resist the urge to unveil the hidden mystery.

His hand reached to lift the tarp from the backside of the vehicle. As the tarp fluttered away, it revealed a late-model Honda Civic. An oppressive silence enveloped the garage, and the air grew thick with tension. The sight sent shivers down their spines.

Allison quickly volunteered to run the license plate, and she hastened to the car to make the call. The vehicle was locked, but the interior spoke volumes — it unmistakably belonged to Emma.

Within an hour, the farm was swarmed by law enforcement officers, the ominous revelation casting a foreboding shadow over their every move.

Devin had swiftly swung by the resort, poised to take Terry into custody, only to receive the disheartening news that he had never reported for his shift. Panic gripped Mikeal as he absorbed this alarming turn of events.

"Shit," he blurted out, his voice rife with frustration. "He knows we're here, and he's going to run. Get his description out to the troopers and the park rangers down in Yellowstone," he barked, urgency gnawing at him. They couldn't afford to let Terry slip through their fingers, not now.

The case had gone from a painstaking crawl to a breakneck sprint in a matter of moments, and Mikeal felt the weight of the situation bearing down on him. The sprawling crime scene, which included the vast mining area they had uncovered earlier, stretched far and wide, and the sheriff's department was stretched thin.

Devin, perceptive to the concern etched across Mikeal's face, tried to offer reassurance. "Sir, we got this," he said, his voice steady. Mikeal nodded, grateful for the support. "Thanks,

Devin. I know we do, but the worry just creeps in naturally, I guess," he admitted, a touch of vulnerability in his words.

The investigative teams were meticulously cataloging evidence on the plateau and securing the barn area, where they had discovered open mine shafts leading from the structure. The department had reached out to a local spelunkers' club for assistance in navigating the treacherous underground terrain, though they wouldn't be available until the following morning.

With nightfall swiftly approaching, Mikeal and Devin refocused their efforts on the Lynn Family Farmhouse, a sense of urgency hanging over them like a looming storm, as time slipped through their fingers.

As they approached the eerie and abandoned farmhouse, Mikeal issued firm instructions to Devin: he would investigate the rear, while Devin tackled the front. The weight of the situation pressed down on them like a leaden shroud.

Upon stepping onto the desolate back porch, Mikeal's eyes were immediately drawn to the locked freezer. With a sense of trepidation, he reached for his radio, desperately trying to reach Allison. His voice crackled over the radio, "Allison, will you send someone down to the farmhouse with bolt cutters? We have a locked freezer on the back porch, and I'm curious about its contents." Her acknowledgment, "Will do," fell upon their ears before the radio went silent, leaving them in the daunting silence of the old farmhouse.

As Devin reappeared, he relayed that the front door was locked. In stark contrast, the back door, while not entirely closed, creaked open as Mikeal pushed it, and both men cautiously entered the old home. Unbeknownst to Mikeal and Devin, they were retracing the steps Emma had taken a little over four days ago. The back door had been left ajar after Emma's entry, and the two investigators found themselves in the same kitchen where she had been. Their search led them through room after room, uncovering only the remnants of long-abandoned clothing strewn throughout the house.

Returning to the kitchen area, Devin concluded, "Well, she's definitely not here." As he stood waiting further instructions from Mikeal, he picked up on the subtle hum of the refrigerator. "This house still has power," he noted as he opened the refrigerator, his voice laden with disappointment, after finding only a few Gatorade bottles inside. "These bottles were probably purchased recently, I'd say," he remarked. Mikeal nodded thoughtfully before leaving the kitchen and returning to the back porch.

Devin followed him outside and inquired about alerting the state's forensic team. However, Mikeal hesitated, thinking aloud, "I'm not sure if we're ready for the big guns, Devin, but in the front room, I did notice a slight discoloration of the wooden floor. Ask our local team to identify it before we reach out to the state."

The question still loomed in the back of their minds: what could be inside that locked freezer? Devin cautiously broached the topic. "What do you think is in the freezer?" With a hint of apprehension in his voice, Mikeal responded, "Well, I know what I hope isn't in the freezer." The notion was unsettling.

Within a few minutes, Officer Smitty showed up with the bolt cutters. Mikeal wasted no time in dispatching the lock, using the bolt cutters with force, and finally lifting the freezer's door. With a sense of impending dread, they were greeted by the sight of more clothes, heaped inside.

"Why would these be under lock and key?" Mikeal pondered aloud, his voice filled with uncertainty. With resolute determination, he pulled on a pair of blue evidence gloves from his belt. He leaned over the freezer, sifting through the clothes. His fingers brushed against something solid resting at the very bottom of the freezer. "Bingo," he exclaimed triumphantly before extracting the mysterious object. Officer Smitty voiced his initial observation, "A book," to which Mikeal corrected, "Actually, a ledger."

Mikeal shut the freezer with an eerie sense of anticipation and moved to open the ledger. The aged book's pages whispered of decades past. Inside the front cover, the dates April 1st, 1978, to March 31st, 1982, were etched in faded ink. As he turned the fragile pages, it became evident that this ledger was a meticulously recorded archive of projects undertaken during that period—an accounting of the past preserved in the present. After absorbing its contents, Mikeal carefully closed the book before passing it to Devin, who, having anticipated the need for gloves, had already gloved up. The Sheriff returned to his exploration of the freezer's bottom, his fingers dancing in search of answers. Swiftly, he unearthed another volume.

Upon opening the front cover, a breathless moment unfolded. This was what he had hoped to find. The ledger was dated February 2nd, 1970, to March 31st, 1978, a crucial link to the past. With the daylight dwindling, Mikeal acknowledged the pressing need for thorough documentation. He turned to Smitty, their dedicated officer, and urged, "Let's get the crime team out here; we need to catalog everything." As an afterthought, he added, "And inform them about these ledgers; make sure they know we've taken them."

The ride back was marked by a growing exhaustion that clung to Mikeal. As he wrestled with fatigue, he turned to Devin, his voice heavy with weariness. "Devin, mind if I close my eyes for a couple of minutes? I suddenly feel utterly drained." In stark contrast, Devin was a bastion of wakefulness. He replied, "No problem, Sheriff. I'm wide awake." The investigation had reached a critical juncture, and as the shadows deepened, the weight of the day began to take its toll.

Sound asleep, Mikeal felt a slight nudge, rousing him from his restless slumber. With heavy eyelids, he murmured, "What?" A voice replied, "Sheriff, wake up. We're here." His groggy response followed, "What, where are we?" The voice confirmed, "Sheriff, we're back at the station." Sitting up, Mikeal struggled to shake off the cobwebs that clung to his thoughts. "How long was I asleep?" He sought clarity from Devin, who replied, "Almost an hour. It feels like I had barely closed my eyes before you woke me," Mikeal confessed as he stepped out of the vehicle.

Still on the precipice of exhaustion, Mikeal was acutely aware of the time slipping away. If Emma was still alive, her life hung in the balance. He knew he had to press on, prepared to pull an all-nighter if necessary. Carrying the ledger that held answers and shadows of the past, he vanished into his office. Before delving into the ledger, he briefly revisited the Nancy Hulligan case file, confirming the dates of her disappearance —summer of 1970, just as he had suspected.

The ledger was meticulously structured, with each project meticulously detailed. The Kennedy project was the first to catch his attention, noting a street west of town. Flipping through the pages, the next project, Snyder, was listed, beginning on June 8th, at 1738 McKinley Drive, Nancy Hulligan's home street. Each entry was punctuated by a date, a description column, debit and credit columns differentiating between supplies and labor, a reference column primarily denoted by the initials R.L. and a number, likely an invoice. The note section held miscellaneous entries concerning weather, permits, bank draws, and more.

Mikeal followed the entries until August 4th, the day Nancy disappeared. The foundation had been poured, rough framing completed, and roof trusses installed. Debits and credits were meticulously recorded, and the reference column mainly contained R.L. and numbers. However, the note section held the cryptic comment, G.L. # 8. This detail intrigued Mikeal.

Puzzling over this note, he called out to Devin for assistance. Mikeal handed him the newer ledger and briefly explained its layout and what to look for. As Devin walked away, clutching the ledger, Mikeal plunged back into his thoughts.

Clearly, he thought G.L. referred to Gary Lynn, but what did number eight signify? Mikeal scoured the first project for a similar notation but found none. Page by page, he combed through the ledger, seeking a matching reference, until he stumbled upon the entry dated June 19th, 1972, with the note G.L. # 9. Was this related to a specific credit on a project Roy had been tracking for his son? Mikeal flipped back a couple of pages in an effort to determine the location of this project. Three pages back, he found his answer. Scribbled across the top of the page was Summit Mountain Project. Looking at the first date of the project, June 5th, 1975, a chilling realization struck him like a bolt of lightning. Tina Lattimer, who was working at Summit Mountain, had disappeared on Saturday, June 3rd, 1975.

Sitting back and lowering his chin to his chest, he comprehended the sinister code. The realization landed like a heavy burden, shrouding Mikeal in dread. It was more than the family construction business—it was a generational legacy of darkness and predation, handed down from one son to another. The idea that Terry had been groomed by his father to continue this dark lineage sent shivers down Mikeal's spine.

The night grew darker, and Mikeal, teetering on the brink of exhaustion, pressed on, flipping through the remaining pages of the ledger. The G.L. references stopped at #13 in February of 1978, but he knew the continuation lay in the book on Devin's desk.

"Devin!" The sharp yell shattered the eerie silence that hung over the nearly vacant station. "We need to get back to the farm tonight. We have to start searching the mine shafts now," Mikeal instructed with a sense of urgency in his voice. Responding swiftly to the call, Devin retrieved his heavy jacket from the office closet, mirroring Mikeal's urgency. Within minutes, they were inside the sturdy Tahoe, retracing their path from just an hour earlier, heading back towards the farm.

During the ride, Mikeal had brought Devin up to speed on the disturbing revelations he had uncovered in the ledgers. His certainty that Emma, if still alive, was confined somewhere deep in the mines only heightened the urgency of their mission. Devin's eyes remained fixed on the winding road as Mikeal continued to fill in the narrative, the weight of their predicament growing heavier with each word.

But then, a deathly silence enveloped the cab of the vehicle. Concerned, Devin shifted his gaze to the Sheriff, only to find Mikeal had slumped against the window, appearing to be deep in slumber. Returning his focus to the road, Devin's eyes briefly caught the digital clock on the dashboard. It read 10:00 that night, and they had at least another hour's drive ahead of them before reaching the ominous farm.

Devin and Mikeal returned to the farm, the clock ticking past 11:00 p.m. At the mountain's summit, a makeshift command station had been hastily set up in one of the dilapidated, long-forgotten trailers. Allison emerged from the trailer, her expression reflecting her surprise at seeing Devin back at the site. "I wasn't expecting to see you until morning," she admitted.

Devin, driven by the urgency of the situation, answered with unwavering determination, "Change of plans. Sheriff believes Emma's down in the mine."

Concern etched across her face, Allison questioned, "Where's the Sheriff? Were not expecting the spelunker team to arrive for a couple more hours."

Aware of the Sheriff's ailing health and the importance of the mission, Devin replied, "He's in the Tahoe. We need to let him rest. But I need you to show me the entrance to the mine."

With a tinge of disbelief, Allison took two cautious steps towards Devin's parked Tahoe, her gaze fixed on the Sheriff slumped against the passenger window. Concern etched into her voice, she asked, "What's wrong with him?"

"Show me the entrance, and I'll explain on the way," Devin instructed, the urgency evident in his voice. They both headed towards the old barn, the gravel crunching underfoot, with Devin outlining what he knew about the Sheriff's brain tumor along the way. Allison couldn't help but feel a twinge of devastation upon hearing the news. The turmoil within her was twofold—a mix of concern for the Sheriff's well-being and a sense of exclusion as she realized Mikeal had only confided in Devin.

The barn, carved into the mountainside, loomed before them. The massive main door stood ajar, revealing a bare, rocky dirt floor within. Two vintage tractors from the 1950s sat parked side by side on the right. Dead ahead, the entrance to the mine beckoned. "This wasn't what I was expecting," Devin expressed his disappointment.

Allison, refocusing on their mission rather than her emotions, replied, "You were thinking a vertical shaft, weren't you?"

"Yeah, that's what I assumed. Why else would we have called in the cave divers?" Devin replied with a hint of frustration. A smile crept across Allison's face as she said, "Follow me."

They ventured into the mine, its cavernous opening illuminated by four banks of temporary lights with an intensity that could light up a football field. Deeper into the depths they went until they reached a larger chamber. "Here you go, is this more like what you were expecting?"

In the center of the room stood an ancient mechanical elevator, likely dating back to the early 1900s. "I guess I was expecting an open vertical shaft, not one with an elevator. Has anyone gone down?" Devin inquired.

"Not yet. We've been waiting for someone to deem it safe to use," Allison explained. Devin approached the winch system, operated by a hand crank, and inspected the inch-and-a-half metal cable, remarkably free of rust. The gears, too, were surprisingly well-preserved, still bearing traces of grease.

Devin then focused on the steel cage and climbed the outside to examine the pulley system on top. Excited, he shouted down to Allison, "Allison, this elevator is still being used."

"How do you know that?" she asked, puzzled.

Devin climbed back down and displayed his grease-smeared hands. "Allison, I'm no expert in mechanics, but I do know that metal parts have to be greased regularly. I think it's safe. Will you lower me down?"

Scratching her forehead thoughtfully, Allison hesitated before responding, "Shouldn't we wait?"

Devin's determination was unwavering. "Allison, Emma is missing and could be down there. We can't afford to wait. Can you lend me your flashlight for a backup?" The atmosphere was charged with tension, and time was running out.

Allison hesitantly approached the winch system, her gaze shifting between the simple controls and Devin preparing to enter the elevator. "Devin, I can lower you down, but there's no way I'll be able to pull you back up," she voiced her concern.

Undeterred, Devin stepped into the elevator. "Great, we'll worry about that later. I'll stay in touch with the radio; I'm ready when you are."

The elevator began its slow descent into the depths of the shafts. The first fifty feet revealed nothing but the cold and damp chiseled rock face. "Hold up for a second," Devin's voice crackled over the radio. The reflection of his flashlight suddenly disappeared from the rock face, replaced by a well-carved, timber-framed opening in front of him, extending about twenty-five feet into the darkness.

"Allison, how much cable do we have left?" Devin inquired. "Plenty, we're maybe at half capacity," she responded. "I'm at a horizontal shaft, but I don't know – if you were hiding something, would you place it here or go deeper?"

"Deeper," Allison replied. "Yep, that's what I figured. Let's keep lowering." The elevator descended another twenty, then thirty feet before coming to a halt. "Allison, I've hit the bottom," Devin reported. A cool burst of air caressed his neck. He turned around, shining his light on the wall, revealing another horizontal shaft stretching into the unknown. "What do you see?" Allison's voice came across the radio.

"A lot of nothing," Devin responded before stepping out of the elevator.

Slowly, Devin ventured further down the shaft, supported by timber framing every ten feet or so. About one hundred feet in, he reached another shaft branching off to the right. Thus far, he hadn't seen any signs of human presence, and he began to question his decision to bypass the first shaft. Aware that Allison couldn't pull him back up, he had no choice but to continue exploring. The right-hand shaft was smaller than the one he was currently in. Anticipating it would likely terminate within fifty feet, he decided to investigate. The first twenty feet remained nondescript, lacking any timber framing. As he proceeded deeper into the darkness, around fifty feet in, the tunnel began to widen, and timber framing reappeared. The suspense in the underground labyrinth was palpable, and Devin's every step seemed fraught with tension.

The walls of the narrow mine shafts disappeared abruptly, and Devin found himself in a natural cave. The cavern was vast, with a ceiling soaring at least fifty feet above him and a width of around one hundred feet. The uneven, damp floor featured pockets of standing water, creating a disconcerting atmosphere that weighed heavily on Devin. The once comforting feeling of the narrow mine shafts now gave way to an eerie and unsettling sensation.

As he explored the cavern, Devin clung to the walls, fearful of potential drop-offs concealed in the darkness. His flashlight guided him along the left perimeter of the cave, where he hoped to discover another opening. Finally, the beam of light illuminated what seemed like an entrance. However, as he approached, his foot struck something solid. The light revealed a Gatorade bottle on the ground, providing evidence that someone had been in this desolate place.

A few feet ahead, Devin reached the opening he had spotted earlier. Upon entering, he realized it was not another shaft but a small room carved into the rock. Along the back wall, a mantel displayed what initially looked like jars. However, as he drew closer, the horrifying truth became apparent.

"Jesus Christ," Devin exclaimed before attempting to reach Allison on the radio. The radio remained silent, and the gravity of what lay before him began to sink in. Neatly stacked against the back wall were human bones. What he had seen before in case files now existed in tangible, nightmarish reality. Human skulls lined the "shelves," a gruesome display that raised the body count to fifteen. Devin's emotions swirled in a mix of revulsion, fear, and determination, as he realized he had to continue his exploration. With his radio signal failing and the underground becoming more sinister with each step, he was compelled to move forward.

As Devin ventured into the deeper recesses of the cave, the cool breeze had changed to a stale, suffocating air. However, within the small enclave, he felt the cool breeze once more. Investigating, Devin identified a two-foot gap behind the shrine on the left side, leading to another tunnel. The headroom grew lower, forcing him to crouch as he progressed. The walls became damper, indicating a proximity to the surface. The slow pace and the repugnant odor of human excrement in the narrow tunnel heightened Devin's apprehension.

Ten feet in, he spotted a wooden door to his right. Devin cautiously approached, finding it locked with a mechanism similar to the freezer lock back at the house. He called out "Emma," but received no reply. Determined to break through, Devin positioned himself for leverage in the cramped tunnel. Placing his legs against the door, he began stomping it with his feet. The wood creaked and cracked with each impact until it finally yielded. Devin, greeted by the noxious smell he had detected earlier, pushed his way in.

Square tins and discarded Gatorade bottles littered the floor. A tarp covered something in the corner. Devin hastily uncovered it, revealing Emma's lifeless body. His heart sank, and he feared the worst as he checked her pulse. Although her body was cool, it wasn't cold, and he managed to detect a faint heartbeat in her neck. "Emma," he called out, but there was no response. Realizing the urgency, Devin knew he had to get her to the surface immediately, as time hung in the balance in the eerie depths of the cave.

Devin swiftly removed his heavy coat and wrapped it around Emma's lifeless form. With great care, he positioned her on the tarp and began dragging her through the eerie room toward the cavern. Every strained movement felt like an eternity, and he couldn't shake the feeling of urgency that gnawed at him.

In the midst of his struggle, he thought he heard a voice, distant but unmistakable. Still, he pressed on, inching Emma toward the narrow opening. Then, as he attempted to pull her through the tight space, the voices became clearer and more insistent. "Over here!" Devin yelled back, his voice filled with desperation.

In the blink of an eye, two spelunking team members materialized, their presence providing a jolt of hope. Devin didn't waste a second, his adrenaline surging as he shouted, "She's still alive! We've got to get her out of here now!"

With his call to action, more team members converged on the scene. Without exchanging words, they seized hold of the tarp, their strong hands lifting Emma's fragile body. Together, they hurriedly carried her to the elevator, where she was hoisted to the surface. Waiting paramedics swiftly transferred her to an ambulance, which sped away toward the hospital in Bozeman. The tension remained palpable, but a glimmer of hope had broken through the darkness.

CHAPTER 28

Six hours earlier, the piercing sound of the rescue crew's arrival had stirred Mikeal from his deep slumber. He sprang into action, reaching for the Tahoe's radio to contact Devin and Allison. Within seconds, Allison's voice crackled through the speaker, relaying the concerning details to the Sheriff. Devin had descended into the mine over an hour ago, but contact with him had been lost for more than half an hour. Mikeal swiftly updated her on the arrival of the spelunking team and the ambulances waiting at the scene. Time was of the essence, and Allison was keenly aware.

Determined and resolute, Mikeal emerged from the Tahoe, seizing command of the unfolding crisis. His tone was unwavering as he directed the team before him: "Get your gear on quickly and follow me!" Eight men and women, geared up and ready, fell in line, ready to execute their mission. They marched in step with Mikeal, following his lead toward the ominous mine entrance. As they approached the mine, Allison appeared, a beacon of authority amidst the chaos.

Mikeal stopped and watched as Allison waved the team forward to follow her deeper into the mine. With a last glance back at Mikeal, who stood alone, resolute at the mine's entrance, they turned the corner, disappearing into the darkness of the mine. The race against time had begun.

Allison had just witnessed Emma's safe rescue and, despite her exhaustion, felt a sense of relief and satisfaction as she returned to the station in the early morning hours. However, she was taken aback by the unusual commotion surrounding interview room number one. A cluster of officers congregated by the entrance, creating a strange scene. Curiosity piqued, she inquired, "What's going on?" A departing officer muttered, "Sheriff's on a roll," before heading away. Her persistence eventually granted her a glimpse into the room.

Inside, the table was strewn with open volumes of books, each brimming with data and information. The walls were plastered with oversized sheets of paper that seemed to have been hastily extracted from an easel pad, resembling a frantic brainstorming session. The Sheriff's back was the first thing she noticed as he furiously jotted down dates, numbers, and other cryptic symbols, shuttling back and forth between the books and the paper sheets. Stunned by the spectacle before her, Allison raised her voice, calling out, "Sheriff!" Her interruption prompted the onlookers to disperse, but Mikeal remained undistracted. With a growing sense of urgency, she approached him, resting her hand on his shoulder before calmly repeating, "What's going on?"

In response, Mikeal halted his relentless scribbling, turned to Allison, and said, "Look, I'm sure you have questions, but give me another twenty or so minutes to finish this, and I'll answer any questions you may have." Disheartened by his unyielding focus, she left the room.

Mikeal continued for the next half-hour, oscillating between the books and the wall, capturing everything he deemed

crucial on the sheets of paper. Meanwhile, Allison sensed
someone passing behind her on their way to the kitchen.
Mikeal's voice reached her as he inquired about coffee, to
which she replied, "Just made a fresh pot." He added, "Great,
I'll explain everything when I get back." Her eagerness to
understand the situation spurred her to her feet, and she
headed back to the interview room.

On the wall, three sheets of paper were prominently
displayed, bearing the headings "Roy," "Gary," and "Terry
Lynn." Each sheet was annotated with a number, date, and
what seemed to be a reference to a street. The "Terry" sheet
was surprisingly empty, in stark contrast to "Roy," which had
twenty-two entries, and "Gary," which boasted twenty-seven.
Focusing on the table, she began flipping through the pages
of the ledgers they had seized from the farmhouse, engrossed
in her investigation.

Upon Mikeal's return, Allison couldn't contain her curiosity
any longer and asked, "What is all of this?" The Sheriff's
response was chilling. He said, "Well, Allison, if my theory is
correct, this is potentially the largest mass murder in
American history, carried out over several generations by a
family of killers. These guys make Manson look like a
novice." Her brows furrowed as she contemplated the
significance of it all. "Why is Terry's sheet blank?" she
probed. Mikeal's voice was tinged with uncertainty as he
admitted, "Good question, one to which I currently don't
have an answer." A bewildered Allison returned her attention
to the sheets hanging on the wall and voiced a haunting

realization, "We found twelve more skeletal remains in the mine today. With the three earlier finds, we have fifteen. This indicates forty-nine: Sheriff, we have thirty-four more bodies to find?"

A heavy silence hung in the room as both Mikeal and Allison grappled with the gravity of this revelation. The quietude became increasingly uncomfortable, prompting Allison to break it by saying, "I spoke with the hospital on my way in; Emma's suffering from severe dehydration, but other than that, surprisingly, she's in good shape." Mikeal inquired, "Did they say when we could speak with her?" Allison responded, "Hopefully tomorrow."

Mikeal's sense of urgency was palpable as he declared, "That's not going to work. With Terry unaccounted for, we need every detail she can provide to find him." Allison, displaying empathy for Emma's current condition, questioned the rush, saying, "I don't understand, Sheriff. Terry didn't kill Emma. Maybe he's nothing like his father and grandfather."

Mikeal's gaze remained fixed on his notes lining the wall, each mark representing someone's lost loved one, their lives unexpectedly extinguished without clear understanding. He responded gravely, "Allison, we won't know for sure about Terry's intentions towards Emma until we speak with her. There's the possibility that he's not a cold-blooded killer like his father, but perhaps he left Emma in the mine to die a slow death because he's a coward who can't look his victims in the eye as he ends their life."

Mikeal swiftly shifted the conversation, addressing Allison, "When I realized we were going to have a sizable body count, I checked our database for unsolved missing persons in the area since 1960. We have seventeen, in addition to the two we were already aware of." His gaze fell upon the table, every inch of it covered by ledger books and paper. He locked his eyes on the computer printout, which he snatched up, saying, "I'll need you to cross-reference their disappearance date with what's on the wall, see if we can get a match. If we've lost our opportunity to prosecute the killers, hopefully, we'll at least be able to provide some sort of closure to a few families," Mikeal remarked. Allison pondered, "So you're thinking Terry Lynn was aware of all this and carried on the family business of murder?"

Deep in thought, Mikeal remained silent for a moment. "Sir, Terry Lynn, do you think he's involved?" Allison pressed. Finally, looking up, Mikeal responded, "Yes, probably. At a minimum, I'm sure he was aware of what his father was doing."

Devin had remained at the Lynn farm throughout the night, directing the rescue team as they navigated the treacherous mine, desperately searching for additional bodies. As the adrenaline of finding Emma wore off, he left the farm and began the journey back to Bozeman, navigating the winding mountain roads with heavy eyes. Exhaustion weighed on him, and the prospect of a few hours of sleep beckoned.

However, only a few miles into his trip, a call about a vehicle fire crackled over the radio. The location was one of the forest service roads near where the three bodies from Hebgen Lake were found. Devin, without hesitation, informed dispatch he was thirty minutes away.

As Devin arrived, no visible flames greeted him, but dark smoke still billowed from the truck. The remoteness of the area made it unlikely that anyone had spotted the smoke from a distance and called it in. Devin suspected that whoever set the fire made the call after safely escaping the area.

Approaching the vehicle, the intense heat radiated from the metal, forcing Devin to keep a cautious distance. He recognized the truck from his visits to the resort during the Sammy investigation—it was Terry Lynn's. Unbeknownst to Devin, Terry observed his every move from the deep woods through a pair of binoculars. Terry had strategically positioned himself about seventy-five feet from the road, elevated on a ridge, looking down at the road and the remnants of his sinister bait.

Devin surveyed the area, contemplating whether Terry had fled into the woods or had an accomplice who likely made the vehicle fire call. Fatigue weighed on his legs, but he resisted the urge to retreat to the cruiser until backup arrived. Unaware of the impending danger, he paced around the vehicle, a mere seventy-five feet away from the ridge where Terry lurked.

Terry placed the binoculars on the ground, opting for his scoped bolt-action rifle and aimed it towards the road. He had chosen the site carefully, while he was hidden in lush vegetation, he had a clear firing lane to the vehicle below.

Understanding the reasoning of someone with severe mental issues was nearly impossible. Rationality often evaporated, yet occasionally, actions hinted that a real human being still existed deep within their damaged mind. Despite Terry's ruthless intentions for Emma to die from starvation in the mine, a trace of empathy led him to leave her with meager rations, cruelly fostering hope of survival. As he zeroed in on Devin's back through the rifle sight, he grappled with unexpected difficulty controlling his breathing and heart rate. An experienced hunter, he had mastered the art of a calm trigger pull, but this was uncharted territory. He could shoot Devin through the back at any time; however, suddenly something unsettling about that entered his subconscious.

The Lynn family's deviant legacy always involved preying on singular female victims with a sexual element. Unlike his father and grandfather, Terry lacked their sexual urges, turning the family business into a twisted game, each victim emboldening him.

Devin had infuriated Terry multiple times during the Sammy investigation. After their confrontation around the Jeep Wagoneer, Terry had decided that Devin would be his first male victim. With a deep breath, Terry once again aimed his rifle at Devin's back, right below his left shoulder blade, and waited for him to turn and face the woods.

Devin, oblivious to the impending danger, continued to stand with his back toward the forest as he retrieved his cell phone from his pocket. Realizing there was no cell coverage, he walked towards the Tahoe to use the radio. Terry cautiously followed Devin's movements with the rifle until the trees reappeared in the rifle scope. "Damn!" Terry sat back against the tree, losing his clear firing range. Devin managed to get through to dispatch on the radio and was quickly connected to Mikeal.

"Sheriff, on my way in, I responded to a vehicle fire close to where we found the Hebgen Lake bodies. It's Terry Lynn's truck. The truck's burnt to a crisp. He's either headed into the forest or he had an accomplice who helped him get away."

Devin only heard silence on the other end as Mikeal contemplated their next move. They had been unable to establish a connection between the Lynn Family and Steve Taylor; however, there was still the unresolved issue of how Tina Lattimer's bloody clothes ended up in the Taylor warehouse. The possibility of Terry and Steve working together could not be discounted, but something in the Sheriff's gut told him otherwise.

"We've found Terry's truck," Mikeal informed Allison, who had entered his office. "Devin believes he fled on foot into the mountains. Devin, sit tight; we'll get reinforcements out there ASAP."

"Great, I'll be ready. Where?" Allison asked.

"I need you to stay here. When Emma wakes, we need to find out what happened. Maybe she has an idea of where Terry's headed." Dejected at being left behind once more, deep down, she understood the necessity of someone staying.

"Reception in the mountains will be spotty, so no need to call me. I'll check in when possible for updates. Do you need anything from me before I head out?"

"No, Sheriff, I'm good."

Mikeal arrived at the site of the vehicle fire around noon. A roadblock had been established where the forest road branched off of Highway 191. After clearing this checkpoint, it was about three-quarters up the road to the burnt-out truck. The site was bustling with activity as Mikeal pulled up. "Morning, gentlemen," he said, approaching a group of men huddled around the front of Devin's Tahoe. Most replied back with a greeting. "Sheriff, there's a well-defined ridge line about a half-mile up this road that feeds into the backcountry. If I were a betting man, that's where I'd place my cash," Devin offered.

Mikeal stepped back and surveyed the surrounding geography. A sense of unease crept over him. The road cut through a narrow mountain pass, steep banks on both sides veiled by trees and dense vegetation. It was the perfect setting for an ambush. He felt momentarily paralyzed. Should he warn the others, risking gunfire in response? But where could they take cover? Both sides of the road offered ample opportunities for a sniper's hideout.

While the other officers continued their discussion at the front of the Tahoe, Mikeal realized he hadn't been noticed. Quietly, he decided to slip away into the woods on the left side of the road.

During the early summer, as part of fire containment efforts, the forestry service cleared the ditches lining both sides of the fire roads in Montana. The ditch dropped about three feet below the road, presenting a five-foot vertical climb to reach the forest. Jumping the ditch was easy for Mikeal, but another two feet up was impossible. His only choice was to descend into the ditch and find a sturdy tree to use for leverage.

Spotting a young tree that might suffice, he gripped its base tightly, testing its strength with a few tugs. Satisfied, he awkwardly struggled to pull himself up into the woods, relying on the tree for support.

He swiftly scrambled to his feet, stealing a glance over his shoulder at the officers below, still absorbed in their discussion, before refocusing on the forest ahead. No flat ground lay ahead, prompting him to seek higher ground. Using trees as leverage, he ascended deeper into the woods, pausing occasionally to catch his breath. The road and the voices of the officers vanished behind him, obscured by the dense trees. Hindered by the foliage, he estimated he was roughly fifty feet away from the road.

The climb lessened a bit, allowing Mikeal to finally move parallel to the road. The ground became muddy, scattered with softball-sized damp rocks that impeded his progress. Continuing forward, he noticed an unmistakable boot print in the mud. Mikeal swiftly crouched down, hoping not to draw attention. The print was fresh, but abruptly vanished after a few steps. He unholstered his service revolver, a realization dawning that he must be close.

Mikeal's gaze swept the dense foliage, but everything remained eerily still. The wind barely made its presence known, leaving the forest in an unsettling silence. Only the distant birdsong broke the haunting tranquility. With limited options, he pressed forward.

Below, the officers concluded their talk. "Seems like a plan. What do you think, Sheriff?" Devin turned, expecting Mikeal, but the Sheriff was nowhere to be seen.

Cautiously, Mikeal crept ahead on all fours, endeavoring to blend with the forest floor's lush cover, keeping his movements hidden.

Devin glanced back at the Sheriff's patrol vehicle, but the intense glare on the windshield obscured any view inside. Closing in, he was just a few feet away when he could finally confirm: Mikeal wasn't in the vehicle. Perplexed, he redirected his attention toward the burnt-out vehicle some fifty feet away.

After a brief crawl, Mikeal halted and scanned the clearing. Light penetrated the once-thick forest, revealing the patrol vehicle below. As he fixed his gaze on the road, a noise from slightly behind him caught his attention. Whipping around, he spotted movement amid the vegetation near a sturdy tree.

"Sheriff!" Devin called as he neared the burnt vehicle's driver's side. Mikeal sprang up, ready to shout a warning, but fire erupted from the foliage, followed by the unmistakable gunfire echo. A sudden, sharp noise like a metallic clang pierced the air. Devin, diving into the ditch, felt something zip past him.

Simultaneously, Mikeal aimed his revolver toward the movement but was met with a muffled pop—a misfire. Cursing internally, he saw Terry rise, aiming his rifle. Mikeal, diving for cover, lost sight of Terry. The officers below unleashed gunfire toward the initial shots, bullets zipping overhead and hitting trees.

Meanwhile, having lost sight of Terry, Mikeal wasn't sure if his target had been hit or had taken cover, perhaps even retreating deeper into the woods. With no functioning weapon, once the gunfire slacked, Mikeal urgently called out to the officers below, "Cease fire!" Devin, securely positioned behind the five-foot barrier rising from the ditch to the forest floor, shouted back, "Sheriff, where are you?"

"I'm roughly fifteen feet from where the shot came from, but my gun misfired," Mikeal yelled in reply.

CHAPTER 29

Allison had proactively contacted the hospital earlier that morning, leaving her details and requesting an immediate call once Emma regained enough consciousness to converse. Several hours passed without a response, prompting Allison to opt for an unannounced visit. The Bozeman Deaconess Hospital, established in 1911 through community collaboration with the Methodist Church, had evolved into an eighty-six-bed facility by 1986. Though Allison wished for a discreet arrival, reality demanded she ask for directions to Emma's room, forfeiting any element of surprise.

As she entered the front door, Dr. Vermeulen promptly greeted her, expressing sincere apologies for the delayed response to the deputy. "Emma has positively responded to the saline and electrolytes we administered. I spoke with her roughly an hour ago; she's quite coherent."

Inquiring about the incident, Allison pressed, "Did she mention anything about what happened?" To which the doctor responded, "I didn't inquire, and she didn't offer any details."

Arriving at Emma's room, Dr. Vermeulen announced, "Emma, you have a visitor." Her voice held a hint of disappointment as she responded, "Deputy Allison, I was expecting the Sheriff." "He was unexpectedly called away," Allison explained, "but he promised to stop by to see you." "How are you feeling?" the deputy inquired. "Better, but I still have a throbbing headache," Emma replied. "Do you feel like talking about what happened?"

Emma paused, her eyes fixed straight ahead as she took a deep breath before slowly exhaling. "Well, eventually I'd have to, so let's get started." "Since we're not at the station, I'd like to record our conversation. Would that be alright with you?" Allison asked. Emma nodded in agreement, her gaze still fixed on the wall before her. "Alright, in your own words, walk me through what happened on the day you disappeared."

Emma started her story without making eye contact. "I had left the police station earlier that day. It was my day off, and I was planning to go back home, but I started to doubt whether the police would follow through on my request to speak with Terry. So, I decided to approach him myself. After a few unsuccessful attempts to call him, I drove out to his trailer. Nobody was there, so I checked the farmhouse. The back door was unlocked, so I went inside to look around. When I returned to the kitchen, Terry was standing in the doorway."

Emotion overwhelmed Emma, and tears started to flow freely. "I'm such an idiot. My hatred for Mr. Taylor blinded me from considering anyone else."

"Emma, he had everyone fooled. Let's take a break and get you some water," Allison responded. She walked over to the water pitcher beside the bed. "It's empty. I'll refill it. Just try to relax, and we'll continue when I return."

Emma closed her eyes, thinking only a few minutes had passed. Upon waking, she found Allison seated, casually flipping through a magazine. "I'm sorry, must have dozed off for a few minutes."

Allison chuckled and moved closer. "You were out for about an hour. They brought you some food. Would you like to eat before we continue?"

"What is it?" Emma inquired.

"I'm not sure. Looks like your standard hospital mystery meat," Allison replied. Emma spent the next fifteen minutes devouring whatever was on her plate, draining the recently filled water pitcher as well.

"You feel like continuing?" Allison gently asked. "I think so," Emma responded.

Emma recounted the entire ordeal, starting from the farmhouse and leading all the way to the depths of the mine. "Do you remember what you talked about when he held you captive?" Allison pressed, seeking any crucial details.

"He kept saying it was some sort of game," Emma replied, her voice trailing off without further elaboration.

"Did he mention if anyone else was part of this game?" Allison pressed urgently. Emma paused, pondering for a moment before shaking her head. "Wait, he did mention his father and grandfather. He said it was a game to them too, they even kept score." A wave of revulsion swept over Allison, her mind racing back to what the Sheriff had revealed at the station—the ledgers found at the farmhouse were their scorecards.

After gathering herself, Allison focused and continued, "Did he ever mention Steve Taylor's involvement?" Emma finally turned to meet Allison's gaze. "He mentioned planting evidence at Steve's warehouse."

Allison swiftly reached for her phone, her urgency palpable as she dialed to update the Sheriff.

Devin and the other officers scrambled up the hillside towards the point where the shot originated. By the time they arrived, Mikeal was already there, actively scouring for clues. "I haven't found any traces of blood, so I doubt he was hit," Mikeal explained, gesturing about ten feet away. "But look here," he continued, pointing at broken branches and the disturbed vegetation. "It seems like he crawled away to this spot and then snapped this branch, likely pulling himself up to his feet."

Devin peered down at the disturbed ground, the very spot where the bullet, if accurate, would have snuffed out his life. The ferns lay flattened, suggesting that Terry had lingered here for hours. Scattered about were remnants of an empty beef jerky bag and two discarded Coke cans. As Devin grappled with the proximity of his near miss, Mikeal's voice broke the silence from behind him. "The bastard set a trap for us," Mikeal declared, stepping up beside Devin. Together, they stood, shoulder to shoulder, gazing down the ominous firing lane toward the charred remains of Terry's truck.

Mikeal felt his phone buzz in his pocket, and he swiftly retrieved it, finding Allison's name flashing on the screen. "Yes, Allison," he answered. Devin couldn't help but observe the Sheriff. Mikeal's pants from the knees down were smeared with mud, his breath came in heavy, labored pants, and his chest rose and fell with visible strain. Allison quickly briefed Mikeal on the planted evidence. Finally breaking his silence, Mikeal responded, "Understood. Get the tracking dogs here immediately. Gather as many officers as possible and head out here. Terry's fled into the mountains, and we'll need every resource available to track him down."

Mikeal slid his phone back into his pocket before addressing the group. "Obviously, we can't wait for the dogs to arrive, so we're going after him." Devin signaled for Mikeal to join him away from the others. "Sir, it might be best for you to wait here and set up a base camp; the terrain past this ridge-line will get challenging." "I appreciate your concern, Devin, but I'll manage," Mikeal insisted. Devin looked skeptical. Mikeal wagged a finger at Devin. "Alright, no need for a lecture. I skipped my appointment—no chemo. I'll be okay to do this,"

Mikeal disclosed. Before Devin could respond, Mikeal turned his attention back to the other officers.

Devin and the other officers swiftly trailed behind Mikeal as he traced a path marked by disrupted soil and snapped twigs. It was clear that when the return fire erupted, Terry's utmost concern had been to flee the area swiftly. His haste left a trail even a novice could follow. It led directly up the mountain, then plateaued, merging back with the ridge-line. Along the crest, the trail was a mere five feet across at its broadest points, often narrowing to a mere three feet. This slender width was barely enough to erase the overt signs of Terry's retreat. Mikeal surmised that Terry aimed to put as much distance as possible between himself and his pursuers, willing to risk staying on the more visible path.

The group advanced in a single file, ascending steadily into the towering mountains. Hours passed before they reached a modest clearing. Likely the aftermath of a landslide a few months prior, a cluster of trees had been uprooted, offering the team a vantage point overlooking several valleys below. Mikeal approached the edge where Devin stood, peering through his binoculars at the expanse below. "Do you reckon he was much of an outdoorsman?" Mikeal speculated, his eyes scanning the rugged terrain.

"Terry?" Devin replied, a hint of puzzlement in his voice. "Oh, undoubtedly. He grew up around here, so he'll have the upper hand navigating these mountains."

"We'll have him, or at least his body by nightfall, I'm certain of it," Mikeal reassured Devin. Suddenly, another officer called out, having discovered boot tracks in the soft, exposed earth created by the uprooted trees leading into the valley below. Kneeling down, Mikeal examined the distinct impressions. He surveyed the immediate area, finding it all a bit too straight forward. Keeping his suspicions to himself, he sensed this was a deliberate diversion. There was rougher ground where Terry could have easily avoided leaving such clear tracks. Standing back up, Mikeal weighed his options before directing three officers to trail the tracks down into the valley. He, Devin, and the two remaining officers would persist along the crest trail.

Over the next hour, Mikeal and his team navigated the rugged trail that intermittently led them downwards, only to thrust them into another steep climb up a ridge. The path transitioned from gravel and roots to a sloppy, muddy mixture, making the ascent even more challenging. Frustration simmered within the group as they slipped and struggled through the mire. With every step, the landscape grew more rugged, the dense forest enveloping them in an air of impenetrable wilderness. Doubts about Terry's choice of fleeing this deep into the forest started to circulate among the officers who remained with Devin and the Sheriff.

Approaching the crest of the next ridge, Devin, leading the team, caught the distant hum of a highway. The group came to an abrupt halt, reevaluating their approach. "Sounds like we're edging closer to the highway," remarked Devin. Mikeal leaned in, formulating a plan. "We'll proceed in that direction." Turning to the other officers, he ordered, "You two, backtrack and make sure he hasn't looped behind us." The officers, visibly weary but relieved that the return path sloped downhill, started to move away. As they turned to leave, Mikeal's realization struck. "Wait a second!" he called out urgently before they moved too far. "My revolver's jammed; I'll need to borrow one of your pistols," he instructed. Both officers exchanged a quick glance before one offered up his firearm.

Waiting until the officers had vanished from sight, Mikeal refocused on Devin, his gaze piercing the dense foliage ahead. "We'll keep searching until we reach the highway. You've seen the signs as well – no indication he left the main trail. He's either hiding ahead or already made it to the highway. We might stumble upon a few game trails as we descend the mountain. Let's minimize our noise until then." Taking the lead, Mikeal and Devin descended from the ridge, the trail's downside returning to its dry, root-filled course.

After about fifteen minutes, the distant sound of rushing water pierced the silence. Rounding a bend, they discovered the source: a towering rock formation, its cascading waters feeding the valley below. Approaching cautiously, they found what appeared to be a small clearing under the colossal rock feature, which they cautiously approached. Communicating only with hand signals, Devin indicated he was moving in closer. Once he reached the edge, Mikeal motioned for him to halt, before grabbing a sizable rock and tossing it through the opening. Other than the echo of the rock hitting the cave walls, silence greeted them.

Simultaneously, Devin, his flashlight now clipped on the side of his pistol, aimed his beam into the cave. The shallow nook, extending only about ten feet inside the mountain, bore signs of sporadic use as a shelter over the years. Teenage graffiti covered the walls, while beer cans were scattered across the ground. With the waterfall's roar masking any sounds from the cave, Mikeal felt comfortable enough to speak.

"This is the first fresh water we've found in hours. If he came this way, he'd have stopped here to hydrate," Mikeal stated. "Yeah, but look at all this," Devin replied, pointing his light at the litter scattered across the ground. "How are we going to tell?"

Mikeal knelt down, examining the cold rock-lined fire pit. Picking up a charred piece of wood, he realized no recent fire had been lit. Edging closer to the outside opening, feeling the splash of water against his pants leg, Mikeal scanned for any signs of soft ground that might have captured evidence of Terry's passage. Yet, all he found was solid rock.

Doubt crept into Mikeal's mind for the first time that afternoon. They might have lost him. He hoped the returning officers might have caught Terry off guard by doubling back, but it felt like a slender thread of hope.

Reeling himself back to the present, Mikeal masked any despair on his face, addressing Devin with determination. "Here's the plan: Radio silence until we reach the highway. I'll follow the creek bed down the mountain; Devin, you continue on the trail, and we'll rendezvous at the highway."

Devin nodded affirmatively before vanishing around the cave's edge, returning to the original trail they had been following for hours. Alone now, Mikeal's focus returned to the water cascading into the valley below. Initially, it was a steep descent from the trail. The creek, which had swiftly expanded to about five feet in width, roared as it thundered over football-sized rocks, gaining momentum as it rushed into the depths of the valley.

As Mikeal followed the creek's violent path, he grappled with the small trees to slow his pace. Eventually, the ground leveled slightly, and he spotted what seemed to be a game trail terminating at the water's edge. The transition from trail to water was marked by a change from solid ground to muddy terrain. Amid the deer tracks etched in the mud, Mikeal discerned a boot print, initially concealed by the trampled ground. The depth of the mud hinted at recent movement, a silent testament to someone passing through.

Mikeal left the water's edge and followed the trail, which was little more than a footpath, back into the forest. The creek soon curved, aligning itself with the trail. Walking alongside it, Mikeal encountered the same footprint intermittently imprinted in the soft dirt. He estimated he was likely a few miles away from the highway, yet the roaring water obscured any distant sounds, leaving him in a state of uncertainty.

Continuing his pursuit, the creek carved deeper into the earth, creating a stark five-foot abyss between the pathway and the water below. The once thunderous roar of the creek softened, its flow now contained by encroaching walls. The landscape dried out, leaving no traces of recent footprints. Mikeal's realization hit hard—he knew Terry had likely reached the highway by now. A momentary pause revealed the gnawing hunger in his gut; fatigue was setting in, his legs aching. Weariness weighed heavily on his focus. Yet, before he could dwell on it, a glimmer in the sunlight filtering through the trees snagged his attention.

As he approached the shiny object, his radio suddenly crackled to life, shattering the veil of silence and announcing his proximity to civilization. He hastily silenced it, cursing himself for the careless mistake. Disgusted and distracted, he kneeled to inspect the glimmering item—a sardine tin. Its pungent odor filled the air, but Mikeal's thoughts lingered on his blunder. And then, everything took a dire turn.

In an instant, Mikeal's senses jolted as he glimpsed the baseball bat-sized tree limb hurtling toward his skull. Instincts kicked in just before impact, his body lurching to the side, softening the blow enough to avert unconsciousness.

Before he could regain his bearings, Terry pounced, wielding the branch with malicious intent, aiming to suffocate Mikeal. Summoning every ounce of strength, Mikeal strained against the crushing pressure on his windpipe, his arms struggling to stave off impending doom. Desperation flooded his thoughts: fueled by adrenaline and the sheer will to endure, he quickly calculated if he could reach the pistol holstered on his right side. The window of opportunity was infinitesimal, hanging precariously between survival and the abyss. Hesitation was not an option; adrenaline surged as Mikeal maneuvered, shifting to access his pistol and create a gap between himself and the ground.

Yet, Terry anticipated his move, abandoning the choking attempt and grappling for Mikeal's firearm. Fierce struggle ensued, each vying for control of the weapon. Mikeal, gasping for breath, managed to retain his grip, leveraging the holster's design to thwart Terry's attempts to remove it. Mikeal, with his free hand, sought the discarded limb, now his only chance at reprieve. Swinging it desperately, Mikeal landed glancing blows, the strikes feeble against Terry's relentless onslaught. With no retreat, Mikeal persisted, with little impact. But Terry, increasingly annoyed by Mikeal's persistence, retaliated with a solid punch to Mikeal's chin, momentarily dazing him.

Although dazed, Mikeal seized the opportunity, snatching the gun from its holster, but in his haste, the shot missed by a mere inch, sailing above Terry's shoulder. Panic surged as Mikeal realized his predicament. Terry, now with a firmer grip, wrested control of the firearm, looming above, aiming squarely at Mikeal's head.

Terry wiped the sweat from his forehead. "Well, Sheriff, you're forcing me into something I didn't want to do."

"Terry," Mikeal responded, "you're in control here. No one but you can decide how this ends. I know you're not a killer; it was your father and grandfather. Now you'll have to answer for what you did to Emma, but that's a hell of a lot better than murder," Mikeal pleaded.

"You're wrong, Sheriff. I've killed before, and I can do it again if needed!" Terry shouted back.

Mikeal's expression shifted to confusion, prompting Terry to elaborate. "Emma was a friend, so I couldn't directly hurt her, but like you, she put her nose where it didn't belong."

"I'm just doing my job, Terry. Besides, I've seen the scorecard in the company books; none of the entries implicate you. As far as I'm concerned, the pursuit of justice ended when your father died," Mikeal explained.

"My father... what a coward of a little man, always in his father's shadow," Terry replied. "He said he never had a choice, 'kill or be killed,' he always told me."

"Terry, are you saying your grandfather forced your father to murder those women?" Mikeal inquired.

"Either do it or end up like your Uncle Henry," Terry recounted. "When I turned twelve, he started using me as bait, just as his father used him. A man out with his young son, telling his sad story about how his wife had died, never failed to lure them into the devil's den. When they finally realized it was a charade, it was too late—fate sealed. When I was a bit older, it was my turn. I followed all my dad's rules and picked out the perfect victim. She was a former teacher of mine, which allowed me to get close without alarming her."

Terry paused, as though reliving the experience before continuing. "I had her in my truck and let her escape. That earned me the biggest beating I ever received, and my father called me a failure for the rest of his life."

"See, that shows you're different from your father and grandfather," Mikeal finally spoke up. "If you were a true killer, you would have tried again."

"Sheriff, are you not listening? I told you I have killed," Terry emphatically stated, shaking the gun in Mikeal's face. Putting his hands up in self-defense, Mikeal replied, "I'm not trying to provoke you."

Terry's face twisted with agitation as he began pacing back and forth, the gun constantly aimed at Mikeal's head. Finally stopping, he took several strides forward, standing directly above Mikeal's body, still lying on the forest floor.

"My father was already eaten up with cancer when one night, I guess he thought he could free himself from the guilt. He explained that my mother found out what he and his father were doing, confronting him with an ultimatum: either he stopped or she was taking his son and leaving. He did what most cowards do—agreed to her face to stop, but the first chance he got, he told his father," Terry recounted. "My mother, who I had been told all my life had abandoned me, never left. She ended up with the other women at the bottom of the mine. That was the final straw. I thanked my father for giving me closure before grabbing a pillow and placing it over his head. It was a cruel irony, the way he kicked his legs and pulled at my hair as he fought for air to continue his life. It was just like what I saw with the women he kidnapped, valiantly struggling to prolong their time on earth. Unfortunately, Sheriff, it's once again time for closure. Thank you for letting me finally verbalize the story I've wanted to tell for decades. Hopefully, you can retell it in the afterlife."

In an instant, Terry felt icy metal press against his right ear. Devin's calm voice cut through the tense air, instructing him to slowly raise both arms and toss the gun aside. Complying swiftly, Terry soon found his legs swept out from under him. He hit the ground hard, the impact driving the breath from his lungs as he struggled to regain air. Before he could react, Devin expertly maneuvered, mounting Terry, yanking his arms behind his back, and securing cuffs in a swift and practiced motion.

"Can you walk, Sheriff?" Devin inquired. Mikeal, now propped up on his elbows, nodded affirmatively, indicating he could manage it. The trek of a little over a mile to the highway was largely silent, interrupted only by Terry's occasional complaints about his broken ribs. "How did you know I was in trouble?" Mikeal finally asked, curiosity piqued. "I heard your radio and thought you were signaling," Devin replied. Mikeal chuckled softly, a wry smile on his face. The mistake he made, which inadvertently led to his distraction allowing Terry to sneak up on him, ultimately saved his life. "What's amusing?" Devin queried. With a tinge of melancholy, Mikeal just shrugged, his silence speaking volumes.

When they finally reached the highway, a whirlwind of activity greeted them. Devin, having reestablished radio contact earlier, transmitted his coordinates before picking up Mikeal's radio signal, prompting his swift return to the woods to offer assistance. Officers promptly joined the group, taking charge of Terry and swiftly guiding him to a waiting van, which sped off toward Bozeman.

With the rush of adrenaline waning, Mikeal began feeling light-headed. "Sir, are you okay?" Devin's concern was palpable in his voice. "Yeah, I'll be fine, but I really need to —" Mikeal's words were cut short as he started to collapse forward, thankfully caught and eased to the ground by Devin. Paramedics, already on-site, rushed over to assist.

Lying flat on the asphalt, one of the paramedics removed Mikeal's jacket, fashioning a makeshift pillow for his head. As the medical team checked his vitals, Devin gazed down at the Sheriff, helpless and worn. The ordeal seemed to have aged Mikeal ten years in just a few hours. His face bore the brutal marks of the confrontation with Terry.

When Mikeal regained consciousness, he stubbornly protested the mandatory trip to the hospital, his determination to return to the station palpable. Yet, Devin stood firm, unwavering in his decision. With gentle insistence, they carefully lifted Mikeal onto a stretcher, Devin walking alongside as they wheeled him toward the waiting ambulance. As they loaded him in, Mikeal, drained but fixing his gaze on Devin, watched silently from the stretcher. His tired eyes locked with Devin's figure standing in the midst of the highway. Devin's presence seemed unwavering, a reassuring anchor amidst the chaos. Mikeal held that connection until the ambulance slowly faded from view, a silent understanding passing between them, an unspoken promise of camaraderie that transcended words.

ABOUT THE AUTHOR

Detroit native I.B. Alexander swapped the Motor City's energy for the sunshine of Tampa, Florida. There, he builds a life with his wife, Marjorie, and their feline first mate, Sebastian. By day, I.B. navigates the world of finance, but his true passion lies in crafting captivating stories.

When crunching numbers take a break, you can find him:

- **Lost in the melody:** Music ignites his creativity, whether crafting original pieces or jamming with loved ones, his trusty guitar always close by.
- **Casting a line:** He seeks peace and quiet on a fishing trip, a chance to reconnect with nature.
- **Embracing adventure:** Any activity in the great outdoors, from hiking to rafting, sparks his imagination.

The global pandemic became a turning point. With newfound focus, I.B. poured his energy into writing. The result? His debut novel, the first installment in a thrilling three-book series. Buckle up and get ready to be swept away by his imaginative world!